MOUNTAIN GODS

JOHN STONEHOUSE

Copyright © 2024 by John Stonehouse

All rights reserved.

No part of this book may be reproduced in any form or by any electronic or mechanical means, including information storage and retrieval systems, without written permission from the author, except for the use of brief quotations in a book review.

This book is a work of fiction. Names, characters, places and incidents are either a product of the author's imagination or are used fictitiously. Any resemblance to actual people, living or dead, events or locales, is entirely coincidental.

ISBN 13: 9798303166837

Cover Design by Books Covered

ALSO BY JOHN STONEHOUSE

IN THE JOHN WHICHER BOOKS:

An American Outlaw

An American Kill

An American Bullet

An American King

An American Reckoning

South Country

Mountain Gods

Wildburn

CHAPTER ONE

Carlsbad, NM.

AN ARC of light around a pole lamp cuts the pre-dawn sky as Deputy US Marshal John Whicher tightens the straps on a ballistic vest.

In the lot of a tractor supply off Highway 62 in Carlsbad, New Mexico, he taps down the Glock holstered against his leg, hitches the M4 carbine at his shoulder.

Around him, five members of the task force apprehension team move in near silence—two US Marshals, a Carlsbad police sergeant, two Ramos County Sheriff's deputies, all dressed in tactical gear.

Whicher pulls an arrest warrant from a cargo pocket. Scans it, out of habit.

The two US Marshals in the team, Brent Hogan and Reva Ferguson watch him.

Reva Ferguson catches his eye.

Whicher nods.

Marshal Hogan takes a pace forward. Heavy-set, his dark

hair pushed back from his face. He turns, addresses the group. "Alright. Everybody 'bout ready?"

The two sheriff's deputies, Billy Drummond and Andre Parrish move in closer.

The police sergeant, Shannon Towne steps beneath the glow of the pole lamp. Alert. Pawing at a goatee beard. Short-cropped blond hair picked out in the light.

"Two arrests we're looking at this morning," Hogan says. "Number one—Karl Ramsay. Armed and dangerous—wanted on a UFAP warrant. We have Marshal Whicher with us, out of Western Division, Texas…"

"El Paso issued the warrant on Ramsay," Whicher says. "I got the job bringing him in."

"We'll pull in Ramsay first," Hogan says. "Then head across town, make the second bust, Alvaro Nunez."

Sergeant Towne speaks; "Karl Ramsay was at an address on the east side of the lake on Anderson yesterday, according to local intel. But we think he moved overnight."

"I have a search warrant for the Anderson address," Whicher says, "but nothing for anything new…"

"So, the plan is, we take Ramsay in the street," Hogan says.

The two sheriff's deputies, Parrish and Drummond, blow on their hands, breath fogging in the chill air.

Sergeant Towne continues; "Ramsay's been on the move the last couple days, probably headed for Roswell or the Q. He likes to move in the morning."

Whicher looks around the group. "Just so everybody's clear on the ID before we move on this… We're looking for a white male, thirty years old. Five-eleven, around a hundred-eighty pounds. With mid-blond hair. File picture shows him clean-shaven, but he may now have a beard or other facial hair." The marshal holds up the picture attached with the warrant. "The guy's hooked into every form of organized crime—narcotics, money laundering, illegal export of firearms; armed robbery, you name it."

The female marshal, Reva Ferguson speaks; "We know Karl Ramsay in the valley." She looks to the sheriff's deputies and Sergeant Towne.

They nod, grim-faced.

"Alright," Whicher says, "so y'all know him. You know how this all is. So, let's be careful…"

Few lights show in the windows of the houses on Pike Street—a residential area of family homes and one-floor ranches four blocks over from the lot of the tractor supply.

Whicher sits behind the wheel of his Chevy Silverado. Marshal Reva Ferguson beside him in the passenger seat—at thirty, the youngest member of the apprehensions team.

She pushes a pair of ballistic glasses up into her midlength, dark brown hair.

A single pickup rolls along the street—its driver noticing nothing—the task force vehicles concealed along adjoining roads.

Just in view through the truck's windshield is an unmarked Chevy Blazer; in the driver's seat Marshal Hogan, Ferguson's partner from the Roswell office eighty miles to the north. Along with Hogan is Shannon Towne from the city police. The pair of them parked closest to the suspect house.

Reva Ferguson checks her watch.

"Think he'll move soon?" Whicher looks across at her.

"According to Towne."

"How's he know that?"

"Local informants."

"He know where Ramsay will be heading?"

"Up the valley, we think," Ferguson says.

Between the house and US 62 a half-mile over, the sheriff's deputies wait in two separate cars; Ramsay likely to make for the highway. Hogan and Towne primed to follow in the unmarked Chevy—Whicher and Ferguson positioned to take station behind them—the sheriff's units ready to circle around, get out front—to box Ramsay in, leave him no place to go.

A burst of static hisses on the radio.

Hogan is on the line; "All units—we have two—repeat, two—unidentified white males leaving the building. They're getting into a white Toyota Corolla."

Whicher starts the motor in the Silverado. "That his car?"

"He's switching it up," Ferguson replies.

"Suspect vehicle is now leaving the property," Hogan says. "They're headed west on Pike."

A white sedan drives into view at the end of the street—moving quickly.

Whicher waits for Hogan's Blazer to pass the intersection.

He pulls out from the curb. Feels his heart rate tick up.

"Be advised," Hogan says, "both occupants are dressed in hooded tops and ball caps. It's hard to see who's who. Over."

Steering to the intersection at the end of the street, Whicher makes the turn onto Pike.

The Blazer is almost out of sight—no sign of the Toyota.

Whicher accelerates as Hogan makes a turn at the end of the block.

Reva Ferguson sits forward, stares straight ahead through the windshield.

The radio crackles again; "Vehicle is now headed north—toward Highway 62. Let's get out in front of them, people."

The marshal pictures the sheriff's deputies, Drummond and Parrish moving off.

At the end of the block, he makes the turn to follow after the Blazer—the white Corolla visible again now, beyond the roadside houses—moving fast.

The car makes a left at a four-way intersection.

In the Blazer, Hogan picks up speed.

Pushing down on the gas, Whicher closes in.

Ferguson fits the ballistic glasses. Unfastens the retaining strap on a semi-automatic Glock.

At the intersection, Whicher powers the Silverado through the turn, engine note rising.

A short stretch of road is ahead—he sees the Toyota, the Blazer close behind it. The two black-and-white SUVs from the sheriff's office crossing over a four-lane highway out in front of them; Parrish and Drummond, maneuvering to put in a block.

The Corolla swerves, sharp, violent.

Whicher accelerates to flank Hogan; shut off the way back.

The Toyota screeches to a halt—sits ninety-degrees across the street.

Parrish and Drummond have both stopped—they're out of their units, weapons drawn.

Marshal Hogan veers to the front end of the suspect vehicle.

Whicher steers to block it in from the rear.

The doors fly open on the Blazer; Marshal Hogan and Sergeant Towne jump out. Both men level AR-15s on the sedan sitting sideways across the road.

The hooded figures in the car move; agitated.

Whicher sees what happens next as if in slow-motion; hyperreal.

The man in the passenger seat reaching toward the console.

Deputies Parrish and Drummond shouting out—yelling for them to stay where they are.

Marshal Hogan running forward.

The passenger in the Toyota whipping up an arm.

Drummond firing his weapon—twice.

Marshal Hogan tight to the vehicle.

Glass exploding out from the car.

Sergeant Towne ducking—Marshal Hogan reeling back—collapsing.

Deputy Drummond bracing—firing over and over.

Both figures in the Toyota slumped.

As Whicher grabs the M4, jumps out—levels the rifle. Repeated shots ringing out. *"Cease firing,"* he shouts, *"Hold your fire…"*

Reva Ferguson runs to Hogan, lying crumpled on the ground.

Towne is at the driver's side window—rifle angled in.

Drummond standing rooted.

Parrish crouched, arms locked out; pistol levelled.

As Whicher puts a hand to the door.

The man in the passenger seat is against the front console. A Smith & Wesson semi-automatic in his hand.

The marshal rips the door wide, takes the gun from him.

Towne opens the driver's door—the hooded man flinches.

The sergeant grabs him, drags him out onto the street.

Whicher heaves the man in the passenger seat upright—pushes the ball cap off his face.

Vacant eyes stare lifeless.

Beside the car, Reva Ferguson kneels to Hogan—blood pooling around him.

"Roll EMTs, now," Whicher shouts, *"get 'em moving…."*

Deputy Andre Parrish grabs his radio.

Whicher turns to Towne; "Is it Ramsay?"

"Not him…"

"Is he still alive?"

Towne only stares back.

The marshal steps away from the car. "We need ambulances down here—fast."

CHAPTER
TWO

ROUNDING THE BEND ON PIKE, the suspect house is directly in front of Whicher—no sign of movement from the tan-rendered, one-floor ranch.

Sergeant Towne points the muzzle of his AR-15 into the footwell.

The marshal stops the truck just short of the property—no vehicle is in the driveway, nobody in sight.

Whicher jumps out, reaches in back for a door ram made of hardened steel. Thinks of the ambulances back at the highway, city cops, the county sheriff on site.

Towne hustles out of the truck. "We're going to break in?"

The marshal grips the ram, slings the M4 carbine onto his shoulder.

"There's no warrant…" the sergeant says.

"Exigent circumstances…"

"Your call."

Running tight along the side of the house, Whicher leads to the front entrance. He takes in the door, takes in details—no hinges showing. "*US Marshal,*" he shouts, *"open up."*

No answer comes back.

He tries the handle—it's locked.

Towne snugs the butt of the AR-15 to his shoulder.

Whicher puts a foot against the door, taking the slack. The lack of hinge on the outside showing it will open inward. He swings the ram, drives it onto the wood beneath the lock.

The door flies open—he steps aside, throws down the ram, grabs the M4.

Towne moves for the doorway. *"Police officer—entering..."*

Whicher follows the sergeant inside—sweeps the kitchen—takes the lead into a hallway, stops short of an open doorway to a center-fed room.

Arcing around the opening, he moves just fast enough to process what he sees—careful not to break the plane of the door threshold with the barrel of the gun.

The room is a living room—nobody in view inside.

At the far side of the doorway, he points the muzzle of the M4 at the ceiling—indicating to Towne he's seen nothing; signaling to enter.

Towne maneuvers behind his rifle, steps inside the room.

Whicher follows. Checks for dead spaces.

Opening the door to the next room, Towne repeats the same steps.

At the sergeant's signal, Whicher enters—sees a bedroom. Sees nobody.

They move fast to the next room—again, empty.

A bathroom door is open, the marshal kicks it wide.

Nobody in there.

The sergeant moves to a corner-fed room.

He steps past the opening, panning, checking behind the rifle.

Whicher sets up at the doorframe, Towne steps in, covers the tight angle along the wall.

Whicher moves to cover the wide expanse of the room.

A suitcase is open on the floor—automatic pistols in it, ammunition, blister strips.

"Fentanyl," the sergeant says. "A ton of it."

Whicher shoulders his rifle. Grimaces. "No Karl Ramsay..."

Law enforcement cruisers and SUVs surround the white Toyota—a uniformed patrol officer mans a roadblock across the street.

Whicher holds the USMS badge out of the window of the Silverado.

The officer waves him through.

The marshal eyes the crime scene techs in zip-suits combing the inside of the Corolla, evidence officers searching the surrounding site on hands and knees.

The two sheriff's deputies, Drummond and Parrish, stand apart—accompanied by plain-clothes detectives. Whicher recognizes a senior officer in dress uniform, Eugene Garton, the chief of police.

Standing at Marshal Hogan's Chevy Blazer is Reva Ferguson—out of the ballistic vest now, a dark blue USMS jacket snug about her.

Whicher stops the truck, kills the motor.

Sergeant Towne pushes wide his door.

Whicher climbs out.

"Ferg?" Towne approaches the Blazer. "You okay?"

Smoothing back a hank of dark brown hair, she nods.

"How about Hogie?"

Ferguson lets out a breath. "First two rounds were stopped by the vest. The one in the shoulder..." She indicates with a hand. "Pretty messed up."

Whicher takes in the pool of dark blood on the asphalt. "He conscious?"

"Just about," she says. "EMTs said hitting the ground knocked him cold. They got him out of here, got him over to the medical center."

Whicher glances at the Toyota. "How about the two in the car?"

"One fatality. The passenger. Second guy, the driver, is in the hospital now."

Sergeant Towne looks across the street to the sheriff's deputies. "How about Drummond? He alright?"

Her eyes cloud.

"Parrish?"

"I guess."

"They had a bunch of fentanyl in the house," the sergeant says, "plus firearms."

"Any sign of Ramsay?"

Towne shakes his head.

Whicher studies the tall, uniformed officer with the sheriff's deputies and the plain-clothes detectives. "What's Chief Garton have to say?"

Marshal Ferguson cuts a look across at the intersection. "They were resisting arrest…"

"And posing an imminent danger," Towne puts in.

Whicher lets the words sit. Breaks off, crosses the road.

The chief spots him.

The marshal gestures with a hand. "What's going on with Marshal Hogan? He going to be okay?"

Chief Garton moves up the sidewalk toward him. "Looks like," he says. "But he lost a lot of blood…"

Whicher steps into the parking lot of a Mexican restaurant. "We entered the suspect house, searched for Ramsay. If he was there, he's sure as hell gone now."

The chief regards him with a steady gaze.

"We found a quantity of fentanyl, plus firearms…"

"Least that's something…"

"You have news crews arriving?"

"They will be."

"Think you can keep 'em quiet?"

Garton looks him over.

"I need to bring this guy in." The marshal stares along the street to Deputy Drummond. His eyes darken. "Firing into a vehicle…"

Garton frowns, adjusts his cap.

"Not a good look," Whicher says.

"Well, listen, I've spoken with the Ramos County Sheriff," the chief says. "Told him what happened. They've placed Drummond on administrative leave already."

Whicher studies the young deputy across the street—Billy Drummond; out of his tactical gear now, in urban camo.

"But he was part of a task force, here," Garton says. "That puts him under federal rules; Marshals Service rules."

Drummond runs a hand over high-and-tight cut hair. Slumped against a black-and-white sheriff's department Explorer. His body gym-pumped, T-shirt riding muscular arms.

"He ought to be okay," Chief Garton says. "Not his fault it went down this way…"

Alongside Drummond, Deputy Andre Parrish smokes a cigarette. Still dressed in olive cargo pants, a Kevlar vest. Whicher takes him in. Dark-complexioned, calm-looking. In his mid-thirties, an experienced guy. "The driver of the car?" Whicher says. "He going to make it?"

"Over in the hospital," Garton says. "Didn't look real good."

―――

Walking back along the street Whicher approaches Brent Hogan's SUV as Reva Ferguson shuts off a call on her phone.

"Chief marshal wants the second warrant served," she says, "I just spoke to the office…"

"You want to execute that?"

"We have a search warrant, along with an arrest warrant.

Search warrant expires today, we already put this back," she says, "for you to go after Ramsay…"

Whicher looks at her.

"I've spoken with Sergeant Towne. Deputy Parrish says he's good to go… assuming you can step in for Marshal Hogan?" Ferguson leans into the Blazer, picks Hogan's AR-15 off the passenger seat. Drops the box magazine, checks it.

"This guy Nunez?" Whicher says.

"Facing multiple charges…"

"Violent?"

Ferguson turns, looks him over, a question in her face.

"He probably knows half the guys Karl Ramsay knows," Whicher says. "If word already hit the street…"

"They're all violent," Ferguson says.

The marshal surveys the scene around the white sedan—mid-morning sun now on shattered glass and blood and the numbered markers of bullet casings littering the road.

Ferguson slams the magazine back into the receiver of the rifle. "Not having it," she says. "Not having two get away."

Whicher eyes her.

Somewhere across town, above the hum of traffic is the pop and wail of more sirens, drifting. Something in the air, he can sense it.

Feel it.

"Yeah," he says. "This could be trouble…"

CHAPTER
THREE

OUTSIDE OF THE cream-painted clapboard house on Glendale, a Ram truck and a Honda SUV sit nose-to-tail on a twin strip of concrete drive.

Whicher pulls over at the curb in front of the property.

From the riverside end of the street, he sees the Ramos County sheriff's deputy, Andre Parrish, approaching slow behind the wheel of a black-and-white Ford Explorer.

Between the back of the house and the next street over is a dirt service alley.

Sergeant Shannon Towne turns up it in a Police Interceptor—to block off the rear way out.

Reva Ferguson pulls in behind him. Whicher breaks out the M4 carbine, steps from the truck.

Exiting the Blazer, Ferguson puts on the ballistic glasses—takes Hogan's rifle from the back seat.

Deputy Parrish is parked now—out of the SUV—tightening the chinstrap on his helmet, shouldering a short-barreled AR-15.

He looks to Ferguson—she nods back.

Parrish moves off, doubling to the front entrance of the house.

Whicher follows—Ferguson brings up the rear.

Rapping on the door, the deputy calls out; *"Police. Open up…"*

He steps to one side.

Whicher watches the front openings; two picture windows, blinds drawn.

Parrish steps forward, rifle leveled.

The door opens.

A young Hispanic woman in jeans and a T-shirt stares out, eyes rounded.

"Ma'am, we have a warrant to search the property."

"Whoa… what's going on?"

Reva Ferguson barks; "Is anybody else inside?"

The woman glowers. *"Nadie…"*

"Nobody?"

"Ma'am you need to step aside." Parrish brushes past, leads with the rifle.

Whicher enters, sees a hallway corridor—a corner-fed room visible through an opening, a kitchen. The door hangs open on a bathroom.

The woman steps to block the hall. "What warrant?"

Ferguson pulls a copy of the search warrant, shoves it at her.

"Police…" Parrish calls out.

Whicher paces forward into the hall; team leader in the two-position.

Ahead, Parrish stops at an open door, raises his rifle. He steps outward—past the opening, panning inside the room.

At the far side of the doorframe, he stops, raises the rifle.

Whicher sets his weight, puts a foot at the threshold, readies the M4. He steps through—to an empty living room. Dead space is behind a couch, he checks. Moves back out.

Parrish rolls off the doorframe, pushes down the corridor, sets up on the kitchen.

Back down the hallway, Ferguson hustles the Hispanic woman into the empty living room.

Whicher gets in place.

Parrish enters the kitchen. Sweeps the barrel of his AR15 left and right. "Alright, clear…"

The marshal checks the bathroom; nobody.

Reva Ferguson clips along the corridor, waits at the door to another room.

Parrish runs forward, turns the handle on it, kicks it open.

Whicher steps fast—balanced, ready to fire, enters the room—a king-size bed is in its center, no sign of anyone.

Ferguson steps in by him, rifle at her shoulder.

The marshal hears Parrish behind them—not waiting—rushing past alone along the corridor.

He catches Ferguson's eye. "The hell's he doing?"

"Go. I got this." She sees his concern. "Go with him."

Whicher holds her look, makes sure.

"Go ahead," she says.

Backing from the bedroom, the marshal re-enters the hallway.

Parrish lunges for another door.

"Wait… hold up…"

The deputy twists the handle, kicks it open.

Whicher sprints, sweeps a second bedroom with the M4—no one in view.

Parrish bursts past.

From back down the corridor is a crash—the sound of Reva Ferguson—voice raised—a man shouting.

Whicher turns—sees the woman—now out in the hallway, shouting.

He runs for the bedroom—steps in behind the M4 carbine.

The doors to an armoire hang open on their hinges, a man in a vest and jeans stands—pointing a pistol at the back of Reva Ferguson's head.

"Put down your weapon…"

Ferguson stands frozen, rifle angled at the floor.

Whicher stares in the man's eyes—sees panic, fear, raw aggression. "*Drop the gun…*"

Behind him, Parrish runs at the Hispanic woman, shouting, "*Get on the floor, get down on the floor…*"

The man with the pistol twitches—his face contorts, he inches the gun closer to Ferguson's head.

Whicher drills his eyes into him; willing him to back down. The urge to kill is in the man's face—a wave of primal fear, violence. "*Drop it. Drop your weapon…*"

Eyes shining, the veins in the man's neck stand out.

Whicher holds on him, finger poised on the trigger. "*Drop it—get on the ground, now…*"

The man hesitates—slowly lowers the gun.

Reva Ferguson steps sideways—whips the butt of the rifle to the side of the man's head; "Get down, get down, now…"

The man drops, hits the floor.

Ferguson kicks the gun away.

She grabs an arm, pulls it behind him, pins his back with a knee.

Grabbing the other arm, she zip-ties his wrists.

Whicher leans out into the corridor.

Parrish has the woman against the wall, arms behind her back, a pair of silvered cuffs on her.

From the far end of the hallway is the sound of breaking glass.

The marshal whips around.

Parrish pushes the cuffed woman to the floor.

Whicher runs to the final closed door at the far end of the corridor—he sets himself, raises the butt of the M4 just above his shoulder, to turn with it fast.

Parrish sprints as Whicher opens the door, pushing at it.

The deputy races through.

Whicher steps in, sees a smashed-out window—moving to it he sees a fleeing figure—a man in a hooded top running through the back yard. He jumps a concrete block wall to the dirt lane behind the house.

Whicher looks at Parrish. "Get on the radio—Sergeant Towne is out there."

The deputy steps to the broken window. "I'll go after him…"

"Tell Towne," Whicher says, "give him a heads up. I'll get around the front, he could go for a vehicle."

The marshal runs back through the house, stops at the bedroom.

Reva Ferguson looks at him, stunned.

"Runner. Getting away. You got this?"

The man in the vest is face down on the floor. The cuffed woman sitting on the edge of the bed.

Ferguson nods back.

Whicher sprints for the door—runs out to the Silverado.

Sergeant Towne's voice is on the radio; "All units—I have a suspect fleeing to the riverside end of the lane—I can't get out, I got a truck blocking me. Repeat, he's going toward the riverside end. Over."

The marshal fires up the Chevy. Floors out the gas, barrels to the end of the street.

Trees and grass of a public park are beyond a ribbon of road.

The man in the hooded top runs to a Dodge Challenger—rips open the door.

Deputy Parrish steps from the end of the dirt lane behind a half-ton pickup.

The Dodge fires into life, pulls out, tires squealing.

Parrish kneels, takes aim at the car.

Whicher sees people in the park, jogging, walking dogs—he stamps down on the throttle.

The Challenger lurches into the road, smoking rubber.

Whicher drives straight for him, heart rate racing—steering the front edge of the Silverado to the back corner of the Dodge. He matches speed, hits the car behind the wheel well. Pulls a quarter-turn—accelerating hard.

The back of the Dodge breaks loose, rear tires sliding.

Whicher keeps the throttle buried, straightens up as the car spins around back on itself.

He gets off the gas.

In the rear-view, sees the Dodge—now facing a hundred-eighty degrees in the opposite direction—facing Parrish.

Sergeant Towne is out in the roadway on foot—rifle at his shoulder.

Whicher turns side-on, to block the street.

He brakes, jumps out, takes aim at the driver of the Dodge through the optic of the M4.

He goes forward, he's into Parrish and Towne.

Goes back he runs right into Whicher.

No way out.

CHAPTER
FOUR

AT THE JAIL facility in downtown Carlsbad, Whicher looks over the file on Alvaro Nunez on a desktop computer.

Both men from the house on Glendale are booked into holding cells—the armed man in the vest, Nunez, suspected of supplying meth, plus assault with a deadly weapon.

The marshal looks briefly at the file on the man that fled the scene; Luis Rios—wanted by law enforcement in Alamogordo—charges pending for assaulting an airman at Holloman Air Force Base.

Pulling a gun on Marshal Ferguson would get Alvaro Nunez an additional federal charge.

At the doorway to the office room, Reva Ferguson appears with two cups of coffee.

She steps inside, hands one to him.

Whicher takes it from her. "Thanks."

She nods.

"You okay?"

"Chief Garton's here." She avoids his eye. "Asking to see us. He wants a verbal report."

"Oh?" The marshal takes a sip on the cup of coffee. "On the Nunez warrant?"

"Both incidents," Ferguson says. "He just came from the city hospital."

Whicher follows her from the room down a short stretch of bright-lit corridor, Ferguson staring straight ahead.

"Towne called," she says. "They're ripping apart the house on Glendale."

Through the open door to an office room, Whicher sees the police chief seated on the edge of a desk, speaking fast into a phone.

Garton sees them, abruptly shuts off the call.

Whicher enters with Ferguson.

Stress is etched into the chief's face as he speaks. "We've got residents calling the department, complaining—that's a family park out there by the river—people feel like they're in danger…"

"Because we're dealing with animals," Ferguson says.

Garton stares at her. "They're seeing lawlessness on their streets."

"People on apprehensions list are violent, a threat to the community…"

The chief rocks back, grunts.

Whicher cuts a look at Reva Ferguson.

"What happened back there?"

"Nunez was hiding in an armoire," Whicher replies. "He pulled a gun on Marshal Ferguson."

The chief glances at her. "I heard. How come it all spilled out into the street?"

"The runner was in another part of the house," Whicher says. "Luis Rios. We didn't know he was in there. He busted out a window, took off out back."

"Maybe you needed more people," Garton says, "before you went in?"

Ferguson's face clouds with anger. "We brought in Nunez. And Rios."

"We were part-way through the search of the house,"

Whicher says. "We made our arrest. No intel suggested a third party would be in there. You'll get a written report from the task force, the same as for the shooting incident on the Karl Ramsay warrant this morning."

Chief Garton shifts his weight, sits forward at the edge of the desk. "They're removing bullet fragments from Hogan's shoulder. The driver of the Toyota underwent a bunch of surgery, they've got him in ICU. Antonio Pittman."

"What do we know on him?"

"Pittman's an associate of Ramsay. Involved with narcotics plus various illegal activities in the valley area. The deceased's name is Jorge Salazar, he had a warrant on him issued by the Albuquerque DA…"

"Which will be why he went for a gun," Reva Ferguson says.

Chief Garton looks at her. "Did you actually see him go for it?"

"He had a weapon in his hand," Whicher says, "by the time I got to the car."

The chief's expression is pinched. "Drummond shot it up pretty badly…"

Ferguson's voice is tight; "We're not required to de-escalate."

"There any ideas on why Karl Ramsay wasn't at the property this morning?"

"You getting flak already?" Whicher says.

"News people see a story," the chief answers.

Ferguson cuts in; "We're permitted to fire into cars."

"Most departments won't allow it, you know that," Garton counters. "Marshals Service, the rules are different. But not every news report makes the distinction. Even if they do, they'll talk it up…"

Whicher folds his arms. "You speak with Deputy Parrish? Or Drummond?"

Garton nods.

"They make any report?"

"They say they got out in front of the suspect Toyota. Marshal Hogan and Sergeant Towne came in from behind. They got out of their units, approached the vehicle, the dead guy went for a gun."

"Is about it," Whicher says.

"You'll get it all," Marshal Ferguson says, "in the written report."

Her jaw is tight as she steps for the door.

———

Back across town near the river on Glendale, Whicher parks the Silverado at the curbside in front of the cream-painted clapboard house.

He studies the Ram truck and the Honda SUV in the driveway, takes in officers from the search team executing the warrant—three men entering the building, two exiting with plastic evidence bags.

Sergeant Towne is in the front yard, now dressed in chinos, a sweat top, sports sunglasses in his cropped blond hair.

Reva Ferguson rolls to a stop in Marshal Hogan's Blazer.

Whicher climbs from the truck, nods to Towne. "What's going on in there?"

"Whole lot of tick-tick. Meth. Powder and rock," the sergeant says. "Looks like it's from a bunch of different sources. Pink powders, yellows, whites. And there are firearms, we need to get it all checked out."

"We know who owns the cars?"

Towne glances up at them. "Nunez and the woman of the house. They took her downtown, put her under arrest. She says the guy that ran, Rios? Showed up yesterday, stayed overnight, she claims not to know him."

Marshal Ferguson approaches.

The sergeant regards her, with hooded eyes.

"We've got IDs on the two men shot on the Karl Ramsay bust," Whicher says.

"Oh?"

"Antonio Pittman. The driver. And a Jorge Salazar, the passenger. Now deceased. Known to law enforcement, according to the chief."

Towne addresses Ferguson; "Any news on Hogan?"

She shakes her head. "I'll head over to the hospital."

"I'm here till the search is finished," Towne says. "I'll try to see him later."

Ferguson fastens the zipper on her USMS coat. "What's happening with Parrish? And Deputy Drummond, do you know?"

"Parrish is taking him back up to Ramos County." Towne looks along the street—at folk in the neighboring houses, standing, watching from behind fluttering lines of black and yellow tape. "It was a justifiable shooting. We all saw that." He shrugs. "At least it wasn't Parrish—one time, you know?"

Whicher looks at the sergeant.

At Reva Ferguson, only standing. Stone-faced.

Beneath the trees in the public park at the water's edge, a cold December breeze blows in off Lake Carlsbad and the Pecos River.

A handful of people are scattered across picnic and rest areas. Whicher eyes a parking lot half-filled with cars and trucks.

Reva Ferguson finishes a call to the medical center.

Stepping by him, she walks on down the path by the side of the water.

Whicher falls in step.

"He's out of theatre," she says. "The doctor said to call back in a couple of hours."

The marshal lets his gaze run out to the sparse line of trees on the opposite bank of the river, to white sky beyond it. "The house on Pike this morning. Why you think Karl Ramsay wasn't there?"

Ferguson walks on, doesn't answer.

"You okay with how it went down?"

She stops suddenly. Angles her head.

"Not talking about Hogan," Whicher says. "I'm talking about Drummond. Billy Drummond. A sheriff's deputy opening up like that..."

"Suspect inside the car was going for a gun."

She walks on.

Whicher walks on with her.

"You saw it," she says.

"I saw the guy with a gun—by the time I got there."

Marshal Ferguson only stares straight ahead.

"You think Drummond could've seen that," Whicher says, "from thirty yards away?

She stops. Looks at him.

Walks on once again.

"The guy bent double in the front seat, the way he was?"

Still she doesn't answer.

"You know them?" Whicher says.

"I know Parrish. Worked with him before."

"And Drummond?"

"No."

"What did Sergeant Towne mean? Back there. About it not being Parrish, 'for once'?"

She shakes her head. Keeps on walking. "Andre Parrish has kind of a rep. But he's a good officer. Been on the task force a long time. A lot of tough situations to deal with. He's handled them..."

At a bench by the water's edge, Whicher stops.

Ferguson pulls up short.

"When we were searching the house back there," the marshal gestures with his thumb. "Only reason I left you alone, before we made certain the bedroom was cleared…"

"Was because of Parrish," she cuts in, "going right on to the next room, on his own. I know."

"So?"

"So, I know it's not good. But it's the way he is. He was pushing on…"

"Look, that son of a bitch Nunez never could've jumped you…"

"If we'd done it the right way," she says, "checked everything, checked the armoire. I know. He was probably trying to make sure nobody else was in there. Maybe Nunez would've just shot me anyway when I opened the door." Her face blanches.

Whicher walks on again, eyes the shining surface of the lake.

Ferguson falls in step beside him.

"So, what now?" he says. "You taking Nunez back up to Roswell?"

"I want to see Hogan."

"After that."

"I don't know." She glances at him. "You?"

"I have to call my boss."

Through the line of trees, Whicher studies the road abutting the end of the dirt lane where the runner, Luis Rios, fled from the house. He thinks of ramming the man's car with the Silverado.

A frown is on Ferguson's brow. "It's stacking up to be quite the mess…"

The marshal nods. "And Karl Ramsay's still out there."

―――

Back on Glendale, behind the wheel of the Chevy, Whicher watches law enforcement activity in the yard of the property —an officer in coveralls hauling a disc-cutter from the back of a police panel van. In the rear-view mirror, he sees Reva Ferguson pulling out from the curbside, headed downtown for the Carlsbad station.

He keys a call to his boss back in Reeves County—Chief Deputy Marshal Martha Fairbanks. Pictures her at her desk; slim with steel-gray hair and metal-frame glasses. Most of her career spent back in Houston; Big City tough. But well-liked in the Pecos office.

The call picks up.

Whicher pushes back in the driver's seat. "We got some trouble out here…"

"Oh?" the chief marshal says. "I was wondering why I hadn't heard?"

"Karl Ramsay. Guy wasn't at the house. We followed a vehicle leaving out of there, stopped it. And a sheriff's deputy opened fire. Killed a guy inside, put another in the meat locker."

Fairbanks exhales into the phone.

"Plus, a marshal here, Brent Hogan, took a couple of rounds."

"Really?"

"Going to be okay, I think, but he's in the hospital, in surgery."

"What's happening now?"

"I'm going over to see him."

Fairbanks is silent on the line a moment. "Nothing's been reported…"

"I asked the chief of police to keep it quiet."

"Why's that?"

"In case Ramsay doesn't know yet."

"You have someplace else you think he might be?"

"Mainly, I was calling to ask do you want me to stick around or head back?"

"I'll call El Paso," Fairbanks says, "see how badly they want Karl Ramsay."

"After this," Whicher says, "they're going to want him pretty bad."

CHAPTER FIVE

FROM THE WINDOW of a third-floor ante-room in the hospital recovery ward, Whicher studies the perimeter of a construction site, new-built condos pushing out into the flat scrub bordering the river, shadows outside lengthening, dusk starting to settle across the desert land.

A nurse enters the room.

Marshal Reva Ferguson pushes up out of a two-seat couch, a can of soda in her hand.

"Five minutes I can let you have with him," the nurse says. "But he's still pretty heavily sedated. He may not say much, he may not be lucid."

"I have to go talk to his wife," Ferguson says. "Like to let her know he's okay."

The nurse nods, steps from the room into the hospital corridor.

Whicher follows Ferguson into the recovery room.

Marshal Brent Hogan is hooked up to an IV, multiple dressings covering the shoulder wound. His face is flushed, puffed out, eyes unfocused. Dark hair a mess.

"Brent," Reva Ferguson says.

He half turns his head.

"How you doing?"

He lies motionless a moment. His voice weak when he speaks. "Okay..."

Whicher takes a step toward the bed. "Doing good, the docs say."

Hogan's eyes move onto him. "You get him?"

Whicher inclines his head.

"You get your man?"

"We made arrests," the marshal says. "Took a couple off the board. It's ongoing, don't worry about any of that..."

Hogan breaks off, stares at the ceiling. "I don't remember much..."

"I'll go see Mary tonight," Ferguson says. "Go over. Let her know I've seen you, let her know you're okay."

Hogan nods, his eyes half closing.

"The chief marshal's spoken with her. But I'll go over," Ferguson says. "She'll want to know what happened. All you need right now is to rest up."

Whicher takes a pace from the bed. Catches Ferguson's eye. "I'll go on and wait outside..."

Stepping back into the ante-room, the marshal pushes the door closed.

Staring out of the window into growing night he catches his own reflection in the darkening glass. Six-one frame—upright, in shape. Wide-set eyes above a broken nose. He shifts his focus, stares straight out at lights now threaded across the city. Not difficult to imagine himself in Hogan's place—stopping multiple rounds. Lying blank-faced in a hospital bed. Maybe worse.

The door from the corridor opens.

Sergeant Shannon Towne enters the room.

He looks at Whicher, his eyes wary.

"In there." The marshal gestures at Hogan's room. "But he's pretty out of it."

"I just got done on Glendale." The sergeant runs a knuckle

over his short goatee. "Came right over. Heard he lost a lot of blood."

"Internal bleeding."

Towne searches his face.

Whicher breaks off, changes tack; "What's going on with the house?"

"We got it all, we think," the sergeant says. "Dealer quantities of methamphetamine in there, we're running traces on the guns. Looks like one of them could've been used in a murder."

"Really?"

"Could be."

"You getting home anytime soon?"

Towne shakes his head. "Waiting on a warrant for the other house—on Pike Street. Chief Garton wants the place searched, we're expecting to do it tonight. Life on the task force, huh?"

"You got a night service endorsement?"

"What I'm waiting on," Towne says. "There's noise already, Chief needs to justify what happened today."

"Task force op; not his call."

"His town," the sergeant says. "He'll end up answering the questions. For what it's worth, we're hearing Karl Ramsay was definitely at the house last night. He either left early—or he stayed behind when we followed the Toyota out of there."

"Think he sent them out to take the fall?"

"I don't know how he could've seen us." Towne looks at the door to Hogan's room, the corners of his mouth downturned. "Look, I don't know what happened…"

Whicher follows the sergeant's gaze. "You going in?"

"You?"

"I'm headed home."

"Back to Texas?"

Marshal Ferguson steps from Hogan's room, shuts the door softly behind her. "Falling asleep," she says.

Towne eyes her. "He okay?"

"Did you need to see him?"

The sergeant shakes his head. "It can wait."

"I've got a two-hour drive to see his wife," Ferguson says. "I need to get out of here, she'll be waiting."

"We speak tomorrow?" Whicher says.

"You heading out?"

"Headed home."

Towne shifts his weight, looks around the room. "You know the chief says the guy driving the Toyota? Antonio Pittman? May not make it through the night..."

Ferguson looks at Whicher, her face grim.

"That kid Billy Drummond," Whicher says. "He sure shot up everything pretty good..."

―――――

Outside in the hospital parking lot, the marshal takes out his phone, checks for calls, sees two missed—one from his wife Leanne, the other, Chief Marshal Fairbanks in the Pecos office.

He breathes the cool night air, strides long, listens to the hum of traffic. Reaches the Silverado, keys a call back to Fairbanks. Waits for it to pick up.

"I missed your call," he says, "I've been over at the hospital."

"Just wanted to let you know I've spoken with the Marshals Office in El Paso," Fairbanks says, "on the Ramsay warrant."

"Somebody has to find him," Whicher says, "before he can be arrested."

"Yeah, that's why I was calling... They want you. They want you on it. They know you're good," Fairbanks says. "The Valley Task Force has the best network of officer personnel to get you Ramsay, they can help..."

"This was just an apprehension team," Whicher says.

"I know. But I'm talking about the full High Intensity Drug Trafficking Task Force. All of it. Karl Ramsay's already part of their investigations, El Paso had to run a deconfliction check to make sure nobody else was about to pick him up."

"We got enough trouble," Whicher says, "last thing we need is any blue-on-blue action."

"They need you to find him."

"Ma'am, I came here to arrest him."

"Well. All that changed."

Whicher stares across the dark lot, says nothing.

"If they shoot one of ours…" Fairbanks says.

"I get it."

"They need you to bring this guy in, John."

Whicher leans his weight against the truck.

"Faster you can expedite the arrest, the sooner you can get back here."

Across the lot, Shannon Towne heads fast toward his vehicle.

"Get yourself a room, get set up," Fairbanks says. "Stay on it. Find out where he could be."

Whicher pushes off the Silverado.

"Let me know what's happening."

The marshal clips across the lot toward the sergeant. He waves at Towne, catches his attention. "Ma'am, I have to go…"

"Call me."

"Understood." Whicher finishes the call.

The sergeant stops.

"You get your warrant?"

He gives a thumbs-up. "Judge gave it the okay. Search team's already over there…"

"I follow you down?"

Towne looks him over. "Thought you were headed home?"

"Plans changed."

CHAPTER SIX

FIVE MILES south off of Highway 62 at the house on Pike Street, Whicher parks the Chevy behind Sergeant Towne's unmarked SUV.

Police vehicles are in the driveway of the one-floor, tan-rendered ranch, working lights set up, search team officers moving in and out of the building.

Towne steps from the car as Whicher climbs out.

A search team officer approaches the sergeant across the front yard. "There's a false wall panel in there, in back of the kitchen," he says. "A space inside it. Packed with Mexican Ice."

"Whoa. Show me."

The search officer turns back up the driveway.

Towne runs a hand over his short-cropped blond hair, follows.

Whicher falls in step.

Entering the building, the marshal glances at the lock—thinks of smashing it open with the door ram that morning.

"Just make sure not to touch anything," the search officer says.

Stepping through the house to the kitchen, past evidence

techs, the way is clear to a rear lobby leading out into a back yard.

A panel of drywall rests on the floor against the lobby door.

In the wall void, plastic-wrapped packages fill the space from floor to ceiling.

Inside the packages are glass-like shards.

Whicher stares at a solid wall of crystal meth.

Towne turns to the officer. "Son of a bitch... you find anything else?"

"There's a couple laptops we should be able to take a look at."

"The owner of the house," Whicher says, "he a known dealer?"

Towne makes a face. "I'd have to check. Owner's the driver of the car this morning—Pittman, Antonio Pittman, the guy in the hospital. He has convictions for robbery, possession, assault."

"He under surveillance?"

"Nothing from DEA," the sergeant says. "But lot of agencies could have been interested in him."

Whicher nods. "El Paso Marshals Office ran a deconfliction check. If there was something outstanding it would've come up."

"So long as it was in the system." Towne taps Whicher on the arm, indicates for him to step outside.

The marshal follows out of the back door, around the side of the house, into bright lights now set up in the front yard.

"They've got enough already—for the chief." Towne looks back toward the house. "The fentanyl we found was retail quantities; probably going out to motorcycle gangs, street vendors, whatever..."

"But not the ice," Whicher says.

"That ice is worth a ton, that's high-level. That's major money; synonymous with serious violence."

"Chief Garton doesn't have to justify it," Whicher says.

"Not to you, maybe." The sergeant looks off along the street. "I've been on since four-thirty a.m. They got this, let 'em finish the search…"

"What do you want to do?" the marshal says.

Towne angles his head, grins. "I want to go get dinner."

———

At a roadhouse two miles north up the highway, the marshal takes in the few other diners scattered around the bar and grill—truck drivers and working men, at ease in the down-home brick and tile décor. Couples and groups eat, spread among the tables and booths, college kids are set up at a neon-lit bar.

Shannon Towne sits where he can see the entrance. Eating smoked brisket, corn and slaw.

Whicher works a plate of ribs and fried okra. "So, how long you been on the task force?"

"Pecos Valley task force? Around twelve years."

"They keep you busy?"

"Pretty much," the sergeant says. "Think you're getting on top of one thing, something else comes along."

Whicher takes a sip of sweet tea. "You work with Reva Ferguson much? Marshal Hogan?"

"I work with 'em plenty. USMS office up at Roswell deputizes some of the local law enforcement. They're involved, same as every other agency."

"The deputies from Ramos Sheriff?" Whicher says. "They get their fed status from the Marshals office?"

"Parrish and Drummond? Far as I know."

Whicher thinks of the two men from the morning's first arrest. "You work a bunch with them?"

"Parrish, yeah. Drummond, that's the first time. For me, anyhow. Why's that?"

The marshal eats, doesn't answer. "What's going on—in the valley, right now?"

"Pecos Valley?" Towne takes a forkful of smoked brisket, thinks it over. "Hundred years ago they tapped the aquifers, flooded the whole place with water—turned it from a desert into a regular garden valley. Grew crops. Fruit. Folk had food. Now it's flooded with drugs and guns..."

"How's that working out?" Whicher says.

The sergeant holds his fork upright. "Since ninety it's been designated—part of the New Mexico High Intensity Drug Trafficking Area. Prime transshipment corridor for illicit drugs. We have a hundred-eighty-mile border..."

"Try twelve hundred," Whicher says.

Towne gives a dry laugh. "No, y'all are welcome to that. Whatever, our corridor runs north all the way up to Albuquerque—then out into the whole country. Flowing the opposite way to the drugs is money and weapons—headed back across the border. But interdictions are on the up."

Whicher cuts into the dish of ribs, leans into the table.

"We shut down the supply of prescription-controlled drugs; ephedrine, pseudoephedrine. The mom-and-pop meth labs go out of business," Towne says. "But then the Mexican labs move closer to the border—they make 'em bigger, turn them into super-labs." The sergeant takes a pull at a longneck bottle of beer. "We had folk cooking in chicken sheds and trailers, but those guys are running labs turning out ice by the ton. Pure crystal—purer, stronger, for less money, shipping it UPS, FedEx, on trains, on Greyhound buses. Truckers bring it in big rigs, low-lifes drive it up in the backs of their cars."

"Where's Karl Ramsay fit? In all of this?"

Towne sets down the bottle, returns to eating. "Well, for everything, there's a deal to be done. Palms to cross, wheels to grease. The money keeps on growing—and the money's just as bad as the ice. Poisoning everything it touches. Karl

Ramsay's a facilitator. What I know of him. Down there on the border, in El Paso. Into everything that goes on—headed up or headed down."

"What kind of intelligence y'all have?"

"On him specifically? I don't know," the sergeant says. "I was just out to bust him, same as you. You'll have to look him up in the morning."

"The warrant's for unlawful flight from prosecution."

"DA and the HIDTA task force will have been watching," Towne says. "They must've decided it's time."

Whicher nods, eats. "Why's he come here? Less heat?"

"Could be. But Pecos Valley task force is hooked up with every LEO in the southwest," Towne says. "ICE, Homeland Security, DEA, FBI, you guys. We have our own informants, too. That's how we know where he's been."

"But this morning?"

"He got lucky. It happens, you know that. He must've moved. But we'll find his trail."

Whicher looks at him. "You sound pretty confident."

"Been doing this a while."

The marshal takes another mouthful of rib.

"If you're sticking around, I'll find you his case notes," Towne says.

"Don't need to make a case. I just need to nail him."

The sergeant shrugs, scans the room.

Whicher checks his watch. "What did you mean about Parrish, today?"

"Andre Parrish?"

"You said; 'at least it wasn't him'?"

Towne laughs. "I mean, you saw what happened. Right?"

The marshal looks at him.

"Drummond's lacking experience. I grant you. But he opened up on that car, he was doing the right thing."

"On a county sheriff bust he could never do that."

"I couldn't do it on a police shift," Towne says. "But you

deputize us, make it federal, it changes up the game. We're in harm's way; bringing violent criminals to book..."

"You think he was justified?"

"Dumping a mag into that car?"

Whicher nods. "Based on what he could see?"

"Not my call," the sergeant says.

The marshal sits back from the table. "And Andre Parrish? That the kind of thing you've seen him do?"

"Andre Parrish has a reputation," Towne says, eyes guarded now. "He's a hothead, maybe. Look him up, if you want."

Whicher doesn't reply.

"A guy like him has done a lot of good," the sergeant says. "Billy Drummond's young, he lacks experience. But he shot first—kept us safe."

"Brent Hogan took multiple rounds this morning."

Towne takes another slug of the beer. "I don't know what to tell you. What do you want?"

Whicher turns back to eating. Eyes the man across the table. "All I want is Karl Ramsay. And I'll be on my way."

———

The highway is quiet, little traffic moving on it as Whicher turns into the lot of a two-story hotel on the south side of Carlsbad. He pulls into a parking bay, keys a call to his wife ninety miles back across the Texas state line.

Leanne answers on the third ring.

"Been a long one," Whicher says, "sorry..."

"I was wondering if you were going to call."

"I went out to eat. With a guy on the apprehension team."

"Is everything okay?"

The marshal shuts off the motor on the truck. "The bust this morning—not good."

"Oh?"

"Guy wasn't there. But we followed a suspect car, stopped it—some sheriff's deputy got spooked, opened fire."

Leanne is silent on the line.

"One of ours got hurt. Passenger in the car was killed. Driver's still in the hospital."

"Is everything alright? Are you alright?"

"I'm fine. I called Chief Marshal Fairbanks, she said to stick around, least for now." Whicher takes the keys from the ignition, steps from the truck. "They want this guy bringing in."

"You have somewhere to stay?"

"Just about to check into a hotel."

"You have something with you?"

"Change of clothes, a go-bag..."

"How long you think you'll be away?"

The marshal stares at the rendered façade of the building in the hotel uplighters. "Couple days? We'll need to move fast—longer this guy's running the harder it'll be."

"Lori was hoping to see you..."

"Yeah. She up?" The marshal pictures his daughter, not far shy of her thirteenth birthday.

"She went to bed."

He opens the rear of the cab, checks the custom-fit gun safe, checks the M4 carbine and the tactical vest are securely locked inside. "I'll call her tomorrow."

"Try to find time..."

Grabbing a canvas carryall from the back seat, he locks up. "I will."

"So, this guy?" Leanne says.

"Yeah, he's a runner. Charges pending in El Paso. A dealer, fixer."

"Is he dangerous?"

"If he made the list for the apprehensions team..." The marshal thinks of the long day; leaving the family home at three a.m. arriving in Carlsbad in the pre-dawn.

"So, what now?"

"I'm pretty beat. Fixing to take a shower, turn in."

Whicher listens to his wife's silence on the end of the line.

He softens. His voice is warm when he speaks again. "Don't worry. You know? I'll be careful."

Across the city, in the still night air, the rumble of a freight train sounds somewhere—and the keening of another siren is drifting.

CHAPTER
SEVEN

MORNING SUN STREAMS through the window at the Carlsbad Police Department. Whicher sits at a computer terminal in an empty office, in a dress shirt, chinos, and a tan, Resistol hat.

On the desk, the monitor displays law enforcement files on Karl Ramsay. A picture on screen shows his face; expression confident to the point of arrogance. Defiance in the pale blue eyes. His mid-blond hair is cut short, his features square, the jaw prominent. Lines across his brow make him older-looking than his thirty years. Compared to the photograph with the warrant documentation, a marked hardness shows, a brutal quality, over and above the self-assurance.

The marshal takes a notepad and pen from a navy ranch coat on the back of his seat. Flips it open. Turning back to the computer terminal, he opens up another file, studies an onscreen map of the New Mexico High Intensity Drug Trafficking Area. The graphic extends from El Paso, on the border in Texas, east through Carlsbad—then north to Artesia and Roswell on the Pecos River. Beyond that is Albuquerque, Santa Fe, Farmington. Three interstates furnish access to the wider country.

Whicher focuses on the low to mid-portion of the Pecos River valley—from Roswell to Carlsbad, away from the urban centers.

Ramsay had been in Carlsbad, he could be laying low in the rural land—away from surveilled interstates, from big cities with networks of snitches, prying eyes.

Clicking onto a summary report, Whicher reads a passage describing Ramsay's history of deals including with the Juarez and Sinaloa cartels—neither fully controlling the ports of entry to the US, each ascending, dropping, reascending in turn.

A recent cartel deal was with La Familia Michoacana—for supply to street gangs in the HIDTA area—plus a deal for black tar heroin—aimed at high-school-student consumption in the northern counties of the state.

The marshal makes a series of notes on the pad, pushes back from the desk, thinks of his own daughter. He glances again at the image of Karl Ramsay. His gaze lingering on it. Locking it in.

A knock sounds at the door.

Whicher calls out, "Come…"

Shannon Towne enters the room, carrying two cups of coffee.

"Mornin'."

The sergeant hands a cup to Whicher. "You get breakfast?"

"At the hotel."

Towne gestures at the shoulder holster at Whicher's side. "Nice rig."

The marshal cuts a look at the large-frame Ruger revolver finished in stainless steel.

"You carry that plus the Glock?"

"Habit. From my army days."

The sergeant looks at him.

"Faster draw in a vehicle."

Towne thinks about it. Nods.

"So, what's happening this morning?"

"We're fielding heat," the sergeant says.

"Already?"

"Chief Garton's scheduled for press around noon. He wants me there. Fergie's coming down—to represent the Marshals office. Make clear we've got one of our own in the hospital, you know? Listen, she asked if you could meet with her? She's driving down this morning—there's somebody she has to see."

Whicher looks at him.

"A source," Towne says.

"Informer?"

The sergeant nods.

"Where at?"

"Up by Severn Rivers," Towne says. "Brantley Lake. Take you about a half hour. It's right up two-eighty-five. Let me give you her number."

Whicher writes it onto the notepad. "What's going on at the hospital?"

"With Hogan?" the sergeant says.

"Antonio Pittman. He survive the night?"

Towne's face darkens. He takes a pull at his cup of coffee. "Going into a briefing with the chief, now. Guess I'll find out, either way."

The land north of Carlsbad along Highway 285 is flat, desert country of low hills and rock, a hard pan of caliche covered in mesquite and scrub.

Whicher scans the horizon from behind the dust-streaked windshield of the truck.

He spots the turn from the four-lane highway onto the Capitan Reef Road—takes it. The asphalt of the winding county lane scarcely distinguishable from the bleached earth.

Beneath a hazed blue sky, evidence of wildfire burns is everywhere—singed and blackened clumps of brush stripped back to skeleton-like spines.

Crossing the Pecos River two miles on, he catches site of the Brantley Dam. Part of managing the sinuous river—eking out life from it, in the dry desert soil.

The turn off for the lakeside park is ahead, he takes it. Steers in the direction of the reservoir. Passes a deserted campground, no vehicles in sight. Cresting a small hill, he can see out onto the water.

Farther down the stony track he sees a group of picnic benches by the reservoir's edge— shade trees lining a parking area. In a scenic overlook a stationary silver-gray Tahoe.

The marshal checks his rear-view, sees no one, continues down.

He takes in the vehicle.

The driver door opens on it.

Marshal Reva Ferguson steps out, in a gilet and jeans. Dark brown hair back from her face, a pair of aviator sunglasses on the top of her head

Whicher pulls into a space beside her.

He shuts off the motor, climbs out.

"Marshal." She looks him over.

He nods, tilts the brim of the Resistol down a notch against the glare off the lake. "Mornin.' How's Hogan? You spoken to the hospital yet?"

She shakes her head. "They'd call if there was anything…"

"You see his wife? She alright?"

Ferguson makes a face. "It's been a shock. She said she spent half her life praying nothing like this would ever happen."

The marshal watches sunlight on the surface of the water. Thinks of many times his wife Leanne has said the same.

Ferguson studies the primitive road down from the hill. "I didn't really know what to tell her."

Whicher nods, eyes her. Thinks to change the subject. "This guy we're meeting?"

"Should be here any minute. His name's Grady Owens. Driver for a local trucking company," she says, "servicing the oil and gas fields. DEA busted him a couple years back. For possession. Told him he could cop an early parole deal."

"Oh?"

"Now he's their guy. By way of theirs, ours."

"The task force team?"

"Right," she says. "Owens moved down from the Q, somebody at the DA put in word to his parole office, got him a job here. He's in and out of every drill site and store and parts supply. The major trafficking organizations know all of the routes, all of the freight capacities, they know who they can get to. He's a useful source. Nervous, though."

"How so? You leaning on him?"

"Six months after he got out," Ferguson says, "he was caught in possession of a bunch of stolen tools. From a drill site."

"No kidding?"

"He was headed straight back for prison, somebody offered to make it go away…"

"In exchange for what?"

"Whatever we need to know."

Whicher looks at her. "Could be a dangerous line of work."

She nods, unsmiling. "So could prison."

At the head of the hill, a Ford pickup rolls into view. It steers slow toward the reservoir.

"That's him."

The marshal takes it in as it approaches.

Behind the wheel of a battered-looking Ford Ranger, Grady Owens picks at the sleeve of a T-shirt, skinny arms scrolled with tattoos.

He peers out from beneath the bill of a ball cap. Drives the remainder of the track. Parks beneath the trees. Stares out at Reva Ferguson, eyes cutting to the big man in the coat and hat. He shuts down the motor, slides out.

"Grady," Ferguson says.

Long black hair shows from beneath the ball cap. His jeans are cut low, rucked over hi-top boots. Small, dark eyes look out from the pitted skin of his face. Owens pulls out a pack of cigarettes, lights up. Blinks behind the trail of smoke.

"You know why you're here?"

"Guessing it's 'cause of yesterday," Owens answers.

"You see the news?" Ferguson says.

"Out of Carlsbad?" Owens nods, takes a draw on the cigarette.

"This is one of the US Marshals present yesterday."

The man squints at Whicher.

"There's a lot of pissed off people in law enforcement," Ferguson says.

"I heard one of the guys y'all stopped is in the morgue," Owens answers.

"Karl Ramsay; we're going to need to know where he went."

Owens bugs his eyes.

"He was at a city address," Ferguson says. "Left before we could get him. Where'd he go?"

"The hell should I know?"

Whicher addresses the man; "So far, what have you heard?"

Grady Owens takes a pull on the smoke, shivers in the cold breeze. He meets the marshal's eye a moment, breaks off. "I heard he found out they were going to bust his ass—in El Paso. So, he lit out. Word is, he's looking for money. Looking for some payback, too."

Ferguson regards him.

"You know? Smoking somebody."

Whicher says, "You know who?"

Owens shakes his head. "Some Mexican. What I heard on it. Some beef on a black tar deal."

The marshal makes a mental note. "Somebody around here?"

"Couldn't tell you."

"You know what Ramsay was doing here?"

"Why would I?"

Ferguson cuts in; "Because it's your job to know, Grady. That's the only reason you're still out."

Owens takes another drag on the cigarette. Blows smoke out sideways.

"Where you picking up your information?" Whicher says. "Guys on sites?"

"Some."

Reva Ferguson folds her arms over her chest. "We want to know where he went. Where he is. Where he's going to be."

Owens shrugs. Throws down the cigarette butt, grinds it out. "How am I supposed to know that?"

"Talk to people."

"I can't ask where Karl Ramsay is at. You know what kind of freak he is? Evil. Nobody likes him. You know he killed his own girl?"

Whicher looks to Reva Ferguson.

"A young woman was murdered," Ferguson says, "six months back, in Roswell. Supposedly a girlfriend. It's unsolved, there was speculation about him…"

"What I heard, he strangled her, dumped her body, he was out drinking, laughing about it the same night."

"There was no evidence linking him," Ferguson says. "He was questioned over it, he had an alibi."

Owens looks out across the lake water, rubs at his tattooed arm. "I don't want to be anywhere near that son of a bitch. You think I can go around asking about him?"

"There'll be TV briefings today," Whicher says. "Use that. Talk about what went on, is all, see what people know. You don't need to ask about Ramsay specifically, find out what anybody heard."

At the top of the scrub hill, an RV pulls into view. It stops at the top of the slope, the driver and a passenger leaning forward to look out over the lake.

"I got to get to work," Owens says, "I can't be seen with y'all." He takes a step toward his Ford truck.

"Grady." The tone of Ferguson's voice stops him. "I brought along the marshal here—because there's something you need to understand. The Valley Task Force will be all over this. So will the US Marshals, now. We're going to bring Ramsay in. Anybody around him, anybody like the two yesterday morning; Pittman, Salazar—anybody that gets in the way of that, they better know what's coming."

A bitter twist is in the man's face as he stares at her.

"That includes you. Find out where Karl Ramsay went."

"I have to go—I got work to do."

"You need to get to work for me."

Owens opens up the truck door. Climbs inside.

"You'll be hearing from me."

He fires up the motor, backs around.

Whicher watches the RV on the hill turn toward a picnic area, Owens working his way up the grade. "Where's he get his information?"

"In the valley, it's all about transshipment," Ferguson answers, "what comes in that's only ever going out. On up to Denver. Chicago. Back to Florida. Coming in from everywhere—California, Arizona, Texas. It's all about freight. And Grady drives a truck every day, he's part of the whole transportation network…" She reaches for the door handle to her Tahoe. "That's how he knows. That's how come we need him."

CHAPTER EIGHT

IN A CONFERENCE ROOM of the Carlsbad Police Department, lights and cameras are set up on stands in front of a long table, microphones spaced at short intervals along its top. News media crews sit in rows of plastic chairs in the center of the room. From the back, Whicher watches technicians connect lengths of cabling, position boom mics, test mixing boards and lamps.

Around forty people are present, reporters from outlets in the valley locale.

He checks his watch—nearly noon.

A set of double doors opens—Reva Ferguson steps out, leading Shannon Towne and Eugene Garton, the city chief of police.

Stepping behind the table, they settle down into seats.

Chief Garton surveys the assembled group. "Good morning." He scans the faces before him. "If we're all set, I'll begin right away… On behalf of the department, I've called this briefing to address questions that I know have arisen regarding the incident yesterday—in which a federal officer was injured executing an arrest warrant, and in which a suspect was fatally wounded and another hospitalized."

The chief glances at a set of notes.

"First I'd like to outline the nature of the operation yesterday," Garton continues. "A federal task force apprehension team was in process of executing an arrest warrant—issued for an individual, name of Karl Ramsay—under investigation as part of the Organized Crime Drug Enforcement Task Program."

He looks up from the notes, scans the room.

No questions.

"The program runs under the Department of Justice—and comprises federal agencies and their local counterparts, in this case the US Marshals Service, plus an officer from my department and deputies from Ramos County Sheriff. I'll note that persons wanted in these types of investigation are invariably armed and dangerous—and violent." He turns to Reva Ferguson. "That was the case regarding the suspect in question, Karl Ramsay?"

Marshal Ferguson nods. "It was."

"Alright," Garton goes on. "So, an arrest warrant of this type is rarely easy to serve. Yesterday morning, at around six-fifteen a.m. task force members were observing a house where the suspect was believed to be. While observing the house, a vehicle left the property—with two men in it, a driver and a passenger. Task force units followed it. The vehicle was stopped at an intersection off Highway Sixty-Two in the south of the city. Officers approached the vehicle—the passenger was seen to make purchase on a weapon..."

Whicher picks up on the phrase—eyes the chief.

"This individual did not comply with a lawful command to drop their weapon. He was subsequently fired on..."

A male reporter in a sport coat raises a hand. "Chief, the act of firing into a vehicle is against policy."

"Police department policy," Garton says. "But the apprehension team is designated under USMS control. Marshals Service is under no such restrictions."

The reporter continues, "Why were the task force trying to arrest the suspect in the street?"

Garton inclines his head. "Apprehending a fugitive in the street or in a vehicle instead of in a home is generally safer. Serving this kind of warrant inside of a person's home can prove extremely difficult. There may be firearms in the property, multiple individuals could be present—there's the opportunity for fugitives to take up defensive positions. Everything connected in serving this type of warrant is inherently dangerous…"

"But neither of the occupants of the car was Karl Ramsay," the reporter says.

A female reporter in a windcheater raises a hand. "Was either occupant of the car directly threatening the task force?"

"The deceased was seen to make purchase on a weapon, as I said before… and both occupants of the vehicle were known to law enforcement."

"Why wasn't there any attempt to de-escalate before the task force opened fire?"

"Chief," Ferguson cuts in, "if I could take that?"

Garton nods.

"We're not required to," Ferguson says. "Before using force. We're issued a federal warrant, we're required to execute it."

"With lethal force?"

"Up to and including lethal force," Ferguson says.

"Who were the occupants of the car?" the reporter in the sport coat says.

"The driver's been named as Antonio Pittman," Ferguson answers. "And the deceased man was one Jorge Salazar."

"It was Salazar who had the weapon?" the reporter says.

Shannon Towne speaks; "Salazar was in possession of a Smith & Wesson nine-millimeter semi-automatic."

"What was he doing with it? He had it in his hand?"

"He was holding it."

A bald reporter in a short-sleeved shirt and tie raises a finger.

"Yes," Chief Garton says.

"Why was nobody on the task force wearing a bodycam?"

"It's not required," the chief replies.

"Am I correct in thinking the officer that actually carried out the shooting was a Ramos County sheriff's deputy? They routinely wear bodycams," the reporter says.

"An officer serving on a federal task force is legally deputized," Ferguson says, "and subject to federal rules while in pursuance of that duty."

The young woman in the windcheater speaks again. "The deceased's family has indicated it may look to the county DA to prosecute over the shooting."

Chief Garton's face is bleak. "The county DA would have no authority to do that, ma'am."

The first reporter raises his hand again. "What's the condition of the driver of the car?"

"Antonio Pittman's condition is a matter for the medical team at the hospital," the chief says.

"Who owns the property under surveillance?"

"Mister Pittman is the registered owner."

The woman in the windcheater speaks again; "What can you tell us about the men shot in the car?"

"A search of the property uncovered substantial quantities of illegal drugs," Chief Garton says. "Crystal methamphetamine, commonly known as Mexican Ice. Along with quantities of fentanyl and several firearms. I'd draw your attention to this in regard to the fact that the people involved in this incident, although not the subject of the original arrest warrant, were nevertheless participating in highly illegal activity of a type known to involve the ready use of violence—at any time."

The chief looks around the room.

A female reporter in jeans and a fleece jacket raises her

arm. "What can you tell us about the second arrest made by the task force yesterday morning?"

"Ma'am, we're not here to discuss that..."

"But a suspect fled the scene of the arrest there—and a car was subsequently PIT-turned at speed in a residential street. Local residents have expressed concern, isn't that right?"

"That's a completely separate incident—the arrest of an individual with a history of violent offending," Garton says. "It was expedited under difficult circumstances, with not a single shot fired."

The reporter in the shirt and tie raises his hand again. "Both of these incidents involved the use of a federal apprehension team. What assurances can you give residents who may be worried about incidents like this happening in their neighborhoods?"

"That all is an entirely different matter," the chief says. "This briefing is limited to furnishing details on the attempted arrest of Karl Ramsay. At this point in time, that's all the information we want to make public, in view of the fact this is an ongoing operation. So I'd like to thank everybody for their time. And if there are no further questions, I'll wish you all good day."

From the end of a busy corridor, Whicher sees Chief Garton's office, the door wide open, Marshal Ferguson and two uniformed officers inside with the chief.

Shannon Towne stands in the doorway. Spots the marshal, steps out. "Message," he says, "while we were in the briefing."

"Oh?"

"From a source on the street. Guy I know spray paints cars at a custom body shop, here in town. Says an auto dealer named Delmar Sadler reckoned to see Karl Ramsay two nights back. At the house on Pike."

"Really?"

The sergeant strides down the corridor toward a drinks vending machine.

Whicher follows.

"This guy owns a used-auto yard," Towne says, "like, a mile away."

"We go pay him a visit?"

Reva Ferguson steps from Chief Garton's office, moves down the corridor. "How you think it went?"

"The briefing?" Whicher says.

"Chief thinks it's giving the whole thing legs, maybe it did more harm than good…"

Towne works the machine, doesn't reply.

"That kid Drummond opening up on the Toyota," the marshal says. "Either of you see the guy in the car 'make purchase' on the gun?"

The sergeant looks doubtful.

Marshal Ferguson doesn't answer.

Towne looks across the lobby. "What do you want to do about this auto dealer?"

Ferguson regards him. "What's this?"

"A guy that saw Karl Ramsay, at the house on Pike. We need to go see him."

"I have to head to the hospital, see Hogie."

"You know how he is?"

She shakes her head.

The sergeant looks to Whicher. "You want to take a police unit?"

"Let's take my truck, go unmarked," the marshal says. "Don't want to let him see us coming…"

CHAPTER
NINE

TRAFFIC IS light on US-62 as Whicher steers past the fast-food restaurants and tire shops and auto-parts stores. He spots the sign for the used car business. In front of a brick office a handful of vehicles are parked in line on a tattered lot.

Whicher eyes the faded blinds on the office window. "Where's your source get his information?"

"This guy Sadler brought up a vehicle to the body shop my guy works out of," Towne says. "First thing this morning. Some truck in need of a respray."

The marshal hits the blinker. Pulls in.

"They were yakking about the news yesterday," the sergeant says, "the shootout with the cops. Sadler told him he'd been over at the house on Pike the night before the bust."

Whicher glances at the highway running south. "Pike Street can't be far from here…"

"It's five minutes."

The marshal studies the vehicles for sale—a mix of older-model pickups and sedans. He shuts off the motor. "Let's see what Sadler has to say."

Stepping out, he peers at the glass front of the office. In the air is the sound of a high-pressure water hose.

Whicher tracks along the side of the office with Towne to a lot in back.

A young Hispanic jet-washes a half-ton Ram truck. Watching on is a thickset man in jeans and a striped shirt, his face weathered, hair graying, his beard worn short.

Whicher pulls out his USMS badge and ID. "United States Marshals Service."

The young Hispanic steps around the truck, takes the men in, wary.

Towne shows his own ID. "Carlsbad Police—with the Pecos Valley Task Force."

"Mister Delmar Sadler?" Whicher says.

The older man's eyes move quickly. He nods.

"Sir, I need to ask you a few questions."

"What's this about?"

The marshal glances in the direction of the man washing the truck. "If we could step away a moment?"

Sadler inclines his head, leads the way back onto the front lot.

"It's in connection with an incident yesterday—you may have heard something about it?" Whicher says. "A shooting during a law enforcement operation."

"I did hear something about it," Sadler says. "I don't see how I could be of any help."

"Sir," Sergeant Towne says, "did you make a visit to a house on Pike Street the night before last?"

Stepping to the door of a compact Nissan parked on the front lot, Sadler adjusts a sign in its windshield. "Why do you ask?"

Whicher eyes the man.

"Alright, as a matter of fact I did."

"What was your business there?" Towne says.

"I was delivering a vehicle."

The marshal steps toward him. "What vehicle?"

"Chevy SUV. I sold a Chevy SUV to a gentleman the day before yesterday. I was asked to deliver it."

"You sold it to someone at that address?"

"Yes, sir, I did."

"Who?" Towne asks him.

"Well, a man named Jorge Salazar."

Whicher glances at Towne. The sergeant shows no reaction at the mention of the man shot dead by Deputy Drummond. "This somebody you know?"

"No. Not at all. I just sold him the vehicle—I took it around to the address he gave, seeing how it's not at all far."

"Did you enter the house?" Whicher says.

Sadler's expression is clouded.

"We're conducting a thorough search of the property, sir. If your prints or DNA are in there…"

Swinging the door shut on the Nissan, the man scowls. "Alright, I did go inside, yes. I was asked in. I gave the man his keys, gave him the paperwork. I stayed just a minute. Then that was it, I left."

"Who was in the house?" Whicher says.

The noise from the high-pressure hose stops suddenly—the lot falls silent.

Sadler looks around. Lowers his voice. "I saw three people."

The marshal pulls out a picture of Karl Ramsay from the arrest warrant documentation. "Did you see this man?"

Blowing the air from his cheeks Sadler nods. "Yes, sir. He was one of them."

"Karl Ramsay. You saw him inside the house?" Towne says. "Do you know him?"

"I don't know any of them. But I know 'of' him," Sadler says. "I know him by reputation, that's all."

"You know what he was doing there?" Whicher says.

"No, sir, I don't. I went to deliver a vehicle to a customer. I was invited in. I went in, handed over the keys and the title. I only spoke with Mister Salazar—the other two men were in the living room, I was in the kitchen…"

"But you recognized Karl Ramsay?"

"He's pretty well known," Sadler says. "Most people in business around here know who he is. But listen, I don't have anything to do with him or anyone else who was in that house—I don't know any of them."

"This vehicle?" Whicher says.

"It was a Chevrolet Traverse. Six years old. Silver in color."

"We're going to need the registration plate."

"Well, sure thing. But why do you need that?"

Whicher takes out his lined notepad. "Because we're going to have to find it."

―――

On the enclosed terrace of a Mexicali restaurant overlooking the city courthouse, Whicher sits with Shannon Towne—eying the late-thirties mission-style building beyond the trees across the square. On the table before them is a dish of flautas compuestas with chicken—and Towne's phone—the call to the state police already made to get a stop order on the car.

"You think Delmar Sadler knew any of the people at that house?"

The sergeant thinks it over. "Even if he did, it's not a crime to sell somebody a car."

"Think Salazar bought it for Ramsay's use?"

"Do you?"

"Would be my guess…" Whicher eats a forkful of the side of salad and beans on his plate.

"We could pull in Sadler for questioning?"

"We could," Whicher says. "We don't have reason to charge him with anything. You get the impression he was lying?"

Towne shrugs.

"He known to law enforcement?"

"Not by me."

The marshal watches cars and trucks rolling past the courthouse. "I need more on Karl Ramsay. How come he's known to people outside of his circle? People like Delmar Sadler?"

Towne takes a chunk from the flautas. "Ramsay's into straight business—as well as non-legit. Property. Transportation..."

"As cover?" Whicher says. "Or to launder money?"

"Mostly it's just business. A whole lot of blurred lines," Towne says. "Guys like Ramsay don't make a distinction whether it's within the law." The sergeant's phone rings. "I should get that."

He picks up, listens.

Whicher eats, scans the faces of the few other diners on the restaurant terrace.

"No..." Towne says. "That's okay, we know who that is..."

The speaker on the other end of the line continues.

"No, we're good on that... Yeah. We checked it out already. Listen, I'll be back in soon, I'll see you then. Okay." The sergeant clicks off the call.

Whicher looks at him.

"Detective at the department," Towne says. "Chief Garton had officers go door to door on Pike—collecting witness statements. One of the reports says some neighbor kid saw somebody visit the house—the night before we executed the warrant."

The marshal makes a question with his face.

"Delmar Sadler. Right? I told him we already know about it."

Back at the police department, a group of uniformed patrol officers gather for a shift change, a watch commander with briefing notes headed toward them down a corridor. Officers in jeans and hooded tops and jackets make for the exit door. Whicher spots Marshal Reva Ferguson emerging from an office.

She sees him, raises a hand.

Ahead, Sergeant Towne continues on to a squad room.

"You have a minute?" Whicher says.

She steps back inside the small office.

"Ramsay has a vehicle he's likely using," Whicher says. "Chevy SUV. You have any idea where he might go?"

"Somewhere up the valley. Roswell," she says, "or the Q?"

Whicher nods. "There any news at the hospital on the driver of the car; Antonio Pittman?"

"They put him in an induced coma. He might not make it."

Whicher looks from the room out into the corridor. "How was Hogan?"

"Okay."

"He doing much talking? You ask him about what happened?"

"What do you mean?"

"He was closest to the car, closer than anybody," Whicher says. "He remember much about it?"

"Like what?"

"Did he see Salazar go for a gun?"

Reva Ferguson looks at him. "You mean before Deputy Drummond opened up?"

"Did you ask him?"

Ferguson eyes the corridor, takes a hold of the door, pushes it closed. "That's something we should probably leave alone..."

Whicher takes a seat at the edge of a metal desk.

"Things are sensitive with Ramos County Sheriff."

"Why's that?"

"There have been incidents—in the past." Ferguson leans her back against the door. "With Deputy Parrish, for one thing."

"What kind of incidents?"

She stares at the far wall of the room. "If you look into this, you're going to find it anyway, I might as well save you the bother. Andre Parrish has shot four people over the course of his time on the task force."

"*Four* people?"

"Two were fatalities, the two others survived..."

The marshal only stares at her.

"All of the incidents took place during high-risk fugitive apprehension missions. But Parrish didn't fire a shot yesterday." Ferguson presses her lips together. "Look, Deputy Drummond has been placed on admin leave; if it gets out he opened fire too early..."

A knock sounds at the door.

Reva Ferguson levels dark eyes on the marshal. "The passenger of that car still shot Hogie three times. Jorge Salazar. Whatever the timing of it."

She turns, opens up.

Shannon Towne is in the corridor. "Bureau of Indian Affairs is reporting the presence of a fugitive we have a warrant for—up on the Mescalero rez."

"Task force has a warrant?" Ferguson says.

"Traxler, Curtis Traxler. Warrant from the District Court in Albuquerque. Federal charge of methamphetamine tracking. BIA are requesting assistance on the arrest."

"You know why?"

"He's been seen at some trailer home. They can go get him, but they want to hand him over into federal custody, they don't want to house him."

"Where is this?"

"Up in the hills somewhere," Towne says. "Whitetail Springs, or something…"

Marshal Ferguson looks at Whicher. "We should probably do this—you might be able to talk to the guy. Traxler was on a pool list, along with Ramsay—a list the DA were looking at, before El Paso put out your warrant. He's intel."

"On Karl Ramsay?"

Ferguson nods, "Curtis Traxler's a known associate."

CHAPTER
TEN

WINTER SUN SITS LOW in a cloud-streaked sky above the forested hills lining US 70 on the Mescalero Reservation. Whicher slows the Silverado approaching the turn for a road marked *Indian Service Trail 3*.

Beside him in the passenger seat, Marshal Reva Ferguson studies a DEA folder.

Moving into the turn lane on the highway, Whicher sweeps across, steering the truck over a rusted cattle guard.

A grit road ascends a steepening grade between swathes of white fir, ponderosa pine and one-seed juniper. Shadows fleck the road from the dark-green canopy of forest. Within the woods striated light cuts shafts among the boughs and the trunks of trees.

"You come out here much?" Whicher says. "What's going on?"

"Same thing that's going on everywhere else."

"Ramsays of the world shipping drugs in?"

Ferguson nods. "It's growing. Fewer people are out here, it creates more impact. Fuels a rise in thefts, violent crime. Domestic abuse gets worse…"

The road rounds a bend, emerging into a small clearing of

Gambel oak and the stumps of felled pine—a feeling of isolation already present in the air.

"Bureau of Indian Affairs are working on it," Ferguson says. "Along with the DEA and the Valley Task Force."

"What do we know about this guy, Curtis Traxler?"

Marshal Ferguson glances at the folder in her lap. "He's been running a network."

"Dealing meth?"

"Dealing whatever. Meth, heroin. Plus, he launders."

Whicher cuts a look at her.

"Some of it through the casinos," she says, "not much. A lot of it will go in bulk currency transportation. Either out of state, cross country or back into Mexico."

"How they making that work?"

"It goes through the black-market peso exchange. DEA says he has a network of small-time dealers working for him, street-level, retail-level. My guess would be one of them shopped him."

"Somebody from here?"

"There's always bad blood. Deals gone south, scores to settle."

Ahead, the road climbs steadily, twisting, turning with the contours of the mountainside.

"How about elsewhere in the state," Whicher says. "Traxler do business farther afield?"

"South-eastern New Mexico, right up the Pecos Valley," Ferguson answers. "Along with Karl Ramsay."

"Think we'd be able to pressure him? Get him talking?" Whicher glances over at her.

"He's looking at a statutory minimum of ten years," she says. "Maximum of life. Unless he wants to cut a plea."

"How about turning state's evidence? Would he be useful enough?"

"For us to make him an offer?"

"I'm talking witness protection," the marshal says.

Ferguson puts her head on one side. "Maybe."

Whicher steers on, thinks it over. Eyes the light and shadow within the trees. "So, how about the arrest—BIA law enforcement expecting this guy to be trouble?"

"They didn't ask for much by way of backup. I guess we'll find out."

Ten miles onto the reservation the road is packed dirt now, starting to top out from the depths of the forest onto a forbidding plateau of high mountain grasses, fir and oak and pinyon pine.

Ahead, at the toeslope of an outcrop of limestone and mesquite, two tribal police vehicles are parked—an SUV and a full-size Ram pickup—three uniformed officers standing looking back along the road.

The marshal slows.

Reva Ferguson sits forward in her seat. "That's Robert Decoteau." She points through the windshield. "A lieutenant in the BIA police. Older guy, in the campaign hat."

Whicher takes him in.

A tall, raw-boned officer stands to the lieutenant's left. To his right, a thick-set younger man.

"We need to talk to 'em," Whicher says. "We don't want any repeat of yesterday."

He drives in close, brakes the truck to a halt, shuts down the motor.

Marshal Ferguson climbs from the cab. "Lieutenant," she says.

He nods a greeting.

"This is Marshal Whicher."

Decoteau turns steady eyes onto the marshal.

"He'll be assisting on the arrest."

Whicher steps forward, offers a hand.

The lieutenant takes it. Indicates a curve in the road beyond the outcrop of rock. "Trailer's just around there a ways. We think he's holed up. With a young woman."

"You know who?" Ferguson says.

"Jena Velasquez. From the rez. She's been away, living in Artesia, but the trailer belongs to her."

"You get a look yet?"

"No need to go ahead and show him we're out here," Decoteau says. "We know the ground. Word is he's in there. Been hiding out three days."

Whicher eyes the tall officer and the younger uniformed man.

"Officers Roanhorse," the lieutenant says, "and Kee. They'll make the arrest. We'll hand him over to you, you can take him out of here. Just back us up. And ship him out."

The marshal fixes him with a look. "One thing—we need to keep this low key…"

Decoteau studies on him. "Traxler sees us all, I don't imagine he'll be trouble."

Ferguson says, "You see the news yesterday?"

"The bust in Carlsbad?" The lieutenant nods.

"We don't need another incident."

"Unless he turns violent," Whicher says.

Decoteau looks at him. "What then?"

"Then you can shoot his ass."

The lieutenant grins.

Whicher doesn't return it. "Only if he comes out firing."

———

Set back among the trees where the dirt road finishes, the single-wide trailer sits on a patch of bone-hard caliche at the foot of a wooded ravine.

The tall officer, Roanhorse, steers the police truck toward a half-ton GMC pickup parked out in front. Officer Kee in the passenger seat, an AR-15 rifle propped in the footwell.

Behind them, Reva Ferguson rides with Decoteau in the lieutenant's SUV.

Whicher rolls forward in the Silverado.

Roanhorse parks at the side of the GMC truck.

Decoteau peels right to block it in from the rear.

Continuing past the lieutenant's vehicle, Whicher steers to where he can see around the back of the trailer. A patch of bare earth and stone is behind it, the ground littered with auto junk and old lumber, reels of fence wire, split wood posts.

At the tree line is a shelter made from metal siding.

Roanhorse and Kee step from their unit—both men in tactical vests.

Kee swings up the AR-15.

Roanhorse unfastens the retaining strap on a semi-automatic SIG.

Lieutenant Decoteau gets out, followed by Marshal Ferguson as Officer Kee tracks around to the rear of the trailer.

Roanhorse approaches the front door.

Ferguson stands to the side in the yard—watching the window.

Roanhorse knocks—steps back.

Whicher leaves the motor running, rolls both windows.

Wind is picking up across the plateau—moving through the pine and fir and oak—no other sound above the engine idling.

Roanhorse calls out; "Police. Open up."

The lieutenant takes a step to one side of the door.

Marshal Ferguson draws her Glock, aims at the window.

Roanhorse moves forward again toward the trailer—then stops.

The door opens a crack.

A dark-complexioned young woman with bleary eyes looks out. Her hair unkempt, face a mix; surprise, incomprehension. "What's going on?"

"Ma'am, open up, please. I need to take a look inside."

She stares at Roanhorse. At the lieutenant—at Marshal Ferguson.

Whicher shifts his gaze past the side of the trailer—a feeling ticking inside.

He comes off the brake, the truck starts to creep forward.

From in back is a series of sharp sounds.

A flat crack.

A man's voice shouting; "*Stop. Police officer—stay where you are…*"

Piling past the woman, Roanhorse and Decoteau rush the trailer through the open door.

Whicher hits the gas, weaves around rusted oil drums at the side of the trailer—sees Officer Kee, rifle at his shoulder—aiming at a man running for the trees in back.

He shouts to Kee; "*Hold it—hold your fire…*"

The fleeing man disappears into the shelter.

Kee lifts his head from his sights.

The noise of a motor barks into life.

An ATV blasts out from the shelter—its rider jumps a drainage ditch, powers up a bank of shale and scrub, disappearing out of sight.

Whicher whips the steering around, floors out the gas.

The truck lurches forward, rounds the bank of shale into a steep-sided valley—covered in dense scrub and trees.

The ATV rider swerves, brakes—drops from sight over a long, flat ridge of earth.

The marshal follows—sees the drop from the ridge's edge—a thirty-foot descent into a dry creek.

He angles the truck across the slope, tires breaking loose in the crumbling ground.

Plummeting to the bottom, he hits hard against the bed of the creek.

The ATV kicks up a high spray of dirt and gravel as Whicher pushes down on the throttle—following through the bottom of the steepening valley, the truck picking up speed, tires jolting over clumps of brushwood and stone.

In the rear-view mirror, Lieutenant Decoteau's SUV is a quarter-mile behind in a cloud of dust.

The phone rings.

Whicher answers.

Reva Ferguson speaks; "He's headed up toward a spring, the lieutenant says—Whitetail Spring."

"What's after that?"

The line is silent.

"Can he get away?"

"Lieutenant says he can get down into Bear Canyon. Onto seventy."

"You need to roll units down there."

"Lieutenant's doing it now…"

Whicher grips the wheel. "Let's see if we can't get the son of a bitch stopped…"

Ahead is a dip in the creek bank where the water course runs shallow. The marshal steers to it, floors out the throttle, the truck tears up the bank to where the valley floor is flat— hard dirt, with only light scrub.

He can go faster.

Back down in the creek bed, dust billows from the ATV. The rider steals a look behind, over his shoulder.

Sees Whicher closing in now.

Standing suddenly, he jumps the ATV.

Whicher sees all four wheels suspended in mid-air.

It crashes down—to the opposite bank of the creek.

The rider flattens to the tank—steers directly at a rock-strewn hill of pine and fir.

Whicher gets off the gas—cuts back down into the creek.

Up and out the other side—no sign of Decoteau's SUV behind him.

The motor on the ATV wails—the rider attacking the acute angle of the grade.

The marshal starts after him in the Silverado—then lets the gas pedal go—no way he can follow with any speed.

Staring, he hears the engine revs on the ATV spike.

Sees the front wheels bucking—arcing into the sky as it turns over.

It falls back, careering downward on its side, the rider falling, hurtling backward. Tumbling, rolling down the side of the hill.

The ATV crashes against the trunk of a tree—it cuts out.

Whicher stands on the brakes, jumps out, whips the large-frame Ruger revolver from the shoulder holster.

Above him on the slope, the rider tries to rise from the ground.

Whicher runs uphill, eying a dark-haired man—wincing, face contorted in pain.

"Curtis Traxler?"

The man in the hooded sweat top only glares back.

Whicher holds the big Ruger directly at him. "US Marshals Service. You're under arrest."

―――――

Back at the side of the creek, Lieutenant Decoteau's SUV sits parked alongside the marshal's Chevy—Officer Kee dragging the crashed ATV from the hill with a top-mounted winch in the bed of the Ram.

Curtis Traxler sits in the rear of Whicher's truck—cuffed and chained to a D-ring in the floor. His hands and face are cut up, clothes bloodied, grimed with dirt.

In the back of Decoteau's SUV, the young woman from the trailer, Jena Velasquez, sits wide-eyed, looking out.

Decoteau finishes up a call. Approaches Kee working the winch. "We get that ATV loaded, we're done."

The officer nods back.

The lieutenant looks to Ferguson. "You need anything? Or you want to head out, take your prisoner?"

"We should hit the road." Ferguson looks at Velasquez. "What do you plan on doing with her?"

Decoteau takes a pace closer. Lowers his voice. "You want her?"

"We need people talking," Whicher says. He glances at Curtis Traxler in the Silverado. "What do you know about him?"

"Traxler?" The lieutenant shrugs. "He was living out here a few years back. Suspect on a couple of burglaries. Assaulted a couple guys. I busted him for possession. I was glad when he left."

"How come he wasn't prosecuted?" Ferguson says.

"Lack of admissible evidence."

"He shows up here now and again?" Whicher says. "That it?"

"I got a call. Heard he was seeing Ms Velasquez. Folk on the rez know her. She's been away a while herself."

"Think he'd talk to you?" Whicher says. "Maybe coming from a BIA cop, instead of a regular fed…"

Decoteau eyes him.

"We need intel," the marshal says. "If you could get him interested."

"Why would he want to do that?"

"Marshals Service could protect him."

The lieutenant's eyes are hard. "In return for helping you?"

"For turning state's evidence," Whicher says.

The lieutenant stands a moment. Gestures with his head. "I'll go ask him."

Reva Ferguson looks at Whicher; "Is now a good time? To hit him like this?"

"He lawyers up, things can all get different."

Decoteau hitches his gun belt, walks toward the marshal's truck.

Ferguson watches. "Anything Traxler says would still have to be okayed."

"We get the idea working on him is all," Whicher says.

Leaning into the rear of the Silverado, Decoteau speaks to Curtis Traxler. The man sits slouched, expression blank. Face unresponsive.

The lieutenant continues talking.

The conversation one-way.

Finally, he turns back—mouth downturned. He shakes his head.

Whicher steps to the truck, takes out his keys. Addresses Traxler. "We're taking you on back to Carlsbad. After that you'll be going up to Albuquerque. To the District Court."

The man's eyes cut to him.

"Trafficking methamphetamine. Laundering. Resisting arrest. It ain't going to be good…"

Traxler juts his chin.

Marshal Ferguson approaches. "You don't have to be a chump your whole life. You're looking at thirty years on a prison yard…"

Whicher leans up against the side of the cab. "What do you know about Karl Ramsay?"

"What do you know about trafficking in the Pecos Valley? In the south of the state?" Ferguson says. "Who do you know?"

Traxler stares back. Screws up his face. "I don't know a damn thing, lady."

"That right?"

"They're talking about witness protection," Lieutenant Decoteau says. "Starting over, muchacho."

Traxler turns his eyes on Whicher. "Ain't nobody going to tell you a damn thing about Karl Ramsay. Not me. Not anybody else."

―――――

Roanhorse has the tailgate down on the Ram pickup, a set of steel ramps fitted to the edge of the bed.

Officer Kee positions the wheels of the ATV in line with the ramps—starts the winch.

In the rear of Decoteau's SUV Jena Velasquez stares out forlornly.

Whicher steps to the lieutenant; "You have a jail facility here?"

Decoteau grunts; "Marshals Service want to charge her?"

Jena Velasquez looks out at him. "I didn't do nothing…"

"You understand what harboring a felon is?"

Color drains from the woman's face.

"How long has he been here with you?" Whicher says.

"Couple days. He just wanted to go someplace. Get away."

"You're living in Artesia?"

"Still got my place here," Velasquez says.

Marshal Ferguson approaches the vehicle.

At the Ram pickup, Officer Kee has the ATV in the bed.

Roanhorse breaks out a set of ratchet straps to secure it.

"You shelter somebody accused of a federal offense," Whicher says, "you're going to prison."

Velasquez shakes her head.

"Anything from one year to five." He keeps his eyes on the young woman. "You known Curtis Traxler a long time?"

"I don't know… I guess a while."

"Know people he runs with?"

"What's that mean?"

"You know a man named Karl Ramsay?" The marshal sees a thought pass behind her eyes.

Velasquez sinks in her seat.

"I need to find him."

Her voice is small when she speaks. "I know a girl… a girl he sees."

"A girlfriend?"

"I mean, I've seen him come around. In Artesia. I know she sees him. Been going on a while…"

"I need a name."

Lieutenant Decoteau cuts in; "You want her, marshal?"

"Can you book her into the county jail?"

"On what charge?"

"Suspicion of harboring."

"If the Marshals Service want her, you best charge her," Decoteau says.

Reva Ferguson fixes the lieutenant with a look. "I have to get Traxler to Roswell. He's going on to the Q. We can't take her too, we have to find Karl Ramsay. Can you take her to the county sheriff?"

The lieutenant scowls.

Marshal Ferguson steps to where she can see the young woman in the back of Decoteau's car. "You know something about these people? You need to think about your situation here. Start talking."

Whicher looks at Velasquez. "I need the name of the girl."

CHAPTER ELEVEN

OUTSIDE THE WINDOW of the office at the Carlsbad Police Department the sky is full dark, light streaking the parking lot, sets of headlamps moving fast down Guadalupe Street.

Whicher drinks from a steaming hot cup of coffee, eats take-out chicken and green chile tamales; on the desk in front of him a computer terminal—with multiple screens open.

The marshal eases back in his chair. Studies the Valley Task Force files on Curtis Traxler. Thinks of calling his boss, Chief Marshal Fairbanks, back in Pecos; to talk about pushing for a charge on Jena Velasquez—if only to get the woman to talk.

A knock sounds at the door.

Marshal Reva Ferguson appears from the hallway. "I'm looking to head out. I'll take Traxler to Roswell tonight, somebody can ship him up to Q-town in the morning."

"You get him secure?"

"Leg irons and cuffs and a Martin chain, the watch sergeant fixed him up."

"Work on him," Whicher says, "if you get the chance."

Ferguson cants her head.

"We need something…"

"It could take a while."

The marshal takes a sip on his cup of coffee. "I don't have a while. Like to see about this girlfriend of Karl Ramsay."

"Even if you found her, you really think you're going to find him?"

Whicher eyes the computer monitor. "There any more from the hospital?"

"Hogan's wife is down to see him." Ferguson looks out along the corridor. "Listen, I ought to hit the road."

"Watch the guy…"

"Traxler?" Ferguson grins, "I'll watch him." She steps sideways from the room.

The marshal eats some more of the tamales, clicks onto another set of computer files. He skim-reads a preliminary report on the attempted arrest of Ramsay. A second set of files on the warranted search of the house on Pike. A third report listing out door-to-door inquiries from the general locale.

He reads it again—sits looking at the screen a long moment.

A witness statement.

Male witness at the neighboring house.

Witness reporting somebody arriving at the Pittman property the evening before the arrest.

He checks the time.

Given as ten p.m.

He thinks of the used car dealer—Delmar Sadler. Sadler delivered a car there that evening. He'd seen Karl Ramsay, inside the house, along with Pittman and Salazar.

The marshal pinches the bridge of his nose. Sits forward.

He should call. Check what time Sadler went over—tie off the loose end.

He takes the notepad from his coat. Flicks through, finds

the number. Keys a call. Steps to the window. Looks out over the few police units and civilian cars in the lot.

"Delmar Sadler."

"Mister Sadler—this is Marshal Whicher, we spoke this afternoon—about an automobile you sold?"

"Marshal..." Sadler's voice is guarded. "There something else I can do for you?"

"Just checking a few details," Whicher says, "this should just take a moment. You told us you delivered a vehicle to Mister Jorge Salazar—at an address on Pike Street?"

"Yes, I did. A Chevrolet Traverse..."

"What time would that have been, sir?"

"What time?" Sadler says. "Well, I guess around five-thirty."

"Five-thirty in the afternoon?"

"Around that."

Whicher writes the detail on the pad.

"Right after work," Sadler says, "after I got done closing up the yard. It couldn't have been any later than six."

"That's just fine, sir." The marshal pats down his pockets for the keys to his truck. "I just needed to check."

"Was there anything else?"

"No sir, that was all. Thank you for your time. I appreciate it."

The marshal clicks off the call. Grabs his hat.

Heads for the door.

———

The residential street across town is dark save for yard lights and a few lit windows in the houses. Outside the Pittman property on Pike is a police department cruiser. Black and yellow tape seals off the perimeter—signs reading *No Entry* are posted at the windows and doors.

Whicher pulls alongside the cruiser. Rolls the window, holds out his USMS badge and ID.

The officer behind the wheel cracks the door.

"Need to speak to the folks in the neighboring house, that okay with you?"

The patrolman nods. "Go right ahead, marshal."

Whicher steers the truck to the curb in front of the neighboring property—takes in the one-floor gray-rendered ranch —two cars parked in its front yard, a suburban and an SUV.

He shuts down the motor on the truck. Steps out. Fits the Resistol. Buttons his coat.

Ornamental cypress lines the concrete drive, floral planters dot the watered, green lawn.

Whicher strides to the front door, presses on the bell.

Moments pass—before a man in his late-thirties opens up—dressed in slacks and a golf shirt, his dark hair receding.

Whicher shows his badge and ID. "Sir, good evening. US Marshals Service."

The man's eyes are rounded behind steel-frame glasses. "Uh. Is this about next door?"

"Yessir, it is."

"We gave statements already," the man says. "We didn't know Mister Pittman, we don't know anything about him. We've only been out here six months. To tell you the truth, we're really just completely shocked…"

Whicher eyes the Pittman property next door. "Sir, a witness at this address said somebody showed up about ten o'clock the night before last. The night before the incident involving Mister Pittman. Is that right?"

"Oh. You mean, Greg? Gregory?"

"Gregory Joyner," the marshal says.

"Evan's friend."

"Sir?"

"Our son, Evan."

Whicher looks briefly into the hallway of the house. "I come in a moment?"

The man exhales, his face anxious. He steps aside.

Whicher enters. "Sir, you are?"

"Myron Coleman."

A slim woman emerges from the kitchen, dressed in jeans and a green cotton top.

"US Marshals Service ma'am."

"This is my wife, Caitlin."

"Is something wrong?"

"It's about that statement Greg gave…" Coleman says.

Caitlin Coleman's face goes slack. "Look, none of us saw anything. Evan's friend told a police officer he'd seen someone. He was staying over for the night. Greg said he looked out of the window—and saw someone show up there, that's all it was."

"The statement said it was around ten?"

"That's right, that's what he said…"

Myron Coleman looks at his wife, then at Whicher. "The officer didn't think it was significant."

"Greg's mom came over to pick him up, what with everything that's been going on…" Caitlin Coleman puts a hand to her chest.

"Did he describe the man to you?" Whicher says. "The witness statement says white male, around thirty to forty."

"That's what Greg told us." Coleman throws a nervous glance toward his wife.

The look she gives in return is fleeting. Shadowed.

Whicher regards her.

Myron Coleman blows out his cheeks.

"Sir? Is something wrong?"

Coleman runs a hand through his thinning hair. "Well…" He glances at his wife again. "Later—later on—he said the man he'd seen was a cop."

Whicher holds his gaze steady. "Sir?"

"I know, it's ridiculous..."

"How'd he know that? Are we talking about a cop in uniform?"

"No." Coleman's voice is dry in his throat. "No, he said not."

Caitlin Coleman clears her throat. "The TV news was on yesterday. Myron and I still can't believe it—I mean, drug traffickers, right next door..." She stops herself, looks away, suddenly. Swallows. Begins again. "They were watching the local news on the shooting at the highway. And Greg suddenly said; 'That's the man I saw'..."

The marshal keeps his eyes on her. "Y'all see what the man looked like?"

Myron Coleman shakes his head. "Neither of us saw him. It was just a short news piece. And we told Greg it must've been some mistake." Coleman looks at the marshal. Alarm in his face now, eyes wide behind the steel-frame glasses. "But that's it isn't it?"

Whicher eyes him.

"That's it. That's the reason you're here."

———

Back outside in the street, Whicher sits entirely still behind the wheel of the Silverado. Light spill from the yard of the Coleman house reflecting in the windshield of the stationary cruiser, wind moving in the branches of a live oak at the opposite side of the road.

The marshal sits. Only watching. Thinking.

Finally, he stirs.

He takes out his phone, keys a number. Listens to it ring.

Hears it pick up.

"Hey, stranger."

"Leanne."

"Didn't know if we were going to hear from you."

He pushes back in the driver's seat. "I know. It's been a long day."

"You coming home?"

His gaze runs out to the Coleman house. "Not coming home." He eyes the lit window at the front, thinks of the young family inside. "Wish I could."

"You okay?"

"Yeah. How's Lori?"

"She's okay," Leanne says. "Asking how long you'll be staying out."

The marshal thinks of his daughter. Nearly thirteen.

"You know she never likes it..."

"I know."

"So, are you expecting to stay out," Leanne says, "till you can make an arrest?"

"We've got one dead," Whicher says, "one in the hospital. One of ours pretty messed up..."

"Oh," Leanne says.

The marshal hears the lightness in his wife's tone. Used to it; used to hearing it, knowing it for a mask to hide the worry inside.

He pictures her, misses her, suddenly. "El Paso want this guy..."

"Your boss wants her best investigator out there..."

Whicher stares out along the street. "I'm here to bring the guy in. Unless something changes. There's heat on yesterday, Chief of Police gave a press call..."

"Did they push you out there? On camera? I'm sure you loved that."

Whicher cracks a grin, doesn't answer.

"I'll take that as a no."

"I had to go make an arrest on Indian land. Tribal reservation over in Mescalero," he says. "With the BIA. Not related. It might get us a couple leads." The marshal regards the police unit outside of the Pittman property.

"Is everything alright?" Leanne says.

"Uh-huh."

"You sound... a little down."

Whicher rubs a hand over his face. "Ah, there's a kid I need to find. Bunch of things going on... And something I don't like..." The marshal stops himself.

"What do you mean?"

"I don't know," he says, "just a feeling."

"What feeling?"

"About all this," Whicher says.

"John, you need to get some rest. Eat. You have a room, right? A hotel. Go get some food."

"I know."

"Okay? Get some sleep. Nobody's ever gotten away from you. Why would this be any different?"

Whicher thinks of Myron and Caitlin Coleman. Of the fear in their faces. Of the drywall in the neighboring house, stashed full of Mexican Ice. A ton of it. Wholesale quantities—amounting to fortunes. Deadly amounts. The violence around it always extreme.

And an innocent kid.

Overlooking a late-night arrival from a bedroom window.

Not just anybody.

Not anybody.

A cop.

"Yeah," he says.

"What do you mean, yeah?"

"Nothing."

A note is in Leanne's voice now. "Come on, what's going on?"

He feels a tightness—low, in the pit of his stomach. "I don't know... but this here..."

"What about it?"

He stares out along the dark street. The Ruger tight against his side beneath the ranch coat. Thinking of rounds slamming into the white Toyota, rapid fire exploding into it. The limp bodies of the men shot up inside.

"This all right here…"

He thinks again of a cop.

A cop in a place he never should have been in.

"This all could get real nasty…"

CHAPTER
TWELVE

THE ROAD through Otero County rises steadily into greening, wooded hills. Stands of Douglas fir and pine line the slopes of the Lincoln National Forest, interwoven with patches of oak and juniper in the early morning sun.

Whicher drives the deserted two-lane—twisting through a rugged country of rough meadow and fenced pasture—signs for hunting outfitters and horse trails and campgrounds by the sides of the road.

Entering the settlement of Twin Forks he sees the elevation marker—at over eight thousand, one hundred feet.

The road is still rising. He shifts behind the wheel, steers along the snaking highway through a forested mountain valley—past dilapidated barns and a few new-built houses set back in grassland now flecked with clumps of white.

Whicher takes in the strangeness of his surrounds—the height of the land cooling, rarefying the air, ushering year-round rains.

Rains now turning to winter snow.

In the old Western mountain village of Cloudcroft, the marshal drives a main street lined with plank-front stores and timber walkways. Galleried saloons and hotels mix with tourist cafes and hipster joints. Dirty snow is pushed to the sides of the road, white powder layered onto the roofs of cars and pickups.

A bright-painted food truck is set up in the street selling breakfast tacos.

Whicher pulls in, shuts off the motor in the Silverado.

He slides out from behind the wheel.

A bearded man in a flannel shirt and watch cap regards him from the food truck.

The marshal approaches, scans the menu board. "Morning."

"Morning to you, sir," the man says.

"I could use some breakfast."

"We got that."

"I'll take the flour tortillas—with eggs, pico de gallo, carnitas and refried beans."

The food truck vendor smiles to himself. In his sixties, sharp-eyed. "Fine choice." He sets to making up the order. "You out of Texas?"

The marshal nods.

"I can always tell."

Whicher surveys the buildings and businesses lining the intersecting streets. Thrift stores and art supplies vie for space with truck and auto parts dealers—crystal emporiums and jewelers sit alongside micro-breweries and bakeries.

"Here to explore the great outdoors?" the food vendor says.

"In a manner of speaking."

"I get you something to go with this?"

"Cup of coffee."

He glances along the street. "If you want it spiced with

pumpkin or blackberry mocha or whatever, your craft coffee is over yonder."

"Yeah," Whicher says. "Regular is just fine."

"Here on business? Visiting, enjoying the Lord's great country?"

"Looking for the Osha Trail Road."

The man points along the street. "Down thataway. Couple blocks from here you'll see a dirt road, make a left."

The marshal looks past the storefronts.

"It gets kind of rough."

"Am I good in a truck?"

"Unless the snow's real bad."

The marshal inclines his head. "Looking for a property up there."

"Well, there ain't much." The vendor assembles the tortillas, fills them. "A few cabins. Log homes. Couple houses. There's some trailers. And campgrounds over by two-forty-four, if you're going over that end."

"Looking for an artist."

"You'll find a bunch of 'em out here," the man says. "Big arts community. Painters, sculptors. All kinds of folk."

Whicher pays for the food and the coffee. Eyes the singular mélange of storefronts and businesses making up the street. "Quite the mix out here…"

"People come from all over…"

The marshal takes his change from the counter, gathers up breakfast, picks up the cup of coffee.

"Enjoy," the man says. "And good hunting."

———

Out at the back end of town the grit road follows the side of a wooded hill through pine and fir, sunlight breaking through the canopy onto snow on the ground, swift cloud moving overhead.

The last of the regular houses is miles back, only a few cabins and trailers sit back from the road.

Whicher sees an A-frame wood house and barns in a patch of white-over meadow.

A posted sign scrolled with hand-carved lettering reads, *Tall Firs Artists' Retreat.*

The marshal turns up the drive onto the property, studies the house and a deck built to one side; a counterpoint to the steep pitch of the A-frame roof. He steers toward an old-model Jeep Wrangler parked out in front.

Coming to a halt, he kills the engine. Takes the Marshals badge and ID from his pocket. Steps out.

Beyond the house and the deck is an overlook down into a secluded valley.

Stepping to a lacquered timber front door he knocks hard.

He takes a pace back. Listens. A silence hits him—deep silence. He takes a lungful of breath. A mild ache is in his head—he thinks of the heightened altitude, the thinness of the air.

The door opens.

A woman stands looking out—dressed in paint-stained jeans and a threadbare sweater. Her eyes clear, dark brown, her face open, unkempt black hair falling to her shoulders.

"Ms Joyner?"

"Is this about the booking?" she says. "In December? The painters' workshop? Acrylics and oils?"

Whicher holds up his badge and ID.

Her face clouds.

"I'm from the Marshals Service."

"Is something wrong?"

"It's about an incident, a couple of days back. Down in Carlsbad."

"You mean that awful shooting?"

"Yes, ma'am."

"Those drug dealers…" She puts a hand to the door. Her body stiffens. "We don't know anything about any of that…"

"Ma'am?"

She only stares out.

"If I could come in? For just a moment."

She lets out a short breath. Steps back.

Whicher follows her inside.

The living area of the house is bathed in light from picture windows and sliding glass doors—sun warming the timber-lined walls, lighting up a mismatch of furnishings and décor and original art.

"You're aware of the incident?" Whicher says. "At the property next door to where your son was staying?"

"At the Colemans, yes I know."

"I spoke with Mister Coleman last night. And his wife. They told me about your son. Giving a witness statement."

Annaliese Joyner rubs a paint-stained hand across her brow. "This whole thing is such a shock." She shakes her head. "I mean, for Caitlin, for Myron, they just can't believe it—they've only lived there a few months."

"Your son is friendly with their son?"

"From when we lived in Artesia," the woman says. "Greg and he went to the same school. The Colemans were living there at the time. We moved here about a year ago. Then they moved there to Carlsbad…"

"Your son gave a statement—that he'd seen somebody arrive at the house the night before the shooting incident?"

She nods.

"He told the Colemans the man he'd seen was a cop."

Annaliese Joyner looks at him a long moment. She swallows, doesn't make any reply.

"Is your son here ma'am?"

"No."

"He in school?"

"He's homeschooled. A friend of mine's running class today. There's a group of us, we share the teaching…"

"Ma'am, did your son talk to you about it? Did he tell you what he saw?"

"Look," she hesitates. "He said he saw a news clip on TV. Later on. At the Colemans. After he'd given his statement, after the police had gone away. I think he was confused… he thought one of the men looked like the man he saw."

"One of the officers in the news clip?"

The woman's face is anxious. "Look, why are you here?"

Whicher doesn't answer.

"Is this… serious?"

The marshal scans the room, lets his gaze run out to the view of the ravine-like valley beyond the picture window.

"I mean why would a police officer visit a house a drug dealer was living in?"

"Ma'am, I need to talk to your son. I need to see him."

CHAPTER
THIRTEEN

A MILE farther up the Osha Trail Road, Whicher follows Annaliese Joyner's Jeep Wrangler onto private property toward a log house and clapboard barns set back among the trees in a small, snow-covered clearing.

In the doorway to one of the barns, a woman with graying, dreadlocked hair looks out—wearing a mountain fleece, a hand-printed tunic. Knee-length, fur-topped boots.

Annaliese drives her Jeep up to the house, parks.

Whicher pulls in alongside her, eases out of the truck.

Annaliese steps from her vehicle. "Grace."

The woman glances at her, takes in Whicher. "Everything alright?"

"I need to talk to Greg."

The woman keeps her eyes on Whicher. "You sure everything's alright?"

Whicher holds out his badge and ID. "Ma'am. Everything's just fine, Gregory's not in any trouble. I just need to see him a minute."

The woman looks to Annaliese. "Is this about... that Carlsbad thing?"

Annaliese nods. "It's okay."

The dreadlocked woman turns to Whicher. "You're a marshal?"

"Yes ma'am."

"This is Grace Pires," Annaliese says.

Pires regards him, her face doubtful. "Alright. Well, I'll send him on out."

———

Standing with the boy at the edge of the woodland clearing, Whicher watches from the tree line—as Annaliese Joyner leans against her Jeep.

She stares at the two of them, head canted to her chest—arms folded across a duck down coat.

Gregory Joyner is slight, his hair down to his shoulders, eyes lively. He wears old jeans, muddy sneakers, a baseball jacket over a hooded top.

Standing, looking at Whicher, he stuffs his hands down into his pockets.

"You don't need to be nervous. You're not in any trouble, it's just about what you saw."

The boy flicks hair from his eye.

"It's about what happened at the Colemans place," Whicher says. "When you were staying over. With your buddy, Evan."

Gregory looks up at him, searches his face.

Whicher sees the openness—the same lack of guile as his mother. "You gave a statement to a police officer. Told him you'd seen a man arrive the night before the shooting happened up the road? At the neighbor's house. That right?"

The boy looks afraid. "He asked if I'd seen anybody coming or going."

"It's okay," Whicher says. "I just want you to tell me what you saw."

"Well, Evan was setting up a new game."

"Y'all were playing video games?"

"I got up to use the bathroom. When I came back in the room, I heard a car door close. I looked out of the window. I saw a man next door, walking up the yard."

"You see the vehicle he arrived in?"

Gregory shakes his head. "I couldn't see to the street. I just heard a car pull up, I heard a door closing. And then this guy was walking up to the house."

"What time was this?" Whicher says.

"About ten."

"Ten o'clock at night?"

"Around that."

"What happened then?"

Gregory takes his hands from his pockets. "Well, he walked up to the door. He looked like he pressed the bell." The boy mimics the action. "Then he went in."

"What did he look like?"

"I mean, he just looked like a guy, a regular guy. Wearing jeans, a jacket…"

"Was he big, small? Young, old?"

"I don't know, I guess like Evan's dad."

"About that age? Late thirties? Early forties?"

"I don't know, I guess. Not old."

"In his thirties?"

The boy nods.

"You get a look at his face?"

"He was kind of dark. With real dark hair. Kind of pushed back off of his face. He looked… Italian or something…"

"Dark?"

"Yeah."

"Hispanic?"

"I don't know. I don't think."

"There anything else?"

"Well, he was smoking. He was smoking a cigarette."

The marshal regards Gregory—his eyes are still, his face neutral.

"He was smoking it walking up the driveway. Then waiting at the door. He turned his head and blew out his smoke. That's how I saw his face."

"He see you?"

Gregory shakes his head, eyes rounded.

"You sure?"

The boy swallows.

"You have the light on in Evan's room?" Whicher says. "You would've stood out."

"We had the lights out."

"You were playing in the dark?"

"We could still see."

"Alright, what happened after that?"

"He went inside."

"You see him leave?"

"No."

"You hear him? Or hear his car?"

"We got back into gaming," Gregory says, "we had the sound up and all. I don't know what happened. I didn't think about it..."

Whicher eyes the barn, the house. The boy's mother glaring from the Jeep. "Can you tell me anything else? This guy seem relaxed? Nervous? In a hurry? Taking his time?"

Gregory thinks about it. "He walked up fast. Like, he wasn't hanging around."

"You see the person who let him in?"

"I just saw the door open. Then he stepped inside."

"You get another look when the door opened? In the light from the house?"

The boy nods.

"So. You got a pretty good look. Couple looks."

Gregory stares at the marshal. His eyes cut away.

"Later on," Whicher says, "you saw something else. That right?"

The boy doesn't answer.

"It's okay," Whicher says. "I just need to know what else you saw."

"It was a news report... because of the shooting. They were showing it on TV. And then I saw him again. Right there."

"The man that came to the house?" Whicher feels the twist in his gut. "You recognized him? What was he wearing?"

"Like... army pants. A bulletproof vest..."

Whicher feels his mood descending.

"He was with the other cops..."

In Gregory's face is anxiety, confusion.

"Was he wearing anything on his head—like a helmet, along with his other gear?"

"He was just standing there. He didn't have anything on his head. He was with another guy. Dressed the same." Gregory's voice rises. "And he was smoking a cigarette. And he had the dark hair, all pushed back. So, I recognized him, right away..."

He stops.

Whicher lets the moment pass. Keeps his voice measured, even. "You recognize him again? If you saw him?"

A wariness steals across the boy's face. His eyes cloud, his body tensing.

No matter.

You have your answer, the marshal tells himself.

Despite the silence.

The boy knows what he saw.

Who he saw.

No doubt in the marshal's mind.

No doubt in Gregory Joyner's.

———

Back down the snow-covered road at the A-frame house, Whicher keys a call to Marshal Reva Ferguson.

It picks up.

"You get your prisoner delivered?" Whicher thinks of Curtis Traxler—Ferguson transporting him up to the city of Roswell.

"Last night, yeah," she says, "he's headed up to Albuquerque later on today."

"Get anything from him on the ride up?"

"Hardly said two words," Ferguson says. "What are you doing about the girlfriend? You go talk to her?"

"Not yet. I'm working something..." The marshal shifts in the driver's seat of the truck.

"So, are you going to kick her loose?"

"I'll go see her. Did you hear back from your source yet? Your trucker? Grady Owens."

"Called this morning. Said he hadn't heard a thing. He mentioned the Mexican again; the guy he says Ramsay's looking for."

"On the black tar deal? You have any idea who that could be?"

"I'm checking Valley Task Force files..."

Annaliese Joyner steps from the house out onto the adjoining deck, her face dark. She stares out into the woods, over the valley at the back of the property.

"I spoke with an agent at DEA," Ferguson says. "They reckon Ramsay's in and out of Artesia, where Jena Velasquez is at."

"That's what, thirty, forty miles from Carlsbad?"

"About that."

"You think he could be there?"

"Could be. He could be anywhere."

Annaliese turns to look directly at Whicher in the truck. "Listen, I want to talk to Deputy Drummond. You know him?"

"Billy Drummond? Not real well. I know they put him on admin leave. How's that going to help you find Karl Ramsay?"

The marshal doesn't respond.

"USMS don't investigate officer-involved shootings," Ferguson says, "you know that. Did Chief Garton ask you to talk to him?"

"It's nothing like that."

"Oh?"

Whicher hears the doubt in Reva Ferguson's voice. "My boss is going to need to know what happened."

On the deck, Annaliese Joyner breaks off looking at him—she turns, re-enters the house.

"I can get you a number."

"I'd appreciate it."

"Alright," Ferguson says. "Let me know if you hear anything on Ramsay?"

"Likewise, if your man has something, call."

Pine and fir and snow and rock descend into foothills of endless forest. The call of birds and the wind are the only sounds. From the timber deck the view of the valley shows an undisturbed tract of nature.

Annaliese eyes the marshal, guarded. She leans against the railing at the side. "Are you going to ask my son to give a second statement?"

Whicher regards her.

"You don't seriously think he saw anything, do you?" She holds her arms folded across her sweater. "We don't want anything to do with any of it. The police. Drugs. Those awful people next door to Caitlin and Myron. The whole reason we moved out here was to get away from all of that. Gregory's twelve years old," she says, "he has friends from his old school caught up in it…"

"He wouldn't have to come to Carlsbad," Whicher says. "I could take his statement here."

She snaps her head away, stares back out into the valley. "He made his statement, that's it. He's not giving another."

"Ma'am, he says he saw a man he later recognized—as a law enforcement officer."

Her voice is tight; "He only thinks that…"

"He saw him at the house next door to the Colemans." The marshal studies the untouched valley, an Eden, unsullied, an innocent dream.

"Why does it even matter?"

Whicher steps closer to her. "Because we had a task force assembled to arrest a man there."

In her eyes is fear, incomprehension.

"And next morning," the marshal says, "the man we were looking for was gone."

CHAPTER
FOURTEEN

TWENTY MILES west in the town of Alamogordo, Whicher pulls the Chevy into the lot of the Otero County Sheriff's Office off of White Sands Boulevard.

Eying the one-floor building, he shuts down the motor, steps out.

He crosses the lot, squares the Resistol, enters reception, sees a round-faced deputy in tan uniform shirt behind the counter.

A female dispatcher in the room behind stares at a flat-screen monitor.

Whicher holds out his ID. "US Marshals Service—I called on my way over, about a young woman you're holding? Jena Velasquez?"

"Brought in by the Bureau of Indian Affairs?" The deputy picks up a pair of eyeglasses from the countertop, puts them on, searches in a file tray. "Sheriff says there isn't room to hold her."

"Oh?"

"You'll have to take her someplace else if you want to keep her. We've got no space in gen pop. BIA said the hold was just one night." The deputy finds the booking form, gestures with his head toward a secure door. "She's in there. Right on down at the end of the corridor."

Whicher checks the custody release form and booking document.

The deputy slides a security card over the counter. "I'll need that back."

Crossing to the door at the side of the reception lobby, Whicher slides the card into a reader, sees the unit flash, presses on the switch to enter.

A corridor is on the other side. Strip lighting. The smell of disinfectant.

The marshal passes a series of closed cell doors, reaches an open-sided cell, fitted out with floor-to-ceiling steel bars.

Jena Velasquez sits on a fold-out cot—looking out through heavy-duty wire mesh between the bars. Her long dark hair is draped over her shoulders. Stress etched into her face, her eyes burned out, fatigued.

"Ms Velasquez. Here to talk to you about yesterday."

The woman glares at him.

"You thought about what I told you?"

Velasquez slumps an inch on the cot. "I don't know what you want…"

The marshal steps to the bars of the cell. "I want Karl Ramsay. Want to find him. Arrest him, take him in. You were harboring an associate of his…"

She shakes her head.

"Curtis Traxler at your property—a wanted felon."

"I didn't know…"

"Good luck telling that to the judge."

She lifts her face, looks at him. "We just went back to the rez. To get away."

"From what?" the marshal says.

The woman lets out a breath.

"That's the whole reason you're in this mess. You his girlfriend?"

Velasquez shrugs.

"In a relationship?"

Her look is blank. "I known Curt a long time… I mean, sometimes yes, sometimes no…"

"But you're not living there anymore—at your trailer?"

She shakes her head. "I'm over in Artesia."

"Doing what?"

"I work in a store. A clothes store, my cousin owns it—and you're going to get me fired…"

"You just took off?" Whicher says.

"Curt came over. He said he wanted to kick back, get high. Whatever."

"That it? You went on back to Mescalero, to the hills? Like that?"

"I told my cousin I got sick." Velasquez spreads her palms in her lap. "What do you want from me?"

"Want you thinking about your future."

She holds his look a moment. Her head drops between her shoulders.

"You want to spend the next five years of your life in prison?"

She stares at the floor.

"You expect anybody to believe you don't know your boyfriend is a wanted criminal? I bring it to the DA, they're going to want answers…"

Velasquez sits silent, mouth clamped shut.

"You told me Karl Ramsay had a girl. Someone you know?"

She looks up from the cot.

"I want a name."

"Alright. Charlene."

"Charlene who?"

"Kingbird."

"She from the reservation?"

"Navajo Nation," Velasquez answers. "But she's in Artesia, living there."

"She see him often?"

"I don't know."

"Regular?"

Velasquez nods.

"She work?"

"No."

"How's she live?"

"He pays." Velasquez makes a face, bugs her eyes.

"He pays for a place? Gives her money?"

"She's his girl."

Whicher takes out a pen and the lined notebook from his ranch coat. "I need an address."

She only stares.

"I get an address, I'll see about getting you out of here."

———

Headed back down US 82 east Whicher scans the low hills descending from the Sacramento Mountains outside the settlement of Mayhill, trees of the Lincoln Forest starting to thin now, along with the snow. Road signs for deer are still everywhere despite two thousand feet of elevation drop.

He keys a call to Sergeant Shannon Towne back at the Carlsbad Police Department. Sets the call to speaker.

It picks up—the sergeant comes on the line. "I spoke with Fergie this morning," Towne says. "She told me you got Traxler. She said he ran like hell."

Whicher slows rounding a sharp bend on the highway. "I just got through with a girl we picked up with him, a young woman—Jena Velasquez. She gave me the name of a girlfriend of Ramsay's—Charlene Kingbird. Ever hear of her? Or Velasquez?"

"I don't think."

"I had the BIA put Velasquez in the jail at Otero County. Threatened her with harboring."

"Fight dirty, huh?"

"Maybe. I went over this morning, broke her out of there. Dropped her back at the reservation." He thinks of her; subdued, anxious. Wary of her own shadow. "The address I got for this Charlene Kingbird is in Artesia. I'm going to stop by on my way back."

"Oh?"

"Probably a long shot…"

"Yeah, if she's just some squeeze."

"Ramsay keeps her. Maybe she's more than that."

"Yeah? Well, she'll most likely blank you."

"There been anything more on Antonio Pittman?"

"You mean, from the hospital?"

"They put him in a coma."

"Billy Drummond put the douche in a coma," Towne says.

"Last I heard it wasn't looking good. He still alive?"

The sergeant's voice is dark when he answers. "I don't know. I didn't hear he wasn't."

CHAPTER
FIFTEEN

BOX STORES and fast-food restaurants line the highway into Artesia—an oil and gas town of new-built hotels and businesses along the main strip, ice cream and burger joints interspersed among realtors and construction supply.

The marshal passes a pristine Baptist church; sees a new-looking high school football stadium—the feel of money in the air.

He makes a right at an intersection by a gas station—onto West 13th. Follows a broad street under live oak.

At Missouri Avenue he makes a left onto an unremarkable residential road.

A mix of new and older houses line the street—in white-painted clapboard, rendered in tans and creams.

At the corner with Sixth is a brick and stucco three-bed property. Red tile roof and an attached garage. No vehicle is in the driveway.

He pulls over at the curbside, studies the house—sees no outward sign of life.

Catty-corner across the street is an elementary school. The marshal eyes it. Shuts off the motor, slips the keys from the ignition, steps from the truck.

Walking up the front yard to the house, the sound of children playing drifts in the air.

At the front door he knocks. Hears nothing from within the house. "*US Marshal,*" he calls out.

He scans the neighboring properties. Sees no one.

A path leads along the side of the house, the marshal takes it.

He walks around to the yard in back. Along the rear façade is a double-wide kitchen window, a door—and then another, smaller window set high, likely one of the bedrooms.

The marshal steps to the kitchen door. Raps a knuckle against the glass. "US Marshals Service. Anybody home?"

He looks through the picture window. A few dishes sit in the sink. Cups and glasses are on a table, along with a crumpled grocery bag.

No sign of Charlene Kingbird.

He turns around, scans the empty yard—little more than a patch of dead grass and bone-hard earth. Empty planters sit in a row by a chain link fence.

Turning back to the kitchen window, he peers in further. He can make out a corridor—beyond it, part of a living room.

He stops short.

Puts a hand against the glass.

White sneakers are on the floor, legs—dressed in jogging pants—a figure lying prone.

He steps back, slips the Glock semi-automatic from the clip holster at his waist. Searches the window for a place to break it. Grabs the handle of the door—tries it—it's unlocked.

He opens up, steps inside.

Leads with the pistol.

Moving through the kitchen he calls out; "*US Marshal...*"

He moves fast, enters the living room.

A young woman lies prone. Her eyes are closed, mouth open, arms splayed at her sides.

In front of a couch is a table—on it, a small glass pipe, a wrap filled with chunks of clear crystal.

The marshal kneels, puts a finger to the woman's neck—a young woman, Native American, barely out of her teens.

There's a pulse. Weak.

She's breathing; but only just.

He moves fast, checks the bedrooms, the bathroom—makes sure nobody else is in the house. Running back to the living room, he turns the woman half-prone. She's unresponsive. He checks her airways, listens to her labored breathing.

He grabs his phone, dials 9-1-1.

A male dispatcher answers.

"This is Deputy US Marshal Whicher—I need an ambulance at Missouri Avenue—I have a female overdose victim—still breathing, but not conscious."

"Copy that, marshal."

"She's not in good shape."

"We'll roll a unit right away."

"She's on the floor," Whicher says, "I don't know if she passed out—or had a heart attack, or a seizure. There's crystal meth and a pipe beside her. I just got here, I don't know how long she's been like this…"

"There any sign of co-use?" the dispatcher says. "Could she have taken anything with it—opioids? Anything else?"

"I don't know…"

"Can you stay with her?"

"I'll stay."

"Can you give me the full address?"

The marshal says it out loud.

"You're five minutes from the hospital, somebody will be there right away."

He stares down at the young woman, hardly more than a girl.

"You still there, marshal?"

"Still here."

"They're rolling now, they just minutes away."

Whicher kneels, takes in the striking face of the young woman—the frailty of her slim body, inert, crumpled like a child.

He feels an anger rising. Speaks softly; "It's alright, just hold on..." No reaction registers. "Just hold on..."

Standing, he moves to the front door, unlocks it—throws it open. He checks the living room for any signs of different drugs, steps again to the front door, looks for the ambulance —hears only the sound of kids' voices from the school.

The attached garage catches his eye—he ought to check it.

Running back through the house into the kitchen, he sees a door leading out to the side. A key is in the lock—he opens it.

Stepping through, he finds a switch for the lights.

Parked in the garage is an SUV; a Chevy Traverse.

In the garage space, stacks of carboard boxes line the back and outer walls.

He opens one—inside are bags filled with shards, glass-like crystal.

He opens another box—the same crystals inside.

Exiting the garage, he runs back in the house, kneels at the side of the young woman. Puts his hand to the pulse at her neck. Hears the wail and pop of a siren's approach.

/ ———

An ambulance stands silent in the driveway of the house—its rear doors thrown open, gurney waiting at the front door.

The marshal keys a call, paces in the front yard.

Shannon Towne answers.

"I found the car—Ramsay's car."

"Say again?"

"That Chevy SUV—the Traverse—the one Delmar Sadler sold?"

"To Salazar? The guy killed on the bust?"

"It's here in Artesia. At Charlene Kingbird's place—I found her OD'd in the house."

"Damn. There any sign of Ramsay?"

"No sign. EMTs are working on the girl now."

"She bad?"

Whicher eyes the house, the gurney. "Pretty bad. Listen, the place is full of ice—Mexican Ice—the garage is half filled with it."

"Ramsay using it as a stash house?"

"Or maybe it's a bug-out deal—for the day it hits the fan."

The sergeant whistles into the phone. "You want to call in DEA?"

"I'm here for Ramsay," Whicher says, "anything else is you guys, the Valley Task Force. I don't want a bunch of drugs."

"It's evidence…"

"I don't need evidence, I'm not investigating him—I already have a warrant. I just need to find the son of a bitch, bring him in." The marshal pictures the half-dead woman lying inside the house. "I intend to do that…"

"I hear you."

"Call whoever you need to call, let 'em know the place is full of crystal meth. For what it's worth, I say leave it in here. We could stake out the house, watch for him coming back." Whicher stares at the closed door of the attached garage. "It's a lure. He's set his own trap."

The sergeant stays silent, thinking it over.

"I'll get Charlene Kingbird to the hospital. If we leave his car, leave the ice, leave the place as it is, Ramsay's probably going to come back."

"What kind of volume on the narcs?"

"There's boxes of it lining the walls in the garage."

At the front door a male EMT appears—talking fast into a radio.

"Alright, look," Towne says, "I should be able to get a couple of guys from the task force right over—can you wait?"

The EMT lifts the detachable stretcher from the carrier.

Whicher covers the phone with his hand, calls across; "You moving her?"

"Going now," the man calls back.

"How is she?"

The EMT gives a shake of the head, a grimace. He re-enters the house.

Whicher uncovers the phone.

"I'll get people out there," Towne says.

"Don't let one of them be Parrish."

The sergeant's voice is a mix; surprised, guarded. "Why not?"

"Just find someone else."

The marshal hangs up.

CHAPTER SIXTEEN

A BLOCK and a half back from the house on Missouri Avenue, Whicher watches the property, thinks of Charlene Kingbird—thinks of her lifeless face as the EMTs wheeled her out to the ambulance.

He thinks of Karl Ramsay. He would have driven there, left the new-bought vehicle from Delmar Sadler; everything worked out ahead of time. Another car likely waiting for him to switch into—the Chevy left behind as backup.

What car would he be driving now?

Did Charlene Kingbird have a car?

The streets are deserted, the sidewalks of the residential neighborhood empty—barely any traffic moving. Whicher focuses on the house, on its immediate surrounds.

Taking out his phone, he scrolls the list of contacts. Keys a call.

It rings, picks up.

His boss, Chief Deputy Marshal Fairbanks answers.

"I just found a vehicle Karl Ramsay's been using."

"In Carlsbad?"

"Artesia. About forty miles north of there."

"Any sign of Ramsay?"

"Not yet."

"It sounds like you're getting close?"

Whicher stares through the windshield out into the road. "Wherever he goes, I'm going to find him..."

Fairbanks picks up the tone of his voice. "Everything alright?"

The marshal checks his rear-view mirror—sees nothing behind. "I think we could have a problem."

"What kind of a problem?"

"I think somebody on the task force tipped off Karl Ramsay—let him know we were coming the other day."

The chief marshal is silent on the line.

"This morning, I went to see a witness—a kid that says he saw somebody at the house—the night before we tried to make the arrest. The kid later recognized him as law enforcement..."

"Is this a credible witness?"

"I think so."

His boss lets out a long breath.

"The guy this kid saw has a questionable record," the marshal says.

"How so?"

"He's been involved in four shootings on the task force. It's dangerous work—I know that. But I think there's something there, maybe something more than that."

"The officer-involved shooting on the Ramsay arrest," his boss says, "is this who we're talking about?"

"No, ma'am. It's his partner."

A half-ton pickup noses around the corner at the end of the block—Whicher watches it—a man in a snapback behind the wheel.

"But you have a witness who says he saw this person?" Fairbanks says. "At the house. And you believe him? Who else knows about this?"

"Nobody." The marshal tracks the pickup—watches it turn past the elementary school, continue along the road.

"John, if you think there's something there, I'll back you."

Whicher takes in his boss's words—the sound of her voice measured; guarded.

"But you need to be careful. And you'll need this cleaner than clean—this was your op, your attempt at an arrest. It was your intervention for USMS Texas—even if it was a New Mexico task force."

"I know that, ma'am."

"What do you intend to do?"

"I'm going to see the guy's partner. Tell him I just want to see if he's okay. See if he wants to talk about what went down."

"You know," Fairbanks says, "you need to think about this. This could be real bad news. It might be better I withdraw you—let El Paso find somebody else."

"I don't want to do that."

"You think this is a lone actor? Could there be others?"

Whicher doesn't answer.

"Do you think your witness is safe?"

The marshal stares along the street at the house on the corner of Missouri Avenue. "Nobody knows about this kid, ma'am. And I intend for it to stay that way."

Two phone calls and a twenty-minute wait on civilian support at the Pecos office show no vehicle registered with DMV in Charlene Kingbird's name. Wherever Karl Ramsay was, he wasn't in any vehicle belonging to her.

Whicher sits. Keeps watch on the house. Thinks of Cloudcroft, up in the mountains. Thinks of Annaliese Joyner. No way she wanted her son testifying against a law officer in any court.

He thinks of talking with the chief of police, Eugene Garton. Or telling somebody else on the task force. Too much of a risk.

Gregory had been confused, afraid—as if witnessing a thing could make him part of it. In some twisted way it did; the boy knew it, instinctively, his mother knew it, too.

Dig deeper, Whicher tells himself. Tell nobody else.

A gray Ford Explorer moves slowly down Missouri Avenue in his rear-view mirror.

It pulls in to the curb a half-block behind him.

The marshal sees a lone man at the wheel.

The driver sits, makes no move to get out.

Whicher's phone rings—he picks up.

"Shannon Towne. Right behind you."

The marshal eyes the silhouette—of Towne in the rear-view.

"Thought I'd come up. Help you stake out the house. I called Artesia PD and the DEA, they're sending people."

The call clicks out.

Shannon Towne steps from the unmarked vehicle. Dressed in jeans and a wool jacket. He moves up the sidewalk. Arrives at the truck.

Whicher gestures for him to get in.

Towne opens the door. "Seen anybody?"

Whicher shakes his head.

The sergeant climbs in. "Could be a long wait, huh?"

"Could be."

"Which is the house?" Towne settles into the passenger seat.

Whicher points through the windshield. "Corner of the next block. Brick and stucco with the red tile roof and the attached garage."

The sergeant stares out at it.

"Ramsay will probably try to call the girl sometime,"

Whicher says. "He'll want to know why she's not there. Not picking up calls."

"Unless he left," Towne says. "Just split. For Q-town, or out of state…"

"Yeah…"

"You don't think?"

"There's a ton of crystal meth in there," Whicher says, "boxes and boxes. It's all along two walls. What's it go for?"

"Eight ball on the street will run you seventy to a hundred," the sergeant says.

"Could be a couple million there, easy."

"They cut it, right, it could be more."

The marshal rubs a hand across his jaw. "No way he's leaving that."

"Unless it's not his."

"Then how come it's hidden in his girlfriend's place?"

Towne nods. "So we watch the house, rotate people."

"You have enough officers with task force status?"

"Got multiple officers sworn in," the sergeant says. "We should be able to keep a presence, at least for a while. If DEA want to remove the product, that's their call."

Whicher thinks about it.

Towne looks at him. "There any news on the girl?"

"I'll have to call the hospital."

"She was alive, when they took her out?"

"Just about." Whicher's mood darkens.

The sergeant turns to studying the neighboring properties at either side of the street. "You believe Ramsay filled his girlfriend's place with ice?"

"It's right opposite from an elementary school." The marshal points it out.

Towne peers along the street across the intersection to the schoolyard and buildings. "Yeah. That could be a problem."

"Surveillance teams will need to factor it in."

"I ask you something?" Towne turns in his seat. "How come you didn't want Deputy Parrish here?"

"Karl Ramsay's my bust. My warrant," Whicher says. "This all is your beat—the Valley Task Force, the whole operation, the High Intensity Drug Trafficking Area program..."

"But?"

"I've got a federal warrant. I intend to serve it. Take in Ramsay." He cuts a look at the sergeant.

"What's that have to do with Andre Parrish?"

"I don't need anything going sideways."

Towne bridles.

"Considering the last time," Whicher says.

"A low-life pulls a gun on a vehicle stop—you don't think that can happen? People get shot up, it's not what anybody wants..."

"I'm hearing bad things around Andre Parrish. He's out."

The sergeant sits back in his seat. Eyes the street.

"He's been involved in four shootings serving on federal task forces," Whicher says.

"You look him up?"

"Two of them fatal. That's one hell of a hit rate for a Ramos County sheriff's deputy."

"More than it ought to be, I grant you..."

"And nothing's happened over any of it? Nobody brought any charges?"

Towne shakes his head. "Local DA's don't have authority to prosecute federal officers."

"Right," Whicher says. "And while he's on the job, he's a fed..."

Towne looks at him. Color in his face. "This work can get crazy—you know that. Officer fatalities on task force ops—way higher than anything else. We're dealing with violent criminals, psychopaths some of them. There's not a damn thing for them to lose. Sometimes it gets rough. Hell, you PIT-turned a guy in the street with your truck—on the Nunez bust…"

Whicher says nothing, lets the sergeant speak.

"Parrish is a good guy. He goes in loud, stays loud. You know? He'll go in hot. So far, nobody got the drop on him—but he didn't fire a shot on the Ramsay bust—or on the second bust; Alvaro Nunez. Considering the jerk stuck a gun against Fergie's head, I say that shows quite some restraint."

"That would never have happened if he hadn't blown the search going through the house too fast."

"He's okay, alright? We're happy to have him…"

"Keep him away from this," Whicher says.

The sergeant eyes him, none too friendly.

Whicher meets his look. "I don't want him here. I don't want him any part of this."

CHAPTER
SEVENTEEN

A SIGN for livestock and farm supply sits high on metal posts off of East Second in the city of Roswell. Opposite is a Western-style diner—Whicher pulls into a lot filled with trucks and panel vans and old-model sedans.

He backs the Silverado into a bay, beneath a line of bull mesquite. Stepping from the truck, eyes the parked vehicles, wonders which belongs to the young sheriff's deputy—Billy Drummond.

The smell of food drifts from the kitchen in back—fried chicken, home-baked pies. Whicher feels his hunger sharpen.

Drummond had been reluctant to meet. Neutral territory always a good move.

The marshal enters the diner. He sees the young man—installed on a brown, leatherette bench seat at a booth by the window.

He's dressed in a checkered shirt, the sleeves rolled on his muscular arms.

Spotting Whicher, he sits back; eyes darting to left and right, scanning people at the other tables.

The marshal takes in his surrounds—paintings of cattle

drives, rodeo posters. A working crowd is in, dressed in denims and plaids and battered Western hats.

Reaching Drummond's booth, Whicher slips in behind the table.

The young man takes a sip on a cup of coffee.

"Appreciate you coming out." Whicher eyes the busy four-lane highway beyond the diner window. "You order?"

"I was waiting on you."

The marshal picks the menu card off the table. Looks at Drummond. "So, how you been?"

The young deputy shrugs. "I've been sitting around, doing nothing. Since they stuck me with admin leave."

"Right. You talk to anyone about it?"

The young man angles his head.

"They tell you what they want to do?" Whicher says. "At the sheriff's office?"

Drummond glances around the room again, turns to studying on the menu. "They just said to wait it out. That there's going to be an investigation."

"You know who's going to be doing it?"

"Why you want to know that?"

The marshal looks toward the counter—catches the eye of a waitress. Turns back to the booth. "It was my arrest."

"What difference does it make?"

"I have to file a report. Check with everybody. Make sure I got everything straight."

The young man rubs at his nose, sniffs. "What is there to get straight?"

"Yeah, nothing much," Whicher says.

A slim woman with tied-back auburn hair approaches the table. "Gentlemen. What can I get you?"

The marshal reads from the menu. "I'll take the chicken-fried steak—with green chile cornbread. And the salad side."

"I'll just take a sandwich," Drummond says. "Chicken, bacon, Swiss."

The waitress nods. Makes a note on the order pad, turns back for the counter.

"I wanted to talk to you," Whicher says, "get your take."

"What do you mean, my take? You saw it go down, you were there."

"I was two cars back. Behind Marshal Hogan. And Sergeant Towne. Y'all were out front, you and Parrish. I was back aways. Couldn't see real good."

Drummond looks at him, a question in his face. "See what?"

The waitress returns with a pot of coffee, fills the marshal's cup, refills Drummond's.

Whicher glances at her. "Thank you."

She smiles. Heads for another table.

Drummond leans in. "Will the Marshals Service be investigating?"

"Can't do that. It'll be PD. Or another law enforcement agency the sheriff's office contract with. But you and I can talk." Whicher feels the young man's tension. Eases off a fraction. He turns his gaze out of the window to follow a semi slowing for stoplights on the highway. "So, you handling it okay?"

Drummond doesn't answer.

"Kind of thing would make me wish I never quit smoking…" The marshal cuts a look at the young deputy. Grins.

Drummond runs a knuckle across his brow, his eyes hunted. "Yeah? Well, I never smoked. Never wanted to."

Whicher thinks of Gregory Joyner's description. Dark haired male, late thirties to early forties. Smoking.

He runs an eye over folk eating in the diner. Listens a moment to the burr of conversation in the room. "Whyn't you tell me, in your own words, how it all was? From your point of view."

The young man laces his fingers together on the booth top. Guns the muscles in his arms. "We were supposed to get out front, you know? Stop the suspect car—let you guys approach. We came in from the highway, tried to block off the road. The vehicle swerved right over sideways."

Whicher remembers the Toyota careering to a halt.

"I got out of my unit, Deputy Parrish was out of his. Marshal Hogan drove his truck up to the car." Drummond looks at Whicher. "You went around back—to stop it reversing?"

The marshal nods. "That's how come I couldn't see."

Drummond leans in, takes a breath. "Marshal Hogan and Sergeant Towne got out—they had their rifles. The guys inside the suspect car were moving all around…" He mimics their motion. "The one in the passenger seat went for a gun."

"You saw him get a gun?"

"They took a Smith & Wesson nine-millimeter off him…"

"I took it off him," Whicher says.

Drummond looks at him. "We told them to hold still—we were shouting at 'em. And then Hogan was running in—I saw the guy in the passenger seat—his arm came up—I opened fire."

"You remember how many shots you fired?"

"Two? Three?"

Whicher remembers; two.

"The guy in the passenger seat shot at Hogan," Drummond says. "I saw Hogan fall back—so I fired on them, I kept on firing…"

Whicher says, "Until I shouted for you to stop."

Drummond's eyes go wide. He looks up as the waitress approaches the table.

She puts the plates of food down.

Whicher glances up at her. "Thanks."

Drummond only sits still, his face drained.

The waitress turns away.

Whicher breaks off a piece of bread, cuts a slice of the chicken-fried steak.

He takes in the young man opposite in the booth. Distressed—not the battle-hardened look he'd seen in Andre Parrish. "This all a new thing to you? The apprehensions team?"

"Pretty new."

"How many ops you done?"

"Eight. Counting the last one."

Whicher nods. "You work with Deputy Parrish?"

"Yeah."

"All of them?"

"Department tries to put newer deputies with an experienced guy."

Whicher takes a forkful of salad, breaks off another piece of chile bread. Picks his next words carefully. "How is he?"

Drummond stares at the tabletop. "I mean he's good." He takes a bite on the sandwich.

"He talk to you—about how to approach the job?"

"What do you mean?"

"About what all to expect? What kind of thing might happen?"

The young deputy chews on his mouthful of food. "That's why they put the older guys with the new ones. Like a mentor type deal…"

The marshal eats. Silent. Trying to gauge the influence of Parrish on the younger man.

Drummond takes another bite on the sandwich.

"Deputy Parrish didn't fire a shot that day," Whicher says. "Why you think that was?"

The young man blanches, doesn't answer.

The marshal eases back in his seat. "Y'all had about the same viewpoint. But Parrish didn't fire a round. You think he didn't sense danger?"

Drummond swallows, his eyes go flat.

"He talk to you about how to react?" Whicher says. "You know? In a live situation?" The marshal cuts another slice of the steak. "Sometimes older guys, experienced guys feel like they need to warn you—not to come off second best, you know? Not to let the bad guys get the drop?"

"What's that have to do with anything?"

The marshal keeps his voice even. "Just thinking on how come you fired a total of—twelve rounds. When Deputy Parrish didn't fire any. Wondering, maybe. Whether you might have been psyched a little, going in?"

Drummond's voice tightens in his throat. "What're you trying to say?"

"Over-amped, revved. You know?" Whicher meets the young man's stare.

"You trying to say Parrish put me up to shooting those two pricks?"

The marshal shakes his head, tears off another piece of green chile cornbread. "I'm saying I need to know how this all happened. When folk come asking. And they will."

The young man only stares at him.

Whicher eyes the sandwich on his plate. "Don't let it go cold on you, son."

CHAPTER
EIGHTEEN

OUTSIDE THE ROSWELL city limits the county two-lane runs through farm and ranchland—stands of leafless fruit trees intercut with fields of winter corn. White-painted post-and-rail fences line the sides of the road—Whicher passes stud and livery stables, thinks of the Kentucky grasslands. He spots the brick entranceway to a horse ranch—worked iron eagles topping ornamental columns.

Slowing the Silverado, he turns in. Drives a graded road toward a collection of agricultural buildings and a large house set at one side.

Big rigs and trucks and horse transporters are parked on hardstanding by barns and stabling. Reva Ferguson's silver-gray Chevy Tahoe over by a fenced paddock and corral.

He pulls in alongside her vehicle, shuts down the motor.

Staring out through the windshield he sees her—riding a chestnut mare, a big one, maybe sixteen-hands high.

She works the horse around the paddock in a rising trot—in knee-length boots, an equestrian helmet, hands together at the horse's withers. Controlling it with only slight movement from her hands.

Climbing from the truck, he leans against the fence. Takes in the poise of the mare, thinks of roping horses he's ridden. Power and pace to spare, none of the finesse.

Ferguson spots him—turns the horse. Elegant, precise.

He sees the balance—her skill as a rider.

Bringing the horse to a walk, she crosses the beaten earth of the paddock to stand at the fence.

"Saw the ranch," Whicher says, "from the road."

She nods.

"Like you said. Gate with the eagles."

Swinging a leg over the mare's back she dismounts.

Atop the horse is a compact saddle, open stirrups, no fender.

"See why you need the boots."

She brushes the horse's flank with her hand. "Yeah, I like to ride hunt saddle. Ever tried it?"

"Grew up on a farm," Whicher says. "I've done some riding. Never in an English saddle."

"If I get time off in lieu, it's what I like to do. A little eventing. Low level. I don't have time for anything more."

The marshal rubs the horse's muzzle.

Ferguson ties the reins to the rail. Unfastens the chinstrap of the helmet, takes it off, loosens her hair.

Whicher scans the handful of horses spread out in paddocks around the stables. A few head of beef eat from bales of hay in an open barn. Beyond it, a male rider circles a palomino in a large corral. "What news on Marshal Hogan?"

"Med team is happy with him," Ferguson says. "I think they're letting him home soon."

"Good news."

She nods. "So, you get to talk with Billy Drummond?"

"We just got done," Whicher says, "back in town."

She lets her gaze linger on the marshal. "How'd it go?"

"He told me how it all was—his point of view."

She turns to the horse, unfastens a girth strap.

"I'm just looking to get a read," Whicher says, "maybe figure out why he opened up the way he did."

"Why he fired on a suspect vehicle containing an armed man?" Ferguson unbuckles the strap beneath the horse's belly, yanks it free.

"I need to know if there was undue influence."

"You mean, from Andre Parrish?"

"Guy's his partner," Whicher says.

Ferguson lifts the saddle from the horse's back.

"He's got that record..."

She carries it to the fence, places it on the top rail. "I keep telling you to let that alone."

Untying the reins of the mare, she walks the horse to a gate in the fence, strides through.

Whicher falls in step alongside her. "I saw Curtis Traxler's girlfriend this morning. At the county sheriff."

"Jena Velasquez?"

"She gave me a name. An address in Artesia. Of a sometime girlfriend of Ramsay. Name of Charlene Kingbird—ever hear of her?"

"I don't think."

"Riding back from Alamogordo, I stopped by."

Ferguson leads the horse to a long barn. She stands at the threshold.

"I found her OD'd on the floor at the address. Called an ambulance. EMTs took her to the hospital."

The mare shifts weight, one foot to the other as Ferguson looks at him. "What happened?" she says. "She going to be okay?"

Whicher dips his head. "Didn't look okay."

Leading the horse on into the stable barn, Ferguson opens up the door to one of a dozen stalls.

"I searched the property," Whicher says. "Found the car

Delmar Sadler sold to Jorge Salazar. The guy killed in the bust."

Thoughts pass across Reva Ferguson's face. "So, Ramsay was there? At this girl's place?"

"Left the car—along with a garage full of crystal meth."

Standing dead still, Ferguson regards him.

"I called Shannon Towne. Valley Task Force are going to stake out the house, put it under surveillance—in case Ramsay shows up."

"You think he could?"

"There's a ton of Mexican Ice in there. He could go back. Load up with it. Try to disappear."

Ferguson walks the mare inside the stall, sets to taking off the bridle. "He wouldn't use the car, now that we know about it."

"Yeah," the marshal says, "that's just it."

Turning from the horse, Ferguson eyes him.

"The only person who knew about Karl Ramsay getting that car—is dead."

"What's that mean?"

"Jorge Salazar. The man who bought it for him? He's dead. Because Billy Drummond shot him to death. Your young sheriff's deputy."

Reva Ferguson's eyes are cold and hard.

"Whatever happened that morning," Whicher says, "however anybody thinks it went down—those guys getting shot up—worked out pretty good for Karl Ramsay."

———

Back outside of the barn, Whicher waits at the Silverado.

Marshal Ferguson emerges, in jeans and running shoes and a padded mountain jacket. She takes out the keys to her Tahoe. "What's happening with Jena Velasquez? You going to charge her?"

"Kicked her loose," Whicher says. "Drove her back to the reservation."

"You let Lieutenant Decoteau know?"

"I'll call the BIA."

"Arrest was on their land."

"Right. I'll talk to him."

"I don't suppose he'll be happy to know she's back."

"Don't imagine she'll stay."

"What do you want to do about surveilling this house," Ferguson says. "You think the Marshals Office needs to get involved?"

"Valley Task Force can handle it," Whicher answers. "We don't have the personnel. But this is still a USMS warrant. I'm still holding paper on Ramsay."

She unlocks the door to the Tahoe. "You know, I think you're wrong about Billy Drummond. And Andre Parrish for that matter. I don't know why you'd think something went on —other than an unexpected consequence—to a high-risk law enforcement action."

"You see Jorge Salazar make purchase on his weapon?" Whicher says. "Before Drummond opened fire?"

"I saw Marshal Hogan shot down by Salazar."

"Not what I'm saying."

"I saw Hogie approach the car, I saw Salazar shoot him."

"After," Whicher says. "After Drummond already fired on the car."

A flash of heat steals into Ferguson's face.

She takes off her jacket, takes her phone from a pocket. Glances at the screen, reads it. "Owens."

"The truck driver?"

"My guy." She looks up. "Missed it." Keying to return the call she puts the phone to her ear.

Out of the corral, the rider on the palomino canters the horse along the fence line of an empty field. The marshal watches. Shades low sun from his eyes with the brim of his hat.

Reva Ferguson exchanges brief words with her confidential source.

She finishes the call. Looks at Whicher. "Says he's got something. Says he wants to meet."

CHAPTER
NINETEEN

COLD WIND BLOWS from the surface of Lake Brantley. The battered Ford Ranger belonging to Grady Owens makes its way down the gravel road through scrub and hard caliche to the deserted parking area beneath the trees at the water's edge.

Whicher stands by the Silverado—Marshal Ferguson alongside him at her own vehicle.

Owens steers the last yards, pulls in, leaves the motor running. He rolls the driver's window, stares out. Wearing the ball cap, a plaid overshirt. Lit cigarette in his mouth.

He glares in Whicher's direction.

The marshal holds his look.

"Three's getting to be a crowd." He speaks his words to Ferguson, keeps his eyes on Whicher. "Don't want no audience every time we do this."

"So maybe you ought to not steal folks' tools out of rig sites," Ferguson says. "Especially when you're already on parole for possession of meth…"

A scowl crosses Owens's face, creasing the pitted skin.

"So what's going on?"

"Word on Ramsay. Says he's looking to organize a shipment. Move a lot of drugs."

"Who for?" Whicher says.

Owens takes a pull on his cigarette, blows out a stream of smoke. "That, I don't know. But a couple of drivers I'm buds with say something's coming up. The word's gone out. They don't know what it is. They know to turn a blind eye when the time is right. Leave their trucks unlocked. And don't ask no questions about what all they're carrying in back."

"So how come they know there's a Ramsay connection?"

Ferguson speaks; "He's well known as a broker. A trans-shipment guy."

"Plus, he's around," Owens says.

Whicher looks at the man. "He's been seen around?"

Owens flicks his ash. "Man comes and goes like he owns the place. Folk see him. He don't give a damn. Guys like him, they know they're—you know…"

The marshal looks in at Owens slouched behind the wheel of the Ford Ranger. "They know they're what?"

The man's face is set, implacable, his eyes dead. "Untouchable," he says.

Whicher waits for him to go on.

Owens only smokes in silence. "Word is, he's after money," he finally says. "Looking to collect."

Ferguson steps toward the truck. "I need more than that. And so will the DEA. We'll need to know who he's setting things up for—what they're moving, whose narcotics it is."

"And where they're going," Whicher says.

"The where," Owens says, "I can maybe help out."

"You know the destination?"

"I don't know that. But those drivers will know where to stop someplace, pick up somebody to navigate for 'em. Wherever it is they're going. They'll know to drive west on ten, north on twenty-five, whatever. And get off at some exit. Lay up in some truck stop."

"Find out where," Whicher says. "What do these guys get in return?"

"A bunch of green nobody has to know about." Owens gives a bleak grin.

Reva Ferguson approaches the man's window. "What about the Mexican?"

The man's eyes are hooded looking back.

She angles her head. "You said Ramsay was looking to 'do' someone. On a black tar deal?"

"Ain't nobody talking on that."

"Somebody must know something."

"Who *do* you know about?" Whicher takes a step toward the battered Ford pickup. "Who's selling Mexican black tar?"

Grady Owens takes a long drag on his cigarette. Shakes his head at the marshal. "Who ain't?"

An hour later, the polished tile floor of the corridor in the Carlsbad Medical Center is bright beneath overhead lights.

Whicher strides with Reva Ferguson to a patient room at the corridor's end.

A female nurse appears at the threshold; Latina, a slim woman in her forties.

Ferguson shows her USMS badge.

The nurse checks, nods them inside.

In a room lit with sun from floor-to-ceiling windows Marshal Brent Hogan sits upright in a large-frame hospital bed. He looks at Ferguson and Whicher in turn.

The nurse takes a reading from a computer monitor. Writes it onto a clipboard, checks the medication dispenser by the side of the bed. "I'm right down the hall if you need me." She steps out, closes the door behind her.

Ferguson says, "You doing okay?"

"Pretty much." His voice is hoarse when he speaks.

"About ready to get out of here—if you can think of a way of busting me out." He nods at Whicher. "You might have to wheel me…"

Ferguson grins. "They looking to keep you in?"

"Another day or so. Just keeping an eye on things, so they say." He checks the door is shut. "Anyhow. What's going on, you pick up Karl Ramsay?"

Whicher drags two chairs from either side of the window. "That's what we wanted to talk about." He slides a chair to Reva Ferguson, sits on the other himself.

Ferguson sits. "We just came from a meet with Grady Owens."

Hogan looks at Whicher. "You check your wallet?"

"Yeah, he's a delight, as ever," Ferguson says.

"He have news?"

"Maybe. Marshal Whicher found something, though, this morning."

Hogan looks at him. "Oh?"

"Car he's using," Whicher says. "Plus a ton of Mexican Ice."

"You sure it's him?"

Whicher nods. "It was at a property up in Artesia, belonging to a sometime girlfriend. I'm pretty sure."

"What's the name of the girl?"

"Charlene Kingbird."

Hogan shakes his head. "Don't know her—I don't think."

"Grady Owens says Ramsay could be looking to move some product," Ferguson says. "Put a shipment together."

"He knows we're coming for him," Hogan says. "Could be looking for a payday before he hits the road…"

"There's a lot of crystal meth at that Artesia property," Whicher says. "We don't know whose it is. Likely his—he could be holding it for someone else."

"You talk to the girl at the house?"

"She was OD'd."

"Dead?" Hogan says.

"Alive. Not conscious."

Ferguson leans forward in her seat. "How reliable do you think Grady Owens is?"

Hogan looks at her.

"Is his information credible?"

"It has been in the past," Hogan says.

"If we're looking to set up something, surveille the property long-term, or intercept a transshipment, we need resource."

"You need to talk to Frank Niemann. At FBI."

"From the Farmington office?"

"He works out of Las Cruces, too," Hogan says. "On HIDTA stuff, major trafficking. If you're looking at an interdiction, he's probably your man."

"How about intel?" Whicher says. "You think he'd have any? On this specifically?"

"If anything made it to the intel network, he'd likely know about it. He's tight with the DEA."

Ferguson dips her head. "He'll have pull, federal leverage."

"If you're talking vehicle stops, SWAT team intervention, you'd need him," Hogan says. "If it's surveillance for the property in Artesia, you'd have to talk with local forces." He looks at Whicher. "You're after bringing this guy in, huh?"

The marshal nods, doesn't answer.

Ferguson stands. "I'll call Chief Garton. He might want to put it up the line to the Valley Task Force." She takes the phone from her jacket, steps from the room. Pulls the door to.

Whicher leans back in his seat. Takes in the view from the window. The edge of the city giving out to winter scrub beneath a hard, clear sky. "So how do you like getting shot at?"

"Thank God for tac vests," Hogan says. "Ever copped a round?"

The marshal nods. "Hurt like hell."

Hogan laughs, coughs. "Yeah, I wouldn't recommend it."

Low sun lights up the walls and ceiling of the room. A faint hum of electrical equipment is the only sound.

"You remember much about it?" Whicher says.

Hogan looks at him.

"Or is it gone? You hit the ground, it knocked you cold."

"I remember it, partner. Remember it pretty good."

"I spoke with Billy Drummond today," Whicher says, "that young sheriff's deputy. From Ramos County."

"How's he doing?"

"Doing admin leave. Learning what the world can look like."

Marshal Hogan slumps an inch in the bed.

"You remember approaching the car?"

"Yeah."

"You were first in," the marshal says. "Closest. Parrish and Drummond out in front, out of their units. You remember what happened?"

"The guys in the car were moving; agitated. Parrish and Drummond shouting for them to stop. I got tight to the car." Hogan hesitates. "And then there were two shots—Drummond fired into the vehicle."

"You see either of the guys in the car do anything?"

"Like what?"

"I don't know," Whicher says. "Anything."

Marshal Hogan shakes his head.

"You were right up close, maybe six feet from them?"

"About that."

"Either of the guys in the car threatening you?"

Hogan stares at the back wall of the room.

"You see a weapon in anybody's hand?" Whicher says.

"No..." Hogan's eyes cut back, his gaze sharp. "So what? What're you saying?"

"Not saying anything. I'm just asking what you saw."

"A lot of movement," Hogan says, "both guys acting out—and then one of them shot me, the guy in the passenger seat. After that I don't remember much."

Across town at the Carlsbad Police Department, Whicher settles into a chair in a blue-walled meeting room fitted with large-screen TV monitors. Through the open door is a view out into a lobby area—he sees Sergeant Shannon Towne with Reva Ferguson, in conversation, cups of coffee in their hands.

He checks his phone—looks for any message from his wife Leanne back in Texas. He should call.

Ferguson clips across the lobby with Towne, the two of them approach the meeting room, enter.

Chief of police Eugene Garton appears at the far end of the lobby space—alongside him, a plain clothes officer in a dress shirt and black suit.

Ferguson sets down a cup of coffee for Whicher.

Sergeant Towne nods a greeting. "Chief wanted to speak to us."

"You know what about?"

"Some angle on the Ramsay case…"

Garton crosses the lobby with the man in the suit.

The marshal takes a pull on the cup of coffee. "How is it over at the Kingbird house?"

"Couple of officers from Artesia PD are on it. DEA are sending people."

"There any news on her?"

"On Charlene Kingbird?" Towne shrugs, gives a shake of his head.

The police chief enters the room with the suited man—rangy, in his thirties, with fine, sandy hair.

Garton closes the door, clears his throat. Looks at Whicher. "This is Detective Trenton Allen. From our criminal investigations unit. Trent; Deputy Marshal Whicher, Western Division, Texas."

Whicher and the detective exchange nods.

The chief of police moves into the center of the room. "I've asked you here to make sure everybody's on the same page—following talks with Marshal Ferguson. Also in view of Marshal Whicher's discovery this morning of a vehicle—along with wholesale amounts of crystal meth at a house in Artesia."

"The vehicle was recently acquired," Whicher says, "just in the last days."

"Valley Task Force will be surveilling the property," Chief Garton continues. "We'll supply officers alongside of local LE agencies and the DEA. However, I know from speaking with Marshal Ferguson there's a possibility the drugs at the house might form part of a transshipment about to take place."

Sergeant Towne looks at Ferguson. "How do we know that?"

"Intel."

His face shows surprise.

"My intel," Ferguson says.

Garton goes on; "Any interdiction on that, we'll need larger numbers. Marshal Ferguson's talking to Frank Niemann at the FBI. A federal officer getting shot we'll likely get the green light. Meantime, I've asked Detective Allen along to give his thoughts on another thread—raised by Marshal Ferguson." He looks at her.

"Right," she says, "intel Ramsay could be looking to carry out a revenge kill—on a Mexican dealer."

Towne looks at her. "Really? I'm not hearing any of this."

"Over a black tar heroin deal. You've got your sources, I've got mine. But I'm looking for thoughts—on the dealer's identity."

Chief Garton gestures at the detective. "Trent's my best-placed man for that. He's handling intel for Valley Task Force."

Trenton Allen glances at Ferguson and then at Whicher. "We could come up with names, people to check out, I don't know how strong that would be. We'd want to narrow down the focus—are we looking for a local independent? Or a known retail distributor?"

"We've got nothing on that," Ferguson says.

Allen thinks it over. "We're seeing an uptick of activity in the Las Cruces area."

"Black Dragon chasers are all over," Sergeant Towne says, "so are the suppliers."

The detective turns to Chief Garton. "Frank Niemann or the DEA might know better. Maybe they could pinpoint names?"

Whicher runs a knuckle across his jaw. "We can't watch everybody."

"We just need a couple of lines to work," Sergeant Towne says, "someone's going to know where Karl Ramsay is at."

"I might have something on that," the detective says.

"Oh?" Towne looks at him. "And what's that?"

"We've been going through interview statements, for the chief. From the door-to-door inquiries, from neighborhood folk. One of the witness statements talks about a visitor to the property on Pike—late, the night before…"

Whicher studies the detective, feels a tick of alarm.

"Do we know who it was?" Ferguson says.

Chief Garton cuts in; "We weren't looking at it before, it didn't appear to be significant. Plus, the witness was unavailable, it was some kid staying over in the next-door property."

The marshal keeps his face neutral. He takes in Sergeant Towne and Reva Ferguson in turn.

"So, maybe we need to find him," Allen says. "Try to identify who it was the kid saw."

The chief nods, "If this person who came by the house is

the man Ramsay's now looking for—if we identify him, we could put a watch on him—that might be a way for you to bring Karl Ramsay in."

"A used-car dealer bought a vehicle around to the house on Pike," Sergeant Towne says. "Delmar Sadler, we know about that. He went over there the prior evening. Drove over. With the SUV you found..." He looks at Whicher.

"This was late," Detective Allen says. "Ten at night, or after."

Lines of stress show in Chief Garton's face when he speaks. "Maybe we need this kid. This witness..."

"Somebody should speak with him," Ferguson says.

The marshal says nothing—feels apprehension rising, feels the tension in the room.

"Maybe we need to get the word out," Garton says. "Have somebody go out. Find him. Bring him in."

CHAPTER
TWENTY

OUTSIDE THE CARLSBAD law enforcement center, Whicher walks with Marshal Ferguson and Sergeant Towne to a fenced lot under a darkening sky. Evening traffic moves down Guadalupe, headlamps blazing on trucks and pickups, windows of the neighborhood houses lit along the street.

Ferguson's Chevy Tahoe and Whicher's truck sit among the police Chargers and Interceptors and unmarked units.

Ferguson takes the keys from her pocket. "I ought to hit the road, get back up to Roswell." She glances at Shannon Towne. "Unless you think we'll be needed? On surveillance at the Kingbird house?"

"PD and the DEA are going to cover overnight," the sergeant says. "We'll get a roster drawn up, see how it looks." He turns to Whicher. "What do you want to do about that witness? The kid?"

The marshal shrugs, keeps his voice even. "Guess we need to look at everything…"

"You're not that interested?"

"I have to check in with my boss," Whicher says, "and we need to set up a meet with the FBI guy."

"Frank Niemann," Ferguson says, "I'll call him."

Towne eyes his vehicle, an unmarked gray Explorer. "We done for today?"

Whicher nods. "I'll head back to my hotel. Make some calls."

"And I'll arrange a meet with Niemann," Reva Ferguson says. "Soon as I know, I'll let you know."

Whicher unlocks the door of the Silverado. Feels Towne's eyes upon him.

"Anything happens," the sergeant says, "call."

Snow falls from a full dark sky, the headlamps of the Chevy lighting up trunks and low-slung branches of fir and pine and oak at the sides of the two-lane highway. The climb is steady into the hills, lights winking through the trees from houses ahead—in the settlement of Twin Forks.

Two hours on the road through the folds of a cold, black night—maybe ten more miles to go into the mountains.

Whicher checks his watch—coming up on nine, he should make a call to Leanne.

He lights up the phone on the dash stand, keys a number.

It rings, picks up.

"I would have called earlier. Been a busy one, kind of working late..."

"Oh? Are you getting anywhere?"

He reads the sound of his wife's voice—bright. Tired. A little forced.

"I think."

"So, is Fairbanks letting you come home?"

"It's El Paso," the marshal says, "not Fairbanks."

"How so?"

"Court there issued the warrant."

"Yeah? Let them serve it..."

The marshal steers along the tire marks in the snow on the road, doesn't answer.

"You have enough help?"

"Enough," Whicher says. "Anyhow, what's going on, how's Lori, how are you?"

"Lori's out. She's in rehearsals. For the high school musical. I have to go pick her up. It's a dress run, or something. Technical run."

"She having a good time?"

"She is, it's fun, it's really good for her."

The marshal thinks of his daughter; more independent, more complicated by the day.

"You better be here to see it," Leanne says. "Did you find the kid? That boy you were looking for?"

The marshal stares out through the windshield, doesn't answer.

"Everything okay?"

"Mm-hmm."

"I'll take that as a no." Leanne's tone changes; "Oh, there was a call here. At the house today. For you. I wrote it down. The Ramos County Sheriff."

Whicher pulls himself upright at the wheel. "They called the house?"

"Somebody from Ramos County Sheriff," Leanne says, "wanting to speak to you."

"They say who?"

"They just said they were from the sheriff's office."

The marshal considers it. "A woman? Or a man?"

"A man. Why?" His wife's voice is suddenly troubled. "Is something wrong?"

"No… No, it's okay…"

"Alright," Leanne says, unsure. "Well, look, I ought to run, I told Lori I'd get there in time to catch the end—they have this big ensemble number... Don't forget to eat."

"I won't."

"So, you didn't eat yet?"

The marshal grins.

"I have to run, call if you need me."

"I will."

Leanne blows a kiss, finishes the call.

———

In the mountain village of Cloudcroft, Whicher steers through a fresh fall of snow beneath the few streetlamps. Cars and trucks are angled along the snow-covered side of the road at lit-up bars and half-filled eateries.

He broods on the thought of the call to the house from the Ramos Sheriff's Office.

They would have called the USMS office uptown if they thought he'd returned back to Texas.

They wouldn't call his home.

He thinks of the meeting with Billy Drummond, up in Roswell—meeting with the young deputy could have triggered it. He pictures Drummond at the diner; defiant, but unsure.

The image of another man comes to him—Deputy Parrish. Andre Parrish.

'Some man wanting to speak', Leanne had said.

No message.

Except maybe for one, the marshal thinks.

A simple message.

I know.

Where you are in Texas; where your home is.

Where your family is at.

I know.

Now I'm letting *you* know.

———

The grit service road up the side of the wooded hill is white-over—snow gathered in the boughs of pine and fir, clumps lit up in the hi-beams of the truck. No tire marks are visible; no vehicle has passed recently on the road. Few cabins and trailers show from out of the darkness this far up.

Rounding a bend, the façade of the wooden A-frame house is suddenly picked out. A sea of white surrounding it; the adjacent meadow snow-covered, lit with moonlight.

Beyond the clearing, dark depths of forest swallow all light. He passes the sign board—*Tall Firs Artists' Retreat*.

The Jeep Wrangler is parked out in front of the house.

Whicher steers his truck up the driveway, scans the lit windows in the house.

He brakes to a stop, shuts down the motor. Sits a moment in the silence.

She'll be alarmed—at his presence, this late, unannounced. Not much he can do about it. He buttons the wool ranch coat over the large-frame Ruger in the shoulder holster and the Glock at his hip. Steps out into the snow, feels a cutting wind against his skin. Takes in the blackness of the night, an iron-taste in the air.

Pulling down the brim of the Resistol, he crunches over ice and snow to the front door.

He knocks. Rings on the bell.

A moment passes—then an outside lamp flicks on.

Whicher steps back as Annaliese Joyner opens the door—she peers out into the night. A blanket shawl about her shoulders, the same paint-stained jeans, a heavy sweater now engulfing her slim frame.

She puts a strand of black hair behind her ear.

"Ma'am, I'm sorry to trouble you this late."

She only stares out, dark eyes searching his.

"You think I could come inside? It's about Gregory."

"Has something happened?"

"Ma'am? Is your son here?"

She glances over her shoulder. "He's here. Why? What do you want?"

"If I could come in?"

She holds a hand to the side of her neck, lets a moment pass. Eyes still on his, dips her head.

The marshal knocks snow from his boots.

He enters the hallway.

Beyond it, sees the main living space, lights low, flame bright behind the glass of an iron wood stove.

Gregory is nowhere in sight.

"What are you doing here?"

"Do you have someplace else you could stay?" Whicher says.

Her eyes widen.

"Tonight. Maybe for a few days."

"Why would I want to do that?"

"I think it would be better—safer," Whicher says. "For Gregory. For you."

"What do you mean?"

The marshal lowers his voice. "Your son's existence as a witness has come to light. It's possible someone may try to find him…"

"Who?"

"Ma'am, I'm not at liberty to say that."

Heat is suddenly in her.

"But I believe a threat may exist. Over Gregory's wellbeing..."

"You can't tell me that, then not tell me why he's under threat—who he needs protecting from…"

"My job to protect him, ma'am. That's why I'm here."

Annaliese stands silent in the hallway, thoughts running behind her eyes.

"Where is he?"

"Upstairs," she says, voice shrill. She turns, stalks into the living room.

The marshal follows.

Standing before the wood burner, she presses her hands to her temples.

She whips her hands away, her eyes drill him. "This is everything we wanted to get away from." Her voice is tight in her throat. "*This. You.* People like you, your world. Everything about it, everything that's wrong. We left Artesia to get away from all of this—from drugs, crime, all of the madness—your whole way of life."

The marshal looks at her.

"Everything to do with you people," she says. "We came to get away, to be closer to my kind. The Apache. My mother's tribe, Mescalero Apache. I wanted Gregory… to have a foot in both worlds… I should have taken him to live on the reservation…"

Annaliese stops, her face is suddenly still.

Whicher listens for any sound in the house, hears nothing. Only the crackle of wood burning in the stove; flames lapping against the glass. "If I can find you," he says, "others will be able to find you."

Her eyes are on him once more, intense.

"We should move you. Even if it's just a precaution…"

"Where?"

"Friends? Family? Someone you know, someplace out of the way."

The marshal unbuttons the heavy ranch coat.

From the hallway is the creak of a tread on the stair.

Gregory Joyner descends the wooden steps. Leans across the banister. To stare at Whicher. Eye the revolver and the semi-automatic at his hip.

Fear rising in his face.

CHAPTER
TWENTY-ONE

THE LOG HOUSE and clapboard barns of the Joyner's neighbor Grace Pires sit hunkered beneath the falling snow as Whicher searches out a signal for his phone. Looking back across the white-over clearing, wind whips through the branches of overhanging trees at the forest's edge. No sign shows of Annaliese's Jeep or his own truck; both vehicles hidden now—out of sight behind the larger of the barns.

The marshal bunches his shoulders against the cold, holds out his phone.

There should be coverage back down near the Osha Trail Road, according to Pires.

Two bars of network show.

He holds the phone close, keys a call to Lieutenant Decoteau at the Bureau of Indian Affairs.

He checks his watch—gone ten, now—nobody likely to pick up.

Taking in the undisturbed snow on the road, he eyes his own footsteps through the clearing. Thinks of how long it will take for fresh fall to cover his tracks.

A gruff voice answers.

"Lieutenant?"

"Who is this?"

"US Deputy Marshal Whicher. Calling to let you know I turned Jena Velsaquez loose from the county sheriff's jail this morning. I wasn't expecting anybody to answer..."

"You charge her?" Decoteau says.

"Not at this time. She's back on the Mescalero Reservation. She gave me the name of a girl Karl Ramsay's been seeing. I went after the girl—name of Charlene Kingbird, you know her?"

"I don't think," the lieutenant answers. "What's happening with Curtis Traxler?"

"Up in Albuquerque, court's holding him."

Decoteau grunts.

The marshal pictures the bleak mountain plateau—Traxler trying to flee. The terrain around Whitetail; unfrequented, remote. "So, Velasquez is out. I wanted to ask—did you search her trailer?"

"We checked it yesterday," Decoteau says. "Something on your mind?"

"Maybe." The marshal stares into the leaden black sky, steps further beneath the overhang of trees. "Curtis Traxler's an associate of Karl Ramsay. Word is, Ramsay's looking to move some kind of bulk narcotics shipment out of state. I know where he's keeping some of it. But there'll be more."

"So?"

"So, he has to be keeping it somewhere," the marshal says. "Seems like there could be some spots up there; where we picked up Traxler—places folk don't go, parcels of land out of the way."

"We keep an eye on everything," Decoteau says.

"It's remote land, you don't have unlimited officers."

"Trying to tell me I've got a problem, marshal? With drug running in my back yard?"

"Not telling you that. Just letting you know on Jena Velasquez."

A beat passes. The lieutenant speaks again. "We searched the cabin."

"Alright," Whicher says. "So long as it was checked."

"And if Karl Ramsay shows his face up here," Decoteau says, "I'll arrest the son of a bitch on sight."

Inside the Pires house, Gregory Joyner sits with his mother at a plank table, eating baked tapatias, Grace Pires feeding split oak logs into a fireplace set within a stone hearth and chimney.

Whicher sits, drinks coffee. Takes in the pieces of art on display—paintings, watercolors and oils, carved wooden objects and ceramics. Trinkets of jewelry and beads on the lampshades glint in the low-level light of the room.

Gregory glances across the table at his mother. Eats, his face sullen, shoulders slumped.

At the fireplace, Pires gathers gray dreadlocks from her face, ties them behind her neck with a length of braid.

"Why do cops in Carlsbad even care about me?" Gregory says.

Annaliese looks at Whicher.

"I don't know anything about what happened back there..." The boy speaks his words to his mother. "I just stayed over at the Colemans—with Evan, that's all."

The marshal sips on his cup of coffee. "It's alright. It's just a precaution."

Gregory eyes him from the table.

"There's just some problems—with what the police are working on," Whicher says. "US Marshals get called sometimes. To make sure things stay straight, make sure everybody's okay."

At the fireside, Pires huddles in her mountain fleece. She looks at Whicher. "If you're headed down to Cloudcroft—you ought to think about moving. Before the snow gets any worse." She indicates a long, low couch. "Or you could stay…"

The marshal thinks of the journey back in the worsening weather. Hours, it'll take him, to reach the hotel in Carlsbad. "If it's not too much trouble?"

She shrugs, unsmiling. Walking into the open kitchen at the side of the living room, the woman takes a dish from the stove. "There's some tapatias. With avocado, refritos, vegetarian cheese." She takes a plate from the cupboard.

Gregory finishes up his food, pushes the empty plate aside. Stands.

"You want to get settled for the night?" his mother says.

The boy pulls a small backpack from under the table.

Pires sets down a plate of food for Whicher.

"Thanks," he tells her.

"I'll take him," Pires says. She leads Gregory from the room.

The marshal looks at Annaliese.

"The bedrooms are in back," she says. "Grace converted the adjoining barn."

Whicher eats, resists an urge to check the place.

Annaliese stands, crosses to the fireplace. Tension emanating from her. She sits in a hide-covered armchair.

On the wind is the screech of an owl.

She wraps her arms around her knees, stares at the board floor.

The marshal looks at her.

"That's bad…" she says. "An owl."

He returns to eating. "It's just an owl in the woods."

She shakes her head. "An omen."

The marshal regards her.

"Bad omen. We believe in a dark side. You know? That a dark side exists in life…"

He watches her in the moving light from the fire.

"That it's present? Alongside the light? At the same time? Apache people believe it. I know it's different, your world."

"Not so different," Whicher says.

She glances at him.

"Things I see. In my work. I see the same presence. Seen it many times."

She turns her face back toward the fire. "The world you live in is filled with it. I don't just mean, your world... your work, in the law. I mean all of it. All of your world."

Whicher mops sauce from the plate with a corner of baked enchiladas, doesn't respond.

"We believe we're blood relatives—to the rocks and streams and trees of this place," she says. "To these mountains. That's why we came here, why I brought us back—why I brought Gregory back, to be here."

Whicher nods. "Well. You made a good choice."

"You think so?"

"I do."

She lets a moment pass. Listens to the night sounds, head canted.

Only the wind moans through the trees.

"How long do you suppose we'll have to do this?"

Whicher doesn't reply.

"What lesson should my son learn—from what you bring from your world?"

"Your son's not the problem..."

"Then why can't he sleep in his own bed tonight?"

The marshal meets her eye at the fireplace. Leaves her question unanswered. "Is there anyplace else you could go? After tonight."

"Why should we?"

"Just until we know we can deal with any threat."

"Running," she says. "Hiding. That's what you want?"

Whicher eats. Thinks about his words, what to tell her. "You have people someplace else? On the reservation?"

She doesn't answer.

"Would you be safe there?"

"We'll be safe anywhere." Her face is suddenly hard. "The mountains are filled with spirits. With gods. Do you know that?" She looks at him. "I know you don't. But there are gods in these mountains, there always have been—that call upon the winds and the rain. To banish the evil that comes to our lands, drive it out, drive it away."

The marshal finishes up his plate. Leans into the table, shoulder holster pressing against the worn oak boards.

"Let your people come. Whoever it is. Whoever threatens us," she says. Her voice even, weighted with a flat resolve; "Whoever threatens my child. Our flesh and blood is everywhere. All around us here. Our people are here. They've always been here, they always will be. Nobody will push us out. These are our lands. Our ghosts walk them. Our gods hold sway."

CHAPTER
TWENTY-TWO

TRAFFIC MOVES brisk down the tree-lined boulevard in the town of Artesia, the low sun of a winter morning pale in a hazed-over sky.

Whicher turns in on Missouri Avenue.

Three blocks from Charlene Kingbird's house on Sixth, he sees stationary vehicles parked at either side of the road. One of them will be Valley Task Force surveillance—the marshal picks out an unmarked gray, Ford Explorer.

He slows, steers up behind it, brings the Silverado to a halt. Studying the Ford SUV he thinks of Shannon Towne, the sergeant from the Carlsbad PD—he drove one like it.

He thinks of the missed calls to his phone overnight. Towne had tried to get in touch—but left no message.

The rear windows on the vehicle in front are blacked, he can't see inside.

Shutting off the motor, Whicher unhooks the seat belt, rubs at his shoulder. Stiff from a night on the couch in the Pires house. He pictures the log-built property, up beyond the snow line in the Sacramento Mountains. Gregory Joyner still sullen, Annaliese defiant. The woman, Grace, unsmiling. Watchful.

But nobody had come. And there was work to do, he'd had to leave.

They'd need to move—to somewhere better protected.

He'd found them; anybody in law enforcement could probably find them.

He pops the door of the truck, steps out onto the sidewalk. Eyes the three-bed stuccoed house ahead along the street at the corner with Sixth. Opposite the house, the little elementary school—climbing frames and slides in the fenced-in schoolyard.

Walking up behind the Ford he draws level with the passenger window. Pauses—looks in for Towne behind the wheel.

Andre Parrish stares back at him from the passenger seat.

The driver, a female officer in a ball cap, turns her head.

The passenger-side window opens.

Parrish glares out, eyes intense.

"The hell are you doing here?"

"Observing a property," Parrish says. "On behalf of the Valley Task Force. What're you doing?"

Whicher looks at the driver. Shows his USMS badge.

In her face is mild confusion.

"You want to step out here a moment?"

Parrish grabs the door, swings it wide.

Whicher crosses the street, walks a half-block beneath denuded trees to stand out of sight of the Kingbird property alongside a two-story house.

Parrish steps down the sidewalk, dressed in jeans and sneakers, a long sweater covering his badge and gun.

He stands square in front of the marshal.

Whicher eyes him. "You need to back the hell up."

The deputy juts his chin. "You need to back the hell off, is what you need to do…"

Whicher stares at the man.

Parrish shifts his weight to the balls of his feet. "I'm

carrying out legitimate duties. With my team. You got a problem with that?"

The marshal regards the deputy.

"I know what you think," Parrish says, eyes wide in his face. "I get this shit all the time."

"That right?"

"People talking behind my back—saying things; that I'm trigger-happy..."

The marshal doesn't respond.

"That I get off killing bad guys. That I shoot first; ask questions later—you think I don't know that?" Parrish's face is accusatory. "Well, let me tell you something—not a single charge has ever been brought against me. Not by any agency—nobody's raised so much as a concern—let alone a complaint. Let alone any charge. Not one."

"You done talking?"

Color rises in the deputy's face. "I know you spoke with my partner. Billy Drummond. What makes you think you have the right to do that?"

"He killed a man on my warrant."

Parrish eyes him, hands curling into fists. "He told me what you said—wanting to know did I put him up to it?"

"There'll be an investigation," Whicher says. "Your record will come up."

"Yeah? Well, I didn't fire a goddamn shot."

"I won't have a federal case compromised," the marshal says. "Your partner blew the arrest on Karl Ramsay, you blew search of the second property that day—on the Nunez warrant."

The deputy's face tightens. "How the hell you figure that?"

"You left Marshal Ferguson exposed. I had to run after your ass, you raced through the house so fast..."

"It's my fault some piece of crap put a gun against her head?"

The marshal looks along the sidewalk to the unmarked SUV on the avenue. Thinks of Nunez, his pistol pushed into Reva Ferguson's hair. Thinks of the phone call—to Leanne—from somebody at the county sheriff's office. Dialing back a rising anger, he eyes the man in front of him. "Listen. The best thing you can do right now is get yourself transferred off of the case."

Parrish's voice is tight. "You're just a day-tripper, Tex. This all is my beat—you know that?"

Whicher stares down the street at cars rolling past the SUV.

"Sergeant Towne tried to reach you last night," Parrish says. "Clear it with you. About all of this. Said you had 'concerns.' And whatever bullshit. But he couldn't find you. Nobody could..."

The marshal turns to the deputy.

"Got some line you're working?" Parrish says.

Whicher picks up unnatural stillness in the man's face; an effort to conceal intention.

"How come he couldn't reach you? Where'd you go?"

"You get done with your shift," the marshal says, "call it a day." He gestures at the unmarked surveillance car. "I'll talk with your boss."

"The sheriff?" Parrish says. "Sheriff's right behind his officers..."

The marshal looks him in the eye. "Head on up to Roswell..."

Deputy Parrish stares, unblinking.

"You head on back there. I don't want to see you. You got that? You don't come back."

Flat terrain of ranchland and desert scrub stretches out to either side of the Severn Rivers Highway. A sweep of sky arches overhead to a far-off horizon. Whicher steers the truck out of Artesia down an empty road.

The image of Leanne and Lori is in his mind's eye.

The uneasy feeling inside—at Parrish—or somebody from the Ramos County Sheriff's Office tracking down his address, finding the family home.

Instinct is in him—an instinct to go for Parrish by the throat.

The phone on the dash lights up.

Whicher presses to answer.

Reva Ferguson comes on the line. "I spoke with Frank Niemann. He's agreed to meet with us. At Las Cruces. This afternoon."

"Oh?" Whicher says. "You tell him Ramsay could be looking to move a shipment?"

"I did."

"He buy it?"

"Yeah, it sounded like it..."

Whicher pictures the truck driving informant, Grady Owens, squinting out of the battered pickup at Brantley Lake. "So, your guy's information could be right. There anything more from him?"

"So far, no," Ferguson says. "Shannon Towne was looking for you last night..."

The marshal shifts his grip on the wheel. "I'm headed into Carlsbad, the PD. I'll try to see him. You know what it was about?"

"He didn't say. Maybe they're looking for the kid Chief Garton wants to find—the witness?"

Whicher lets a beat pass. "You hear anything on that?"

"It could have been about Pittman," she answers. "Antonio Pittman? Driver of the Toyota—the guy in the hospital? He died last night."

The marshal sits back, stares out along the road ahead.

"Never came out of the coma," Ferguson says, "they

switched off his life support. There were complications, no chance of any recovery."

"Does Billy Drummond know that?"

"I don't know. You think one of us should tell him?"

Two down, Whicher tells himself.

Two fatalities.

"Listen, the drive to Las Cruces takes a while," Ferguson says. "You know it? We should head out as soon as we can…"

The marshal only listens to the sound of the truck tires humming against the road. "Chief Garton or Ramos Sheriff can talk to Drummond," he says, finally. "I'll see you at the PD."

He reaches forward, clicks out the call.

From a second-floor window of the law enforcement center, Whicher stares out at an auto repair business on the opposite side of a four-lane highway. Cars and pickups pulling in, headed out, vans bringing in parts, a constant flow of vehicles in and out of the yard. He thinks about transportation, transshipment, the flow of goods and services—from individual units like a local repair shop—to interstate haulage, innumerable journeys, impossible to adequately survey. Crossing the floor of the small office room assigned for the Valley Task Force, he pushes closed the door, clears away the remains of coffee and a drive-thru steak sandwich from the top of a veneered desk.

He scrolls his phone, keys a number.

It rings, picks up.

His boss, Chief Marshal Fairbanks comes on the line.

"Ma'am, good morning. I'm calling from the PD in Carlsbad."

"I was going to call you."

"We're still looking for Karl Ramsay."

The chief marshal clears her throat. "What about your other... situation?"

Whicher lowers his voice. "The existence of a witness is now known."

"This is the child?"

"PD detectives uncovered it going back over statements," the marshal says. "Police chief here wants him found."

Whicher sits at a corner of the desk, eyes the closed door to the room.

"That's going to make your life harder," Fairbanks says. "You still think you're dealing with a lone bad actor?"

"Hard to say. But a second guy from the Ramsay bust died last night, the driver of the car. If the op was compromised the way I think it was..."

"The stakes just got higher," Chief Marshal Fairbanks says. "Anyone involved will want to make it go away."

Whicher lets his boss's words sit. Listens to noises outside in the corridor—the sounds of a busy law enforcement center. "Ma'am—did Ramos County Sheriff call the office yesterday?"

"Not that I know," she says. "Why?"

He stands again. "No matter."

"John, if you need El Paso involving on this, let me know?" she says. "It could be escalating. What are you going to do about the kid?"

"Starting to think about WITSEC," the marshal says. "For the mother and the son."

Fairbanks is silent a moment. "I won't say it couldn't happen. But we'd need a deal with the District Attorney's office."

"The deputy identified by the witness showed up on a surveillance team this morning—at the house we're monitoring for Ramsay. I told the task force sergeant here to keep him away. The whole stakeout's likely a bust from here on in

—Karl Ramsay probably knows we're sitting outside of there."

"Because your suspect told him?"

"Best case, yeah. Worst case, somebody else involved..." Whicher crosses back to the window.

"Can you share this with anyone?" Fairbanks says. "Anybody on the team?"

"I figured the sergeant here for a safe guy..."

The chief marshal thinks it over.

Outside in the lot he sees a silver-gray Chevy Tahoe pulling in—Reva Ferguson arriving. He checks his watch. Three hours and change to Las Cruces. "Ma'am, I have to go —I'm meeting with an FBI agent this afternoon."

"Oh?"

"Looking into an interdiction on a transshipment deal Ramsay could be part of. It could get us closer to him."

"Let me know what's happening."

"I will." The marshal shuts off the call.

He grabs his coat, fits the Resistol, heads out into a busy corridor—uniformed officers and civilian staff moving along it in ones and twos.

To one side of a lobby, in an open-plan office area, Shannon Towne works at a report writing station. The sergeant sees him—holds up a hand, emerges from around the desk. "Got a minute?"

"Headed out," Whicher says. "Got a meet with Frank Niemann."

"I was trying to reach you last night," the sergeant says. "You weren't at your hotel."

Whicher doesn't respond.

"Only I spoke with the Coleman family last night—from the neighboring house on Pike?"

The marshal regards him.

"I went out there—spoke to them about this witness the

chief talked about. They said a marshal already talked to them." Towne stares at him. "They said you talked to them."

"That's right, I did."

The sergeant makes a question with his face.

"You tell anybody else about this?"

"I wanted to speak to you first."

Whicher indicates a stairwell. "Walk with me…"

Towne falls in step—the two men head toward a set of stairs to the floor below.

"I just came from Artesia," Whicher says, "the Kingbird house? Andre Parrish was one of the officers there."

"I tried to tell you that, last night," Towne says. "He was rostered on, I was going to clear it with you."

"You tell him I didn't want him there?" Whicher starts down the stairs.

Towne descends beside him. "I know you don't like the guy. But if he's put up for duty on the task force, I can't refuse—unless I have good reason."

"You know the driver of the Toyota died last night?" Whicher cuts a look at the sergeant. "I don't want any officer from Ramos County on this warrant. I told Parrish that. I'm ready to make it official."

Towne stops on the half-landing of the staircase. "What about this witness, this kid?"

The marshal stops. "I'll handle it."

"Chief Garton wants him located."

"US Marshals Service will handle it."

"You go out and find him last night?"

Whicher eyes the sergeant. "If I need to take this federal, I will."

The sergeant only stares, unmoving.

"And right now," the marshal says, "I have a meeting to make with the FBI."

CHAPTER
TWENTY-THREE

THE SAWTOOTH RIDGES of the Organ Mountains rise against a clear blue sky to the east of the city of Las Cruces. Whicher exits light traffic on I-10, steers down an off-ramp toward a truck and travel stop.

He follows a service road past a gas station, past fast-food restaurants. Enters a parking area lined with live oak and cypress.

In the passenger seat beside him, Reva Ferguson points out a blond-haired man sitting at a bench beneath the trees.

"That him?" Whicher spots a black, GMC Yukon with tinted windows—drives toward it, pulls in to an empty bay. "How well you know this guy?"

"Niemann? Not well," she says. "I've met him a few times with Marshal Hogan."

Whicher takes in the seated man now watching them; poised looking, in a sport coat, eyes guarded, his face sharp.

"Why?" Ferguson says.

"No matter." Whicher shuts off the motor, steps from the truck.

Panel vans, sedans and pickups half-fill the lot. At the picnic bench, the FBI agent stands.

"Appreciate your meeting with us." The marshal offers his hand.

"Not a problem." Niemann shakes with him. Turns to Ferguson. "I was sorry to hear about Hogie—he going to be alright?"

"Getting out today," she answers, "discharged from the hospital."

Niemann looks at Whicher. "Initial attempt with Ramsay didn't go so well…"

"Two fatalities, so far."

"I buy you folks a cup of coffee?" The FBI agent steps from the picnic bench. Indicates a food mart and convenience store at the side of the lot. "Karl Ramsay's pretty well known, this part of the state. As a broker, facilitator. Bureau and the DEA keep tabs on him."

"That right?"

"He's on ATF radar. He was looking to move a cache of firearms out to California—to smuggle into Mexico." Niemann leads the way past a parked row of Freightliners and Macs to the entrance of the travel center. "What can I get you?"

"Just some water," Ferguson says.

He looks at Whicher.

"Coffee, no cream, no sugar. Thanks."

The FBI agent orders at a drinks stand.

Whicher watches traffic—rolling in from the interstate—eighteen-wheelers, concrete trucks, a steady stream of cars and pickups, SUVs and vans. He turns to Ferguson. "I called Lieutenant Decoteau, last night, at the BIA—let him know about Jena Velasquez."

Niemann passes Whicher a cup of coffee in a cardboard holder. "I know Bob Decoteau."

"We made an arrest out there," Ferguson says, "an associate of Ramsay's."

"Wouldn't read too much into it." The FBI agent hands her

a chilled bottle of spring water. "Doesn't mean he's going to be out there."

"You get out on the Mescalero Reservation?" Whicher says.

"Not much. Decoteau's a good guy, he does a good job. But they're under-resourced." Niemann leads the way back outside. "So, you hear Ramsay's after moving some product?"

"That's the word," Ferguson answers, "I have a pretty good source."

"He know the Marshals Service is looking for him?"

"He knows," Whicher says.

Niemann glances at Ferguson. "You said on the phone Ramsay has a stash of Mexican Ice?"

"Back in Artesia."

"What kind of volume?"

"It's lining two walls of a garage at a house," Whicher says. "I don't know what the value would be."

"How's it stored? Is it bulk? Wrapped?"

"Wrapped packages."

"Retail-ready, even better."

"For what?"

Niemann reaches the picnic bench beneath the trees, sits. "You know what 'shotgunning' is?"

Whicher looks at the FBI agent.

"Start with a large quantity of narcotics—divide it into multiple smaller shipments. Send it all out at roughly the same time. If law enforcement stops one or two or more of the vehicles, most of the shipment still reaches its intended destination."

Whicher sits at the table with Ferguson. "That's what he'll do?"

"A lot of them do that," Niemann says. "Ramsay will even throw in a couple of sacrificials. Vehicles they expect law enforcement to stop and seize. They get attention focused onto that, get it focused the wrong way."

"People know they're getting thrown under a train for him?"

Niemann grins, looks around the truck stop. "Yeah, he's that much of a son of a bitch…" He blows on his cup of coffee, takes a sip. "They use this place sometimes. They'll double-shotgun—split a partial load into even more loads."

Ferguson scans the lots, the restaurants and food concessions—an overpass carrying the raised interstate, vehicles everywhere. "Not a bad spot."

"Close to the interchange," Niemann says. "I-10 and I-25."

"There any specific intel?" Whicher says. "On what Ramsay might do next, where he might go?"

"I wanted to talk to you about that."

"Oh?"

"DA here could be interested."

The marshal shifts his weight on the bench seat. "Karl Ramsay's already facing charges in El Paso."

"Right. I understand that," Niemann says. "But Las Cruces DA are interested—there's a chance to net multiple offenders here."

Whicher takes a pull on his cup of coffee.

"You're watching the guy's stash?" Niemann says. "At a house in Artesia?"

Ferguson nods.

"How about if we kept watching—but we let him take it out of there? Let him split it, arrange to move it. Us watching. We get him out in the open, him and everybody else. Get 'em thinking they're good to go, we take a whole bunch of them out."

"We'd need Valley Task Force," Reva Ferguson says. "Plus law enforcement elements from the HIDTA area. DEA, the Bureau, local police."

"If USMS agree it, I could likely get the manpower,"

Niemann says. "With the DA onboard we make it strategic. We'd be looking at top-down support."

"El Paso court already issued a warrant," Whicher says. "They'd have to agree it."

"But USMS would want to do it?"

"I'd have to talk to my boss."

Reva Ferguson regards the marshal.

Agent Niemann runs a hand through his short-cut blond hair. "Something tells me you're not really going with this, marshal?"

"I'm here to take Karl Ramsay back to Texas is all."

In the FBI agent's eye is a hard glint.

"You're talking about a large-scale interdiction. I'm looking for Ramsay, nothing more."

"I hear you. But to get to him," the FBI agent says, "you might have to cut somebody in."

The phone in Whicher's pocket starts to ring. He takes it out checks the screen; Otero County Sheriff. "I need to get this." He rises, steps away from the table, keys to answer—puts a hand over his ear to shut out the noise of a passing semi. "Whicher."

"Sir, are you the marshal that was in here yesterday morning? About an arrestee from the Mescalero Reservation? Name of Jena Velasquez?"

"Yes, I am."

"We've just had an officer from the BIA police in here. Officer Roanhorse. Saying Jena Velasquez has been assaulted. Injuries were pretty severe, he brought her into Alamogordo for medical treatment, but now he says she's disappeared…"

CHAPTER
TWENTY-FOUR

THE CLIMB IS long up US 70 into the mountains east of Las Cruces—snow and ice at their peaks despite the day-long sun.

High above the ranchland and the scrub-covered hills, wind buffets the cab of the Silverado as Whicher steers up the four-lane, passing rigs and trailers shifting gears for the ascent.

Beside him in the passenger seat, Reva Ferguson stares out of the window. "I don't see what you hope to get from this…"

Whicher glances over at her, feels her tension—aware of it since leaving Niemann at the interstate stop. "You don't think it's strange?"

She turns, looks at him. "About Velasquez? I wouldn't know what was strange in her world."

The marshal studies the road ahead, low sun splintering on the windshield—a sense building, he can feel it. Feel an ember smoldering somewhere inside.

Parrish could have gotten to Velasquez.

Parrish, or someone like him.

Ferguson sits forward in her seat. "You know what I don't understand?"

He hears the note in her voice.

"You want to chase after some drug dealer's girlfriend—but you won't entertain what Frank Niemann says…"

Whicher keeps his eyes on the road now curving with the contours of the hillside, starting to top out at the head of the mountain pass.

"He's offering strategic-level escalation—multi-agency resourcing. Call your boss," Ferguson says, "call El Paso. Call the court, they'll all tell you the same thing."

He looks across at her—sees frustration in her face.

"If the FBI set something in motion with DEA and the Valley Task Force—you probably don't even need to be here," she says. "They could execute the warrant. You could go home, go back to Texas…"

The summit of the San Augustin Pass is in view now—a panoramic vista of plains land stretching for miles below. Whicher sees a deserted parking area off the highway—turns from the road into it—rolls the truck to a stop at the edge of an overlook.

Reaching for the ignition, he shuts off the motor. "Something you need to know…"

Marshal Ferguson's voice is cool. "About what?"

He unhooks his seat belt, steps out.

Ferguson follows.

Leaning against the roof of the cab, he eyes her. "The witness. From the house on Pike Street? I found him. Yesterday."

"You found the witness?"

"Right."

"You never said…"

He nods.

"Why not?"

"I saw the interview notes. Before Chief Garton's detective. Trenton Allen. Saw there was a witness, from the neighboring house. Nobody thought it was important."

"I don't understand…"

"The kid saw somebody arrive at the house next door. Antonio Pittman's house."

"Well, so what?" Ferguson says. "What difference does it make?"

Whicher holds her eye. "The man the kid saw—was Andre Parrish."

Buttoning the wool ranch coat against the wind, the marshal pushes down the Resistol on his head. He walks the slope of the parking area toward a monument—to the White Sands Missile Range on the plains below—a white-painted Nike Hercules missile, set in concrete, its outline stark against an azure sky.

Cars and trucks descend the downslope of the highway. Winter cold blowing through the air.

At a green-roofed gazebo housing tourist information boards he stops. Looks out at the horizon, to a distant range of mountains.

Reva Ferguson arrives at his side.

"I don't know what to do with this," she says, finally.

The marshal nods.

"Who have you told?"

"My boss. In Pecos."

"No one else?"

He shakes his head.

"Why not?"

"New turf here."

She looks at him. "You don't know who you can trust?"

He doesn't reply.

"Why didn't you tell me?" Her tone is pointed.

"I'm telling you now."

She lets the thought sit a moment. "And you've met this witness, this kid?"

"I have."

"You believe he's telling the truth?"

He nods.

"Why?"

"Because the kid didn't know what he'd seen."

She looks at him.

"He's got no reason to lie."

"You think Andre Parrish tipped off Karl Ramsay?" she says. "Told him we were coming in the morning."

"Police department in Carlsbad thought they had good information…"

She rubs a hand across her face.

Whicher lets the wind fill up the silence. Glances at her. "Why would a county sheriff's deputy go to a drug dealer's house?"

"I don't know," she says, voice rising, "I don't *know*, I have *no* idea. I know you've been down on him since day one…"

"You had a gun put against your head because of him."

She stares off at the highway. "What are we supposed to do?"

Looking back at him, a wildness is in her eyes.

"This stays USMS only."

"You can't seriously suspect… other people are involved?"

His face is grim. "I guess we'll find out."

Turning from him, she starts to pace in the deserted lot.

"I'm talking with my boss," Whicher says, "about WITSEC."

"You know where this kid is right now? You've talked with him?"

"I have."

Her eyes search his face. "Do you think someone will… try to find him?"

"I think they will."

Ferguson makes no response. Only walks to the edge of the overlook, stands staring out across the limitless plain.

"Whatever Frank Niemann or Chief Garton or anybody else wants to do," Whicher says, "all of it could be a waste of time—if Karl Ramsay's going to hear about it…"

She speaks her words to the wind. "Then what does that mean?"

Whicher bunches his shoulders, turns back for the truck. "It means we're on our own."

CHAPTER
TWENTY-FIVE

LATE AFTERNOON SUN lights up restaurants and big-box stores in the town of Alamogordo. At a Super 8 by a three-block mall, Whicher turns from the highway for the lot of the sheriff's office—a tan-rendered, one-floor building framed against a ridge of the Sacramento Mountains.

Beneath a stand of ponderosa pine is a BIA law enforcement pickup. The tall figure of Officer Roanhorse steps from it. He opens the rear door, reaches in, drags out the occupant; a disheveled male—in his late twenties, Hispanic—in jeans and a black, hooded top.

The man's hair is wild, tattoos scroll his arms and neck. At his wrists are a pair of silvered handcuffs.

Roanhorse straightens him up as Whicher pulls in.

The marshal shuts down the motor in the truck—steps out, along with Reva Ferguson.

The young man pulls away from Roanhorse, kicks out, mouthing something.

The BIA officer pins him against the side of the truck. He flips the younger man around—pushes him forward, face down against the roof of the cab.

"Need a hand?" Whicher says.

Roanhorse leans in, says something to his arrestee. The struggling stops.

"Anybody I know?" Ferguson says.

The BIA officer grunts. "Jose Sifuentes. Air Force Base police picked him up out at Holloman. Domestic disturbance."

Whicher regards the man as Roanhorse pulls him up off the side of the pickup.

"We already had a live warrant," the BIA officer says. "Failure to appear on an auto theft charge. Plus suspicion of breaking and entering."

Sifuentes eyes the marshal. "You looking at, ese?"

"Go ahead," Roanhorse tells him; "mess with a federal marshal, make my day…"

Whicher stares back at the man.

"I'll book him in," Roanhorse says, "be right out."

The marshal turns to Ferguson. "Holloman Air Force Base. Didn't that come up somewhere already?"

The BIA officer hustles Sifuentes into the sheriff's department.

"Guy on the Nunez arrest," Ferguson says. "Luis Rios. The guy you rammed in the street."

"He was wanted for something out at Holloman?"

"Not unusual. Daytime population at the base runs to thousands, they're the biggest employer in the area. There'll be calls on law enforcement—things go on…"

Whicher thinks again of the Nunez bust, thinks of Parrish charging through the house, obliging him to follow; leaving Ferguson exposed. He thinks of PIT-turning the car of the runner, Rios, before anyone could open fire.

Officer Roanhorse exits the sheriff's department.

"They taking him off your hands?" Ferguson says.

"They'll hold him."

Whicher looks at the man. "Appreciate your seeing us."

The BIA officer nods.

"Sheriff's office said you picked up Jena Velasquez earlier?"

"This afternoon, up on the rez."

"Somebody assaulted her?" Ferguson says.

Roanhorse's face is dark. "Somebody beat her up pretty bad, she was hurting. Wandering around outside of Mescalero. We got a phone call. I went out, picked her up."

"What happened?"

"She didn't want to come—I persuaded her, took her to the Indian Hospital. Doc said she needed to stay overnight, there weren't any beds. I said I'd bring her on down here. I got her to the medical center—she was in a wait room, she ran out. I haven't seen her since."

"What do you think happened?" Whicher says.

"She didn't want to talk, didn't want to go to any hospital."

"You found her in Mescalero?" Ferguson says. "You think she was attacked there? She have a vehicle?"

"I picked her up, she was just wandering down the road."

"Where you think she could've gone?"

"About anyplace..."

"She was living back in Artesia."

"Could she have been attacked at her place?" Whicher says. "Where we arrested Curtis Traxler?"

Roanhorse shrugs. "Up at Whitetail? That's twenty miles from where I found her." The BIA officer looks at him. "What's the Marshals Service interest?"

"I'm looking to serve a warrant on a guy named Karl Ramsay. You know him?"

"I know who he is."

"He come up on reservation land?"

"Sometimes. I picked him up on an assault out at the

casino one time. It never went to court, some kind of fight. Nobody pressed charges."

"Jena Velasquez is part of his circle," Whicher says. "She gave us the name of a girlfriend—a Charlene Kingbird. You know her?"

"Kingbird?" Roanhorse shakes his head.

"We found her, put her place under surveillance, it's full of narcotics belonging to Ramsay."

"We should have somebody check Velasquez's place in Artesia," Ferguson says.

Whicher looks at the BIA officer. "You know where she lives?"

Roanhorse shrugs.

"Anybody been up to Whitetail?"

"I've been down here cleaning out the low-life." Roanhorse gestures at the sheriff's office. "And waiting on you."

The marshal turns to Ferguson. "Wouldn't mind taking a look around there."

"She wouldn't go back to her trailer."

Roanhorse cuts in; "I'm headed back to the rez, you want to follow me over…"

An hour later, flecks of snow are on the wind, dusk settling in the forested hills as Whicher follows the black, BIA Ram pickup along deserted service roads—a lonely feeling hanging in the trees, in the fast-chilling air.

"We get done here," the marshal says, "I'll take you back to Carlsbad."

Ferguson notches up the heat in the cab. "You really think Karl Ramsay could have something to do with this?" She gestures out of the window. "With a place like this? This kind of country?"

"Emptiness could be a part of it..." Whicher scans the road ahead, the climb through the silent, wooded hills. "If he was looking for a place to hide drugs..."

Leaning back in the passenger seat, Ferguson considers it. "So, why not talk to Frank Niemann about it? Let him talk to DEA."

The marshal notices patches of snow, now starting to settle. "Because none of it's going to work..."

"You don't know that."

"If information can get back to Ramsay."

She looks at him. "You think Andre Parrish will feed him?"

"Parrish. Or somebody else..."

Letting out a long breath, Ferguson stares ahead out of the windshield.

"Maybe it's not all on him," Whicher says. "Think about Billy Drummond. Guy shot and killed the only man that knew Karl Ramsay bought a vehicle..."

"That Chevy Traverse?" Ferguson says.

"From Delmar Sadler, right. In Carlsbad."

She shakes her head.

"It worked out pretty well," the marshal says, "for Ramsay."

Ferguson turns again to look at him. "How are we even supposed to work this case?"

Whicher follows the BIA pickup in the fading light, doesn't answer. A fork is ahead on the road, now—he sees the taillights of the Ram glow red.

Roanhorse steers toward the smaller road—to the northeast.

Whicher follows.

As the ground rises, the canyon opens onto a high plateau. Sparse scrub and snow and pale mountain grasses stretching to the distance under the darkening sky. The marshal recognizes the ground from the Traxler arrest two days back. A half-mile on is the wooded slope of a hill—beyond it the trailer—Jena Velasquez's place.

No vehicles are anywhere in view. Whicher surveys the immediate surrounds—feels the solitude, the emptiness of the place in the lowering light.

Roanhorse drives up close to the property. Parks in front of the trailer.

The marshal steers in, pulls up alongside the BIA truck.

Roanhorse exits the Ram, eyes the trailer.

Whicher sees the door hanging open. Points.

"Got it," Ferguson says.

Stepping out, the marshal pushes his coat back clear of the Glock.

Ferguson climbs from the truck, looks to Roanhorse.

The BIA officer nods.

Whicher makes for the front door.

Fanning out, Ferguson takes the left side, Roanhorse easing to the right.

"*US Marshals*," Whicher calls out.

He peers inside into semi-dark.

Chairs and tables are upended—items strewn across every surface, scattered about the floor.

The marshal leans out, looks at Roanhorse. "You boys search the place this morning?"

"How's that?"

"I called your boss last night, Lieutenant Decoteau. About taking another look up here?"

"First I heard of it." The BIA officer steps to him, looks inside.

Reva Ferguson calls across from the side of the trailer. "What's going on?"

"Somebody's been out here. Trashed the place." Whicher steps in, takes in the chaos of the living area; disarray in the kitchenette—he checks out a bedroom, finds more of the same.

"Somebody looking for something?" Roanhorse says.

The marshal steps back into the living area.

Ferguson stands silhouetted in the doorway.

"Somebody after something," Whicher says, "or sending a message."

The BIA officer shakes his head. "This girl's a dumpster fire…"

"You think of anywhere she might be out here? Friends? Family?"

"I can check around."

"Why would she come here?" Ferguson says. "We need her address in Artesia."

The marshal steps from the trailer, scans the hills in the twilight. "Wouldn't mind taking a look around here."

Ferguson steps out. "How're you going to do that."

Roanhorse exits the trailer. "You know how to work country?"

The marshal nods.

"Know how to cut for sign?"

"Some."

"In the dark?" Ferguson says.

Whicher listens to the sound of the woods. A feeling in him. A sense of something. Gut instinct. Of something wrong, something out on the land. In the distance is the call of a bull elk—guttering, its eerie finish a high-pitch scream on the wind.

He turns, sees the BIA officer studying him.

"We need the whereabouts of Jena Velasquez," Whicher says.

Roanhorse nods. "I'll speak with the lieutenant. Find out if he sent Kee up here, Officer Kee." He thumbs over his shoulder. "But he wouldn't do that."

Reva Ferguson walks to the Silverado, climbs in.

Whicher thinks of two dead from the arrest in Carlsbad—maybe a third now—a woman he turned loose from the sheriff's jail.

In his mind's eye is the file image of Karl Ramsay in the warrant jacket.

As he traces the line of the deserted road—into forest hills in the failing light.

CHAPTER
TWENTY-SIX

DRIVING down the mountain highway off the Mescalero Reservation, lights at the edge of the village of Cloudcroft pinprick the dark through low-slung boughs of pine and fir.

Whicher checks the clock on the dash—coming on seven in the evening.

Bars of network show on his phone, the first in an hour.

"I need to call Decoteau. And we should get something to eat."

He slows approaching the entry into Cloudcroft. Light snow falls as he steers past construction yards and realtors—a barbecue joint, a tin-roofed motel.

Ferguson scans the streets leading back from the highway. "Let me ask you something?"

He glances at her.

"How come you're okay with the BIA—if you're so damn wary of everybody else? You think they're different?"

Whicher considers it. "They operate on their own terms."

"Oh? You know them well?"

"I've worked with BIA law enforcement."

"Yeah, well, me too…" Heat is in her eyes as she looks at

him. "And I don't have a problem with them. Like I don't have a problem with Ramos County Sheriff."

The marshal shifts his grip on the wheel. "You have a problem with Andre Parrish being on Pike Street the night before we hit it?"

"Says you... says some kid..."

At the side of the road is a gas station—a snow-filled lot. A pole lamp lights up a food cabin, hand-painted. Whicher gestures at it.

"Good," Ferguson nods. "Let's make this fast."

The marshal pulls over. Brakes the truck to a stop.

Ferguson throws open the passenger door, steps out.

Whicher reaches for his phone.

At the serving hatch of the cabin, a round-faced woman in a bandana watches.

Ferguson crosses the lot.

Whicher keys a call to Lieutenant Decoteau.

The line picks up.

"Roanhorse says Jena Velasquez went missing."

"You know somebody beat her up?" Whicher says.

"And wrecked her trailer, according to Roanhorse."

"I was calling to ask—did you go up there?"

"Nobody from the BIA police went by."

At the serving window, the woman in the bandana leans out; she points at a menu board for Ferguson.

"I meant to go up if there was time," Decoteau says, "didn't happen. But we already checked the trailer after Traxler's arrest; nothing was in there."

"Somebody beat her up pretty bad," Whicher says.

"She runs with bad people."

The marshal shuts down the motor, takes out the keys. "You know where she lives in Artesia?"

"I don't," Decoteau says. "I could ask around."

"If you hear anything..."

"Likewise, marshal."

"Got it."

"You ever getting home?"

Whicher grins to himself. "I'll let you know." He finishes the call.

Climbing from the truck, he crosses to the food cabin.

"I ordered already," Ferguson says, her voice cool.

The woman behind the counter looks him over.

The marshal reads from the menu board. "Can I get the brisket burritos? And coffee."

She nods. "Coming right up."

Ferguson steps away toward the main drag, breath clouding around her. Nothing is moving on the street. A set of stoplights at the intersection change from red—throwing green light onto the snow.

Whicher steps across to her.

"You talk to him?"

"BIA weren't up there."

"So, what now?"

Whicher regards her in the light from the streetlamps. Lets his gaze run out to the black night, to snow now blowing on the surrounding hills. He pictures the log house belonging to Grace Pires—the house and barns, up there somewhere in the looming dark.

From the food cabin, the woman at the serving hatch calls over; "Folks—got your order..."

Whicher turns, walks back across the lot.

He takes a pair of twenties, puts them on the counter. Picks up a cardboard tray with the order.

"I'll get your change," the woman says.

"Keep it," the marshal says. "And thanks."

Carrying the tray to the Silverado, he places it on the roof.

Reva Ferguson steps to the truck.

"You want to eat out here?" Whicher says. "Or get in?"

"Out here is fine." She picks up a cheeseburger from the cardboard tray, takes a bite.

Whicher tries the brisket taco. Bunches his shoulders as cold wind blows a dusting of ice through the air.

"So, we have no idea what happened to Jena Velasquez?" Ferguson says. "There's no word from the stakeout team watching for Karl Ramsay. And you don't want to work with Frank Niemann at the FBI." She looks at him over the roof of the cab.

The marshal takes the lid off his carry-out cup of coffee, takes a sip.

"What *do* you want?"

"I'll work with him," Whicher says.

"But you think it'll be a waste of time?"

Whicher eats, stares out along the deserted street. "All I want is Karl Ramsay."

Ferguson eats a handful of fries. "Niemann wants that. He wants the net thrown wider is all..."

The marshal takes another bite of brisket taco. Thinks of Annaliese Joyner. Of Gregory. Isolated in the forest and hills in the blackness of night. Isolation might be their greatest danger; if anyone should find them. He glances at Ferguson. Takes another sip from his cup of coffee. Decides on something, despite himself. "We get done eating there's something I want to show you."

She takes another bite of her food.

In the light from the pole lamp her eyes are wide, focused.

He sees the question in them.

"Somewhere I want to take you," he says. "Somebody you need to meet."

―――

Snow glistens in the hi-beams of the truck, clumps of white powder falling silent from the trees. Whicher follows the road up the hillside—ahead sees the forest clearing. He searches for the entrance to the property, makes out a set of gateposts, the line of a fence.

At the far reach of the Silverado's headlamps, a log house and barns form from out of the dark.

Reva Ferguson squints through the windshield.

"This is it," Whicher says, "this is the place."

He drives in, over undisturbed snow—parks in front of the house, leaves the lights lit on the truck, the motor running. "I'll see if they're still here."

He climbs out into cold air, sucks down a lungful.

Stepping through the snow he knocks at the door.

Above the motor rumbling is the sound of wind cutting through the mass of trees.

Whicher knocks again, calls out, "US Marshals..."

A woman's voice calls back from inside the house; "Who is this?"

"Deputy Marshal Whicher. From last night."

A moment passes. He hears a lock turn, the sound of a bolt being drawn.

The door opens.

The marshal shows his face in the light.

Grace Pires stands with a Winchester deer rifle looking out at him.

Whicher eyes the gun. "Are they still here?"

The woman nods.

"I have another marshal with me." Whicher points back at the truck. "It be alright if we came in?"

Pires lowers the rifle, pulls her fleece top about her—she looks at him; doubtful.

Whicher strides back to the truck, kills the lights, kills the motor.

Reva Ferguson climbs out.

Pires regards the pair of them. Puts the gun by the door, moves aside.

Whicher leads Ferguson to the house, inside, into the small hallway.

Pires bolts the door behind them, leads them to the living area, a bright fire burning in the stone hearth, low-level light on the clutter filling the room.

Annaliese and Gregory Joyner stare out from the attached kitchen—Gregory holding a dish cloth, Annaliese staring from the sink.

The boy's face is pale.

Annaliese's eyes flick from Whicher to Ferguson. "Is something wrong?" She puts down a plate on the drainer, face wary, skin drawn tight around her cheekbones.

"This is Marshal Ferguson—from the USMS office, Roswell," Whicher says. "I wanted her to meet you."

"What for?"

Whicher looks at Gregory, standing mute. "You been here all day?"

The boy nods.

"Doing what? Homeschool?"

"I guess."

"Anybody else come out?"

He shakes his head.

Whicher turns to Pires. "Anybody been out here?"

"No," she says.

"You go anywhere? Anybody try to contact you?"

The woman shakes her head.

Reva Ferguson looks around the living room. Steps to Annaliese. "Your son gave a witness statement? To an officer in Carlsbad?"

Annaliese stares at her, folds her arms across her chest.

"I've spoken with my boss," Whicher tells her. "The way this works, an investigation will need to take place, before anything can happen."

"We can't stay here," Annaliese says. "We've done nothing wrong, why should we hide?"

Reva Ferguson looks at her. "There's no need to be alarmed."

"The Marshals Service will make sure your son is protected," Whicher says, "you, too." He looks to Reva Ferguson.

Ferguson keeps her eyes on Annaliese, nods.

"I'm not turning his life upside down while you people investigate this man, whoever he is." Annaliese looks from Ferguson to Whicher. "We're not going to live in fear…"

"USMS can protect you."

"Who's going to protect us from you? Your people are the ones threatening us." Annaliese's voice is tight. "We can protect ourselves—and we will." She turns, suddenly, to Pires. "Thank you for letting us be here with you…"

The woman says, "You don't have to go."

Annaliese's eyes shine. "We do. And we were leaving. Now. That's enough. It's time…"

―――

Snow on the road down through the woods shows no sign of any vehicle passing. In the rear-view mirror, Whicher sees the headlights of the Jeep behind him.

"We can't stop her," Ferguson says. "If she wants to be in her own house…"

"I found her easy enough," the marshal says. "Someone else could find her…"

Ferguson stares out into the night in the headlamp beams. "You think Andre Parrish would come out here?"

The road rounds a bend through the trees—Whicher recognizes the entrance to the Joyner property. He slows, scans the ground. "Maybe it's not just Parrish we have to think about."

Nothing obvious is out of place—no tracks are present, no churn marks in the snow.

Turning in, the marshal steers up the white-over driveway.

Eyes the A-frame house and timber deck. "Anybody finds them out here…"

Ferguson takes in the property, the press of surrounding trees. "They're on their own, huh?"

Whicher drives on toward the house—sees no lights, sees no sign of any disturbance.

He pulls up in front of the timber deck as Annaliese parks her Jeep in front of the house.

The phone on the dash lights up.

The marshal checks, doesn't recognize the number.

Annaliese steps from behind the wheel of her vehicle, takes out a set of keys.

Gregory Joyner climbs out.

"I better get this," the marshal says.

Ferguson nods, unhooks her seat belt.

"Whicher."

"Marshal Whicher?"

A man's voice, unfamiliar.

"Yes, it is, who is this?"

"My name is Doctor Handley, I'm calling from the hospital in Artesia. We've been caring for a patient, a Charlene Kingbird—under a law enforcement emergency request."

"Something happen to her?"

"Your name was on the paperwork," the doctor says, "on the original request. But she's out of danger, now."

"She's awake, she's conscious?"

"She's responding to treatment. She's conscious, she's pretty weak."

Reva Ferguson turns in her seat. "I can go in with them?" she mouths.

Whicher nods, holds the phone to his ear.

"There's no pressing need for further medical care," the doctor says. "Law enforcement has an interest, but we need to discharge her—so I was calling to ask, do you want to take custody? Or should I speak with the city police?"

Ferguson steps from the truck, moves to Gregory and Annaliese at the front door of the house.

Annaliese unlocks it.

Ferguson puts a hand on the woman's arm, stops her. Enters the house first.

Whicher gets out of the truck. "I need to talk to her."

"Can you come in?" the doctor says.

"To the hospital? Tonight?"

"Or I can call the police department—see if they can take her?"

Whicher steps toward the house, watches lights flick on at the windows. "No, doc. Look, I'll come in, can you give me an hour?"

"If that's what you want?"

Standing at the threshold, the marshal eyes the interior of the Joyner house—nothing seems disturbed. Gregory flops on a couch, Ferguson leads his mother through into the kitchen, checking windows and doors. "Hold her there," he says. "Hold her. I'll come out."

CHAPTER
TWENTY-SEVEN

SIX BLOCKS up from the main highway, bright sodium lighting bathes the hospital car lot as Whicher climbs from the truck out into the night air with Marshal Ferguson.

He eyes the main entrance to the building—a smoked glass atrium, flanked with pillars, the main floors of the hospital extending out behind it.

Vehicles arrive and leave—an ambulance pulls in at the emergency entrance bay, lights flashing and popping.

Ferguson looks at him. "We ever getting home tonight?"

"We get done here, I'll take you on back to Carlsbad." Reaching the building, he holds open the door to the main entrance for her.

"It always like this with you?"

Whicher grins, doesn't respond.

A uniformed security guard stands watch in the middle of the reception space. On the front desk, a thickset man in his forties looks up.

Whicher takes out his badge and ID. He clips across the polished floor. "Deputy Marshals Whicher and Ferguson. Here to see Doctor Handley."

"Sir, ma'am." The reception clerk checks his list. "Doctor said to send you right in—room one-one-eight, it's on down the corridor." He gestures with his head to a set of double doors. "I'll let the doctor know you arrived."

"Appreciate it."

"I'll buzz you in."

Whicher steps with Ferguson across the entrance hallway.

The marshal waits as the latch on the door opens—he pushes through into a wide corridor.

Ferguson follows. "What do you want to do with Charlene Kingbird?"

"Her garage is full of crystal meth. You think Valley Task Force could hold her?"

"As opposed to who?"

"Local law enforcement. I don't want her contacting Karl Ramsay. USMS could take custody. Could you guys take her up in Roswell?"

Ferguson cuts him a sideways look.

"What about the courthouse?" Whicher says. "They have holding cells. If she stays ours, we can protect her."

"Yeah, but how about if she's sick?"

The corridor opens into an area with vending machines, seating, a water fountain. Another corridor extending beyond it. Whicher checks a wall-mounted sign.

"You think somebody's going to get to Charlene Kingbird?" Ferguson says.

The marshal doesn't respond.

"You really think that boy up there in the hills could be under threat?"

"You don't?"

Ferguson shakes her head. "I don't know what to think. The kid's scared, I guess. The mom, too, though she won't admit it."

A row of doors is ahead—a security guard waiting outside

one of them—Hispanic, in his forties. "Looking for one-one-eight?"

"Right," Whicher says.

"I see some ID?"

The marshal takes out his badge.

"She's not cuffed in there," the guard says, "not shackled, either. You arresting her? She a jibhead? Junkie?"

"She was OD on arrival," Whicher says, "in possession. I made the call."

"Thought it was a psyche hold," the guard says, "seventy-two-hour, you know?"

"Why's that?"

"Pretty agitated in there."

Whicher looks at the door to room 118.

"Messed up, you ask me."

Ferguson addresses the guard. "You getting an uptick of this?"

"Street users looking for three hots and a cot," the man says, "now that it's turning cold."

Whicher knocks, enters the room.

Charlene Kingbird sits in a chair by a window, wearing a hospital gown—her long black hair loose about her shoulders. One hand grips the other in her lap.

Reva Ferguson closes the door behind her.

"Ms Kingbird," Whicher says. "We're from the US Marshals Service."

In her face is panic, fear.

"Here to place you under arrest—for possession of controlled substances."

Her eyes burn in her sculpted face.

"Anything you say can and will be used against you."

Reva Ferguson takes a pair of cuffs from a leather pouch at her belt.

"You're also under suspicion of harboring a wanted

felon," Whicher says. "Karl Ramsay. We found his car parked in your garage."

"Not all we found…" Ferguson says.

The door to the room opens. A slim man enters, dressed in a doctor's white coat. He runs a hand through thinning brown hair, eyes magnified through steel-rim glasses.

"Doctor Handley?" Whicher says.

"We spoke earlier on the phone?" The doctor glances at the cuffs in Reva Ferguson's hands. "You're taking Ms Kingbird with you?"

"She's under arrest," Ferguson says, "we'll find somewhere for her tonight."

"Do I need to let the city police know?"

"No need," Whicher says.

The doctor steps to Charlene Kingbird. "You're lucky to still be alive, you know?"

The young woman barely registers the man's presence.

"The level of toxicity you came in with—you're running the risk of heart failure, multiple organ failure. We've had fatalities among people younger than you. You need to seek treatment."

She looks up at him. "In jail?"

"Some facilities have addiction programs."

Whicher looks at Handley. "She likely to need further treatment?"

"There's no immediate clinical need, no. There could be non-critical issues around withdrawal." The doctor looks at Kingbird. "I'm guessing you're an habitual user."

A scowl crosses her face as she looks at him.

"So, I can hold her in a regular jail?" Whicher says.

The doctor nods.

Marshal Ferguson looks at him. "She have clothes when she came in, doc?"

Handley indicates the nightstand by the bed. "In there, I think."

Ferguson steps to Kingbird, pulls her to her feet. Points to a bathroom. "Go on in there. Get yourself dressed. Then we're out of here."

Outside in the lot, Whicher opens up the Silverado.

Reva Ferguson guides Charlene Kingbird to the back seat. "Watch your head as you get in."

The young woman ducks inside.

Swinging in behind the wheel, Whicher fires up the motor.

Ferguson climbs into the passenger seat.

The marshal steers out of the hospital parking—past an all-night pharmacy, onto a street running north south. "I'll get you back to Carlsbad."

"Stay on this," Ferguson tells him. "It'll take us through town, we can pick up the highway."

Whicher rolls to a stoplight on a four-lane. Looks at Charlene Kingbird in the back seat. "You know a woman named Jena Velasquez?"

Kingbird's eyes narrow.

"Been looking for her," Whicher says, "trying to find her."

The young woman turns to stare out of the passenger window, her face blank.

"She disappeared on us. Out in Alamogordo... Not looking to arrest her," the marshal says. "She was assaulted today."

In the rear-view, Kingbird meets his eye, momentarily.

"On the Mescalero Reservation," the marshal says. "Somebody beat her up pretty bad..." He pulls away as the stoplight turns to green. "She was beat up, now she's missing."

Reva Ferguson swivels in her seat. "We're only looking to find her, to help her. She could be in a lot of trouble."

Darkness alternates with light from the streetlamps as

Whicher drives a near-deserted road through the west side of town.

Kingbird's eyes meet with his again.

He holds them. "Seems like I'm getting to make a lot of hospital visits. One way or another. I don't want the next call to be the city morgue."

CHAPTER
TWENTY-EIGHT

THE NIGHT AIR is cold at the entrance to the detention center. Whicher presses on an intercom buzzer. He looks into a CCTV camera. "US Marshals Service. Booking in an arrestee."

Charlene Kingbird stands cuffed alongside him on the deserted sidewalk.

A metallicized voice comes back. "Marshal, go ahead."

The lock on the door buzzes open.

Whicher takes Kingbird by the arm, maneuvers her through the doorway into a bare, cement block lobby, painted white.

At the back of the entrance lobby, a face appears at a glass insert in a reinforced-steel door.

Whicher shows the USMS badge and ID.

A latch in the door clanks open. A black-uniformed detentions officer motions them inside into the booking hall.

At the front desk, a female clerk looks out from behind a safety glass window.

The detentions officer indicates a wooden bench bolted along one wall. "You want to park her over there?"

Whicher leads Kingbird to the bench, unlocks his set of

handcuffs from her wrists, sits her down, cuffs her right wrist to one of a set attached to steel rings in the blockwork wall.

Something of the fight in her eye changes.

She slumps an inch, breath dissipating. Her long black hair hangs forward, loose.

At the desk, the booking clerk slides a paper form through the metal recess beneath the security window.

The detentions officer, a heavy-set man in his forties takes it. He looks at it with weary eyes, begins filling it out.

Kingbird stares at the gray-painted floor.

Whicher glances at her. "You get a chance to fix this."

She doesn't respond.

"Your girl Jena Velasquez might not..." Whicher crosses to the booking desk.

The black-clad officer looks up from the form. "Sir, you are?"

"Deputy US Marshal Whicher. USMS Texas; Western Division. Attached with the Pecos Valley Task Force."

Behind the window, the booking clerk adjusts her eyeglasses. Looks at him, the set of her jaw hard.

The officer writes onto the form. "And your arrestee?"

"Charlene Kingbird."

"Address?"

The marshal gives the Artesia address on Missouri Avenue.

"Charge or charges against her?"

"Possession of controlled substances. Trafficking of same."

The clerk turns to her computer monitor, searches the screen. "How long you need her here?"

"Likely move her out tomorrow," Whicher says. "Take her up-country."

The clerk clicks to another screen.

"Any hold on her?" the detentions officer says. "US Marshals hold?"

"Haven't had time to look," Whicher says. "I don't know

of any federal charges outstanding. DA here will be filing. Right now, I just need her secure overnight."

The detentions officer writes more onto the form. "Alright, marshal…"

Whicher thinks of Reva Ferguson—likely halfway home by now—dropped at the Carlsbad Police station. He crosses back to Kingbird at the bench.

She stares at a spot six inches in front of her face.

"You're going to stay here tonight," he tells her.

Whicher lowers his head into Kingbird's eyeline.

She finally looks at him. "She lives in Artesia…"

"Say again?"

"Jena Velasquez…"

"You know where?"

Kingbird nods.

"Could she have gone there?"

"If somebody beat her up on the rez."

The marshal takes a step back. Regards the booking clerk and the detentions officer. "This somewhere she'd be safe?"

Kingbird's eyes are hollow as she answers. She shakes her head. "Nowhere would be safe."

The run-down street is unlit as Whicher drives the Silverado along fence lines of mesh wire and pallet wood—clapboard shacks and trailer homes intercut with new-built houses.

Battered pickups and older-model SUVs line the aging asphalt on the north side of Artesia. Junkers and abandoned trailers rot in bare dirt lots spotted with agave and prickly pear.

The marshal reads numbers from mailboxes, from the fronts of houses and cement block walls. The final property before the intersection is a double-wide trailer home—tan weatherboarding, white shutters at the windows.

He slows, checks the number painted by the door.

No lights show in any of the windows. On the patch of gravel out front of the trailer is no vehicle.

Whicher pulls over, stares at the property, shuts down the motor.

He steps out, eyes the street.

The thud of music plays from somewhere, the sound of a TV drifts from an open window. No cars pass on the cross streets—in the distance is the hum of traffic still rolling on US 285.

A set of wooden steps is before the front door of the trailer. He climbs them, raps a knuckle against the glass. Hears nothing. Knocks again, calls out; "*US Marshal…*" Thinking of Jena Velasquez—the last time he'd seen her—turning her loose on the Mescalero Reservation.

He takes in the darkness of the place, its silence. The image of Charlene Kingbird in his mind—giving up the address; scared. He could have kept Jena Velasquez in the jail; she might have still been safe.

The marshal scans the barren yard, looks off along the street again. Stepping to the door, he puts a hand against the glass.

The catch of something is in the air; some scent.

He sniffs at it.

Tries the handle.

The door opens.

A smell hits him—heady—the smell of gasoline.

Staring into the living room he sees only dim shapes in the darkness—upturned furniture, objects strewn about the floor. He steps back out, jumps off the stairway—grabs a flashlight from the truck.

In his coat is a pair of nitrile gloves, he puts them on, unfastens the retaining strap on the Glock.

Re-entering the property he switches on the flashlight. He moves the beam over the gasoline-soaked room.

Clothes and furniture are all over—pots and pans from the kitchen scattered on the floor. Tables and chairs are upended, cupboards emptied. In the flashlight beam he sees the carpet wet with gasoline, a slick smear over the kitchen floor. Vapor from it fills the air.

It can't have been there long.

Breathing shallow, he moves through the clutter, steps into a bedroom, checks it—sees the same disarray; the bed turned over, mattress and sheets on the floor. Clothing is everywhere, drawers emptied, the door hanging from an armoire.

The marshal checks the bathroom. Moves through to a second bedroom—finds it empty. Backtracking to the living room, he plays the flashlight over the floor. Gasoline is poured everywhere.

He moves to the front door, steps outside, sucks down a lungful of air.

Pulling off the nitrile gloves, he descends the steps to the truck. He takes out his phone. Finds a number for the city police department, sends a call.

It picks up.

"Yeah, this is Deputy US Marshal Whicher—I'm at an address on North Pine. I'm calling to report a suspected attempt at arson."

"Marshal, you have a fire?"

"No fire—but I'm at the home of a missing person—it's been doused in gasoline."

"Alright, marshal, copy that. Can you give me the address?"

Whicher gives the street number.

"We can send a patrol unit over?"

"Send somebody, they might want to take a look, the place has been ransacked."

"You have a name of the occupant?"

"Velasquez, Jena Velasquez."

"And you say she's not there? She's missing?"

"She was assaulted on the Mescalero Reservation earlier—I believe she may be in danger, I'm trying to find her."

"Alright, marshal, we'll send a unit right away."

"Copy that."

Whicher switches out the call.

At the window of a neighboring house, he sees a face at a window—an older woman looking out across her yard.

The marshal takes out the USMS badge and ID—he holds it up, approaches the perimeter fence.

The woman stares at him, eyes the badge in his hand. She opens the window, scowls out.

"US Marshal, ma'am..." he calls over.

"What do you want?"

"Looking for the occupant, you know her?"

The woman shakes her head.

"You see anybody come by here today?"

"She's not a good person," the woman says, "people come and go all times of the day."

Whicher regards her. "You see anybody today?"

The woman shakes her head.

He feels her reluctance, distrust; her apprehension to speak.

"I don't know nothing..." She pulls the window shut, closes the drape.

Walking back to the Silverado, Whicher opens up, gets in behind the wheel.

The gasoline scent is still strong, he looks down at his feet—at the soles of his boots. Thinks of somebody dousing the entire trailer.

Why not set it alight?

Sitting on the dark lane he thinks of the Joyners, of the isolated house in the hills above Cloudcroft. He thinks again of Charlene Kingbird, of Velasquez. Threatened women, frightened.

Maybe it had been a warning? Maybe somebody was interrupted.

He thinks of home, of his own wife, Leanne, his daughter, Lori. Somebody calling there—sending him a message.

His mood darkens. In his mind, the image of Andre Parrish suddenly forms.

Across town, on Missouri Avenue, surveillance will still be watching the Kingbird house for Ramsay—or one of his to collect the drugs. Nobody will be coming.

He fights a weariness. Checks his watch—too late to call Leanne. Thinks of the warrant in the glove box of the truck—for Karl Ramsay. Somewhere, still out there.

He pushes back in the seat, waits for the arrival of the squad car.

Only staring out into the pitch black of night.

Mind turning.

Fuse inside burning.

CHAPTER
TWENTY-NINE

ON THE DESK in the Carlsbad law enforcement center is a bag of take-out breakfast burritos, fresh coffee, a computer monitor displaying multiple open files.

The sun is not long risen, wind stiffening the state flag outside the office window, a field of gold and a red Zia sun against the pale morning air.

Law enforcement vehicles pass along Guadalupe Street, for the secure parking area in back.

Whicher picks up the cup of coffee, takes a sip. Sits. Returns to studying data from the National Crime Information Center, from NLETS, the law enforcement telecommunications system.

A list of charges pertain to Karl Ramsay—in addition to the outstanding UFAP warrant.

On a separate file on screen is a listing for Jena Velasquez; conviction for possession. Another file shows a DUI on Charlene Kingbird.

The marshal thinks back to the first morning—the pre-dawn raid—the day of the attempted arrest. In his mind's eye sees the white Toyota slewing to a stop in the street—the young deputy, Billy Drummond opening fire.

Both occupants of the car now dead from injuries sustained.

He checks his notes, looks up at the screen, types in two names.

Antonio Pittman. Jorge Salazar.

A list of convictions displays; for assault, larceny. Low-level trafficking.

Karl Ramsay filled Pittman's house with Mexican Ice, he'd had Salazar buy him a car; put them at the center of things. The big leagues. Now both of them were inside of the meat locker.

He thinks of the second arrest of the morning—at the house by the river on Glendale—thinks of PIT-turning the runner, the man named Rios.

Parrish.

Andre Parrish.

Blowing the search. Almost getting Reva Ferguson killed.

He stares at a lined page of his notebook. The name *Alvaro Nunez* is written on the pad—the second warrant of the morning.

He opens up the NCIC screen. Types into a search field.

Nunez. Retail-level meth supplier. Suspect on an assault with a deadly weapon.

Whicher thinks of Nunez—pulling the gun on Marshal Ferguson. He thinks of staring the man down. Of the relief when he'd finally backed off.

The screen listing shows him now in custody—in Albuquerque.

He types in *Luis Rios*. The runner. Driver of the car.

Rios was wanted out in Alamogordo—suspect on an assault at Holloman Air Force Base. The marshal thinks of passing the place the prior afternoon.

He squints at the screen.

No listing for a custody location.

A knock sounds at the office door.

Sergeant Shannon Towne enters the room. "Morning."

"Sergeant."

"Front desk said you were already in. Looking to clear the case?"

"Bust Ramsay's ass," the marshal answers. "Then get the hell out of Dodge."

"You take the meeting with FBI?"

"With Agent Niemann? We did."

The sergeant looks at him.

"They're willing to get involved. Marshal Ferguson's in favor."

"Good." Towne nods. "Cause nothing's happening at the house in Artesia. Nobody's been by, nothing's going on. Maybe nobody wants a garage full of crystal meth…"

Whicher pushes his seat back from the desk. "You know anything about the second bust we did the morning we went after Ramsay?"

The sergeant looks at him.

"Nunez," Whicher says, "guy on the warrant. He's up in the Q now. No record on the second guy."

"Other guy was incidental on the bust, no?"

"He was, but I looked him up. Law enforcement in Alamogordo want him."

"You'd have to talk to Detective Allen. Trenton Allen? Guy the chief has looking for the witness?" Sergeant Towne puts his head on one side. "I need to talk to you about that…"

"Marshals Service will handle it," Whicher says, "like I told you."

"You want to tell that to my boss?" Towne steps to the threshold of the room. Gestures at the corridor with his chin. "Chief Garton's in. Asking to see you."

In the second-floor office at the law enforcement center, Eugene Garton sits behind a large desk, gold badge prominent on his black dress shirt. The room is lined with charts, diplomas, with photographs of men and women from the department, former chiefs of police.

"Good morning, gentlemen." Garton indicates two chairs in front of his desk.

"Chief." Whicher nods. He pulls out a chair alongside the sergeant.

"You making any progress?"

"Detained a suspect last night," the marshal says.

Towne looks at him.

"Charlene Kingbird, the hospital kicked her out last night."

Garton makes a question with his face.

"A woman connected with Karl Ramsay," the marshal says.

"Living at the house the task force has under surveillance," Towne says.

"She was OD'd when I found her," Whicher says, "she's been in the hospital ever since."

The sergeant shoots an eyebrow. "What's she have to say about the boxes in her garage?"

"Not much," Whicher says. "I need to speak with the El Paso DA. They might want a piece of her, since she's hooked up with our man."

Chief Garton sits forward at his desk. "Marshal, I understand you made contact with a witness we discussed—the minor? A boy that gave a statement to one of my officers during door-to-door inquiries?"

"Right," Whicher says.

"I asked Otero County law enforcement to go out to an address yesterday. Up by Cloudcroft. Nobody was home."

Whicher shows nothing in his face.

"Subsequent to that, officers from the Valley Task Force went up..."

"You know who?"

"I don't," the chief says. "But the point is, nobody was there at that time, either. And it's starting to look like they could be gone."

"Chief, this is a Marshals Service case."

"I asked for somebody to find the witness," Garton says, "they could have information material to this. And I don't see any conflict of interest—if witness information can lead us to individuals connected with the case, it could help identify the whereabouts of Karl Ramsay."

"FBI are coming in on Ramsay," Whicher says.

"Listen, I understand you had a marshal seriously injured on this," the chief says. "At the same time, I have two shot dead inside of a vehicle in my town. People require answers..."

Whicher thinks of Gregory and Annaliese—at the Pires property; back home now.

"I'd appreciate if you let my officers talk to this witness," Garton says. "If you know where he is. I'd think you'd welcome it; we get a live lead, we can help on that—you get your man all the sooner."

"Understood," the marshal says.

"So?" The chief looks at him.

Whicher pushes back from the desk, stands. "I don't have him."

———

Traffic slows for a red at an intersection on the four-lane headed east as Whicher follows a cement truck past churches, apartment blocks, an old motor court filled with dirt-grimed automobiles. He keys the number for his boss, Chief Marshal Martha Fairbanks. Sets the call onto speaker.

The chief marshal picks up. "El Paso office have been in touch this morning."

"Ma'am?"

"Over an event deconfliction notice. Triggered by Las Cruces FBI. It's in respect of an interdiction?"

"I met with an FBI agent out there," Whicher says, "yesterday? Name of Frank Niemann." He brakes the truck to a standstill at the lights. "Las Cruces FBI are looking to hit up a bunch of vehicles in transit, along with the HIDTA task force —a transshipment. Ramsay could be involved. It could mobilize a lot of resource..."

"Get you out of there sooner," Fairbanks says. The tone of her voice changes. "What about your other... situation?"

"Ongoing." Whicher comes off the brake as the stoplight turns to green. "Chief of police here wants him located. They're trying to find him."

"How come they can't?"

"I spoke with the mother. Advised her to stay someplace else with her son. It's not going to be enough."

Crossing the intersection at Highway 285, the marshal eyes the expanse of the county court square—watered lawns, live oak and cypress framing the lines of the early Spanish-style courthouse building.

"If you want more protection," Fairbanks says, "you'll have to talk to them about what that would look like. They'd have to cooperate to make it work..."

"If we're talking about witness protection..."

"It's a decision for a DA, I can't make promises."

"I understand," Whicher says. "Maybe they wouldn't need the full security program."

"If you think the kid needs protection, you should go see them," Fairbanks says.

The marshal hits the blinker, makes the turn onto North Main for the county detention center. "The mother has her own ideas."

"Maybe they'll be okay?" the chief marshal says. "Maybe they don't need protecting?"

"Bunch of hospital visits I'm making out here," Whicher tells her. "A young woman I interviewed was assaulted—now she's missing. Last night I was at a trailer home somebody soaked with gasoline. I don't think things are going to be okay…"

CHAPTER
THIRTY

BEHIND REINFORCED glass in the interview room Charlene Kingbird sits in blue prison overalls—Whicher in a plastic chair on the opposite side of the security screen.

Kingbird rocks on her stool, leans into the stainless-steel counter. Meth withdrawal working through her body, eyes half-dead, then wild, darting.

A lined notepad is open in Whicher's lap, pen trailing from his hand. "I couldn't find her. I tried. She wasn't there."

Kingbird only stares.

"Mainly," he says, "I came to talk about what happens next."

A flash of temper is in her eye, mood turning in an instant.

Whicher leans forward in his chair. "I came to talk about a plea, you know what that is?"

Her body snaps rigid, she glares at the floor.

"Plea bargain. You cut a deal on the charges you're likely facing."

He sees the muscle working at her jaw.

"Cop for one of them, on a lesser sentence—in return for skipping out on the rest. A count deal it's called…"

She looks up suddenly, eyes narrow; "Why?"

"Maybe you have something I need."

Her face is sour as she regards him.

"Karl Ramsay—you know him pretty well?"

She doesn't answer.

"Seems like you know him well enough. To let him leave a car at your place. Let him fill your garage with crystal meth."

She slumps. "You think I had a choice?"

Whicher sits back, regards the concrete block wall. "See, there you go. We could use that..." He turns to look at her through the security glass. "I take that to the DA. Tell them you were coerced. Forced into storing narcotics..."

"You don't believe me?"

Whicher shrugs. "I'm never going to know, either way."

Kingbird rocks on the stool.

"But I could make a case to a prosecutor..."

She studies him now, sick-looking, the color drained from her face.

"Maybe get you out from under—if you work with me..."

Her fine-boned features are stark beneath the prison lights.

"You know about Karl Ramsay?" Whicher says. "What he's doing, where he's gone? You help me find him, I can help you out of this."

She sweeps her black hair back behind her shoulders.

In her dark eyes he sees a nascent focus.

"They'll convict on possession," Whicher says. "Question is—for how much? What's in the house, they could let it go for personal use. The boxes in your garage? That's years of your life, right there..."

Kingbird grips the sides of her overalls suddenly. Fingers tightening on the blue cotton of the prison suit.

"You don't want that. You go down for that, you go down hard..."

A sheen is on her brow, perspiration films her skin. She

shivers behind the glass, her body cramping. She doubles over.

Whicher changes tack; "Last night I went to that address—in Artesia. Somebody tore the place apart, they soaked it with gasoline."

Charlene Kingbird raises her head an inch. In her eyes, water starts to well.

"You know any cops?" the marshal says. "Ever see any? Around Ramsay?"

In her face is confusion. "I don't know what you mean…"

"You. Jena Velasquez. Y'all need to think about survival," Whicher says. "She ought to be in a hospital right now. BIA police found her, yesterday, they tried to get her treatment—but she ran out, disappeared. And I'm sitting here looking at you. Nobody's taking care of either one of you…"

Behind the glass, Kingbird sits unmoving. Finally, she lets out a long breath. "How you think you're going to catch him?"

"Only need to find him…"

"He knows, everybody—everybody knows who he is. He knows you're coming..."

The marshal eyes her.

"You," she says, "the law, whoever. He just knows." She sways on her seat, shrugs. "He goes out there—on the rez."

"The Mescalero Reservation?"

She dips her head. "He sells up there. He knows Jena. She sells for him. I've sold for him. I've washed money, everybody washes…"

"He does business up there?"

"There. All over. He's got his crew, his network."

"Curtis Traxler one of 'em?"

Her eyes are hooded.

"Why Indian land?"

"They'll sell local, hook people in. There's places they store drugs, nobody's around, nobody's looking." Her face is suddenly wary. "How do I know you can get me any deal? You're not the judge, you're a cop…"

"You make a deal it's with the DA's office," Whicher says.

"So, why am I talking to you?"

"Right now, I'm all you've got. I bring the DA somebody who'll testify, somebody who knows what goes on in Ramsay's world—you think they won't be interested?"

In her face is fear mixed with the slightest flicker; a way out, hope.

"You need to fight for you, now," Whicher tells her. "Nobody's coming to pull you out. If I find Jena Velasquez—*if* I find her, I'll tell her the same thing."

He stares at his reflection in the reinforced glass screen. Stark-looking in the harsh lighting. Still. Silent in the numb air of the interview room.

She moves behind the screen, catches his eye. "Or?" she says.

"Or maybe someone else will find her first…"

Snow is on the ground in the tree-lined canyon climbing through the Sacramento Mountains, sunlight strobing through the branches of trees, glaring back from stretches of pristine white.

Whicher drives the two-lane highway, the disinfectant smell of the detention center still present in his nostrils, mood dark, thinking of the young woman behind the screen.

He reaches for the phone, keys a number for Reva Ferguson.

It picks up.

"Marshal."

"Morning."

"Where are you?" she says.

"Otero County. I just came from the Carlsbad detention center."

"What's going on?" Ferguson says.

"I went in to see Charlene Kingbird. She's pretty hooked up into Ramsay's business—she knows about some of it," Whicher says. "I told her about Jena Velasquez. Getting beat up. Disappearing. She gave me a lead, an address. I went out there last night—somebody wrecked the place, it looks like they were about to torch it—there was gasoline all over..."

"Really?"

"Some bad people around this," the marshal says. "I let her know we could make some kind of deal."

"You think she'd know enough?"

"Hard to say. Guess we'll find out."

"Frank Niemann was in touch," Ferguson says. "DEA in Las Cruces think something could be happening in the next couple of days. Grady Owens heard the same. Niemann wants to know do we want in?"

"Tell him yeah," Whicher says.

"You want to?"

The marshal hears the doubt in her voice.

"What about what you said?"

Whicher thinks of the likelihood of word getting out to Ramsay in advance. "So far, we've got nothing better," he says. "Then again, if he's expected and it turns out he's not there…"

The marshal leaves the thought unspoken.

"Alright," Ferguson says. "Well, I'll call him back. What do you want to do with Charlene Kingbird?"

"Keep her where she is, I'll square it with the jail. Right now, I'm headed out to see the Joyners. I talked it over with my boss. I think we might be looking at a need for protection. I don't like what I found last night."

Ferguson is quiet a moment. "You think she'd even agree?"

Whicher eyes the hills through the windshield. "She told me they moved to get away from what's going on—crime, drugs, mainstream life…"

"Maybe she'd move again?"

"She's part Apache, that land up there is homeland. That all is part of why she chose it."

"She's there to make a stand?"

The marshal steers the truck around a bend as trees close with the road, gloom thickening, blocking out more winter light.

He gives no answer.

Crushed snow and the dirt of tire tracks lead from the Joyner property. Turning in on the driveway, he sees no sign of Annaliese's Jeep.

He scans the A-frame house.

No lights show in any of the windows.

Bringing the truck to a stop, he steps out, eyes the house, the adjoining deck.

In the air is a noise; a sharp sound—the strike of metal hitting metal.

Whicher turns his head.

Hears it again.

He follows the line of a rick fence—down the slope of a hill. A barn is at the foot of a small escarpment, covered in weathered shingles, snow and ice on its roof.

Gregory Joyner stands with a sledgehammer in front of a pile of pinon and ponderosa pine. He swings the hammer onto a steel wedge sticking from a chainsawed log.

The wedge splits the wood, falls to the ground, the boy leans in, picks it up.

Whicher raises a hand, descends the slope further.

Gregory turns, startled.

Whicher looks at the pile of firewood.

The boy stands slack-limbed, staring.

The marshal stops at the side of the barn. "Warms you three times, they say…"

Gregory only looks at him.

"Got to cut it. Split it. Then you stack it." Whicher adjusts the Resistol. "Even before you done burn it."

The boy makes no response.

"Here on your own?"

"Mom went to the store."

"Down to Cloudcroft?"

"We were out of food."

"She been gone long?"

"An hour, maybe?"

"She left you here splitting wood?" Whicher says.

Gregory shrugs. Sets the tip of the steel wedge into a crack in another log. He stands the log straight. Steps back.

"Quite a pile," the marshal says.

The boy hefts the hammer. He swings it, brings it down—the hammer bounces off, the wedge sticks in the wood.

"Yeah," Whicher says, "they'll get hung up, huh?"

Gregory nods.

"Got to hit 'em again, chase 'em."

"I don't mind it." The boy straightens the log—swings, hits the wedge again—cleaving the wood into two.

Whicher nods, approaches. "You talk to your mom?"

Gregory's eyes slide away.

"About things, all this?"

"Sort of."

"Alright, well, good," the marshal says.

Gregory picks out another log from the stack.

"Anybody been out here?"

"Why would they?"

"Police department are interested," Whicher says. "Trying to figure things out."

The boy slumps, subdued suddenly.

"Law enforcement," Whicher says, "they have to investigate, things like this. There's a detective wanting to talk to you…"

"All I saw was some cop at a house…" The boy's voice rises, trails away.

Whicher picks up a piece of the split firewood. Examines it. "Yeah," he says. "But what it is, that cop shouldn't ever have been out there. And next day a marshal was shot down in the street. Two guys from that house were fatally injured."

Gregory lets out a breath, stares out over the steep-sided valley at the edge of the property—the slopes dotted with fir and pine and scrub oak—in his eyes resentment, his face a mix; hurt, confusion. "All I did was tell the truth…"

The marshal nods. "I know it."

The boy looks at him.

"That's all that matters, son."

Gregory stands motionless before the tract of snow and wild woodland.

"I came out from Texas to arrest a man," Whicher says. "Bad man. Makes a lot of money—making misery for folk. He's mixed up with a lot of people."

Gregory's face is still as he regards him.

"And that cop you saw? That cop told him I was coming for him."

The boy blinks once.

"So now, what I have to do is, I need to take care of that, too."

The shaft of the hammer slips through Gregory's hands—its head hits the ground, snow enfolds it. His voice is small in his throat when he speaks. "What will I have to do?"

"Won't have to do anything," Whicher says. "Except maybe tell a judge what you saw."

Gregory blanches, looks off into the middle distance.

"Something like this happens, the US Marshals are here," Whicher says. "Our job is to protect people. Take care of 'em."

"What if he comes here? The cop I saw…"

Whicher looks out over the pristine valley—takes in its beauty—drifts of pure white snow carpeting the steep descents. Sun reflects crystalline from a world unspoiled. "Somebody might come…"

Above the silence, only the wind moves in the trees.

Gregory swallows, clamps his mouth shut.

"That's why I need to talk with you, talk with your mom. Make sure things are… prepared."

The boy grips the long handle of the hammer, pale-faced.

Somewhere beyond the barn the sound of a motor drifts, now—a vehicle approaching.

Whicher turns, starts back up the slope through the snow.

He loosens a button on the ranch coat, uncovers the Glock at his hip. Scrambling up the the bank, he sees Annaliese Joyner's Jeep accelerating up the driveway.

She stops at the house, jumps out—sees him. Starts to march across the snow-covered ground. "What're you doing here?"

The marshal sees the black, squared-off pistol holstered at her hip. "Came to ask how you were…"

"We're fine…"

"And see if anyone had come out here…"

"No," she says, her voice tight. "Nobody's been. And we don't want you or anybody else."

Whicher eyes her gun, a SIG semi-automatic.

Her face is defiant. "And if they do, we'll take care of it." She steps in front of him, feet planted. "Gregory's been thinking—about what he saw—and he's not so sure about it, about any of it—in fact he thinks he made a mistake; and I think so, too…"

"Ms Joyner…"

"It was late, it was dark, he saw some man show up…"

She spreads her hands wide. "He saw all of this TV footage the next day... he got confused. He doesn't know what he saw."

Whicher eyes the boy's mother.

"He's thought about it, now he knows... better."

"Ma'am, it doesn't work like that."

"The hell it doesn't." In her eye is a lick of flame.

Whicher runs a knuckle along the side of his jaw.

"I don't want you here," the woman says, "you or any of your people. I don't want to see you again. We've got nothing for you."

"Ma'am..." the marshal weighs his words, "this is a live investigation—your son's statement is a part of it. Any prosecuting attorney can subpoena him. Gregory would have to give evidence to the court."

She balls her hands at her sides. "I want you out of here. Right now, I want you gone."

"Ma'am, the Marshals Service can take care of this."

Annaliese Joyner's eyes glisten black. "Just get off of my property."

Whicher turns, sees Gregory—staring at him, now, across the snow.

From the Silverado is the sound of an incoming call. Glancing at Annaliese, the marshal crosses to the truck—opens up, whips the phone from the dash stand. "Yeah, Whicher, go ahead."

"Officer Roanhorse from the BIA police."

Whicher straightens. "What's going on?"

"I just had a report from a neighbor of Jena Velasquez—on the rez."

"Oh?"

"There's a fire burning up there in her trailer—he said smoke is pouring out of it; I'm about to go up—I thought you'd want to know..."

CHAPTER
THIRTY-ONE

THE TRACE of the service road across the mountain plateau is barely visible beneath the snow. Rounding the last of the tree-covered hills, black smoke curls from beyond a wooded slope a half-mile ahead. In his mind's eye Whicher pictures Jena Velasquez's place, wrecked the last time he saw it; roughly searched, trashed.

He stares out through the windshield—at wheel marks carved along the white-over road, keeps his truck tires within them.

Approaching the wooded slope, he steers over toward the Velasquez property in the mouth of the small canyon—the trailer and outbuildings sheltered in the lee of the hill.

Officer Roanhorse's Ram pickup is parked out in front of the trailer, along with an older-model Chevy S-10.

Roanhorse stands with a Native American man and woman—a couple in their fifties, dressed in boots and jeans and heavy coats.

Their faces turn at his approach.

The marshal raises a hand from the wheel. He scans the trailer—a block of white against the slope of pine and fir.

Black smoke rises from it, soot marks are at its windows and doors.

He steers in, slows, brakes the truck to a stop.

Officer Roanhorse steps away from the man and woman.

Whicher shuts down the motor, climbs out. Gestures at the trailer; "That thing out?"

"Good as."

The marshal looks at him.

"Nothing in there left to burn."

"You check inside?"

The BIA officer nods, face dour.

"Nobody's in there, right?" Whicher searches the man's face.

"I looked, couldn't see nothing."

The marshal glances at the man and woman by the Chevy pickup.

"Brandon Holt, the neighbor," Roanhorse says. "His wife Sherilyn."

Both stare back, their faces immobile.

Whicher fastens his coat, takes the few paces to the open door of the trailer.

He looks in. Catches the smell; strong, acrid at the back of his throat. "You let it burn?"

The BIA officer shrugs. "I wasn't calling up the fire department—it wouldn't have made a difference." He steps to the threshold of the trailer, points inside at the floor.

Whicher sees holes.

Burnt through.

A trail of them—signs of an accelerant burning downward.

Roanhorse rubs a finger against charred wood at the foot of the doorframe. He holds his finger to his nose. "That's gasoline."

Whicher presses a hand against the blackened frame. Smells his skin, detects the trace, the hint of vapor.

He thinks of the trailer home back in Artesia. Cranes his neck to see inside. "Sure nobody's in there?"

"You want to see for yourself go ahead. But it's a crime scene, now."

The marshal eyes the man and woman standing over at the pickup.

"Brandon Holt reported it," Roanhorse says.

Whicher takes out his badge, crosses the snow-covered ground to the Chevy. "Sir. Ma'am. Y'all are neighbors with Ms Velasquez?"

The man nods, the woman's face barely flickers.

"You discovered the fire?"

"Saw smoke," the man says.

"Y'all live nearby?"

Brandon Holt raises an arm, points back along the road across the plateau.

The BIA officer speaks; "They're on Running Horse Creek. About a mile from here."

"I saw smoke. Didn't think much about it." Brandon Holt's eyes are dark in his weathered face. "It kept going. So I came out."

"You see anybody?" Whicher says.

The man shakes his head. "Place was burning. I left out, to call down, get somebody."

"You called down to Mescalero?"

"BIA said to wait. They'd come up." The man looks at Officer Roanhorse.

Whicher glances back across the plateau. "Not many tracks out here. There any other way up?"

"Plenty."

"Somebody come out here without you knowing?"

Brandon Holt starts to speak, his wife looks at him, cuts him short.

Roanhorse angles his head. "What?"

Holt shrugs.

"Come on," the BIA officer says.

"Seen a truck earlier."

"What truck?" Whicher says.

"Crew truck. A Ford."

"Where was this?" Roanhorse says.

"It came by." Holt gestures at the plateau. "Along the road."

"What kind of truck?" the marshal says. "Crew cab? 350?"

The man nods.

"Old, new?"

"Old."

"What color?"

"White."

"You get a look at who was in it?"

"Latino guy."

Whicher looks at him. "One man? More?"

"Just a driver."

Whicher gazes over at the trailer. "Could he have come here?"

Roanhorse speaks; "We came up there weren't many tracks."

"Had snow all morning," Brandon Holt says, "fresh cover."

"This truck come by around the time the fire started?" Whicher says.

"Hour before, maybe."

The marshal looks to Roanhorse. "Know anybody with one like that?"

The BIA officer shakes his head. "Could be anybody..."

Whicher regards Brandon Holt. Turns to his wife. "How about Jena Velasquez? You see her recently?"

"She don't live here," the woman answers. "But she was up with that drug dealer."

"Curtis Traxler. Have you seen her since?"

The woman's eyes tell him no.

"If she came up here, would you know about it?"

Brandon Holt cuts in; "We'll see people..."

"On the road?"

The man nods.

"I heard somebody beat up on her," the woman says.

"Where you hear that, Sherilyn?" Officer Roanhorse eyes her.

Her face is a mask. "Word goes around."

"Know anything about it?"

"She makes her bed with thieves and liars," the woman says, "what's she going to get?"

Whicher surveys the burnt-out trailer, the bleak surrounds of the property—the yard shelter, auto junk, offcuts of lumber abandoned, scattered among the snow. "Lieutenant Decoteau know about this?"

"Not yet," Roanhorse says.

"You going to call him?"

The BIA officer nods.

Whicher turns back to the Silverado. Climbs in, studies the man and woman at the Chevy truck.

He keys a call to Reva Ferguson. Watches snow blowing from the tops of pine on the hill.

Brandon and Sherilyn Holt stare out across the wind-blown plateau.

The call answers.

"News—on Jena Velasquez. Somebody torched that trailer she owns."

"Up on the rez?"

"I'm out there now. With Roanhorse. Neighbors saw a fire. There was gasoline in there—like I found at her place in Artesia."

Ferguson is silent on the line.

"Neighbors say a truck came by, a white pickup. Some Hispanic guy driving." The marshal stares at the charred trailer through the windshield. "Your guy Grady Owens said something about a 'Mexican.' Some black tar heroin deal?"

"Yeah…"

"Somebody Ramsay was after getting even with…"

"You think this could be the guy?"

Whicher lets the thought sit, doesn't reply.

"Owens called me," Ferguson says, "word is some kind of shipment's going on the road today."

The marshal pulls himself up behind the wheel.

"Ramsay could be involved."

"You talk to Frank Niemann?"

"He thinks they could put something together."

"Oh?"

"Along with DEA, local law enforcement…"

"Where?"

"Las Cruces. Owens says it'll likely pass through—on one of the interstates."

"You think the tip's good?"

"Been good intel in the past," Ferguson says. "I hit the road already, I can meet you out there? I can call, I can let you know where."

Whicher watches Officer Roanhorse at the BIA pickup, talking into a radio transceiver. "Alright, I get done here, I'll come out."

The marshal switches out, steps from the truck.

Roanhorse calls over; "Lieutenant says he's going to send up an investigator from the fire department at Ruidoso."

"You going to wait?"

The BIA officer shakes his head. "Going to be a while."

Whicher looks at Brandon Holt. "How many vehicles you see up here? On a typical day."

"In winter?" The man's mouth is downturned.

"Handful, maybe?" Roanhorse says.

Holt nods. "Nobody comes by much."

Roanhorse takes a reel of police tape from the Ram pickup.

Sherilyn Holt looks at Whicher—her chin jutted. "You going to find who did this?"

"If I can."

She climbs into the aging Chevy.

Brandon Holt gets in behind the wheel. He nods to Roanhorse, starts the truck, backs around in the snow.

Roanhorse takes a metal fence-post from a pile in the snow—he pushes it into the ground as the Chevy pulls away onto the plateau road. Tying the tape around the post, he unspools a length along the trailer front.

"So, you have any ideas?" Whicher says.

The BIA officer looks at him. "Do you?"

The marshal watches the pickup. "Maybe. What do you want to do?"

"Check out a couple places on the rez," Roanhorse says, "see if I could find that white truck."

"You know where you want to look?"

"Got some ideas."

"What if you find him?"

Roanhorse glances over from the trailer.

"I mean, on your own," Whicher says. "Want some company?"

The BIA officer shrugs. "You want to tag along, be my guest."

CHAPTER
THIRTY-TWO

THE DRIVE through the high mountain country twists through small valleys and forested hills, open pasture at intervals either side of the white-over service road, the sun high overhead, glaring bright on the snowfields, throwing deep shade in the canyon depths.

Whicher follows Officer Roanhorse's Ram pickup. Wind disturbing clumps of white powder in the boughs of pine and fir, to send it cascading. The marshal turns up the heat blowing in the cab.

On a bend in the trail, Roanhorse slows—ahead is a fork in the road; the canyon dividing into two—a main valley stretching away to the north—another, smaller canyon headed roughly northeast.

Roanhorse brings his truck to a stop.

The marshal drives up behind him.

The BIA officer steps from his unit. Walking forward a few paces, he kneels to the snow-covered road.

Whicher opens up, gets out.

Tire tracks are clearly visible—extending along the main service road through the larger valley.

The road into the side canyon is a uniform white—save for twin depressions running in it, barely perceptible.

Roanhorse turns to Whicher. "See it?"

The marshal nods.

"That's a truck," the BIA officer says.

Whicher nods toward the road into the main valley. "Where's that one go?"

"Cattle country."

"There's cattle up here?"

"Summer pasture," Roanhorse says. "There's a ranch. Folk working up there."

Whicher eyes the smaller canyon. "How about that?"

"That's high country," Roanhorse says. "A lot of forest."

"Somebody went up."

The BIA officer stands. He stares into the steep-sided canyon.

"That'd be about a couple hours back," the marshal says.

"Right around the time…"

"The neighbor talked about seeing a white pickup…" Whicher nods. He bunches his shoulders against the cold, thinks of the fire at the trailer. "Why torch Jena Velasquez's place then drive up here?"

The BIA officer doesn't answer.

"It be easy to get on and off of the reservation without folk knowing?"

Roanhorse looks doubtful.

"Pretty remote out here..."

"Back at the trailer," Roanhorse eyes him. "You said you might have some ideas. So, what're you thinking?"

"The neighbor," Whicher says, "Brandon Holt? Said the driver of the pickup truck was Latino?"

"Yeah. So?"

"Guy I'm looking for, Karl Ramsay, has some kind of a beef with a 'Mexican.' Word is he's out looking for him. You know? Looking to settle a score."

"What's that all have to do with Jena Velasquez?"

"Maybe she got caught up in the middle of it."

Roanhorse frowns. "This Mexican dude burns her out?"

"Somebody doused her place in Artesia with gasoline."

The BIA officer considers it.

"There a lot of Hispanic folk on the rez?"

"Some," Roanhorse says. "Some part Apache."

The marshal scans the snow-covered floor of the valley—rough ground, open country, stands of pine and white oak stark in the distance. He checks his watch. Thinks of Reva Ferguson, the drive to Las Cruces. "And you think a person would have a hard time getting in and out of here unseen?"

"I'm not saying you couldn't do it."

The marshal turns for the Silverado. "Somebody ought to have seen that truck…"

Three miles up the road into the north-running valley, smoke curls from the chimney of a house surrounded by corrals and barns and mud-stained snow. A backhoe and two pickup trucks are parked, their beds loaded up with hay. A few head of cattle eat at a feeder, the steam of their breath clouding in the cold air.

Officer Roanhorse steers his truck between berms of dirty snow at either side of a pathway cut from the road by the blade of the backhoe.

Whicher follows.

A Native American man steps from the house onto the porch.

Roanhorse parks, climbs out of the BIA pickup.

The man advances to the porch rail—heavy-set in jeans and a wool coat, his rounded face weathered beneath a Western hat.

The marshal pulls in, kills the motor. Steps out.

Roanhorse approaches the porch. "George."

The man nods.

"This here's a US Marshal."

Whicher takes out his badge and ID.

The man glances at it.

"This here's George Altaha," Roanhorse says. "He runs the ranch up here. You know about the fire? Down at Whitetail?"

"Heard there was a fire," the man says.

"Somebody started it, deliberate."

The man named Altaha barely reacts.

"Looking for a white pickup," the BIA officer says. "Know anyone drives one?"

"A white truck?"

"Older model Ford," Whicher says. "Crew cab. F350."

The rancher stands mute, giving nothing.

The BIA officer eyes him. "Think about it for me."

"Anybody come by here this morning?" Whicher says.

Altaha directs his words to Roanhorse. "Couple of the hands come up. With feed." He nods toward the small herd of cattle by the corral. "We got the water supply froze. Still got these up here, too late to move 'em down, with the snow. They say the wind's going to get up. Maybe drift."

"Yeah?"

"That's all I seen."

Whicher takes a pace toward the porch.

The man looks at him.

"Sir. Are you aware of any folk coming or going? Recently? Folk you don't know."

"People come through."

"Anyone of late?"

Altaha looks off at a pair of heifers pushing a mineral block around in the snow. "Elan had somebody break in his saddle house. Couple weeks back."

Roanhorse nods. "We know about that."

"Had a bunch of gear taken. Some of them saddles run a couple thousand apiece..."

"Officer Kee's looking into it."

"Tweakers, most like. What he told me."

Roanhorse hooks a thumb into his duty belt.

"You had break-ins?" Whicher says.

"Meth heads," the rancher answers.

The marshal looks from Altaha to Roanhorse. "These are people from the reservation?"

"The rez. And off it," the BIA officer says.

Altaha descends the porch steps. "It's out here now, all of that—it's not just in town."

"Folk come in here," Roanhorse says. "From Ruidoso, Alamogordo, wherever. Friends of people living here. Some bringing drugs. Using, selling."

Whicher regards the rancher. "You see folk out here, you stop them?"

The man nods. "I'll ask their business."

"And you don't know anybody drives an old-model F350, white in color?"

Altaha shakes his head.

Roanhorse looks up the snow-covered road continuing past the ranch property. "What's it like up there?"

"You'll be alright out to Turkey Spring. You don't want to go north, up in the hills."

The BIA officer looks to Whicher. "May as well turn around. Plenty other places we can check."

Altaha says, "How come somebody burned that girl's trailer?"

Roanhorse scans the cattle in the ranch yard, doesn't answer.

"Heard she got arrested."

"You heard right."

"Her and some drug dealer—out of Artesia." The rancher breaks out a hard pack of cigarettes, lights one. His eyes narrow. "Seems like folk here need to take care of things themselves. Way it's going..."

Roanhorse's face is dark.

The marshal addresses the rancher. "You see that pickup, you let me know." He takes a business card from inside his coat, hands it to the man.

"Let the law handle things," Officer Roanhorse says.

Altaha turns the marshal's card between thick fingers. He stuffs it into a pocket, unread. Draws on the cigarette, deep.

Whicher takes in the lonely surrounds beyond the house and barns. The feeding cattle—pine-strewn hills, broken pasture, white-over. Silence prevails, but for lowing beasts, the keening of the wind.

Roanhorse eyes the rancher. Steps to his pickup. Addresses the man across the roof of the cab. "You hear anything—call."

Back down the canyon at the fork in the road, Roanhorse pulls over. He gets out, walks to Whicher in the Silverado.

The marshal rolls the window.

Roanhorse points into the steep-sided valley leading away to the northeast. "How about up there?"

"Think it's worth a shot?"

"Your truck good to climb in snow?"

"I guess we'll find out," Whicher says.

"Got chains?"

"Nope."

The BIA officer grins. "Too bad."

"Let's take a look," Whicher says, "if it gets bad we can bail."

"Alright, you want to follow me?"

A mile up out of the high-valley floor, the ranching road follows a path through broken forest of white pine and Douglas fir.

Roanhorse plows ahead through pristine white between the trees, the sky overhead a cold, iron-gray.

Whicher keeps his wheels in the gouged-out tire tracks of the Ram, the grade of the hill starting to top out, finally.

Through the trees are glimpses of wooded country—denuded patches of hillside covered with snow—summer grazing, rough pasture, abandoned for winter.

Ahead, Roanhorse lets his pickup slow. He brakes the truck to a stop. Steps out.

Whicher lets the Silverado come to a halt against the side of the hill.

The BIA officer gestures—at a disturbance in the snow a few feet in front of his vehicle.

Whicher climbs out into a cutting wind. Eyes the forest road. White powder is raised, churned up, then re-covered, smoothed. Beyond it, the ranch road is entirely undisturbed. At right angles is a way between the trees. Looking along it, the marshal sees ground sign—breaks in low branches, flattened vegetation,.

"See it?" Roanhorse says.

"Good spot."

The BIA officer regards him. "Want to go take a look?"

Whicher fastens his coat.

Roanhorse leads the way into the forest.

"Any idea what could be down here?" Whicher says. "Ever been out here?"

"Not that I recall. Got hundreds of square miles we're policing."

"Forest? Like this?"

"Lot of country."

The path through the trees starts to dip, now. Ahead a

shelter is in view—made from sheet-metal, with a rusted tin roof.

The snow around it is churned up, discolored, mixed with mud.

Roanhorse studies the ground.

Whicher sees tire tracks, the marks of a vehicle maneuvering. Footprints. "So, who comes up here?"

The BIA officer looks at him.

"Who knows about the road even?"

"Ranching folk."

"How about hunters?" Whicher says.

"Not here."

"So, maybe a handful of people?"

Roanhorse nods, steps forward.

A length of old chain hangs from a door handle, but no lock. He drags the door open.

Whicher moves up—sees a jumble of wood and iron posts inside, spools of electric fence wire, a heavy hammer, old ropes.

Roanhorse grunts. "They'll corral the cattle when they're moving 'em... Ranchers. Hold 'em in a pasture while they're rounding up."

"They don't bring gear out?"

"They're up on horseback—they'll store it here and there."

Whicher peers at the inside of the shelter—barely half full. In the dirt he sees the clear imprint of a boot; a fresh imprint. "Think somebody came out to pick up a bunch of fencing?"

"In this?" The BIA officer looks at him

"Me neither."

"We can check with Altaha?" Roanhorse says. "See if he sent somebody?"

"We need that white pickup truck," the marshal says. "If it's out here, we need to find it."

―――――

Back at the Silverado, Whicher knocks snow from his boots against a trunk of pine.

From the BIA truck is the sound of a radio call—Roanhorse opens up, leans into the cab.

Whicher listens, tries to make out the voice on speaker.

Roanhorse leans back out, radio transceiver in his hand, stretching the coiled wire. "Report of trespass—somebody driving on a ranch section east of here…"

Whicher looks at him. "The white Ford?"

The BIA officer's face is intense. "Four-by-four vehicle. Caller said a hand recognized the driver—reckoned the man he saw was Karl Ramsay…"

CHAPTER
THIRTY-THREE

FORTY MINUTES LATER, descending from a high, forested ridge behind Roanhorse's truck, Whicher sees a plateau opening up before him—a vast snow field, peaks of mountains towering above it.

In the lee of a rounded hill a half-mile farther, barns and corrals stand to one side of a group of houses and a scattering of vehicles. Cattle are huddled together, fenced in—a herd several hundred strong.

Wind batters the truck as Whicher follows behind the BIA officer—pushing fast on the white-over caliche road.

Two men at an open-sided barn turn at their approach. Both dressed in dirt-stained coveralls, heavy ranch coats—one in a watch cap, the other wearing a battered brown Stetson hat.

Roanhorse steers for the barn.

Whicher follows.

The BIA officer pulls in.

The man in the Stetson takes a pace forward. Eyes deep-set, his face reddened from the cold.

Roanhorse climbs out as Whicher parks, steps from his truck.

"Daniel. Department's been trying to reach you. Nobody was answering."

"Everybody I got is out," the man says.

The BIA officer turns to Whicher. "Daniel Tessay. Runs the ranch operation here." He looks to the second man. "And Nathan Henry."

"Only got three hands out today," Tessay says. "There's cattle to feed. And the water's starting to ice."

Whicher takes out his badge and ID. "US Marshals Service. Somebody on the ranch reported seeing Karl Ramsay?"

Tessay nods. Indicates the man in the watch cap—wiry, but strong-looking, with black hair to his shoulders. "Nathan saw him."

Nathan Henry looks at Roanhorse. "It was over by the Augustine tank."

"Where at?" the BIA officer says.

"Out by Pajarita Canyon." The hand points along tracks in the snow.

Whicher eyes the line of a ranch road headed to the northeast between tree-covered hills.

"Sure it was him?" Roanhorse says.

"Pretty sure, yeah."

The marshal addresses the man. "How come you know him?"

Nathan Henry's face is guarded. "People know who he is."

Officer Roanhorse stares out along the snow-covered plateau. "Ever see him before out here?"

"No. But I know people that have."

Whicher regards the man. "How far away was this?"

"Five, six miles."

"What happened?" Roanhorse says.

"I was taking feed out."

Daniel Tessay cuts in; "We've got a few dozen head out there, up by the canyon."

"I was up by the tank," Henry says, "I put out feed, I was checking the water didn't freeze. There's a service route comes out of the canyon…"

"I know the place." Roanhorse nods.

"I seen him coming down it. Driving a blue pickup. Tacoma, maybe. He just blew by. Like I wasn't there."

"But you got a good look?"

"Yes, sir."

"Then what?" Roanhorse says.

"I went on down to Red Lake. Couple miles from there. South. Got cattle out there, too."

"You see where Ramsay went?"

"He was headed west, there's a route goes by the mountain, Pajarita Mountain."

"You see him again?"

Henry looks to Daniel Tessay. "I come back here."

"And you called the police department?" Roanhorse says.

The ranch operator bridles; "We got trespassing on tribal land. People stealing—now we got a known drug dealer?"

"Alright." Roanhorse eyes the man. "We'll go look for him."

Whicher addresses the hand. "How long since you saw him?"

"About an hour?"

"He'll be long gone." Tessay's face is dark.

"How you think he got in?"

"Folk are coming by Deadman," the hand says. "Got the fence just back of the canyon there."

"The fence to the rez?" Roanhorse says.

The man nods. "There's a spot people come through. Gap there. Service route will bring you right around where I saw him."

Roanhorse looks at Daniel Tessay. "He didn't come by here?"

The ranch operator shakes his head.

"Maybe he went back out again?" Roanhorse glances at Whicher.

"You know where this is?"

The BIA officer looks to Nathan Henry. "South end of Pajarita Canyon?"

"Right out on thirty-three," the man replies. "At the tank. The road from Red Lake Road comes out there. I can show you?"

Roanhorse shakes his head.

"I see him on the ranch land," Tessay says, "we'll take care of the son of a bitch."

"Sir, y'all don't approach him," the marshal says. "Neither you nor the hands."

The BIA officer turns for his truck. "Man's a wanted felon, dangerous…"

"Folk here are getting sick of trash blowing in."

"If he's here," the marshal says, "we'll get him out."

On the high plain, scrub and mesquite cut the snowbound terrain. Above the glare of white, mountains frame the near distance, the rugged land contoured with ridge lines and hills.

In a fenced enclosure, cattle huddle, eating dry grass and cow cake.

Whicher scans the road running into a low canyon to the east.

Roanhorse kneels to wheel tracks in the snow on the service route—the water of the Augustine tank rippling in the wind. "Vehicle tracks here," he says, "recent."

The marshal nods.

The BIA officer gestures at a road heading away to the south. "Nothing's been down there, down to Red Lake. Not since Nathan Henry."

"Yeah, looks that way."

"If nobody saw Ramsay at the ranch, he could've turned around and went back out." Roanhorse stands, pulls down his cap.

The marshal's mood darkens.

"That spot Henry talked about, Deadman Canyon—it's right up the road there," Roanhorse says. "Wouldn't mind taking a look. Anybody crossed the fence line, there'll be more than one set of tracks."

"Think you'd be able to see them?"

The BIA officer nods. "Two sets and he went back out; no point looking for him."

"If not, you have any ideas?"

Roanhorse angles his head. "There's another possibility. A service route. Sixty-four, down by Yellow tank. It heads north. Wouldn't see him at the ranch if he went that way."

"Where's it go?"

"Pajarito Mountain. Or you can cut over on seven, take you anywhere you want."

"Anywhere on the reservation?"

The BIA officer screws up his face. "You want to hold here? I'll check Deadman. See if he went out. Your phone working?"

Whicher takes it out—sees a signal. "Looks like."

"He know you?" Roanhorse says.

"Ramsay? No."

"Choke point." Roanhorse gestures up the road heading east. "Everything goes through the canyon. You see him, let him come by, is all. Then call me, follow after him."

Whicher considers it. "If he headed onto the reservation, we need to get units rolling."

The BIA officer opens the door to his truck. "He's probably gone. I'll be fifteen minutes."

The motor idles beneath the hood of the Silverado, heater blowing warm air in the cab.

With the truck backed around, the marshal sits behind the wheel, studies the route already traveled—the ground west, outrun from the ranch, his and Roanhorse's tire tracks fresh on the road.

Light snow falls from a winter sky by turns leaden, then bright with sun.

Whicher studies the hulking mass of mountain west of his position. Pictures the forested hills and plains beyond it, wild land, hundreds of square miles.

By the water tank, the feeding cattle jostle, turning their backs against the wind.

A pair of hawks search for hidden prey in the flat winter light.

Whicher keys a call.

Reva Ferguson picks up.

"You still on the road?"

"Yeah," Ferguson says, "where are you?"

"The Mescalero Reservation."

"What's going on?"

"Some ranch called the BIA police, told them about a trespasser on tribal land—it could be Ramsay."

"What?"

"This is unconfirmed..."

Whicher follows the flight of the hawks in the air. The only sound on the line the noise from Ferguson's car.

"Well, what do you want to do?"

"Roanhorse is trying to get more information on it," Whicher says.

"If it's him, you need backup."

"He could be gone already—if he was even here."

"You want me out there?"

"No. Go ahead with Frank Niemann."

"Where was the sighting?"

"Pretty remote out here—I think we're near a place called Pajarito Mountain."

"Why would Ramsay be out there?" Ferguson says.

"I don't know. Look, I wanted you to know. That's all. I have to go, I need the line open."

"Hit me back if there is something…"

"Got it." The marshal clicks out the call.

Pushing back in the seat, he eyes the little-used route south—to Red Lake. Emptiness all around—isolation, a stark beauty.

Restless, he moves the shifter into gear, eases onto the gas, drives a hundred yards back along the service route to higher ground—to a vantage point at the top of a bedrock slope.

Checking behind, he can still see the mouth of the canyon —the way down to Red Lake.

He thinks of Ramsay. So close. Then gone. Shadows of the clouds race across the wide, open country.

He stares out of the windshield.

For a few moments, sunlight falls on snow starting to drift along the bank of a shallow ravine.

Whicher stares at it. He can make out a twin delineation— lines running along the length of a dry watercourse.

And then the sun is gone.

The trace as quickly disappears.

He sits a moment. Stares out over the hood of the truck.

Turning, he checks for signs of Roanhorse. He sits forward in the driver's seat. Tries to make out the vanished impression in the drifting snow.

Coming off the brake, he rolls the Chevy down the slope of the hill. At the bottom, he steers cautiously off the road.

The ravine curves, sinuous, flanked with scrub vegetation, with boulders, with limbs of dead wood. He senses the grip of the tires beneath him in the snow—good enough.

Guiding the truck carefully, he stops a half a mile in, descends.

A riffle has exposed a patch of wet dirt, groundwater running in the bed where the snow has melted.

In the dirt is a tire mark. The sides of an imprint. Intact, sharp.

Whicher kneels to it, turns to look back along the ravine.

He can no longer see the service road.

On the wind, above the sound of the Silverado engine idling is the note of another motor.

The marshal stands.

To listen intently.

The sound is coming along the ravine—out in front of him.

He steps forward, trying to see around the bend in the banked terrain.

Fifty yards along the snowbound water course is a stationary blue Toyota Tacoma.

A bearded man stares out at him from behind the wheel.

CHAPTER
THIRTY-FOUR

WHICHER STANDS FORWARD of the Silverado, taking in a face he's only seen before in file video and stills.

Karl Ramsay sits rigid, face immobile, eyes intense.

The marshal reaches for his waist—whips out the service-issue Glock, levels it.

He holds the barrel of the pistol on the windshield of the truck—heart racing, alert for slightest movement.

Ramsay rips the wheel around, reversing the pickup, backing, turning, the truck barely under control.

For a split second the marshal holds on it. Thinks of firing.

He turns, runs for his truck, snatches open the door, jumps inside.

Throwing the Glock on the seat, he hits drive.

Ramsay is gone already—around the bend in the ravine.

Whicher grips the wheel, accelerating, steering into the path carved by the Toyota.

The truck picks up speed, bucking, sliding over rocks and snow.

He thinks of Roanhorse—the phone on the dash shows no coverage, no way to reach him.

Ahead, the course of the ravine turns sharp—he rounds a

bend, a swathe of hackberry and juniper and oak blocks the way.

Whicher searches out Ramsay's wheel marks, follows a tight path through the scrub and low trees.

The white-over hills grow steep at both sides—terrain climbing.

Beyond it, the ground is clearer, scrub thinning—Ramsay's pickup traversing the side of a denuded hill.

Whicher clears the ravine, heads out onto the hillside, feels the truck tires breaking loose, struggling for grip on the steep pitch of the grade.

Two hundred yards ahead, the Toyota swerves, starts to slide in the snow. And then the pickup is headed downhill—at a diagonal—plowing deep white, throwing out a spray—headed for flatter ground.

The marshal feels the Silverado slipping, hears the wheels spin, steers the truck into the slide.

Chopping at the steering, he fights for grip, for traction, tries to keep the truck moving.

Below, Ramsay plunges faster, headed down—trying to circle back toward the service route, motor howling.

The pickup bumps and writhes over the frozen ground toward a stand of bull mesquite.

And then it drops—the nose of the Tacoma diving—back end rearing, axle clear of the ground, wheels in mid-air, spitting snow.

It slams down, front end burying itself in a bank of white.

Not moving.

Rear end fishtailing.

Now stuck.

Whicher steers the path carved by the pickup—closing yardage, the Silverado lurching, bouncing. He scans the ground ahead—the drop at the mesquite trees.

Touching the brake, the wheels lock, the truck slews sideways.

He fights to shed speed, starts to slip, losing way in the mud and snow.

Fifty yards from the drop he hits the brakes again, gets the truck slowed, gets it stopped.

In the pickup Ramsay guns the throttle, inches forward then back, truck tires spinning.

Whicher snatches the Glock from the seat, jumps out, runs downhill through the snow.

At the mesquite trees he stops.

Sees Ramsay turning in the driver's seat, a black, semi-auto pistol in his hand.

Whicher levels the Glock. Shouts out; *"US Marshal—drop your weapon..."*

Ramsay's gun hand comes up.

Whicher holds hard, fixes Ramsay in his iron sights. *"Drop your weapon..."*

The man glares back.

The marshal locks eyes with him—facing him down.

Ramsay stares.

Whicher feels the breath in his lungs, feels his heart racing, finger curling on the trigger.

As Karl Ramsay puts the gun on the dash—slowly—puts his hands in the air.

CHAPTER
THIRTY-FIVE

POWDERED ICE SCOURS from the roof of Officer Kee's BIA unit now parked on the service road at the Augustine tank. Alongside of the Ford SUV, Whicher waits by the Silverado in a raw wind.

Karl Ramsay sits captive, chained to a D-ring in the floor in the rear of the truck. His eyes are calculating, face a mask. He raises cuffed wrists to rub at his short beard, defiance in the set of his jaw.

From out of the ravine Roanhorse emerges, driving the BIA Ram—Officer Kee behind in Ramsay's pickup.

Roanhorse pulls onto the snow-covered road.

The BIA officer rolls the window.

Whicher approaches. "How you get it out?"

"Winch works pretty good on this."

The marshal eyes Ramsay's Toyota.

Officer Kee drives it forward onto the road—brakes to a stop, steps out. He peels back a partially loosened tarp cover over the bed in back. Carryalls and plastic bags are stuffed with tight-wrapped packages. Kee pulls one out—a lump, like roof tar—covered in Saran Wrap.

Whicher regards it.

"Black tar heroin," Kee says.

The marshal folds the tarp back farther—sees more plastic bags, more Saran-wrapped packages—white and brown powder pressed into solid blocks.

"We need to get it off the hill," Kee says.

Roanhorse steps from his truck. He stares into the bed.

"I need to get the guy out of here," Whicher says.

Roanhorse nods. "I have to call the lieutenant."

"This all is evidence, we'll need to process it. Put everything on the federal tab."

The BIA officer eyes Ramsay.

"I need to get him secure," Whicher says, "speak with FBI in Las Cruces. This thing's not done yet."

"We'll handle the truck."

"If that white Ford pickup shows up, y'all let me know?"

Roanhorse lets his gaze run out up the road.

"Or if you hear anything on Jena Velasquez?"

The BIA officer nods. "I'll call."

Moving fast across the white-over terrain Whicher enters the high plains surrounding the cattle ranch. He eyes the huddled beasts in the winter landscape. Sees the hand, Nathan Henry standing out by a feed truck—Henry staring at him from across the snow.

In the rear-view, Whicher glances at Karl Ramsay—in the back seat, the newly-bearded face like stone. "One hell of a load of heroin you were hauling…"

"Not my truck." In the mirror, Ramsay doesn't bother making eye contact. "No idea there was anything in it…"

The marshal pushes down on the gas, listens to snow and mud and stones thud against the underside of the chassis.

He thinks of the contents of the Tacoma pickup. Untold misery laced in every ounce of it; the unraveling of lives.

Beyond the ranch, the service road climbs a ridge into forest of fir and pine.

Whicher shifts his grip on the wheel. "You knew we were coming for you…"

Ramsay makes no response.

"Back in Carlsbad…"

"Don't know what you're talking about, man."

In Ramsay's eye Whicher sees a certain light—arrogance, a self-regard. "What happened, you get lucky?"

The man's eyes meet his in the rear-view.

"Guess you been pretty lucky," Whicher says, "to this point, huh? Ducking out. Nobody putting a glove on you."

Ramsay's eyes cut away. He turns his head to stare out of the window.

"That's some charmed life you been living," the marshal says. In the tree line, light flickers, striating through the canopy of green. "But you're in the back of my truck, now."

———

Speeding down the descending road the signal on the phone is in and out.

Whicher keys the number for Reva Ferguson. Looks again at Ramsay in the rear-view. "You know your girlfriend nearly died?"

"Don't know what you're talking about."

"Charlene Kingbird? The house on Missouri Avenue…"

"Don't know her."

Still the call to Ferguson won't connect.

The marshal glances at the zip-lock bags in the passenger footwell—a SIG semi-automatic—plus Ramsay's phone. "She was out cold on the floor," he says. "Your girlfriend. I had to get an ambulance. You do that to her?"

Ramsay stares out into the wooded hills, jaw tight, eyes hunted.

Whicher looks at him. "You keep all that Mexican Ice right there by an elementary school? Aggravating factor, you ask me..."

Still the man holds himself in a taut silence.

Ahead the forest road enters another, lower valley—snow-covered pasture, the service road barely visible across it.

"Somebody burned your friend Jena Velsaquez out, did you know that?" Whicher sees the muscle working in the side of Ramsay's face. "They burned her trailer—out here on the rez. This morning. They were going to torch her house in Artesia. Doused it with gasoline last night."

In the rear of the cab, Karl Ramsay's face gives him nothing.

"Somebody beat the hell out of her, yesterday. BIA police found her—tried to get her to a hospital. They drove her down to Alamogordo; she ran out. Nobody's seen her since."

Still Ramsay won't waver.

"She be dead, now or what?" Whicher keys the phone on the dash again.

No response.

Off the hill, down at the four-lane highway, traffic moves steady, trucks and semis clearing a path through the snow.

Whicher makes a left, heads south for Mescalero. In his mind, picturing the morning of the arrest—two men leaving the house in Carlsbad in the Toyota—both men now dead.

He thinks of the young sheriff's deputy—in the Western diner; two fatalities now to his name. And the house on Pike —the wall packed with crystal meth.

The frightened neighbors.

The trail of destruction left in Ramsay's wake.

He eyes the man in the rear-view again. "Somebody told you."

Ramsay's expression barely changes.

"They told you we were coming."

A flicker registers in his face.

"That charmed life you've been leading? It's not luck, right?"

Karl Ramsay's eyes come up on Whicher's.

He says, "Think you know something about me?"

"Somebody paid you a visit—the night before we showed up."

Ramsay shakes his head, looks off out of the window.

Whicher feels his frustration building. "You think you're protected. Nobody's going to touch you…"

"That a fact?" Ramsay says.

"But you're mine now."

"Oh?" Ramsay gives a dry laugh.

"I'm not part of all of this…"

"You above it all, cowboy?"

Whicher looks at him.

Ramsay gives an ugly smile.

"Guess you think you're untouchable," Whicher says.

From the back seat of the cab, Ramsay's eyes move back on his, cold now. "You think *you* are?"

Whicher stares back in the rear-view—until Ramsay's eyes slide away.

He follows a Freightliner throwing up a dirty white spray of slush on the highway. Thinking of the phone call to the house in Pecos, to Leanne. The lick of anger stirring in him—at someone looking to intimidate, lay down a mark.

He hits the blinker, switches lanes, overtaking the truck ahead.

Checking the rear-view, he catches sight of Ramsay—the man's face still, now, thoughts running behind his eyes.

Maneuvering the Silverado past the eighteen-wheeler, the marshal notes the fresh snow fall, starting to sweep along the road from out of the hills.

The phone on the dash lights up.

He clicks to answer.

"Marshal?" A female voice, urgent, strained.

Whicher sits forward. "Who is this?"

"Annaliese Joyner…"

The sound of her voice is all wrong.

"Ma'am? Is everything alright?"

She draws a deep, gulping breath. "What have you done with my son?"

"Ma'am…"

"What's happening?" Her voice chokes in her throat; "What's going on, where is he…"

CHAPTER
THIRTY-SIX

PULLING into the Mescalero law enforcement center, Whicher brakes the truck to a halt. He jumps from the cab, unlocks the chain from Ramsay's cuffed wrists—drags him out of the back, pushes him toward the law enforcement building. "Get moving…"

"What's going on?"

"You're staying here."

"What for?" Ramsay cranes his neck to look at Whicher over his shoulder.

"Just shut up."

An ugly grin is on his bearded face. "Something wrong?"

The marshal pushes him toward the door.

"Not part of this world, huh?" Ramsay smirks. "Still thinking that?"

Whicher stops him, wrenches him around. "You know something about this? Something about what's going on?"

The man pulls a face. "I don't know what you mean."

Whicher eyes him.

"Something amiss?"

Shoving Ramsay back around, the marshal pushes him on, opens up the door. "You better hope not."

A desk sergeant in black uniform looks up from the reception counter.

"US Marshals Service. With a federal felon—on an El Paso warrant." Whicher regards the sergeant, a tough-looking guy in his forties with coal-black eyes. "Need him secure, temporarily. I'm on urgent federal business—can you hold him?"

The sergeant comes out from behind the counter.

"Karl Ramsay," the marshal says, "arrested on the reservation."

"With Roanhorse?" The sergeant looks at Ramsay.

"And Officer Kee, right, they're bringing down a truck from the high country. The truck's packing a ton of heroin." He reads the name on the sergeant's badge; *Rodriguez*.

"You need him locked up?" the sergeant says.

"Till I can get back."

Rodriguez takes a pair of cuffs from his duty belt. Steps forward, snaps the cuffs onto Ramsay's wrists above Whicher's set.

The marshal unlocks his own, retrieves them. Looks at Rodriguez. "You know who this is?"

The sergeant nods.

"Don't let anybody take him—I don't care who it is," Whicher says. "You don't give him up."

The sergeant's eyes come onto Whicher's.

"Release him to me only."

"Alright. If that's what you want."

"Nobody else." The marshal heads for the door.

———

Snow lies thick on the two-lane Indian Service Route as Whicher pushes up the road ascending through sparse forest. Groups of prefabricated homes are scattered among the woodland in rough-hewn clearings. He checks, finds a weak network—keys a call to Chief Marshal Fairbanks at the Pecos office.

He listens to the phone ring above the growl of the motor beneath the hood.

His boss picks up.

"Ma'am, I've got him—I picked up Ramsay, I've got him at a BIA police station."

"You found him?"

"Out on reservation land," the marshal says, "trucking a load of drugs. But there's another problem…" The road crests a hill, drops suddenly—Whicher gets off the gas, eyes a zinc wire fence for the line of the road, steers carefully. "I just had a call from the mother of Gregory Joyner—the witness. She says Gregory's missing, he's disappeared."

The chief marshal stays silent on the line.

"I'm headed out there now—I thought you ought to know. Chief of police in Carlsbad set one of his detectives to try to find him…"

"The mother doesn't know where the boy is?"

"Says she's been trying everyone she knows…"

"If it was law enforcement, she'd know about it…"

"She was scared, really scared."

"You need help?" Fairbanks says. "Are you on your own?"

"Right now, yeah."

"What about the marshal from the Roswell office?"

"Went out to the op the FBI were setting up. I went up on the rez to look for a young woman that was assaulted, in connection with this…"

"Who else knows about the boy?" Fairbanks says. "Who would know where to find him?"

The marshal thinks about it, powers the truck up a steepening section of hill.

"You want me to speak with the Carlsbad chief of police?"

Whicher hears the concern in the chief marshal's voice.

Feels the twist in his own gut. "I don't like the way this all is going…"

"I'll call around," Fairbanks says, "if you hear anything—let me know."

At the Joyner property, Annaliese's Jeep is parked in front of the A-frame house as Whicher pulls in on the driveway.

The door to the house is open.

Annaliese emerges from inside.

Shutting off the motor, he steps out.

She stares at him.

He sees the pistol still holstered at her belt.

"You told me he'd be safe."

"Ma'am…"

"I told you I wanted you out of here—all of you; you said we'd be protected…"

Whicher sees pain etched in her face.

She swallows, her eyes drill him.

"Tell me what happened?"

Annaliese steps away from the house, wraps both arms about herself. "We went down—into Cloudcroft. I had to meet a client—somebody looking to rent the studio, to work here, stay here…"

"When was this?"

"We set it for three-thirty. At the hotel there, on the avenue. Gregory wanted to look around town while I saw the guy, I told him fine, it'd be okay."

"This client? This someone you know?"

"It's someone who got in touch weeks back, it can't be anything to do with them…"

"How long was the meeting?"

"An hour?"

Whicher looks at her. "When did you start to think something might be wrong?"

She starts to pace. "He was going to go look around in the stores. The meeting finished, the client left, Gregory still didn't come back."

"You call his phone?"

"He doesn't have one—I told him I'm not paying for that, he's still too young..."

"You can't call him?"

Annaliese Joyner's eyes snap back on Whicher's. "I never needed to call him—I always know where he is—we live out here, we're fine, we don't need all of that..."

"So, it's what, three hours? Since you last saw him?"

She nods.

"Could he have gone off with someone? A friend, somebody he knows..."

"He never does that, he knows not to..."

"You've called around? Places he might've gone?"

The woman's voice is tight in her throat. "I've tried everywhere."

"Did you call law enforcement?"

Annaliese puts her hands to her face, stretches the skin across her cheekbones. "I don't know what to do anymore..."

"We'll need to call local law enforcement..."

"But you didn't want anyone to know—you didn't want anyone involved... If I find who did this..."

"We'll find him."

Anger flashes in her face now; "If you'd done your job, Gregory would be here... this is all because of that man you're supposed to be arresting."

"I arrested him," the marshal says.

Annaliese stops dead.

"Arrested him this afternoon."

Her shoulders slacken. She stands staring at the deck. "Then what..."

"Ma'am."

"What's happening?"

"I need a picture of Gregory—something recent."

In the village of Cloudcroft, Whicher parks in front of a combined police and fire service office set back from the main drag behind a truck and auto parts store.

A single police unit is parked outside in the lot.

Whicher leaves the motor running, keys a call.

It rings, picks up.

Reva Ferguson comes on the line.

"We picked up Karl Ramsay."

"Say again?"

"Arrested him on the reservation. With a truck load of heroin."

"I need to let Frank Niemann know..."

"Go ahead with the op," Whicher says.

For a moment, Ferguson doesn't reply.

"See who you can pick up. When you speak to Niemann, make sure it's only him knows about this."

"What?"

"Just keep a lid on it. The fewer people know about it, the better."

"Really?"

The note in her voice is light, but Whicher hears the tone in it.

"Just let me know what happens."

He clicks out the call.

Shutting down the engine on the Chevy, Whicher steps from the truck, eyes the timber-clad building.

He squares his hat, enters the office.

Seated at a computer terminal, a black-shirted sergeant in a ball cap and rimless glasses faces him.

Whicher shows his ID. "US Marshals Service—Western Texas division. Here to report a missing minor."

The sergeant peers at the badge.

"Twelve-year-old boy. Local, name of Gregory Joyner. You know him?"

The sergeant stands. "This the boy the Carlsbad police have been wanting to talk to? They sent a detective out here. And the sheriff's office went up—nobody was around."

Whicher checks the man's shirt badge—*Harris*. "The boy's a witness in a federal investigation."

"How long's he been missing?"

"Four hours."

Sergeant Harris takes off his eyeglasses. "That's not real long…"

"I have reason to believe he could be in danger."

"We're just a small department here," the sergeant says, "just the three of us. You sure you don't want to contact the sheriff's office—or the state police?"

"I'll do that. Right now, I want local law enforcement aware—in case somebody spots him." The marshal gets out his phone, shows the sergeant the photograph of Gregory given to him by Annaliese.

"That him?"

"I need your people to know to look for him—in case he's somewhere local, or with somebody round here—in case it's nothing…"

The sergeant glances at him. "You don't look like you think it is."

Whicher's phone starts to ring. He checks it. "I need to get this. Let your guys know…"

The marshal steps from the office into the lot outside. Clicks to answer.

Shannon Towne from the Carlsbad PD is on the line.

"My boss just called—to tell me we're pulling the stakeout on the Kingbird house."

"Right."

"You got your man?"

"I did."

"So, you want to get DEA in here? To take the narcotics? Turn the place over to crime scene?"

"Go ahead."

"Alright," Towne says. "I'm in Artesia now, I'll let everybody know. Reva Ferguson called, I thought you'd be on the op, out in Las Cruces?"

"Plans changed."

"Your buddy Andre Parrish will be pleased," the sergeant says. "Guy looks like he hasn't been home in days, he could probably use the rest."

"You have Deputy Parrish out there?"

"He's on the stakeout. Part of the task force team, you know that."

Whicher moves to his truck. "Keep him there."

"What's that?"

"Keep him there, at the house."

"What? What for?"

Whicher eyes the police station. "Can you hold?"

"Yeah," Towne says. "I guess…"

The marshal mutes his phone.

Re-entering the police station building, he addresses Sergeant Harris. "Listen, forget what I just said; roll with an Amber alert…"

"You want me to put out an Amber on Gregory Joyner?" The sergeant's face shows alarm.

"All agencies, all networks. Use that picture," the marshal says. "Probable abduction—risk of serious injury or death."

"Alright, if that's what you want?"

Whicher steps outside into the lot again, unmutes his phone. "Sergeant?"

"Yeah. Still here."

"Keep Parrish there. I'm headed over."

CHAPTER
THIRTY-SEVEN

PUSHING HARD down US 82 out of the Sacramento Mountains, the light is starting to fail, snow from the high country giving out to pasture and ranchland, the sinuous road twisting through mile after mile of thin forest.

Whicher stares through the windshield into the gathering gloom above the truck's lights, thinks of Gregory—the possibility the boy just skipped out. Rebelled against the straitjacket of caution. Got himself caught up with the wrong crowd, out of his depth.

None of the thoughts hold.

The cold reality of the last days is too strong.

The Amber alert would go out to every broadcasting network; radio, tv, online, SMS text—the national Emergency Alert System.

He'd told Annaliese, told her to stay home in case her son returned.

Rounding a bend on the highway, he sees an old hotel built from river stone—beyond the hotel an automated gas station.

He checks the fuel gauge, comes off the throttle. Signals, pulls in.

The phone on the dash lights up.

He brakes to a halt in a wait area by the pumps.

Chief Marshal Fairbanks comes on the line.

"Carlsbad police don't know anything about it," his boss says. "Chief Garton says he had a detective try to get in touch —but he couldn't find the Joyners."

Whicher thinks of Trenton Allen at the PD.

"They didn't make locating the boy a priority," Fairbanks says. "So, it kind of stayed hanging. I told the chief you arrested Karl Ramsay. He wants to know how come you met with the family, but never informed them."

"I told him it was USMS business..."

"That's what I told him, too," Fairbanks says. "That it's a federal investigation—we're not at liberty to share."

"I spoke with local law enforcement," Whicher says, "got them to put out an Amber alert."

"You took it wide?"

The marshal stares into the tree line beyond the two-lane highway, into the dark of the woods.

"Who else knew the boy's whereabouts?" Fairbanks says.

"Anybody in law enforcement could have tracked him down..."

"I mean, specifically? Your marshal out of Roswell—you take her out there?"

"So?"

"So, she knew..."

"Ma'am?"

"You need to think of anybody that might've had access. She with you?"

"No."

"You know where she was today?"

"Driving out to Las Cruces."

"With anyone?"

The marshal doesn't reply.

"You don't really know where she was." Fairbanks clears

her throat. "I'm just saying. With the way things are, with what you've told me—you need to question everything…"

"She won't have anything to do with this."

"Alright, John. If you say so."

Whicher pushes back against the thought. "I'm headed into Artesia—there's a sheriff's deputy back there on the task force, a guy from Ramos County. He's the officer at the center of this. Guy name of Parrish, Andre Parrish."

"You know where he is?"

"I just heard. Task force is running a stakeout on the home of one of Ramsay's girlfriends. I told him to stay away from it. They're closing surveillance down now, but I heard he's there…"

"Could he have been up there? Up in Cloudcroft?"

"It's an hour-thirty away. He could've been."

The marshal drives the truck forward to the gas pumps.

"Be careful with this."

"I hear you," he says.

"Good."

"I'm still going after him…"

―――

Missouri Avenue is dark—nothing moving, no traffic on the road. Windows are lit in the single-floor suburban homes, the marshal sees the flash of blue and red lights on police units at the intersection ahead.

A police cruiser blocks the street.

Whicher rolls the window. Holds out his ID.

A patrol officer approaches.

"Marshals Service. Looking for Sergeant Towne—from the Valley Task Force."

The officer gestures at Charlene Kingbird's house. "Inside, marshal."

Whicher spots Towne's unmarked, gray, Ford Explorer. He

drives up behind it, parks. Steps out, glances up and down the darkened street.

A female uniformed officer exits the house, clipboard in hand.

"Sergeant Towne in there?"

She nods.

"I go in?" He shows his ID.

The officer notes down his name. "You're logged for the scene record."

"Who's on site?"

"DEA. Plus evidence collection."

Whicher moves to the door, steps over the threshold, takes a few paces into the hallway. Working lights are set up—crime scene technicians in zip-suits dusting for prints, examining furniture and floors.

Shannon Towne is in the kitchen, dressed in a police shirt and olive fatigues. "Hero of the hour…" The sergeant cracks a grin. "You got the son of a bitch arrested. I heard he was out on reservation land?"

"You heard right."

"Doing what?"

"Running a bunch of heroin," the marshal says. "I went out with the BIA police."

"You bringing him back to Carlsbad?"

Whicher stares across the kitchen into the living room, doesn't answer. In his mind's eye sees Charlene Kingbird—OD'd on the floor—close to death. "Deputy Parrish still here?"

"Around back," Towne answers. "Helping DEA empty out the garage. Crime scene want that car of Ramsay's, too—the evidence techs want it. I told Parrish you wanted to see him…"

Whicher nods, steps through the kitchen door into the yard at the back of the house.

On the street is a black, Ford Raptor pickup—Andre Parrish behind the wheel, talking into a phone.

The marshal steps through a gate in the fence.

Parrish spots him. Turns in his seat, finishes the call.

Pushing open the door, the deputy steps out—dressed in jeans, a leather jacket, a black hooded top.

Whicher regards him. "I told you not to be around all this anymore."

The deputy's chin juts. "Maybe it doesn't have a damn thing to do with you."

"Just couldn't keep away, huh?"

Parrish tilts back his head. "Last time I looked, I don't work for you."

The marshal eyes him.

"Sheriff's office pays my check. And I'm signed on for duty with the task force," Parrish says, "whether you like it or not."

"Just have to be around," Whicher says.

The man bridles. "The hell's that supposed to mean?"

"You know Karl Ramsay ain't coming back here."

The deputy screws up his face. "You mean; now that you arrested him?"

Whicher says, "That's not what I meant."

Parrish puts his head on one side—an ugly leer on his face. "What the hell is your problem, man?"

"What time you sign in on this?"

"What?"

"On the stakeout here?"

"The hell is it to you?"

"You don't want to tell me, I'll get it from the surveillance record."

The deputy stares. "I pulled six o'clock to midnight. But now that you finally got around to making an arrest, we get this all cleaned up I guess we can all go home? Right?"

Whicher takes in Andre Parrish—a glassiness is in his

eyes. His short hair is rough-looking, unwashed, his skin flaccid, features etched with fatigue.

And a burned-out adrenaline. Stress.

He takes in the man's pickup—on a private license plate, not state; not a sheriff's unit.

Inside, food wrappers and cans lie piled up with crumpled cartons from burgers and fries.

On the passenger seat are empty bottles of soda, screwed up grocery bags. In the light from the streetlamp, he sees the deputy's uniform on the rear seat—a folded, tan dress shirt, black ball cap, the sheriff's department badge on its front.

"Been home lately?" Whicher turns to stare at Deputy Parrish. "You been living in this? Looking for someone?"

The man's face sets like stone.

Whicher steps in close, sees thoughts racing behind Parrish's eyes. "Find who you were looking for?" he breathes. "Seems like you been on the trail a while…"

Parrish glares, leans forward.

The marshal stands his ground.

"You got something to say to me?"

"You're in over your head."

"The hell are you talking about?"

"Whatever you've done to this point," Whicher says, "you go any further, you commit a capital felony, you'll go down for life. And I mean, without possibility of release. You hear me?"

"I never listened to such a crock…"

"I'm this close to busting you, deputy…"

Parrish explodes in his face; *"For what?"*

"You know—and I know…"

"You think you know something about me?" Parrish eyes him, wild. "I swear to God, I have to live with this bullshit, people accusing me of crimes… nobody ever produced a shred of evidence against me…" The deputy stops, stands rigid—breath coming short.

He steps to his truck.

"Where you going?"

"None of your damn business…"

"Out west?" Whicher says. "Up in the mountains? Up to Cloudcroft, maybe?"

Parrish stands, grasping the door handle of the Raptor—eyes drilling the marshal, muscles working at his jaw as he stares.

He rips open the door.

Climbs in.

Fires up the motor, guns it.

Ripping the steering around in a squeal of rubber, he floors it out.

Disappears up the darkened street.

CHAPTER
THIRTY-EIGHT

A FULL MOON shows clear and bright in the night sky above the hills an hour from Artesia.

Looming out of the dark is a white-spired church as the route climbs steadily, the truck's hi-beams reflecting from snow at the sides of the road.

An urge to put out a stop order on Parrish's Ford Raptor is in him. Whicher thinks of the license plate, memorized as the man was pulling away. He thinks again of the interior of the truck; filled with trash and clothing.

Recognizing a stretch of highway ahead, the marshal sees a sign for Mayhill, twenty miles shy of Cloudcroft.

He passes an unlit country store, a closed roadside cafe. By a scattering of houses, he checks for a signal, sees a network showing. Scrolling for a number he keys a call to Leanne.

The road begins a long curve through the foot of a canyon, Whicher keeps his tires off the dirty snow banked to the side.

His wife picks up.

"Meant to call earlier," Whicher says, "been a long day…"

"I was wondering," she says. "Is everything okay?"

"We arrested the guy. Picked him up this afternoon."

"Oh?"

He hears the surprise in his wife's voice.

"Does that mean you're coming home?"

"I wish," the marshal says. "We've got a child missing. Young boy. Witness to some of what went on out here."

Leanne is silent on the line.

"Kid's mother said he vanished this afternoon—we need to find him." Whicher stares out of the windshield at the forest closing in at either side—overhead, the sky a narrow slit, pitch-dark.

"What do you think happened?" Leanne says. "You have any ideas?"

"Couple," the marshal says. "I think my arrestee might know something about it. There's a BIA police station holding him—I'm headed out there, I need to talk to him."

"You're going out there now?"

"I have to see the boy's mother, too..."

The line falls silent again.

"I'm sorry it's not better news."

"Mmm."

Something in the sound of his wife's voice registers. "Is everything okay?"

Leanne doesn't answer.

"Is Lori okay?"

His wife exhales into the phone.

The marshal sits up. The image of his daughter suddenly present in his mind.

"I didn't really want to say anything about it... it's just that she said there was this phone call."

"What phone call?"

"Somebody called the house. While I was out."

Whicher lets the truck slow against the slope of the road.

"She answered... she said a man was asking for me. Asking about me... and then he started asking about her. Like, what her name was, where she went to school..."

"He asked her where she went to school?"

"I know…"

"Did she tell him?"

"No."

Whicher feels adrenaline, a flash of anger.

"No, of course not," Leanne says. "She said it creeped her out. She told him she had to go… she thought it was weird. I could tell it upset her."

"He say who he was?"

"She said no."

"You try the number?"

"I tried, there was no caller ID… I couldn't get anywhere with it. I didn't know what to think, I didn't really want to bother you about it."

The marshal dampens the anger—softens his voice. "You can always tell me…"

"I know things are difficult out there…"

"It's okay."

"There was that other odd phone call to the house—from the sheriff's office…"

"Listen," Whicher thinks of his wife and child alone in the house—thinks of what to say, to not alarm her. "Don't worry too much about it… maybe say to Lori not to answer the phone if she can't see who's calling."

"I already said that. Look, the person who called before…"

"It's directed at me…"

"I don't like it."

"I know," Whicher says, "it's alright…"

"Don't let this get out of hand. Over everybody's heads."

The marshal steers along the deserted road into night. "I won't."

"And be careful."

"You know I will be."

"You sure you can't come home?"

Whicher listens to his wife breathing into the phone. "I'm coming home..."

"I mean tonight."

"I'm bringing back my arrestee. But I've got to find this boy..." Whicher thinks of the gun safe in the bedroom at the house. "If you need something—you know where it is..."

Leanne's voice is quiet. "I know."

In his mind's eye he pictures the compact Smith & Wesson M&P. "Just lock up and go to bed."

"Alright."

"And don't worry."

"Alright."

"Hang tough. Okay," he says. "Everything will be alright."

———

Pulling into the lot of the BIA police station in Mescalero, Whicher sees a silver-gray Chevy Tahoe beneath a single pole lamp alongside a BIA Ram pickup.

A figure is behind the wheel of the Tahoe.

The marshal pulls in, drives to it, rolls to a stop.

Behind the sheen of light on the windshield, he can make out Marshal Reva Ferguson.

He shuts off the motor on his truck, steps out onto frozen snow on the ground.

Reva Ferguson climbs from the Tahoe. Dressed in a ski jacket, jeans, nubuck boots.

Whicher bunches his shoulder against a biting wind. "Marshal."

"I just got here a half hour ago."

"From Las Cruces?"

"We got wrapped on the op, I called Carlsbad—they said Karl Ramsay wasn't there."

In the light from the pole lamp, Whicher sees the cast in her face; cool anger.

"I called the BIA police."

The marshal waits for her to go on.

"They said he was here." She stares at him.

Whicher says, "Something happen on the op?"

She folds her arms over her jacket. "We arrested five people. Confiscated three vehicles. All of them loaded with narcotics."

The marshal eyes her. "Any of them known associates of Ramsay?"

"DEA says so."

"What's Frank Niemann say?"

"He says the same."

He gestures toward the one-floor police station. "So, what's going on?"

She tilts back her head. "I just had a stand-up row with the BIA officer in there—Roanhorse. I asked to see Ramsay, he refused."

The marshal looks at her, nods.

"He said he was their prisoner; said you put a US Marshals hold on him—he said you'd told them only to release to you."

"You wanted custody?"

"I needed to see him. I needed to see him about today, I can't even do *that*."

The marshal breaks off, studies the stationhouse building. "Listen, there's a bunch of things going down…"

She steps to him, heat in her eyes.

"I needed to be sure he'd stay here."

Ferguson says, "You think you have some kind of rights?"

"Ramsay's my arrestee."

"You call me up, tell me you don't want anyone other than Frank Niemann to know you arrested him…"

"He's my warrant, my hold…"

"Karl Ramsay is part of a bigger picture—a much bigger picture of crime around here…"

"Yeah, I see that..."

"Law enforcement has a legitimate interest, including outside agencies."

"Look," Whicher tells her; "you want to see him, you can see him."

She stands in the lot, only staring. "You know what?"

The marshal returns the hostile look.

"You know what? Forget it." She cuts away, angry.

Stepping to the Tahoe, she gets in, fires up the engine.

She guns it out of the lot.

Whicher watches her up the unlit street.

Crossing to the front door of the station house, he presses on the brushed-steel intercom panel.

A metallicized voice answers.

"Yeah, this is Whicher—here to see Karl Ramsay."

The latch in the lock clicks back—Whicher pushes open the door.

He steps in out of the cold into the small reception space.

The tall figure of Officer Roanhorse regards him from the front desk. "We towed the truck to Alamogordo. Got a crime scene facility there."

"Good."

"The heroin's in back here—in evidence. Lieutenant doesn't want it staying here."

"Right. I'll call someone. Get it moved."

The BIA officer looks at him.

"Marshal Ferguson was here, I know," Whicher says, "I just saw her."

Roanhorse searches his face.

"Appreciate it," the marshal says. "You did right."

Roanhorse inclines his head.

"I go back and see him?"

"You taking him out?"

"Can't take him now, I got trouble."

"Oh?"

"You keep him here? On my tab?"

Roanhorse opens a desk drawer. "That's what you want?"

Whicher nods.

The BIA officer takes out a set of keys—throws them over.

The marshal catches them.

Roanhorse turns toward a door off the reception space. Right along there. "Third cell, right at the back."

At the end of a cement block corridor, three mesh-wire panel cells are welded side by side in a row. Stripped out spaces with just a bolted down cot and a chair.

The first two cells are empty.

In the low-level light, Whicher sees Karl Ramsay on the cot of the third cell—now with his head turned, staring at him.

The marshal walks to the front of the cage.

Ramsay sits with his wrists cuffed. Looks at the keys in the marshal's hands. "We getting out of here?"

"I just came from talking with your buddy."

"What?"

"Andre Parrish."

Ramsay stares out into the corridor.

Looks again at the keys in Whicher's hands.

"Deputy Parrish," the marshal says. "Out of Ramos County. You know? Your friend back there. I just came from talking to him. Two hours ago."

"Man, what? What're you even talking about?"

"Yeah, your buddy. Guy who came to see you—out on Pike Street—night before we came by. To bust your ass."

Ramsay gives a dry laugh.

But Whicher sees the thoughts working behind his eyes. "I know he was there."

The man on the cot gives no response.

"I can prove it, too."

"That right?"

"So, you're in a world of trouble."

"Well, you know what?" Ramsay says. "Whatever trouble you think I'm in, I don't need to be talking to you…"

"No?"

"Without a lawyer present."

"Don't need to do a damn thing," Whicher says. "But you're going to listen to me."

Ramsay leans back against the cement block wall of the cell. Stares at the ceiling.

"El Paso court sent me out here with a warrant for your arrest. And I found you. You got a bunch of charges pending, back in Texas. But before you answer for any of that—there's what's happens here. Understand that?"

Ramsay peels his glance from the ceiling.

"A US Deputy Marshal was shot down in lawful execution of the warrant for your arrest."

No response.

"I pick you up trafficking half a ton of black tar heroin…"

"That's not a half-ton…"

"Whatever the hell it is," Whicher says. "I don't care. Cheapest, nastiest god-awful garbage a man ever laid eyes on."

Ramsay gives a shake of the head.

"On top of that, there's kidnap of a minor."

"What?"

"You know what I'm talking about."

Karl Ramsay only sits forward, stares.

"Plus corruption of state officials—officers employed in law enforcement."

"Are you out of your mind, or what?"

"What I'm going to do," Whicher says, "is, I'm going to call up the state prosecutor. I'm going to make them aware of everything that happened here. Front and center will be the kidnap of Gregory Joyner. For that alone, they'll bury you."

The marshal studies the man seated on the jailhouse cot—face hard-bitten, his eyes calculating, shoulders starting to flex.

"You know what?" Ramsay says. "You can take your goddamn speech and shove it."

Whicher steps up close to the mesh wire paneling. "I'll get the DA to bring every single one of those charges, before the El Paso court even starts with you. You'll never see the outside of a prison cell as long as you live; I'll make it my personal business."

Ramsay stands, suddenly—steps to the wire mesh between them. "You go to hell, you hear me?"

The marshal runs his eye up and down the man before him. "Day one, this is. That's all. Every day, the rest of your life is going to be like it. Only thing you can do to change it is talk to me..."

"I don't even want to listen to your bull, let alone talk to you."

"I want that boy," Whicher says. "So, you think about that."

Ramsay only stares. "We done here?"

"Talk," Whicher says. "That's it, that's the only chance you get."

———

Peering out from a back room in the reception lobby, Roanhorse eyes him. "Everything okay?"

Whicher nods.

"Ramsay?"

"Yeah, he's okay."

Roanhorse sniffs. "You should go home. Get some rest."

"I use your office?"

A female dispatcher in the back room turns from a computer monitor to look at him.

"Need to get on a terminal," Whicher says.

The BIA officer nods. "You want some coffee? Look like you could use it."

"Thanks."

Roanhorse shows him to a desk, lights up a computer screen.

Whicher sits, logs onto a secure server. Takes the lined notepad from his jacket, opens it. Finds the last marked page.

The license plate of Andre Parrish's Ford Raptor is written on it.

He clicks onto the state DMV portal, enters the registration.

The listing for the vehicle shows Parrish's home address.

Whicher writes it onto the pad.

CHAPTER
THIRTY-NINE

FRESH FALL of snow is undisturbed on the Osha Trail Road as Whicher runs the truck out back of the village of Cloudcroft into mountain forest. In the glow of the dash the clock reads ten-thirty p.m. He keys a call to Marshal Reva Ferguson.

The call rings, clicks straight to voicemail.

The marshal clears his throat.

"Yeah, this is Whicher. Listen, I don't know if you heard already, but Gregory Joyner is missing—his mother said he went missing this afternoon from Cloudcroft." Staring out of the windshield of the Silverado, Whicher sees the sign for the Tall Firs Artists' Retreat picked out in the headlamps of the truck. "I didn't get a chance to tell you, back at the BIA station. But anyhow. That's how it is. I had local police put out an Amber alert—so we've got everybody rolling on this. If anybody sees the boy, we'll hear about it." The marshal drives on silent, the line still open. Approaching the Joyner house, he sees an SUV—black with a white stripe and gold badge—a state police unit. "It's bad," he says, into the phone. "No way around it. But there's a chance… That's it, that's all I had to say."

He steers on, drives the last yards to the property. Turns in from the road, tries to think of something to say.

To Annaliese Joyner.

He was on her hillside, now. Driving up in the night. Annaliese alone, now. Alone but for cops. Her boy gone.

He'd said he could protect them.

From the kitchen of the A-frame house, the female officer in the black and gray state police uniform brings a pot of hot coffee, sets it onto the wood burner, the uniform at odds with the sanctuary feel of the timbered living space, room lights all turned low, warmed from the fire's heat.

Support Officer Kate Sanderson pushes a strand of dark blond hair behind her ear. She takes a china mug from a table by the couch. Looks at Whicher. "How do you take it?"

"Just black," he says, "thanks."

She pours the coffee, hands it to him.

Annaliese steps through from the kitchen, in ripped jeans and snow boots, her long, dark hair loose, hands shoved into the pockets of a dark red gilet.

Sanderson pours a second mug.

Annaliese looks at Whicher, eyes hard in the firelight.

"We've distributed alerts to all commercial and public radio," Sanderson says. "Plus TV and cable, internet, also the emergency warning system."

The marshal nods.

"We're live on all social media platforms, and search engine by locality. Plus alerts are running on traffic condition signs out on the highways, as well as the automated all-hazards weather service…"

Annaliese eyes the fire. "First, someone has to see him…"

Sanderson inclines her head.

"There's nothing out there on the abductor," she says, "or on any vehicle."

"We'll work this," Sanderson says, "and keep on working it. Nonstop. Twenty-four seven."

Annaliese's face is drawn, her eyes fierce, tension rippling her body.

Sanderson looks to Whicher. "Gregory gave a witness statement about the double shootings in Carlsbad—that's correct? The working assumption is that Gregory's disappearance is connected with that?"

"There's no other reason we know of," Whicher says.

"We've already talked through any other likely possibility," Sanderson says. "Gregory's father is living out in California, there's no history of any issue regarding custody…"

"His father has nothing to do with this," Annaliese says.

"We have to look at everything." Sanderson breaks off, regards the flames lapping behind the glass in the stove. "There's no suspect profile, we have to cover every base."

Whicher drinks the coffee, listens to the wind outside on the hill, the spit and crackle of the burning firewood. "This afternoon, in Cloudcroft? Before Gregory went missing." He looks at Annaliese. "The person you were meeting with?"

Annaliese lets out a long breath.

"This someone you know?"

Sanderson puts in; "We already talked about it…"

"I don't know him," Annaliese says. "But we've been in contact for weeks…"

"He was the last person you were with," Whicher says, "before Gregory disappeared."

A flash of anger is in her, suddenly; "I know that…" She turns to Sanderson. "Kate. If you don't mind—I'd like to speak to the marshal, here. Alone."

Sanderson pours coffee for herself, face composed. "Alright. If that's what you want. I need to radio in to base—I'll be in my car."

Stepping to the kitchen, she picks up her heavy coat from a chair, puts on her police cap.

Annaliese walks her through into the hallway.

Whicher hears the door opening, feels cold air blown in by the wind.

The door closes again.

Annaliese re-enters the room, shakes her head. She looks toward the hallway. "First thing you think… you assume everybody will be bad."

The marshal doesn't respond.

"The guy I met with is from the arts community; alright? He's someone from my world, there was no reason not to meet him, you have no call to ask about him that way…"

"We have to ask…"

"I know—and you know—that it's someone from *your* world; not mine." She stands staring at him, folds her arms across her chest. "Your world of criminals, that man you arrested—or the police officer you say Gregory saw at his house. You said the Marshals Service would take care of it…"

"We will."

Her voice rises; "Like this?"

"I'll find him. I'll find your son."

Her eyes come off his, she glares into the fire.

"Like I found the man at the center of this," Whicher says, "arrested him…"

"That's why they took him…" She turns, faces him again. "You arrested this man—so they took Gregory."

"Whoever took your son couldn't have known."

"You expect me to believe it's a coincidence?" She steps to him, voice rising in her throat; "You said all along this man had help; from somebody in law enforcement—that's what all of this is about. How do you know the news wasn't passed on? You can't know that."

Whicher stands silent as firelight flickers in the room.

Only the BIA police had known.

And his own boss, Chief Marshal Fairbanks.

And Reva Ferguson.

Ferguson again.

Somewhere out there—in transit—on the road to Las Cruces.

He thinks of his boss's words; *how do you know where she was?*

Looking up from the fire, he sees Annaliese studying him.

The marshal shakes his head. "Even if they'd known Karl Ramsay got arrested, they'd assume he'd give us nothing. Whoever took Gregory panicked..."

"Because of you arresting this man..."

"They need the one witness that saw that sheriff's deputy visit the house."

Annaliese's voice is urgent. "What do they expect to gain?"

The marshal pictures Andre Parrish. "Whoever took him will most likely turn him loose. I think they'd turn him loose and run—just get the hell out, there's no way they can make this work."

"What if enough people want it to work?"

"I don't believe they do," Whicher says. "I don't believe we're talking about a lot of people..."

Turning on her heel, Annaliese stalks to the kitchen, body rigid with tension. Beneath her breath she says, "You think it was this deputy..."

The marshal doesn't reply.

"Don't you?" She walks back into the room, holding the semi-automatic SIG. "Then why aren't you looking for him?"

Whicher looks at the weapon. "I don't have evidence against him..."

"You have my son's evidence."

"Ma'am. You want to put that down?"

She shows no reaction.

"I spoke with Karl Ramsay," Whicher says, "before I came

out here. Told him I'd bury him—unless he helped me on this."

She makes a question with her face.

"He's putting up a front—for now."

"So, go after Parrish."

The marshal looks at her.

"Or tell me where he is, I'll go after him."

"Ma'am, you can't do that."

She eyes him. "Maybe you can sit there; it's not your child…"

"Listen…"

"You have kids?"

"A daughter."

"So, what do you think this feels like?" Her eyes burn him. "You have any idea? No. You have no idea, you're there in your own safe, protected world."

In the firelight, her face is tight with anger.

"People like us out here—we're the victims. Never you. Never people like you."

The marshal breaks from looking at her—to stare across the room. Then meets her eye again. "Somebody called my daughter today. Trying to find out about her. Find out where she went to school."

Annaliese only looks at him.

"They called my wife. Two days back. At my house. The family house. Sending me a message; we know who you are—we know where your loved ones are."

"The people who did this?"

"The worlds we live in," Whicher says, "they're not so far apart."

Crossing to a table at the side of the room, Annaliese sets down the gun. The anger in her transformed into something else—in the set of her jaw, a cold resolve. "If this was your daughter, what would you do?"

Whicher doesn't answer.

"Would you wait? Sit it out? Wait for help, hope for somebody to do something?"

Still the marshal doesn't reply.

"What will you do now?" She steps into his line of vision, looks into his eyes. "Would you stay home—if this was your child? Would you sit there? Turn in? Go to bed? Just go to sleep?"

CHAPTER
FORTY

ON THE NORTH side of the city of Roswell, Whicher drives the Silverado along a deserted road lined with rows of pecan trees, their spiny limbs leafless, ghostlike under sparse streetlamps. Reaching an intersection by a city park, he makes a left onto an upmarket suburban street.

Slowing the truck, he eyes the four and five-bed properties in landscaped lots. Late-model cars sit on pristine driveways, mature trees and manicured shrubs interspersed among the double-front garages.

New.

Plush. High-end on a deputy's salary.

Halfway up the street he checks on the house numbers.

Andre Parrish's place is just ahead.

He pulls over. No vehicle is in the driveway. No sign of the Ford Raptor.

The marshal glances at the dash of the truck—coming up on one o'clock in the morning. Last he'd seen of Parrish was in Artesia, five hours back. Parrish bagging it up the road outside of Charlene Kingbird's place.

Artesia was maybe a forty-five-minute drive away.

Whicher stares at the house—all the windows dark, no

sign of life, of any occupant. No drapes or blinds closed. No lights showing.

Forty-five minutes from home.

So, where was he?

The marshal looks up and down the street—nothing moving on it.

Opposite the house is a line of trees, beyond it, the city park.

No one around, nobody watching.

He shuts down the motor, takes a flashlight from the glove box, steps out.

Breathing in the night air, he listens to the faint sounds of traffic. A dog barking somewhere.

Moving off the sidewalk, he clips up the driveway to Parrish's house.

At the front door he sees the security camera. Not bothering to hide his face, he presses on the doorbell, waits.

No sound comes from inside.

Stepping away, he moves along the front of the house, peering into a window. Opening a gate, he passes around the side to the yard in back. He takes in the pool, hardwood furniture, an expensive barbecue.

The windows along the back are all dark, no lights showing.

He stands a moment. Weighs the warrantless search of a fellow officer's house against the urgent need to locate Gregory. He pictures Parrish in the street off Missouri Avenue —amped-up, desperate-looking; hyped.

At the far side of the property, he studies the construction of a kitchen door—latch and dead bolt liable to go straight through wood frame surrounding it.

Eying the neighboring house over the fence, he takes a step back.

He raises a boot, kicks his heel against the lock in the door. Feels it move a fraction.

Raising his foot again, he kicks out, hard. Hears a crack, a splinter.

The door swings open.

Whicher pushes it wide.

He steps in. Calls out; "US Marshal—anybody home?"

Hustling fast through the empty kitchen he enters a dining area—moves on into a rear bedroom. He steps back out, sweeps a large living room in the light from the street.

He checks a bathroom, enters a short hall—finds a master bedroom. The bed unmade, a bathroom at one side.

Backing out into the hall he finds a third bedroom—filled with workout gear.

At the end of the hall is a fourth bedroom. He spots a walk-in closet. Checks it.

No sign.

———

Off the kitchen is another door.

Whicher opens it.

Switching on the flashlight, he sees a utility area—a washer, a dryer. Beyond that, another door in a cement block wall.

He unfastens the dead bolt.

The door opens onto a pitch-dark space.

He breathes in a scent—rubber and oil.

Feeling for a switch, he flips on a light.

A Chevy Camaro SS gleams in the center of a garage. Alongside it, a Kawasaki Ninja motorcycle.

———

Closing the blinds on the windows in the living room, Whicher puts on a lamp. Takes in the couches, made from fine leather, brand new rugs on the floor. Expensive-looking ceramics sit on designer tables made from chrome and glass. The tech is new, high-end, a TV covering the whole of one wall.

He checks the drawers of a bureau—finds brown envelopes—stuffed with large denomination bills.

Turning out the lamp, he moves from the living room back to the master bedroom. He switches on the flashlight, steps to the walk-in closet along the back wall.

Inside, on a shelf above a rack of clothes is a Beretta twelve-gauge, pump-action. Plus two handguns, a SIG, and a Desert Eagle.

Shells for the Beretta. Ammunition for the pistols.

Three unopened boxes—burner phones.

———

From somewhere outside the house is a noise—Whicher stops—stands entirely still.

He listens for any sound from the street, from the night outside—sensing something.

A light flashes across the bedroom window.

He steps out, moves fast to the rear of the house, enters the kitchen.

The Silverado is out in front in the street—Parrish will be sure to recognize it.

Whicher listens for anything, for the front door opening. Feels his heart rate tick up.

Something is moving; someone.

He pushes open the door to the back yard, steps out.

Bright light is suddenly in his eyes, blinding.

A voice shouts; "*Police—put your hands up—stay where you are…*"

Whicher raises his hands. "US Marshal."

A second voice calls out, "*Don't move, keep your hands high.*"

"I'm armed—I have my badge and ID." Whicher squints in the flashlight beam. "I'm a federal officer conducting an emergency search—for a missing minor."

"Stay where you are," the first voice says.

A patrol officer steps in front of him. "Sir, I need you to keep your hands in the air."

"Got ID inside my jacket. I'm wearing a shoulder holster with a revolver—there's a Glock holstered at my hip."

The beam of light moves off the marshal's face.

"Sir, we had a report from a neighbor about a possible break-in."

"Name's Whicher. USMS, out of Texas, Western Division."

———

An hour later, the city of Roswell is behind him in the rearview mirror.

On US 285 south, the clock on the dash shows two-thirty in the morning.

He steers on. Toward Artesia.

No clear plan.

In Roswell, everything would now be logged by the beat officers. By the city police dispatch. The watch commander would be obliged to compile an incident review.

Parrish would likely hear of it, Whicher tells himself. Or somebody in law enforcement might let him know.

If Parrish returned to the house, he'd see his back door kicked in.

He'd know someone was coming after him.

He'd know it.

He'd know who.

CHAPTER
FORTY-ONE

PULLING into the all-night truck stop from the highway, the marshal eyes big rigs and panel vans and pickups scattered about an expanse of asphalt lot. The windows of a diner are lit up alongside of a convenience store—folk seated at the tables; night workers, drivers, gas and oil field crews.

Slowing the Silverado, he steers into a parking bay. Hunger in him, despite the fatigue, despite the hour.

He shuts down the motor, fastens the ranch coat, steps out. Stares across the lot into the night. Breath misting around him in the sodium light.

Nothing is moving on the highway. In the cold air, only a rumble of diesel engines idling in the overnighting semis.

He thinks of home, of Leanne. Of his daughter Lori.

Of Gregory. Somewhere out there.

Of Annaliese Joyner, of her face—of black eyes drilling into him.

Would you stay home? If this was your child?

He locks the truck. Crosses to the store and diner.

Country music plays in the background as he enters. He picks out a box of donuts from a cabinet, selects a wrapped sandwich.

Behind a counter, a heavy-set man in his fifties regards him.

The marshal holds up the food. "I get a large cup of coffee, to go with these?"

"Coming right up." The man keys in the price.

Whicher pays. Waits by the window. Thinks of Karl Ramsay in the cell at the BIA station. Ramsay telling him to go to hell. He pictures Parrish. Deputy Parrish at the center of everything.

The phone in his pocket starts to ring.

He takes it out, looks at the screen.

Marshal Reva Ferguson.

He steps from the counter, clicks to answer; "Whicher."

Hears only silence.

Feels a sense of alarm.

"I didn't expect you to answer…"

In Ferguson's voice is surprise.

"I was just going to leave a message. I thought you'd be asleep."

"Still awake," he says.

"Well, look. I guess I was just calling… about what happened. About Ramsay. I didn't mean to lose it…"

Whicher cuts in. "That's alright. There's no need."

The line falls silent.

The marshal surveys the half-deserted lot outside from the window.

"I got your message," Ferguson says, "about Gregory. I couldn't sleep. Thinking about it."

"You and me both."

"Look—if there's anything I can do to help…" She lets out a breath into the phone. "You think Andre Parrish has something to do with this?"

"I just searched his house," Whicher says. "I just came from there."

"You went in his house?"

"He has a bureau in his living room—filled with envelopes, stuffed with cash. Thousands of dollars. Just lying around in a drawer. Plus a brand-new Camaro, a race-trim Kawasaki…"

"Did you get a warrant?"

"In the bedroom there's a bunch of guns. And burner phones. Unused, unboxed. Why you think he has all that?"

Whicher lets the words sit. Listens to the silence at the end of the line.

Turning back to the counter, he sees the clerk place the cup of coffee alongside the sandwich and the box of donuts. He steps over. Tells him, "Thanks." Takes the food and the coffee as music plays from a ceiling speaker overhead.

"Are you out someplace?" Ferguson says.

"Just driving around. Trying to figure things out."

"Where?"

"Truck stop. All night place. Outside of Artesia."

She says; "Wait for me?"

He takes a sip on the cup of coffee. "How's that?"

"I can't sleep either."

Whicher doesn't respond.

"Thirty minutes, I can be there."

He stares out again at the black night beyond the window. "Alright," he says. "If that's what you want."

―――――

The booth is at the far end of the diner. Reva Ferguson opposite the marshal at the table—in a roll neck sweater, her dark hair piled on top of her head.

She pulls apart a piece of sugared donut from the half-finished box. "Tell me about the Amber alert?"

Whicher sips fresh coffee. "We have no ID on an abductor."

"So, somebody has to get eyes on the kid. What else have we got?"

"We've got Andre Parrish missing. Cash and contraband at his house."

"So, why not make him an official suspect?"

"Not enough..."

"Even with what you saw at his house..."

"Circumstantial," Whicher says, "nothing linking him directly with Gregory."

"Except his having seen Parrish at the house on Pike Street —the night before we arrived."

Whicher nods. Glances out of the window. "And nobody knows about that. It's just some report in the door-to-door interview files."

"You can't go to your boss?"

"I already did." The marshal scowls.

Ferguson's shoulders slump. She finishes the piece of donut. "It bother you? That you broke in?"

Whicher shakes his head.

"If the search wasn't legal..."

"Then I'll see the son of a bitch in court."

Ferguson blanches, straightens.

"I saw him," Whicher says. "In Artesia tonight. At Charlene Kingbird's place."

"You talk to him?"

"They were shutting down the stakeout. Guy looked like he hadn't been home in days. I think he could've been looking for Gregory. He was rostered for surveillance on the house overnight—before they pulled the whole thing. So, he would've had time to be over in Cloudcroft this afternoon—when Gregory went missing."

"You think?"

"We don't know where he was."

"What's he looking to do about all of it?"

"Kid's the only person that can link him to Ramsay."

Strain shows in Ferguson's face. "You think he'd... kill him?"

Whicher only studies the bleak truck stop lot, the laid-up rigs, night slipping away.

With no answer.

―――

The clock on the nightstand in the Carlsbad hotel room shows four-thirty in the morning. No messages from anyone. Nobody in law enforcement. No response from the Amber alert.

Whicher sits on the bed in the numb silence. Under an unseen weight.

Fire burning slowly inside.

Thoughts still turning.

Mind hunting.

CHAPTER
FORTY-TWO

SNOW HANGS IN THE TREES, lies dirty at the sides of Highway 82. Heat cranked in the Silverado, dawn's light breaks behind him, lighting up the tips of the Sacramento Mountains as Whicher rubs fatigue from his eyes.

He glances at himself in the rear-view—face slack from barely an hour's sleep at the Carlsbad hotel.

Reaching for the phone on the dash he keys the number for Kate Sanderson—the support officer from the state police.

He thinks of the ride up from Carlsbad, through Artesia—to check on Parrish's place; still nobody home.

The call rings twice. Picks up.

"Officer Sanderson? John Whicher."

"Marshal. Good morning."

"Has there been any word?"

"So far, no," Sanderson says.

"How's Annaliese?"

"Hanging in—running on something…" The state police officer lowers her voice. "I don't know what. Rage maybe, she's barely slept. We're looking to set up a press conference, the county sheriff's going to make an appeal. I'm talking with

Annaliese, to see whether she wants to speak. Do you want to be here? They're looking at Cloudcroft, or maybe Alamogordo, we don't know yet."

"I'm on the road," the marshal says, "headed to Mescalero."

"Oh?"

"I have an arrestee in the BIA jail there—somebody I need to see."

"About this?"

"Involved," Whicher says. "I need to see him. See if there's anything he knows…"

"We need a perp," Sanderson says, "a vehicle, something more to look for."

"I hear you. When you know where the briefing will be, call me, maybe I could make it."

"I will."

"If you hear anything…" Whicher stares out along the road climbing into the hills. Despite the warm air blowing in the cab, a coldness touches him.

"I have your number, marshal…"

"Whatever it is…"

Whicher finishes the call.

———

Forty minutes later, the reception lobby at the BIA police station is empty but for the custody sergeant, Rodriguez. At the front desk, he eyes the marshal. Takes a pull from a vacuum steel coffee mug. "Roanhorse said there was some trouble. Last night. With another marshal."

"It's dealt with."

"So, what's going on?" the sergeant says. "Are you taking him? You want to move him to a bigger facility?"

"I have to find a missing minor. The kid on the Amber alert?"

"I saw it."

Whicher thumbs over his shoulder. "The guy back there is involved."

Rodriguez looks at him. "With a kid going missing?"

"I need to see him."

The sergeant opens up a drawer, takes out a key, places it onto the desk.

Whicher takes it, nods, turns for the secure door at the side of the lobby.

He opens up. Steps through.

At the end of the cement block corridor, Karl Ramsay is laid out flat on the metal cot behind the mesh wire of the cell.

The marshal approaches.

"Get up," Whicher says.

Ramsay's face is bleary, his voice thick from sleep. "What's going on?"

"Time's running out."

The man sits upright on the cot.

"I want to know where Andre Parrish is."

Ramsay bugs his eyes. "I already told you I don't know what you're talking about."

Whicher steps to the wire of the cell wall. "Yeah, you do. You son of a bitch. Parrish came to see you the night before we showed up. And told you to get out. And you left your two buddies there to take the fall. Both of them are dead now. Did you know that? Pittman, guy that owned the house. And Salazar, the passenger in his car."

Ramsay shakes his head.

"There was a witness—to Parrish showing up. A boy. Gregory Joyner. Just a boy, but he saw him. He gave a statement to police. That's how I know…"

"I got nothing to say to you without an attorney present…"

"I know that you know him. And right now, I need to know you're going to give me the son of a bitch—you're going to give me Parrish. You're going to tell me you and him were hooked up. And I'm going to put out a state-wide, country-wide alert for him, and I'm going to get him picked up."

Confusion is in Ramsay's face.

"That boy is missing. Parrish is missing. And I'm going to tie all of this around your neck and make sure you sink, make sure you drown with it."

Ramsay squints through the wire mesh of the cell. "You know so much about it, why don't you just go after him?"

"Because you're going to give him to me. You're going to admit it. That's all I need."

"I don't care what you need."

Whicher stares at Ramsay for a long moment. "You know what Federal Maximum Security Prison is?"

Ramsay shifts on the cot, glances up at him.

"Out in Colorado? Florence Supermax? Most restrictive, hard-core prison in the United States. That's where you're headed."

"Why don't you leave me alone?"

"Solitary confinement," Whicher says. "Twenty-three hours of every day. Eight-by-twelve cell. Concrete furniture. Slit window, four inches wide."

"Hell, I might finally get some peace…"

The marshal lowers himself to Ramsay's head height. "You sass 'em like that, they'll fire-hose you out of your cell. Extract you with riot gear. That's the rest of your life, every single day of it. Make this place feel like the most beautiful vacation you ever had. You better hope your life is a short one."

"I don't need to hear this…"

"How long you think you'll last?" Whicher smashes the flat of his hand against the mesh wire cage. "A federal law officer was nearly shot to death on account of you. And a twelve-year-old kid is going to die—because of the filth you spread everywhere you go—corrupting everything you touch, everyone you ever meet."

Ramsay springs from the cot; voice tight, "I don't know what you're talking about."

"Your one hope is working with me," Whicher says. "You give up everybody."

The man in the cell only stares at him.

"You cut a plea with the prosecutor; give up your supply chains, all the people you're dealing with, US Marshals Service puts you into the Witness Security program."

Ramsay's eyes are intense as he stares back.

"Everybody goes down. Except for you. You serve sentence, it's in a WITSEC bloc. Every federal prison has one. Then you're out. Into the program. A new life. No one's ever been found."

Ramsay swallows, his face sick-looking. "I need to see a lawyer…"

"You don't need a thing…"

"I can't just… decide… I need an attorney."

"Forget it."

"I need to talk… to *someone.*"

"I don't have the time," Whicher barks.

"Look, what in the hell do you even want from me?"

"Andre Parrish. I want his name from you. You give him up. Burn him. Admit he takes your money. Tell me now."

———

Back in the reception lobby of the station house, Rodriguez regards the marshal from the front desk.

"Nobody talks to him," Whicher says. "Except for me. You don't release him to anybody."

The sergeant regards the marshal, doubtful.

"There's federal charges pending against him," Whicher

says, "he was running drugs on Indian land. You don't need to listen if anybody comes in here—state or anybody else."

Rodriguez's face is hard. "Nobody's coming in here without our say so."

Whicher holds his look. "Alright. I hear you."

The sergeant's eyes are suddenly sharp. "What do you have against him?"

Whicher doesn't reply.

"I see it in you. Something you don't like…"

"Guy's a bad deal."

"Oh? The rest of them ain't?"

The marshal shakes his head. "He's in with some people in law enforcement. Paying 'em."

"You know that?" The sergeant thinks it over. "And you want him here?"

"I'm guessing nobody here is among them."

Rodriguez's eyes are flat.

The marshal's phone starts to ring in his coat pocket—he takes it out, doesn't recognize the caller. "I need to get this."

Stepping out of the lobby into the white-over lot, he keys to answer.

"Yeah, this is Sergeant Harris—from the Cloudcroft Police. I've got a patrol officer just called with a possible lead."

"Somebody's seen him?"

"A store owner—right here in town. Talked with a customer that said they saw Gregory Joyner, yesterday."

"Yesterday?"

"There's some confusion over it, we're looking into it—but this just came in. I mean, it's a sighting, I thought you'd want to know. In case you were in the area."

"I'm thirty minutes away, I'll be right there."

Blurred sun hangs in a bleak-looking sky above the trees west of Cloudcroft. Whicher sees the panel sign marking the limits at the side of the road. Arriving at the first block on the edge of town, he searches for a hardware store among the homes and businesses.

The phone on the dash lights up—Chief Deputy Marshal Fairbanks.

Whicher clicks to answer.

"That Amber alert is still live this morning."

"Yes, ma'am, it is."

"You have anything?"

"Responding to a lead right now," the marshal says. "Local police took a call, we don't yet know if it's any good."

"What happened last night?" Fairbanks says. "With the sheriff's deputy?"

"I searched his house…"

"On what grounds?" Surprise is in his boss's voice.

"Exigent circumstances."

"Because of the kid?"

"Son of a bitch has thousands of dollars in cash, a brand-new pony car, a race motorcycle… plus a bunch of guns. Plus a pile of burner phones in boxes," Whicher says. "Guy's living like a drug dealer."

"Can you break cover on it?"

"I'm fixing to throw that switch."

"The marshal you're working with, did you bring her in on this?"

Whicher slows passing family homes, their windows bright, emanating warmth. Thinks of Gregory—of the decreasing chances of finding the boy alive. "She's in. She's watching his house—in case he goes there."

"John, you know the longer this goes on… If you need more help…" Fairbanks says.

Opposite a mountain inn he sees a sign for the hardware

store. "Ma'am, I have to go, I'm meeting with the local police…"

"Let me know what's going on."

Whicher finishes the call.

Pulling in from the highway, he swings into the lot of the hardware business—parks alongside a black-and-white law enforcement SUV.

Shutting down the motor, he steps from the truck.

Hustling across the lot, he heads inside the store.

At the counter, Sergeant Harris is with a thin-limbed man in a checkered shirt, a John Deere hat pulled low down on his brow.

A flyer is posted on a wall; showing Gregory's face.

"This is Earl Dayton," the sergeant says.

The man stands with his hands in his pockets, pinched-looking.

"He's owner of the store, here," Harris says. "We've got a unit out looking for the guy he had in here. So far, we can't track him down."

Whicher looks at the man. "What happened?"

Dayton takes his hands from his pocket, tips back his hat. "Well, like I told the sergeant, the guy came in here. Bought a roll of chicken wire, a hand saw. Couple boxes of screws."

"This somebody you know?"

"Not exactly," the store owner says. "I know who he is—kind of a local character; name of Doyle Rickard."

"You'll see him about, in town," Sergeant Harris says. "He lives off-grid, out in the woods—got a bunch like him around here."

Whicher regards Earl Dayton. "What'd he say?"

"Well, he come in, picked up what he needed—paid for it. I made his change. He was looking at that picture, there." Dayton points at the flyer. "And then he said how he'd seen the boy. Yesterday."

"When?"

"He didn't say."

"You ask him?"

"He said he saw him right here in town. Here in Cloudcroft. And then I mean the feller took his change, took what he bought—and just took off. I called after him; told him he ought to be telling the police. But he hightailed it."

"Why you think he did that?"

Sergeant Harris speaks; "He likely wouldn't want to have to talk with law enforcement. A good many of those folk don't hold with the likes of us."

Whicher looks at Dayton. "You go after him?"

"Yessir, I did. I scooted out of the store. But he was out of the parking lot already. I hollered. He was making for the highway."

"On foot?"

"Yeah, on foot."

"I don't think he has a car," Harris says.

Dayton picks at the sleeve of his shirt. "There was only me here. I couldn't just up and leave. So, I went on back, called the sergeant at the station."

Whicher turns to Harris. "You get a description, what he was wearing?"

"We did. And he's well known, everybody on the force knows who he is."

The marshal turns back to the store owner. "You believe him? What the man said?"

"Yes, sir, I did. He seemed kind of funny about it. And then he couldn't wait to get out."

Sergeant Harris pushes a pair of rimless glasses up the bridge of his nose. "Sure wish we knew what time the guy saw the boy—it might not be anything. We know Gregory was here in town, with his mother."

"How come y'all can't find him?"

"He was camped illegally," the sergeant says, "out in the woods. Trespassing. The land got bought. New owners kicked him out, he'll have set up someplace else. A lot of folk here, they'll put up a teepee, or a shelter, whatever. And just stay there."

"There's half a million acres out there," Dayton says. "Forest and mountain. That's just the Sacramento Ranger District."

"Already looking for a needle in a haystack," the sergeant says. "Now we're looking for two."

Whicher glances from Dayton to the sergeant. "Finding this guy won't get us the boy."

———

Stepping out into the lot of the hardware store, the marshal leans his elbows on the cab of the Silverado. He keys a number.

The state police officer, Kate Sanderson, picks up.

"You have anything on that press conference?"

"It's happening here," she says, "in Cloudcroft."

"The sheriff's coming?"

"He's on his way now. They're going to set up in one of the hotels. Will you be there?"

"I'm looking for a witness…" Whicher lowers his voice. "Don't mention it to Ms Joyner. We need more information, it could be nothing…"

Sanderson's voice is measured. "Understood."

"Someone reported seeing Gregory," Whicher says. "We're going to need search teams, boots on the ground. Who do I need to talk to at the state police?"

"Major Carlton's handling the response to the alert."

"Major Carlton."

"The sheriff's office are making units available."

"I'll talk to the sheriff, too…"

The door opens at the hardware store.

Sergeant Harris steps out, talking into his radio. He stares across the lot at Whicher, gestures with his hand.

"Can you hold?" Whicher says into the phone.

The sergeant holds the radio transceiver away from his ear. "Doyle Rickard. He's out on the Cox Canyon Highway—he was hitchhiking out of town. Got an officer there now, it's five miles. I can get you right there."

The marshal opens up the phone line. "Listen, I have to go. Say nothing, until we know this is something. Soon as I know, I'll call."

CHAPTER
FORTY-THREE

DOUGLAS fir and juniper and ponderosa pine line the steep sides of the canyon along the snow-flecked highway. Where a grit road descends from the line of trees to meet the asphalt two-lane, a white law enforcement SUV sits parked up.

Ahead of Whicher, Sergeant Harris signals, pulls over.

The marshal follows the sergeant to the side of the road.

Standing at the SUV is a squat-looking officer—and a man in chi pants and jump boots and an Afghan coat. At the man's feet is a dirt-stained backpack. He stands tugging at a long beard, wild black hair blowing in the wind.

The marshal parks, shuts off the motor. Climbs out, looks at Harris.

The sergeant addresses the man. "Doyle. You're not an easy man to find."

Rickard only glares back, wary.

The patrol officer steps forward. "Mister Rickard says he's headed up to the back of Lucas Canyon. Been camping out there."

"I'll give you a ride out myself, Doyle," Harris says. "But first we need to talk."

Whicher takes out the USMS badge and ID. "Sir, I'm a deputy US marshal. Looking for a missing minor. A child we believe could be in grave danger. You told a store owner back in town you saw the boy, yesterday?"

Rickard's eyes dart from Whicher to the sergeant.

Harris takes a pace to him. "We just want to know what you saw, is all."

Rickard scowls, runs a dirt-ingrained hand beneath his nose. "Nothing. I didn't see nothing."

Whicher eyes the man. "Then why tell the store owner that you did?"

Rickard looks vacant, shrugs.

"Listen," Harris says, "this thing's serious, alright? We need information, and we need it now. If you know something, if you saw something, you need to tell us."

"I don't know nothing 'bout any of it."

Whicher holds the man's eye.

"Well, you need to think about that," Sergeant Harris says. "You can help us out here—I might not need to arrest you."

"For what?"

"Hitchhiking on the public highway."

"Where else I'm supposed to do it?"

"No place."

The patrol officer nods. "Against the law to stand in a roadway for the purpose of soliciting a ride or doing business…"

Rickard only stares at Harris, mouth agape.

"I could cut you a break," the sergeant says.

Whicher steps to the man. "I need to know what you saw. They don't arrest you, I will—for obstructing my inquiry."

Harris hooks a thumb into his duty belt. "Let's just hear it, Doyle, huh?"

Rickard shifts his weight one foot to the other. "I was down in the village…"

"Doing what?"

"Nothing."

"Hawking dreamcatchers," the patrol officer says, "and bracelets. To tourists. I moved him on two times." He indicates the backpack on the ground. "That thing's full of 'em."

"You saw the boy in the flyer?" Whicher says. "Gregory Joyner?"

Rickard nods, shrugs.

"Where?"

"He was down by that coffee shop. Out on the end there, by the church. The Baptist place."

"On the end of the avenue?" Sergeant Harris says.

"When was this?" Whicher says.

"I don't know. Around four?"

"Four o'clock in the afternoon?"

"Yeah, it was getting late. Cold. I was fixing to go."

"Tell me what you saw?" the marshal says.

"Nothing, I just seen the kid. Didn't think nothing of it. And then I seen him again on that picture in the store, reminded me of it."

Whicher looks to Sergeant Harris. "That'd fit for the time, what we know of it."

"He running from y'all?" Rickard says. "Or what?"

The marshal regards him.

"He break loose?"

"What's that mean?"

"Seeing how you already had him." The man grins.

Sergeant Harris looks at Rickard. "What're you talking about, Doyle?"

Rickard makes a face. "He was already with a cop."

Whicher stares at the man.

Harris turns to the marshal. "None of my officers spoke with him. We didn't even know he was missing till you reported it. What time was that?"

The patrol officer speaks; "First I heard of it was around five-thirty. Getting dark by then."

"You saw Gregory with a uniformed officer?" Whicher says.

"Yeah."

"Doing what?"

"I don't know. Talking with him. Kid looked kind of scared. Figured maybe he stole something."

"A uniformed cop?" Harris says.

"Huh?"

"A policeman in uniform?"

The man nods.

"What kind? Black," the sergeant says, "like mine?"

"No. Like, olive pants. A tan shirt and whatever."

"He wearing a hat?" Whicher says.

"Ball cap."

"With a badge on the front?"

Rickard nods. "That's right. Yes, sir."

"He just there on the street or he have a vehicle?"

"He had a vehicle. Saw him walk the kid to it. Big ol' black truck. And then I took off after that, I was gone."

Sergeant Harris looks at Rickard.

"I told you; it wasn't nothing…"

Whicher steps to the Silverado.

Harris follows. "So, what do you want to do?"

"That's it," Whicher says.

"That's what?"

"That's it, I'm throwing the switch."

CHAPTER
FORTY-FOUR

EYING the curve of the mountain road through the trees, Whicher places a call to the state police in Alamogordo. Sitting up behind the wheel of the Silverado he waits while a sergeant connects him to the office of the commander in charge of the search.

In the rear-view mirror, Sergeant Harris follows on the road back to Cloudcroft.

The call picks up, a man's voice; "Major Carlton."

"John Whicher, United States Marshals Service. I'm the officer that executed the warrant connected to Gregory Joyner's disappearance. I'm calling to report a prime suspect in the boy's abduction."

The major stays silent on the line.

"One Andre Parrish. Of Roswell, New Mexico. Owner of a black, Ford Raptor pickup." Whicher reads the license plate number and the home address from the open notepad on the passenger seat.

The state police major speaks, finally. "What relation is the suspect to the child?"

"None. He's a serving peace officer. Gregory Joyner was

witness to his presence at an address sheltering a known criminal—a man I arrested yesterday, Karl Ramsay."

At the end of the line, Major Carlton clears his throat. "Marshal…"

"Parrish has disappeared, too, I searched his house last night…"

"Are you… sure about all this?"

"I found evidence likely connecting him to criminal activity in the area."

"How do you know he's with the boy?"

"I just spoke with a witness in Cloudcroft—who saw Gregory with an officer yesterday." Whicher pictures the uniform and cap on the back seat of Parrish's truck. "No law enforcement officer here reported seeing him. I believe the suspect must've followed Gregory, convinced him to go with him."

The major lets out a long breath. "Well, listen, this is a big call, marshal."

"I'm making it."

"We can do it but…"

"Put it out. Everywhere," Whicher says. "State and national."

―――

Driving the main street through the village of Cloudcroft, the marshal spots the turn beyond the Western saloon. He hits the blinker, slows to take the alley up toward the Osha Trail Road. Passing a timber boarding house is the van of a local news channel headed in.

A call lights up his phone, he checks the screen; Reva Ferguson.

He clicks to answer.

"Where are you?" Ferguson says.

"Driving up to see Annaliese Joyner."

"What's going on, what's happening with the Amber alert?"

"Parrish is now an official suspect," Whicher says. "Somebody saw Gregory with a cop yesterday—I think Parrish came out here..."

"To Cloudcroft?"

"It was right around the time Gregory disappeared."

"You think it was him?"

"I hope so." The marshal's mood darkens. "For Gregory's sake. If more law enforcement people are in this, we could be in a lot of trouble."

"Parrish never went back to his place while I was there."

"We need a unit stationed at the house."

"I'll get on it," Ferguson says. "But listen, I was calling about Jena Velasquez."

Whicher takes the turn onto the mountain road, stares out through the windshield. "What about her?"

"A narcotics cop arrested her last night. In Artesia. In some bar they were watching. She tried to sell the guy a couple of wraps. They went to search her house, somebody'd set it on fire, they had to call the fire department."

"Last night?"

"Maybe it was Parrish?"

Whicher slams on the brakes, skids to a halt in the mix of dirt and snow beneath the truck. "Have you seen her?"

"No. But didn't you say Parrish was amped last night?"

The marshal pictures the deputy at Missouri Avenue.

"Maybe she had something on him?"

"Maybe he was looking to get rid of it," Whicher says. "Or her."

"This is getting crazy..."

"Listen, we need places to look, places Parrish goes—we need to talk to the people around him, friends, family..."

"I can get on that..."

"I have to see the mother," Whicher says, "they're setting up a press briefing here this morning."

"You want me out there?"

"Find out what you can on Parrish," the marshal says.

"I'll do that," Ferguson says, "I'll call."

Up at the Joyner property, Annaliese paces on the timber deck adjoining the house. Sun streaking through leafless trees in the clearing, glaring cold off the white, settled snow.

Her face is drawn. She shivers slightly as a gust of wind blows through the broken country of the valley beyond the deck.

Whicher stands at the rail. Hands stuffed into the pockets of his ranch coat.

Annaliese glances at the house, gives a shake of her head. "It's killing me to be in there. I feel like I'm losing my mind."

"State police know we've identified a suspect," the marshal says. "We've got a stop order out on a vehicle. We may be able to raise air units, get some rotary-wing. As well as search teams on the ground, on the roads."

A molten anger is just below the surface as Annaliese looks at him. "That policewoman in there says that if you've got a suspect, you'll be able to dig into background, circulate pictures, the details of vehicles…"

"Right."

"As if it's all easy. Like it will all be routine…" The edge is thick in her voice.

Whicher says nothing, only listens to the sound of wind in the trees.

"Did you sleep well last night?"

The marshal shakes his head.

Her mouth twitches lightly. "No?"

"I was up all night. As a matter of fact."

Head canted to the side, she regards him.

"I broke into the suspect's house," the marshal says. "Searched it. Drove around thinking on how to find him."

Annaliese makes no response.

"Will you appear at the press briefing?"

Her face is hard. "Is that what I'm supposed to do? The 'right' thing?"

"I'd guess…"

She cuts in; "Because doing that has been really working… hasn't it? My son told the truth, look what happened? He did what your people said to do—and it's one of yours who's done this…"

Whicher lets her words sit, lets them fill the air between them. Takes her anger, takes the barely concealed contempt.

"It's one of *you*…"

"One…"

"Oh? That makes it alright?"

The marshal shakes his head.

"I'm not going to be paraded like some… victim…"

Whicher sees the color at her throat.

"My son and I… are not victims. You want me to sit and weep for the cameras…"

Staring out over the valley, Whicher considers it. "If people see you, it hits home harder. Every mother, every parent will see themselves in you."

Annaliese leans against the snow-topped rail, grips it with both hands.

"Maybe it could amount to something…"

"If you don't find this monster," she says, "I will. I'll bring him into my world."

Whicher doesn't respond.

"I don't know how. But I will. And when I do, I'll cut him open from his belly to his throat."

Still the marshal says nothing.

"I'll have my people. Our spirits. Our gods. Help from *my*

world. So, you'd better be quick. Maybe you don't believe me? Maybe you can't imagine it. But no force in this world could stop me. Maybe you don't understand that."

Whicher only eyes her, silent.

She looks at him a long moment. The cast to her face shifting, slightly. She runs her tongue around her teeth. "Or maybe you do..."

The kitchen door onto the deck opens.

Officer Kate Sanderson steps out.

Annaliese pushes away from the rail, alarm in her, now.

"Update," Sanderson says to Whicher, "about the suspect. The sheriff's office have been in touch—with their counterparts—at Ramos County."

"Where he works," Whicher says to Annaliese, "man's a deputy there."

"They've given details of a former partner, a domestic partner," Sanderson says, "a girlfriend. Sheriff's office thought you ought to know."

"They tell you where I can find this person?"

"They gave an address—in Artesia."

"Alright," Whicher says. "You can tell the sheriff's office I'm on my way."

CHAPTER
FORTY-FIVE

A RED NISSAN SENTRA sits in the yard of a pale-brick duplex apartment building on the north side of Artesia. Whicher pulls in from the street—takes in the houses of the neighborhood, a new-built subdivision—brick ranches with gravel yards, late-model cars on their driveways.

The street is quiet, nothing moving.

Shutting down the truck, he steps out.

He squares his hat, approaches the front door to the building. Checks the name by the bell, rings it. Steps back.

A slim woman in a gym top opens the door.

He shows his badge and ID.

The woman's eyes are a bright blue, her dark blond hair neatly groomed.

"Sonia Altman?"

The woman nods, studies the ID card.

"Ma'am, I'm a Deputy US Marshal," Whicher says. "Investigating the disappearance of a minor."

Sonia Altman's eyes cut away from the badge, she looks up. Flexes a well-toned arm. "Ramos County Sheriff called this morning."

"You know what this is about?"

She nods.

"I need to speak with you. It be alright if I came in?"

Stepping back from the door, she leads the marshal inside through a small hallway into a light-filled living room. Beige couches sit either side of an antique coffee table, dried flowers arranged on it in a turquoise vase.

Sonia Altman regards him. "The person that called from the sheriff's office said you're looking for Andre?"

"Andre Parrish, that's right. Have you seen him lately?"

"No."

"When was the last time?"

She spreads the palms of her hands "Couple of months, maybe. I saw him working out. At my gym."

Whicher takes out the notepad and pen from his coat.

"We split up eighteen months back."

"Are you in contact now?"

"We don't stay in touch."

"Ma'am, we have serious concerns about the welfare of a young boy. At the present time we have no idea where to look for him."

In Sonia Altman's face is shock—but something else. He reads tension around her eyes.

"Anything you could tell me might be of help. I take a seat?"

She indicates one of the couches. Sits down opposite.

"Were you together a long time?"

"About three years."

"Do you know if Mister Parrish has any other property? Or access to any other address? Apart from his home in Roswell?"

"No. Not that I know. But then, a lot of things around him I don't think I knew about." The young woman looks at the marshal a moment. She folds her hands together on her lap. "Why would Andre kidnap a young boy?"

Whicher ignores the question. "Ma'am, is there anything

you could tell me? About Mister Parrish—about his life, his friends? Where he likes to go? Anything at all?"

She looks off around the room. "You probably already know about the—controversy around him?"

The marshal studies on her.

"I mean the officer-involved shootings…"

"He talk to you about any of that?"

"We talked about it." Altman puts her hand to the skin at her neck. "They were all criminals—convicted criminals resisting arrest…"

"Multiple fatal incidents," Whicher says.

"But nothing was ever…" she tails off.

Whicher scans the living room for any lingering sign of Parrish in her life, photographs, mementos. "He tell you what happened?"

Her face is suddenly stern. "He said he'd sooner take down any one of them than risk the life of an officer."

The marshal says nothing.

"Does that seem unreasonable?" She looks at him.

"For people to end up shot to death," Whicher says, "a lot of things must've been wrong."

Swallowing, she turns her gaze from him.

"One time… maybe two times even, I could imagine it. More than that?" Whicher lets the question hang, takes in the woman seated across from him. "Ma'am, during the time you were together, did you ever observe anything unusual?"

"Like what?"

"I've seen evidence that suggests an involvement—with people he shouldn't have been involved with."

Sonia Altman edges forward on the seat of the couch.

"Were you ever aware of anything like that?"

Standing suddenly, she presses her hands to her face. "That was part of why we broke up—a big part of it—things were happening, things I didn't understand."

The marshal leans back in the couch, rests the pen against the notepad.

"He wouldn't tell me about any of it, he started to have all this money." The young woman stops. Takes a hold of herself. "I asked him where it was coming from. He wouldn't say. He'd never tell me anything. But... I'm not an idiot..."

Whicher waits for her to go on.

"Money doesn't just come from nowhere, out of nothing. But whatever I said, he wouldn't talk about it, about any of it —he just told me not to worry. But there'd be phone calls. Things happening. Sometimes he'd disappear, he wouldn't say where he'd been."

"That's why you split up?"

"I was frightened," she says. "Frightened of it. Frightened of him."

"He ever threaten you?"

Her eyes dart around the room. "Obliquely."

Whicher puts his head on one side.

"I thought he was joking. He made it sound as if he was. But then I thought about it, about everything that was going on—I thought of all the people that got shot..." She stops again, looks at him. "What did this boy do?"

"He witnessed something."

Her eyes stay on his.

"He saw him visit a known drug dealer," Whicher says. "A guy I arrested yesterday. High-end guy, big noise..."

The color drains from Altman's face.

She sits down in a stunned silence.

"You think he'd be capable of..." The marshal doesn't finish his sentence.

In her look he reads his answer.

He feels the knot tighten in his gut.

Standing again, she stalks to the window, stares out.

"Is there anybody you think I should talk to?" Whicher says. "Family?"

"His family are all back in Kansas."

"You think he'd go there?"

"They're not close," she says. "I went there one time, that's all. To Wichita."

From outside the house is the sound of a vehicle arriving.

Sonia Altman turns her head to look into the street.

Whicher stands, walks to the window, peers out. A silver-gray Chevy Tahoe is pulled in at the curbside behind his truck. Reva Ferguson stepping from it. In a camel overcoat and slacks, her hair pulled back.

She walks up the driveway. Rings on the doorbell.

"It's a US Marshal," Whicher says. "I told her I'd be here." Moving from the living room to the hallway, he opens up. Steps outside.

Ferguson eyes the house, looks at him. "I just came from Ramos County Sheriff."

"What's going on?"

A frown is on her brow, she looks off along the street. "Nobody wants to talk. They're closing ranks. They have a deputy under investigation from the Ramsay arrest—now this."

"They'll have to talk…"

"We'll have to make it official," Ferguson says.

"We don't have time."

Sonia Altman appears at the front door. "I have no idea where Andre Parrish might've gone."

Ferguson regards her, coolly. "Really?"

"I left him eighteen months ago…"

Stepping back, Ferguson considers the woman. "So, nobody has anything to say?"

Sonia Altman flushes. "Have you tried his partner—from work?"

"Billy Drummond?"

"Billy," she nods, "right."

"Deputy Drummond's on administrative leave," Whicher

says. "Under investigation. For shooting two suspects during an arrest."

"Shooting them dead," Ferguson says.

In the doorway, Sonia Altman crumples.

"Do you know Billy Drummond?"

The young woman holds onto the doorframe, mouth open. "I mean, yes… sure…"

"Do you think he might be someone who would help him?"

Altman's face is blank. "I have no idea."

"How about friends?" Whicher says. "There anybody we should talk to?"

Gathering herself, Altman shakes her head. "They're all cops. Everybody he hangs around with. They're all people from the sheriff's office, the police department…"

Ferguson looks to Whicher, frustration in her face. "We have to be able to talk to someone."

The marshal nods. "We have Karl Ramsay. Charlene Kingbird. Jena Velasquez…"

Ferguson looks to Sonia Altman. "You know any of these people?"

"I've never heard of any of them."

"Jena Velasquez is in custody," Ferguson says.

Whicher eyes her.

"At a holding facility two miles from here. We could go see her?"

The marshal takes a business card from his ranch coat, puts away the notepad and pen. He hands the card to Sonia Altman. "If Andre Parrish calls—you let me know."

CHAPTER
FORTY-SIX

IN THE STARK light of the interview room, the bruises to Jena Velasquez's face show a sick-looking mauve and yellow, the dried blood on her skin an ink black.

Reva Ferguson sits directly across the table from her at the police department. Reading from a copy of the booking form from the custody desk.

Whicher stands to one side.

Ferguson glances up from the form. "Possession and attempt to supply."

Velasquez sits handcuffed in prison blues, tension rippling in her.

"You went out like that?" Ferguson says. "Looking to sell drugs?"

A ragged look twists in her face. "I was broke."

"Like, you weren't going to get noticed?"

"No money. Entiendes?"

"Who attacked you?" Whicher says.

Velasquez squints, one eye swollen half-shut.

"Two days I've been looking for you."

She tilts back her head at him. "What do you care, ese?"

Whicher leans against the interview room wall. "I know

you were attacked on the Mescalero Reservation. A BIA police officer took you for treatment. Down in Alamogordo. You disappeared."

Ferguson puts down the booking form. "We tried to find you."

Velasquez leans in to the table, angling her head from side to side, her body twitching.

"Your trailer got torched. BIA police tried to find who did that," the marshal says. "I went looking with them. On top of that, somebody set fire to your place here in town?"

Reva Ferguson leans in. "Why is that, Jena?"

Velasquez stares at the small table, a jagged anger emanating from her.

"I've got a kid gone missing," Whicher says, "over the arrest of Karl Ramsay—my arrest. I need to find him. I know you're one of Ramsay's people…"

She looks up blinking.

"Charlene Kingbird—your friend, she told me. She was worried about you. She's lucky to be alive. She OD'd. On the garbage Ramsay's flooding the place with. I found her. Called an ambulance for her. Looks like neither one of you is going to make it real far," Whicher says, "the way this all is playing out…"

Velasquez looks at him, defiant.

"The pair of you sell for him," Whicher says, "low-level. Charlene told me…"

"That's lies…"

The marshal holds up a hand. "I'm not interested. Not looking to charge you."

Velasquez eyes him.

"Tell me what you know about Karl Ramsay?"

"I don't know anything."

"You get beaten half to death? Somebody tries to burn you out with gasoline?"

Velasquez raises her cuffed wrists, puts her hands on the table. A fierce light in her eye.

Reva Ferguson sits back in her seat. "You know a man named Andre Parrish? A sheriff's deputy. With Ramos County."

Velasquez says nothing.

"So, you just going to let this all happen?" Whicher says. "Stay silent? Till somebody finally beats you to death? Or burns you alive…"

"What the hell are you going to do about it?" Velasquez spits, barely controlled.

Whicher lets a beat pass, regards her.

"You going to arrest the son of a bitch that did this?" Velasquez's eyes dance with anger.

"You about to tell me who it was?" the marshal says.

"And then?" she says. "What then?"

Ferguson looks at her. "What's that mean?"

"You'll do nothing. Nobody does…"

"Why not…"

"He's protected. He knows it, everybody knows it…"

"Wait," Whicher says, "we talking about Andre Parrish? Or Karl Ramsay?"

Velasquez pushes away from the table, the legs of her chair scrape across the tile floor. "That son of a bitch. The Mexican."

Whicher stares at her.

Bitterness is in Velasquez's face. "You going to arrest him? Over me."

She rocks forward in her seat, anger boiling over.

Thoughts sift from the back of the marshal's mind.

Reva Ferguson looks at Velasquez. "Why don't you tell us who this is? Maybe we could do something about it?"

An image is in the marshal's mind now—Grady Owens, the truck driver; out at Brantley Lake. He turns to Ferguson. "Your guy. At the lake; your man…"

Ferguson looks at him. Sits straight. Nods. "What about him?"

"He said Karl Ramsay was looking for some 'Mexican.'"

"Rios." Velasquez's face contorts as she says it; "Luis Rios."

Ferguson turns to her. "You're saying that's the man that assaulted you?"

Whicher takes out his notepad, flicks back through the pages, scanning the scrawled lines. "I know that name..." He stops at a note near the front of the pad. "We arrested him. Day one. At the house on Glendale. The Nunez arrest. Rios was the runner, I had to hit his car. He was released, I saw it in the follow-up report..."

"Eh," Velasquez hisses, "you hear that? Understand, ese?"

"Nunez was sent up to custody in Albuquerque," Whicher says, "the runner was let out..."

"That's what I'm talking about..."

The marshal reads from his notes. "Guy was wanted in Alamogordo—over an assault, at Holloman Air Force Base."

"Always, he gets out," Velasquez says.

Whicher eyes her. "This guy have a white pickup truck?"

She nods.

"He does?"

She only gapes back.

Marshal Ferguson gets up from her seat, touches his arm. "Okay stop," she says. "You want to step outside with me a moment?"

———

In the glare of overhead lights in the secure corridor, Reva Ferguson levels her eyes at him. "We know who this guy is. He's a police informant."

"That's how come he was let out?"

"I'd guess."

"Did you know Rios was known as 'The Mexican'?"

She shakes her head. "Far as I knew he was just some low-life street dealer."

"Your guy Grady Owens told us Karl Ramsay wanted him over a black tar deal. I picked up Ramsay with a truck full of the stuff yesterday," Whicher says. "You think that was part of it?"

Ferguson only blinks back, silent.

―――――

Re-entering the interview room Whicher stands.

Ferguson lowers herself into the chair.

"What did he want from you?" the marshal says.

Velasquez sits slack-bodied, eyes laced with contempt.

"Why'd he come looking for you?"

Still the woman says nothing.

"We can go after him," Ferguson says. "Arrest him—but you've got to help us out here."

"Even if you pick him up," Velasquez says, "they'll only let him right back out. I'll get carved into pieces…"

Whicher tells her, "Not if it's us."

Velasquez clamps her mouth shut.

"Not if it's us." The marshal meets her eye.

"Who else calls him the Mexican?" Ferguson says.

"It's a street name," the woman answers. "He did time in prison there, he talks like a *pandillero*."

"What did he want?" Whicher says.

Velasquez weighs the marshal—anger still smoldering; an eagerness in her—as if some chance were close; the chance to thrust the knife, settle a score.

"Why did he attack you?" Ferguson says.

"Because of Karlo's stash…"

"Karlo," Whicher says, "Karl Ramsay?"

Velasquez nods.

Ferguson says, "He was trying to get you to tell him about a drugs stash?"

The woman sits silent, hands balled into fists, the chain tight between the cuffs at her wrists.

"Where?" Whicher says. "On reservation land?" He thinks of the description of a white pickup, a Hispanic driver at the wheel.

Velasquez sits unmoving.

But the marshal sees the flicker of reaction in her eyes. "I can get you out of here…"

Across the table from him Velasquez's face is feral —calculating.

"But you're going to have to help me."

No answer.

"And I don't have time. Yes, or no?"

CHAPTER
FORTY-SEVEN

AN HOUR LATER, a dusting of snow lies on the scrub at either side of the highway rising into the mountains. In the rear-view, Velasquez sits motionless, head turned to the side, staring out across the land.

The cuts and bruises across her face are stark—something like a burned-out fire in her eyes. Or resignation, maybe, the marshal thinks. Or just the drinking in of open land under winter sun—after block-walls and the bars of a cell.

In the passenger seat, Ferguson holds the release form in her lap—signing Velasquez into US Marshals custody. She checks her phone for messages on the Amber alert. Shakes her head. "I don't see how this is going to get us to Gregory?"

"If this guy Luis Rios knows about a major drugs stash up on the rez, Andre Parrish probably knows about it, too," Whicher says. "Parrish could be looking to disappear. Maybe he'd want a piece of it."

"Maybe…" Ferguson's voice is flat, unconvinced.

"We have to have somewhere to look."

"Right." She gestures out of the window into thin forest and rock-strewn hills; "But out here…"

Whicher accelerates up the twisting highway. "I found

tracks to a shelter on the rez yesterday," he says. "With Officer Roanhorse. From the BIA."

"Oh?"

"Somebody up there looking for something." He inclines his head toward Velasquez in the back seat. "Something big enough for Rios to half-kill her, maybe—burn her house down, her trailer..."

Ferguson looks into the rear of the cab.

"If Luis Rios is this Mexican," Whicher says, "if he's a police informer, could he have been the source? About Ramsay being holed up on Pike Street?"

The marshal feels her eyes briefly on him.

"I'm just thinking out loud, spitballing..."

"The CID detective at the Carlsbad PD said he knew who the source was."

"Trenton Allen?" Whicher says. "Detective Allen?"

"Right."

"You think he knows Rios is known as the Mexican?"

Ferguson turns in the passenger seat to face forward. She stares out through the windshield; gives no answer.

———

Five miles onto the Mescalero Reservation, the gravel road climbs into a steep-sided canyon. A clearing in the ponderosa pine and Douglas fir is visible ahead—at the back of it, at the tree line, a small, squat structure shows.

Whicher slows, checks for signs of any presence—the road mostly white-over—no fresh tracks apparent.

He brings the truck to stop a hundred yards out; turns in his seat. "That it?"

Jena Velasquez peers forward, the floor-chain to her cuffs rattling against the seat.

She nods.

The marshal comes off the brake, drives the truck farther into the gloom-filled canyon.

He eyes the building—a weathered-looking sheet metal barn.

"Curt brought me out here one time," Velasquez says.

"Curtis Traxler?" Ferguson says, "your boyfriend?"

"How come you came up here?" Whicher says.

"Curt was holding," Velasquez answers. "Ice. A lot of ice, for Karl Ramsay."

"They kept it out here?" Ferguson says.

"They'd leave a guard. Nobody on the rez knew about it," Velasquez says. "Even if they did, they wouldn't touch it. You can't steal from people like them, like Karl or Curt…"

Whicher drives the last yards up the undulating road into the valley. He rolls the window. Feels the cold against his skin—the air wet, untouched by sun.

Braking to a halt, he shuts down the motor. "This really someplace Karl Ramsay comes to?"

Velasquez's voice is firm. "He's been out here."

Whicher thinks of arresting him on the eastern side of the reservation—twenty miles or more away. He steps out.

Reva Ferguson follows. She unclips the retaining strap on the Glock at her hip.

Whicher glances at her. "There's a chance Gregory could be in there…"

She returns his look.

"I'm just saying. Let's take care."

The marshal walks toward the barn.

Ferguson tracks wide to see around the side of the metal structure.

Studying the snow and dirt, Whicher sees no ground sign. He calls out; "*US Marshal—anybody here?*"

In the air is only the echo of his voice above the moan of wind in the canyon.

He approaches the door, sees the rusted padlock on a hasp.

Stepping back to the truck, he digs out a pry bar from underneath the passenger seat.

He moves back to the door of the barn.

Reva Ferguson completes a tour around it.

Whicher jams in the bar, rips at the hasp, pushing, pulling, working it back and forth. It pulls away over rusted screwheads.

He opens up the door.

Inside, the space is empty.

Light filters through holes in the rusted walls and roof.

Scattered around are ripped cardboard boxes, tarpaulin sheets. He takes in the rolls of heavy-duty polyethylene, ends of Saran Wrap. "Same packaging," Whicher says. "Same as the garage at Charlene Kingbird's place."

Ferguson nods. "Somebody's been keeping drugs out here —I'll give you that."

Driving back down out of the canyon, Velasquez's eyes in the rear-view dart to left and right.

She shifts her weight in the back seat.

Reva Ferguson puts an arm around the headrest, twists her body to look at her. "This guy Luis Rios beat you up—then burned your trailer and your house over an empty barn?"

"So, it's got to be somewhere else," the woman says.

"If it even exists…"

Velasquez sits forward. "I look like I made this up? Take a look at my face…"

Whicher cuts in; "Karl Ramsay never went back for that crystal meth on Missouri Avenue. Charlene Kingbird's house, her garage…"

Ferguson considers it. "Parrish could've told Ramsay we had the place staked out."

At the foot of the canyon is the turn onto the service road back downhill.

"Where now?" Velasquez says. "Where are you taking me?"

"Down to Cloudcroft."

"Then what? You said if I help you, you help me…"

"So far, none of this gets us closer to Gregory," Marshal Ferguson says.

Whicher broods on the thought, still no reports of any sightings, despite the alert on the Ford Raptor. "Maybe Karl Ramsay never came back to Missouri Avenue because he didn't have to." He looks to Ferguson. "We know a lot of drugs moved yesterday, you caught some of that with Frank Niemann. Your man at the lake knew about it…"

Ferguson nods.

"So, maybe there's a bunch more out there—waiting to be picked up—now that Karl Ramsay won't be coming for them."

Ferguson turns to Velasquez; "You know of anyplace else Ramsay would keep wholesale quantities of narcotics on the rez?"

In the rear-view Whicher sees Velasquez glare at the cab's ceiling. "Think about it," he says.

"One time Curt talked about wolf…something…"

"How's that?"

"I thought he meant that barn. Gray Wolf Canyon. What they call it, where the barn is."

The marshal adjusts his grip on the wheel. "Maybe we should talk with Curtis Traxler…"

"Traxler's in a prison cell somewhere up in the Q," Ferguson says, "We'd have to find him first." She shakes her head. "This isn't getting us anywhere."

Whicher stares into the dark of the tree line beyond the service road. "So far, nothing is."

CHAPTER
FORTY-EIGHT

IN THE VILLAGE OF CLOUDCROFT, vehicles line the curbsides—panel vans and trucks of TV news channels—mixed with units from Otero County Sheriff and the State Police.

In the lot outside the two-room police department is barely enough space for Whicher to pull in off the road.

Reva Ferguson surveys the length of the street.

Whicher finds a place to stop in the lot, cuts the motor on the Silverado.

"Circus sure came in quick…" Ferguson says.

The marshal thumbs over his shoulder. "See if the PD can house her."

Velasquez jerks forward in the rear seat. "You kicking me out, ese?"

"I can't drag you through every mountain and wood on the reservation."

"We had a deal," Velasquez says.

"I'll speak with the DEA," Whicher tells her. "Talk to 'em—about dropping the charges. But I'll need more from you…"

"Like what?"

"We're not done, not even close."

Ferguson opens up the passenger door, steps out.

Whicher follows. Opens the rear of the cab, unfastens the floor-chain from Velasquez's cuffs, pulls her out.

Ferguson takes her arm, leads her across the lot to the door of the station house.

On the opposite side of the street Whicher spots the uniformed figure of Sergeant Harris. He clips across the road between passing cars. "They run the press briefing yet?"

"Ongoing." Harris indicates the galleried hotel. "They're set up in a back room in there."

"You know if Annaliese Joyner spoke?"

"She went on camera. Recorded something earlier this morning," Harris says. "Sheriff and a major from the state police are doing the talking now. There's live bulletins timed to hit the news cycle…"

"Did anything come in yet, any kind of a lead?"

The sergeant shakes his head, looks off down the road at the mountains rising above the snow-covered roofs of businesses and stores. "That's a lot of country out there. I don't like nobody seeing anything. The longer this goes on…"

Whicher cuts him short; "The guy's truck has to be out there somewhere."

"So does the kid," Harris says. "But this is taking too long."

The marshal eyes the press of vehicles along the street. People everywhere; on the sidewalk, townsfolk, tourists, news crew techs. Uniformed officers stand guard out in front of the Western-style hotel. "There enough on this, you think?"

The sergeant shrugs.

"Enough resource?" Whicher says.

"Even if we had more, we're still nowhere—if we've got no idea where to look."

―――

Back at the lot of the police department, the phone is ringing inside Whicher's truck.

He reaches in to take it, sees the name on screen, Chief Marshal Fairbanks from the Pecos office.

He picks up.

"I'm watching a Major Carlton from the New Mexico state police," she says, "talking about your missing boy—and a missing law enforcement deputy. You declared him an official suspect?"

"I did. A witness saw Gregory Joyner talking to a man dressed in a sheriff's uniform, driving a black pickup. It's got to be Parrish."

"The state police major made an appeal—for the guy to come forward."

"He's not going to do that," Whicher says. "He gets put away, his life won't be worth living. The people he shot to death on the outside? You think anyone forgets. Bad enough to be a cop, but add that…"

The chief marshal doesn't reply.

Whicher watches the busy street.

From a side door at the hotel, Officer Roanhorse emerges.

"Maybe somebody will spot him," Fairbanks says, "now that this is all getting out. A lot of eyes are going to be on this."

Roanhorse starts across the road—spots the marshal—changes direction.

Whicher reads the man's face. "Ma'am, I have to go…"

"Let me know what's happening," the chief marshal says.

"Got it."

Whicher clicks the call out.

Roanhorse approaches. "Station sergeant at Mescalero just called me."

"What's going on?"

"Karl Ramsay," Roanhorse says.

"What about him?"

"Asking to speak with you."

"He wants to talk?"

Roanhorse studies the marshal. "He told the sergeant you'd know why."

Across the lot Reva Ferguson emerges from the two-room station house. "How long you want to keep her here? They're asking, they don't have space..."

"Tell them just today," Whicher says. "Or if they can't house her, have the sheriff's office take her back to Alamogordo, hold her there."

She looks at him, a question in her face.

"We have to go; Karl Ramsay wants to talk—in Mescalero."

"You want to do that?"

"If he has an idea where to look for Andre Parrish."

Roanhorse breaks out the keys to his truck. "You want to follow me over?"

Thirty minutes later at the BIA law enforcement center, wind is picking up, bending the limbs on pine and fir in violent gusts—the sky bleak overhead as Whicher enters the office behind Roanhorse and Reva Ferguson.

In the lobby, the custody sergeant, Rodriguez, steps from behind the desk.

Whicher thumbs toward the secure door to the cells. "He still back there?"

The sergeant's eyes are flint in his weathered face. "I can't get any attorney out here. Duty lawyer's not available. You want to interview him, it's going to take some time."

"We don't have time," the marshal says.

Rodriguez folds big arms across the front of his uniform shirt.

"This is by his own request," Whicher says. "We're not

looking to build a case. I'm trying to find the whereabouts of a missing child."

Sergeant Rodriguez looks to Reva Ferguson and Officer Roanhorse. "You want to talk with him, it's on you."

"BIA police concern is duly noted," Whicher says. "USMS takes full responsibility."

Rodriguez unfolds his arms, crosses to the secure door. Takes a key from his belt, opens up.

Whicher steps through with Reva Ferguson.

"You need me?" Roanhorse says.

"Call you, if we do."

Rodriguez relocks the door.

At the end of the cement block corridor Ramsay stands staring out behind the iron bars and mesh-wire of the cell.

"This is Deputy US Marshal Reva Ferguson," Whicher says.

No response.

"She's part of this investigation."

"Not interested. I want representation."

"Well, you can't have it," Whicher says.

Ramsay gapes. His expression pointed. "I want to talk about what you *said*."

"Whatever you want to say to me you can say in front of her."

"About witness security," Ramsay says, "about cooperating on a *deal*..."

"So, talk."

The man steps back, shakes his head. "First of all, I need some guarantees, here..."

"Can't do it."

Behind the bars, Ramsay's eyes are wide, his face marked with an animal fear.

"I'd have to talk to my boss," Whicher says. "She'd have to talk to the DA…"

"You said you could do this…"

"I'm saying we could. For significant evidence. For testimony to convict."

Ramsay steps forward. "That's what I'm saying." His voice is tight in his throat.

"We can deal," the marshal says. "Only, not now."

"Why the hell not?"

Reva Ferguson cuts in; "Because we have to find a missing twelve-year-old."

Anger flares in Ramsay now; "I don't know a damn thing about any of that."

"Tell me where to look for Andre Parrish," Whicher says.

The man gives a flat, disbelieving laugh. "Like I would know…"

Whicher eyes him. "I think he could be here. On reservation land. Trying to retrieve something, something of yours."

Ramsay tilts back his head. "What makes you think that?"

"Your friend Jena Velasquez practically had the life beaten out of her over it. And she was almost burned to death. By your Mexican pal."

Karl Ramsay stares out from behind the bars.

"Yeah, we know about him," Whicher says. "We know he's after a stash of illegal narcotics—belonging to you."

Marshal Ferguson speaks; "Does Andre Parrish know where this cache is?"

Ramsay stands rooted. Turns his back. "How's that any kind of help?"

Whicher steps to the wire cage. "I have to find this kid. We have no idea where he is."

Behind the bars of the cell, Ramsay starts to pace.

"We have no idea where to look. If Parrish shows up for your stash I want to be there. Or if not me, somebody else…"

Ramsay stops, turns around. "You get a hold of Andre, then what?"

"I'll deal with that…"

"Get me an attorney—you get some representation out here we can talk about a deal—I can tell you where to find it."

"I want to know now."

"Too bad," Ramsay says.

"You want to show some good faith?" Ferguson says. "Tell us where to look."

Whicher stares at the man for the longest time, until Ramsay's eyes cut away. "If I don't find this boy," he says. "So help me… I will come back here and I will bury you."

Back in the reception lobby at the front desk, Whicher stands with Ferguson and Roanhorse—the custody sergeant in back watching a TV bulletin in the dispatcher's room. Annaliese Joyner is on the wall-mount monitor, speaking into the camera—face intent, a fierce light in her eye.

Images of the sheriff and the major from the state police flash up on the screen.

"Get him a lawyer," Whicher says.

Roanhorse frowns. "Going to take time…"

"Call whoever you need to call."

The BIA officer nods.

"Tell them it's urgent. Tell them to put it on the federal tab."

"You get anything from him?"

Whicher grunts. "Nothing we could use."

Roanhorse eyes the screen as the feed cuts to a TV news anchor in a studio. "What were you hoping for?"

Whicher blows out his cheeks. "Long shot. Somewhere to look for Parrish. Anyplace."

Sergeant Rodriguez steps from the dispatcher's room.

"Jena Velasquez reckons there's a drugs cache out here," Ferguson says.

Both the BIA officers turn to look at her.

"She took us out to a place—it'd definitely been used," Ferguson says. "Nothing's up there now…"

"Where is this?" Rodriguez says.

"Gray Wolf Canyon?"

"She heard wolf… something," Whicher says.

"She knew about a barn up in a canyon," Ferguson continues, "she thought it must be there."

Whicher looks at Roanhorse. "Curtis Traxler told her."

The BIA officer nods.

"But maybe it's another 'wolf' something…"

"Wolf Tail Mountain?" Rodriguez says.

Roanhorse puts his head on one side.

Whicher looks at the custody sergeant.

"That's what, a dozen miles from here?" Roanhorse says.

The marshal turns to him. "You know where it is? Can you show us?"

CHAPTER
FORTY-NINE

THE ROAD into high country traverses the same terrain of pine and fir and juniper spread across rocky hillsides and stretches of white-over of pasture. Ahead in the black, Ram pickup, Officer Roanhorse hits the blinker. He turns from the main route, steering over a cattle guard up a dirt road disappearing into forest.

Whicher follows in the Silverado. Reva Ferguson in the passenger seat, studying the stark, winter land.

Roanhorse pulls his unit over suddenly.

Whicher brakes to a halt.

Stepping from the pickup, the BIA officer walks the few yards back to Whicher's truck.

The marshal rolls his window. "This the place?"

Roanhorse nods. "There's some people living out here." He points at tire tracks in the snow on the ground. "Not many —a handful of trailer homes, back in the woods."

"You have somewhere in mind we could search?"

"There's some barns. Storage."

"Yesterday we found evidence in a rancher's barn."

"We have no idea who that was," Roanhorse says.

"Either Parrish," Whicher says, "or Karl Ramsay. Or the driver of that white, Ford pickup."

The BIA officer looks at him.

"We know who he is, we think," Whicher says. "Guy name of Luis Rios. They call him 'The Mexican' on the street."

Roanhorse's face shows no sign of recognition.

"Rival dealer," the marshal says.

"He at Ramsay's level?"

"Maybe he wants to be. Jena Velasquez says it was him beat her up. For the mother lode—wherever it is." Whicher takes in the dirt road rising into the tree line up the side of the hill. "People get to thinking they can dump narcotics out here…"

"Never used to be a problem," Roanhorse says.

"Where you want to start?"

"Listen, I'm not saying there'll be anything out here. But there's barns, storage shelters. Part of an old sawmill, too."

Whicher eyes him.

"Just a bunch of wrecked buildings," Roanhorse says, "they tore most of it down. If we're here, we might as well take a look."

———

Two miles up from the valley floor, the forest road crests a rise into a clearing, rock and snow and scrub extending back into the trees.

A hundred yards from the road at the edge of re-grown forest, buildings are visible—a handful timber-sided, their roofs hanging in. Others are made from sheet metal, run-down, half-collapsed.

A swirling wind scours the open ground, lifting flurries of snow into the air like fine, white dust.

The marshal scans the clearing. No tire tracks visible.

"There any other way up here?" Whicher says.

"Dirt roads come in and out of the forests," Roanhorse answers, "there could be other ways to get in."

Reva Ferguson fastens the camel coat up to her throat. "You know the place?"

"Been a while," the BIA officer says.

Whicher adjusts the holstered Glock. Cold wind biting at him, a strong wind, bending the tops of pine and fir. A high, keening is in the air; the sound eerie.

No sign of any disturbance shows. He leads off over bedrock and frozen grass and tracts of crisp snow. Senses alert. Pushing down frustration—at time escaping, slipping away.

To his right, Roanhorse starts to fan out on the flank.

Whicher pushes out to the opposite side, letting Ferguson continue in the middle between them. A feeling starting to tick inside, despite the silence. Despite the emptiness of the surrounds.

From the far tree line, crows lift, squawking, into the frigid air.

And a noise is suddenly present—the sound of an engine. A motor firing into life.

The marshal stops. Listens.

Ferguson and Roanhorse are both now stock-still.

A car motor is running somewhere, out of sight.

Whicher calls over; "Anybody got eyes on that?"

Ferguson shakes her head.

"Nothing," Roanhorse answers.

The marshal starts to kick out wider—a shape registers in his field of vision—he lurches forward, breaks into a run.

In a shaft of light descending through the trees is a black pickup.

He pulls up, stares.

Just as suddenly, it's gone from view.

Spinning around, he puts two hands to his mouth. Shouts back; *"That was Parrish. That was his truck..."*

Roanhorse turns, starts to sprint back toward the BIA pickup.

Ferguson draws her weapon, stares into the trees.

Tearing across the white clearing in the Silverado, Roanhorse's truck opens up a lead.

Whicher steers after him, eyes a gap in the tree line beyond the abandoned mill.

Roanhorse races toward it—disappears down into the woodland.

Whicher follows—sees the primitive dirt route descending through a swathe of pine and fir. He steers down it, hands light on the wheel, the Silverado shaking, bouncing over the rough descent.

"You get a look at him?" Ferguson says.

The marshal shakes his head.

Parrish is gone in the Ford Raptor, now—down the track, out of sight.

"How you think he saw us?"

"Lucked in," Whicher says. "He's about to luck out..."

Ahead, Roanhorse's pickup dips, hits a protruding rock—its rear axle bucks, the back end fishtails.

Whicher gets off the gas, touches the brakes, skids, tries to steer around the rock, loses ground.

Back on the gas he feels his heart rate climbing. He stares ahead at sunlight cutting through the canopy of trees.

Where the edge of the track overlooks the descent of the hill, he sees Parrish in the Raptor, now—a quarter-mile down, almost doubled back toward them.

A bend—there must be, a sharp bend ahead.

He sees Roanhorse hit the brakes, see his taillights flare in the gloom.

The BIA pickup slews around, barely in control.

Ferguson braces, pushes back in her seat.

Whicher slows, dumps speed, steers a straight line braking toward the corner.

Roanhorse wrestles the pickup around the hairpin bend.

Whicher goes wide, foot off the gas, cuts back in, the truck clears the turn.

Back on the throttle, he sees the track below descending fast—trees close, overhanging at either side. But somewhere ahead is light—intense light, a brightness.

Roanhorse pulls away, accelerating on the slope.

The marshal pushes on after him, toward sunlight—iridescent—a glare of white snow through the forest of branches. The slope is tailing off, the woods finishing—beyond them open ground, stark, exposed.

Roanhorse breaks from the tree line.

The Silverado gathers speed.

Whicher steers out into sunlight.

Andre Parrish is out ahead of them, across a flat, treeless plateau a half-mile wide—the BIA Ram pickup behind him, closing.

And then Parrish is slowing.

Roanhorse is flat out—pulling level, tires spitting snow.

The Ford Raptor skews sharp—into the pickup's side—its right front smashing into Roanhorse's door.

Reva Ferguson shifts forward, leans out of the window holding her Glock.

The Raptor and the BIA pickup close again—at speed, this time Roanhorse ramming the Ford truck as it comes across—Parrish now accelerating, cutting in front of the BIA vehicle, powering sideways.

The Raptor bucks, jumps, catches something in the ground—heaves up violently.

It flips.

Rolls over on its side.

Still rolling, crashes down on the roof of the cab.

Rolling again, it throws up a writhing cloud of powdered snow.

Roanhorse shoots by it—turns, hits the brakes to come around.

Whicher steers for the Raptor—then stamps on the brakes, skidding to a halt in the ice and snow on the rock-strewn plateau.

Ferguson jumps out.

"Go around," he tells her, "I'll go at him from the front."

Grabbing the Ruger revolver, he pushes out of the truck, runs forward.

The vehicle ahead is resting on its side—he can see the windshield, its glass crazed, shattered—inside the cab, the driver hanging limp against the seat belt.

Reva Ferguson arrives at the far side—advances on the truck, gun arm out.

"*Not moving*," Whicher shouts.

Roanhorse steers the Ram in—brakes to a standstill, climbs out, holding an AR-15.

The marshal steps forward to the hood of the Raptor. The engine stalled out, no movement from inside the cab.

He stares in, edging closer. Feels his breath come short.

"*Not him*," he calls out. "It's not Parrish." He stares into the bloodied face of the man in the cab. "That's Drummond. That's Billy Drummond inside of there…"

———

The smell of leaking gasoline is everywhere. "We need to get him out…"

Ferguson peers in; "We don't know what injuries he has…"

"This thing catches on fire, he'll burn to death," the marshal says, "if he isn't dead already."

Roanhorse climbs up onto the side of the Raptor. He opens

up the driver's door. Reaches in to Drummond hanging limp in his seat.

Whicher scrambles up alongside the BIA officer, gets both hands onto Drummond, takes some of the weight.

Reaching around, Roanhorse unfastens the seat belt, catches hold of the man before he can fall into the passenger side.

Whicher drags the deputy upward.

Roanhorse pulls Drummond in, hand over fist—rests him against the truck's side.

Jumping down, Whicher takes him onto his shoulder. He carries him from the Raptor.

Ferguson helps the marshal get the deputy onto the ground.

Drummond lies bloody, his body inert.

Kneeling to him Whicher feels for a pulse, finds one, rolls him onto his side.

Roanhorse regards the man. "Think he'll make it?"

The marshal gives no response.

"What's he doing in Andre Parrish's truck?" Ferguson says.

Whicher stands. "If he's here, with the guy's truck, where's Parrish?"

Roanhorse stares back across the snow to the primitive road.

Ferguson puts away her pistol. "What do you want to do?"

Whicher turns to the BIA officer. "You have radio contact? You get anybody out here?"

"Should be."

"Call for backup, a medic."

"State patrol might have a helicopter?"

The marshal nods, turns to Reva Ferguson. "We need to get back up there."

Roanhorse looks at him. "You need me?"

"Stick with Drummond..." Whicher glances at the deputy on the ground.

"You think Parrish will be back up there?" Ferguson says.

The BIA officer steps to the pickup, takes out a two-way radio set. "I carry a spare in the truck." He holds it out to Whicher. "It's set to Tac-1, if you need to reach me..."

At the head of the track through the woods back up to the plateau, Whicher steers into the clearing behind the abandoned sawmill. He circles around to the side of the falling-down buildings. Kills the motor. Gets out.

From the gun safe beneath the rear seat, he grabs a Marshals Service Kevlar vest. He tosses it to Reva Ferguson. "Put this on."

"What about you?"

"I got you into this..."

She hesitates.

"Go on," he tells her.

She pulls the vest over the camel coat, cinches the straps.

Whicher breaks out the Glock at his waist, eyes the handful of dilapidated buildings. "We don't know what's in there—if he's here, he already knows the ground."

Ferguson nods, apprehensive. She checks her own gun over.

Stepping away from the truck, the marshal moves to the larger of two timber-sided buildings. He finds a broken window—squints inside.

Half the roof is fallen in. Snow covers the ground, topping remnants of old machinery and rusted tools. He tracks down the side of the building, comes to an opening, a doorway, its door long since gone.

Ferguson closes up, takes position beside him. She taps on

the planks of the timber wall. "Not much cover to hide behind—if anybody starts shooting."

Whicher calls out; "*US Marshals…*"

No response comes back.

He steps through the doorway to the space inside—sweeps it fast, sees nothing. Calls out; "*Clear.*"

Ferguson moves in, advances past him.

Whicher crosses to a doorway at the far end. Nothing seems disturbed, no sign of any presence shows. He checks step, waits for Ferguson. Exits back outside in front of a smaller, wooden building.

Ferguson takes the lead, moving fast.

At the entrance to the structure, a double-wide door of weathered planks is closed. She waits at it, sets up.

Whicher gets in place at her side. He listens for any noise, hears only wind wailing, blowing through the trees.

No lock is on the door, he tries its ancient iron latch—it lifts up. Grasping the door, he pulls it back.

Ferguson moves the barrel of her pistol side to side over the exposed interior. "Wait," she says, "what's that?"

Whicher looks—sees the rear of a Nissan SUV.

Leading with the Glock, he rolls around the half-open door into the building.

The space is dark, unlit—the SUV just far enough inside to be hidden from sight.

Nobody is in the vehicle. Touching the hood, he feels warmth from the motor.

Ferguson paces along the inner wall, gun arm out.

Scattered about are ancient scraps of lumber, rotted boxes, a rusting hoist.

"Keep moving." Whicher nods toward the SUV. "Parrish has to be here somewhere…"

Backing to the double-door, he steps out—eyes an abandoned office building opposite the wooden barn—its sides made of sheet metal, the roof tin, windows broken in.

Ferguson emerges through the double doorway. She stands at his side, adjusts her grip on her pistol.

Beyond the old office is a clear patch of ground, covered with snow, wind swirling over it. In the sun and shadow faint impressions show—the trace of a trail leading toward another metal-sided building—some kind of storage.

Whicher points at the marks on the ground, turns to Ferguson.

She stares. "Footprints?"

The marshal raises the Glock. He moves to the side of the office, sprints across the open ground. Following the length of one wall along the storage building he reaches the corner—steps around. In front of a doorway, he sees disturbance on the ground.

Reva Ferguson arrives behind him. She keeps her voice low; "There have to be narcotics here... You want to wait? Get back up?"

"Three more minutes we can clear the place." Whicher steps forward, grips the .40 caliber semi-automatic. "If he's here, I want him now..."

Moving up to the door to the building, he gestures at the handle; "You open it, I'll cover."

She tries it.

The door is locked.

In the air is a metallic creak.

A gust of wind blasts through the clearing.

Whicher listens, hears the noise again. Leads Ferguson down the opposite side of the building. Shutters are on a load-bay—one of the shutters loose, moving in the wind.

He runs, yanks at it—feels it give, feels the shutter open sideways on its hinge.

Stepping away, he calls out; "*US Marshals. Anybody in there*?"

Ferguson looks at him. "We going in?"

The marshal nods. "I'll go right side—you watch the left."

He raises the Glock. Runs through the load-bay opening, gets low, sweeps the barrel of the gun.

Ferguson rushes to his left.

Eyes adjusting in the low-level light, he can make out something under polyethylene wrap—in the center of the room.

In the edge of his field of vision is movement—he snaps around onto it, iron sights locking with a shape on the ground.

"*Hold it,*" he calls out, fighting an urge to pull the trigger. "*Hold it, don't move…*"

Reva Ferguson kneels, takes aim.

As Whicher runs forward.

Toward dark eyes staring back at him.

Shocked.

Filled with fear.

In the half-light.

Gregory Joyner.

CHAPTER FIFTY

CARRYING the boy to his truck Whicher feels the cold of Gregory's face against his own skin.

He opens up the door to the Silverado, gets him inside, into the warmth of the cab.

Unfastening a set of handcuffs from Gregory's wrists, he sees the raw marks where the metal has bitten. He throws the cuffs to the floor, takes off his wool ranch coat, puts it around the boy's shoulders.

Reva Ferguson climbs inside the truck, puts an arm around him.

Gregory looks at her, wordless.

She speaks softly; "You okay?"

He nods.

"How long have you been here?"

"This morning," Gregory says, his voice weak, "the man brought me."

"Parrish?" Whicher says.

The boy shakes his head.

"Drummond? The big man?"

"Is that where you were; at his place?" Ferguson says.

"I don't know." Gregory swallows, his face blank. "It was at some house."

Whicher looks at him. "Is he here—the other man?"

"He was… I don't know where he went…"

"It's okay," Whicher says, "it's alright. We've got you. You're safe. You're going home."

The boy only stares back.

The marshal turns to Ferguson. "Stay with him—I'll go check…"

"Call it in," she says.

Whicher steps from the truck. Unholsters the Glock. "Call it in for me."

"At least get Roanhorse up here…"

The marshal scans the sawmill buildings, the snow-bound clearing, the forest—the hard edge of mountain rising beyond it.

At the head of the primitive forest trail, Roanhorse's BIA pickup powers out from among the pine and fir. Crumpled in the bed is Billy Drummond, unconscious, zip-tied to a steel lug.

At the edge of the clearing, Whicher thumbs back toward the buildings, to his truck. "We've got Gregory. Marshal Ferguson's got him."

Behind the wheel, Roanhorse searches his face.

"Parrish is gone. He's not in any of the buildings. But he was here…" Whicher points at the ground, at boot prints visible in the snow.

Roanhorse shuts off the motor, gets out. Stares at the ground.

He eyes the line of footprints leading off into the woods. "You want to go in after him?"

The marshal takes in the mountain forest—the rocky

ground rising sharp. Wind whipping the branches, swaying trunks of trees. "You got someone coming out for Drummond?"

"State police."

Whicher glances at the deputy in the bed of the truck. "EMTs?"

"Rolling." The BIA officer stares into the woods. "That's hard country."

"You don't want to go in there?"

"It's my country," Roanhorse says.

The marshal nods, moves toward the trees. "Alright, then. Let's do it, let's go…"

———

Less than a hundred yards in, the trail breaks.

Animal runs are traced into the woods—lines of worn ground, channels among the trees and thin-grown branches.

Picking the clearest, Whicher moves fast along it.

Fifty yards in, he sees the heel print of a boot; a fresh print.

He points to it for Roanhorse, not stopping.

Hears the BIA officer call back, "Got it…"

The run is a traverse, now, tracking the contours of the rising mountain.

Ahead, it breaks into two distinct paths.

Whicher stops, looks for ground sign—no prints show in the earth or snow.

Where the run breaks into two, a path ascends—up into thin forest, rocky ground, bright patches of snow where the mountainside is denuded.

A second path descends, scribing an arc across the hill, dropping steep.

Whicher eyes the low path. "Got to want to go down…"

Roanhorse nods; "Fastest way to get off the hill."

The marshal looks back along the high trail.

"Got a ridge up there," the BIA officer says. "Pretty bad. Nasty."

"Would he know that?"

"Guess not."

Whicher looks again at the low trail. "Most likely going to go down. Except for one thing…"

"What's that?"

"Do the opposite—do what they don't expect…"

Roanhorse considers it. "So, what do you want to do?"

"I'll go high," Whicher says. "You take the low route. Either one of us finds any trace, any print, get on the radio…"

"He won't go high."

The marshal only looks at him. "You see his boot print; call."

Nothing is on the ground despite the height gain.

Despite five minutes pushing hard in the worsening wind.

Ghost trails appear among the thinning trees—only to disappear again.

Whicher picks a route on instinct. Checks his two-way radio.

No word from Roanhorse.

He pushes on the button to talk; "Whicher—you read me?"

Above the noise of the wind, the static hiss is hard to hear.

No answer comes back.

Ahead is open sky, the limit of the tree line—snow and rock—the hard edge of a mountain ridge. White powder showers into the air from a blast of driven wind.

The marshal pushes on, leaving the tree line.

Parrish can't have disappeared.

Violent gusts hit him, he drops low, works to keep to his feet.

The high ridge is before him now—a length of jagged rock stretching out—maybe half a mile in length. Serpentine. Curving. Towering. A whiplash above vertiginous falls. Black and gray, bare rock, white snow. Like a blade, sinuous. Or like a wolf tail.

Approaching its edge, he squats, kneels, unable to stand in the force of wind.

Steadying against the ground he stares out along the ridge—rattled, barely able to gather thought.

He sees something.

Gone again.

He searches for it—sees it—a moving figure.

A man moving along the ridgeline.

The marshal grabs the radio. "This is Whicher—you read me? Over…"

Clamping the transceiver to his ear he hears a crackle, the line opening up.

"Roanhorse. Over."

"He's up here—he's out on the ridge." Whicher watches the man, moving, scrambling, sees him turn, check behind.

Roanhorse's voice comes back. "Can you get to him?"

"What's on the other side?" Whicher says. "If he makes it across?"

"Don't go out on that," Roanhorse says, "that's a bad place…"

Whicher listens for the voice of the BIA officer—the sound now breaking up, drowned by the roar of air, cut with static hiss.

Parrish is staring back, now—squatting, taking something from behind his back—a dark shape, holding it with both hands. He gets low among the rock and snow—brings the shape to his eye.

Whicher feels the burst of adrenaline. Rolls flat.

Hears the rifle's report, despite the wind.

Leveling the Glock, he aims high—over Parrish—gives back fire—five rounds, six, trying to drive him off.

Ears ringing, he sees the man get up, move again—hurrying along the knife-edged ridge.

Blood up, Whicher scrabbles forward—free hand and the Glock out in front of him, ready to grab for rock should he fall.

He steals a look at Parrish—moving faster.

Driving on, a thought forms in his mind—the ridge is curving around—Parrish will have the flank—he'll be able to make it count, have the range.

The marshal slows, feels his limbs heavy, turns to look—feels his balance go in the onrush of wind.

Sees Parrish, kneeling with the rifle. Sees him set, take aim.

He throws himself down, starts to slide on the face of the rock—lets go of the Glock, grabs at anything, gets a boot hold, hears the volley of shots.

Breath stopped in his throat, he sees the drop below him.

Pinned against the face of the ridge he watches Parrish rise, opening the angle, ready to shoot down.

Whicher rips the Ruger from the shoulder holster—thumbs back the hammer, barely able to hold his arm straight.

Firing over and over he hears the shots of Parrish's rifle—feels his heart pound in his chest.

Sees Parrish—at full height—now stumbling—the rifle falling away.

As he fights for balance, arms windmilling.

Almost lifted from his feet.

By a wind shearing, supernatural, its force suffocating, devastating.

And like a rag doll he's tumbling.

Falling.

Screaming.

Headlong.
Down a razor-sharp face.

EPILOGUE

Texas / New Mexico State Line.
5 days later.

IMAGES ARE ALL he sees in his mind—flashes of moments, sensations; sights and sounds. The body bag on the floor of the DPS helicopter. The smell of unburnt fuel, the clatter of rotor blades, the helo ascending. Roanhorse's coal eyes. Parrish's injuries. His face in death.

Later, the white knuckles of Annaliese Joyner's hands holding onto her son.

Sitting back in the booth of the roadside diner, Whicher stares out through the glare on the picture window. Onto a busy state highway—streams of pipe and concrete trucks, crew transport, parts supply—the hustle of an oil and gas boom.

He focuses. Brings his mind back to the here and now. Pushing back dark thought. Still-raw memory.

Out of the window, beyond the roadway is flat desert. Scrub. Power lines. Fenced-in oil-field camps, RV parks.

Dust clouds blow through the air from the passing trucks and semis. A dirt devil twists between a gas plant and a laydown yard.

He thinks again of the squall wind on the mountain.

The rib aching in his side, from the fall.

Over at the counter end of the diner, a waitress steps out with a pot of coffee.

"I get you a refill, honey?"

He pushes forward his cup. "Appreciate it."

"One for the road..."

The marshal says, "I guess."

She studies the man seated before her. The empty breakfast plate. The charcoal suit, Resistol hat. Straight back. Level eyes. "Where you headed?"

"Across the state line."

"New Mexico?"

"Thereaway."

Filling his cup, she steps back. "Don't look like you're in a hurry..."

Whicher inclines his head.

She gestures out of the window, across the road. "Most folk coming in now want it yesterday. And then they're out of here."

"That right?"

"Nobody has the time. Wouldn't want to be them. Like to be where I am. Don't see the sense, rushing at it like that. Not like it's going to disappear."

"What's that?"

She says, "Whatever it is on their minds..."

The marshal thinks it over. Takes a sip of the coffee.

"You an oil man?"

"No, ma'am."

She looks at him.

"Law man," he says.

He sees her stiffen, used to it. The reserve, a guardedness

stealing in.

She glances off out of the window. "So. On the road? You have far to go?"

He lets his eyes meet hers a moment. Turns his cup. Nods. "Far enough."

Standing in the white-painted cement block lobby of the Carlsbad Detention Center, Whicher waits at the glass insert in the reinforced-steel door.

A black-uniformed officer appears—the marshal shows his badge and ID.

The door latch cranks back in its mechanism, Whicher enters into the booking hall.

At the front desk, Sergeant Shannon Towne stands talking with a clerk behind the safety glass window.

The sergeant nods a greeting.

Whicher steps across the gray-painted floor.

Turning from the desk, Towne indicates a thin-limbed Hispanic male, at the far end of the room. In his thirties, cuffed and chained on the wooden bench bolted along the wall. "Luis Rios…"

Whicher takes him in; his bare arms and neck scrolled with tattoos.

He pictures him at the Nunez arrest on Glendale. Running from the house. Thinks of chasing him down in the Silverado.

"Picked up last night," the sergeant says, "here in town. In possession of a big-ass bunch of skag."

"Black tar?"

"Right."

"Driving a white pickup?" Whicher says.

"I believe he was."

"A lot of that likely came from up on the reservation."

Towne looks at him. "You'd have to talk to the BIA police about that."

"I'll be seeing them, later." Whicher steps toward Rios on the long bench.

The seated man stares up.

"Here to transport you into custody—in Artesia. For the US Marshals Service. You understand the charges against you?"

"Attempted murder," Towne says, "of Jena Velasquez."

"Bullshit," Rios sneers.

"You beat the hell out of her. Went back, set her house on fire."

"Plus, the DA's office is pressing charges," Whicher says, "for transport and transacting in controlled substances."

"Go to hell." Rios hunches on the bench—the wrist chain pulled tight against the fixing in the wall.

The marshal pictures Charlene Kingbird, seated on the same bench. Thinks of Jena Velasquez; of the fear in her. The certainty in her mind of Rios's impunity. "You know a guy name of Parrish? Andre Parrish. Deputy with the Ramos Sheriff?"

"I don't know nobody..."

Towne steps over. "You want to take him?"

Whicher nods. "That free pass of yours is cancelled."

"Alright. Get up," the sergeant says.

Behind the secure window, the clerk passes paper forms through the metal recess. "Rios," the man says, "Luis, A. Signed into custody of the US Marshals Service."

Whicher puts his signature to the release forms. Keeps one, pushes back the other.

Shannon Towne walks Rios to the desk.

The marshal checks his cuffs. "So, you heard Ramsay was going to be at that house on Pike Street? Just couldn't pass up the chance to set him up."

Towne eyes the man. "Too bad you were dumb enough to

hang across town with the next guy we were looking to arrest."

"Yo, ese?" Rios flips him the bird.

The sergeant grins. "For a snitch you don't have much to say."

Whicher takes a hold of Rios by his arm, walks him over to the door.

Behind the desk, the booking clerk presses on a button—the lock snaps back.

"Be a fun ride," Towne says, "guy keeping a vow of silence. Least it's only a half hour to Artesia."

Whicher tips his hat to the sergeant. Pushes Rios through the door. "I don't want to hear it anyway."

Two hours later, a silver-gray Chevy Tahoe sits among the leafless trees in the car lot of the Roswell Medical Center—Marshal Reva Ferguson behind the wheel.

Whicher steers in, parks the Silverado in an empty bay.

Ferguson steps from the SUV in a navy two-piece, her hair tied back.

Whicher shuts down the motor, gets out.

She takes him in. "Looking formal today… the federal investigator…"

The marshal gives a dry laugh.

"You get Rios?"

The marshal nods. "Dropped him at the PD in Artesia—on the way up."

"Quite the charge sheet on him."

"DA says he has links with a couple of the newer DTOs looking to traffic into the area."

"Be good to see the back of him."

"I don't think he'll be missed."

Ferguson locks the Tahoe. "So, Billy Drummond…"

Whicher gazes over at the hospital building—a multi-wing complex, two floors high. "He have representation?"

Ferguson nods. "A defense attorney, name of Sterling. Fulton Sterling."

"This somebody you've spoken with?"

"Yesterday."

"Alright," the marshal says. "Just so long as we're doing it by the book."

He leads off toward the hospital, Ferguson falling into step.

Between the main building and the rear lot is a medevac helipad. Whicher thinks of landing there in the DPS chopper. Deputy Drummond strapped to a spine board in a rescue litter. Parrish zipped inside a body bag.

"Fulton Sterling wished to convey that they're cooperating with the attorney's office investigation," Ferguson says. "That and the internal inquiry."

"All I need is what Ramsay knew—as it pertains to my arrest."

"You seeing him today?"

"At Otero County." Whicher reaches a set of double doors, holds them open for Ferguson.

"I don't know what connection Billy Drummond has to Ramsay," Ferguson says.

"DA's office has enough to hang Ramsay with. I'm just filing the report for USMS. After that... I'm done with him."

―――

The air in the hospital room is dry, overheated, despite the December day.

Deputy Billy Drummond lies secured to the bed—one hand cuffed to a length of chain.

Seated at his side is a fleshy-faced man in his fifties, dressed in a gray suit—his eyes sharp, fair hair thinning.

Whicher sits with Reva Ferguson at the foot of the bed.

In Drummond's free arm, a drip and cannula are attached. He settles the arm at his side.

Fulton Sterling sits forward.

Ferguson switches on a compact audio recorder.

"If everybody's ready," the lawyer says, "I suggest we begin. My client has admitted to being in receipt of monies and other items while a serving peace officer…"

Whicher studies on Drummond.

"In mitigation, he is assisting with all inquiries into this."

"You admit to being on the take…"

"At a minor level," Sterling says.

Drummond's eyes come onto Whicher's.

"And we can present evidence my client was under duress over this," the lawyer says, "from his partner, a senior deputy, no less, a man who exerted a powerful control."

Reva Ferguson looks at Sterling, then at Whicher.

The marshal shrugs. "That's your defense?"

The attorney's face hardens. "Perhaps you'd like to begin your questions, marshal?"

"I'll do that." Whicher sits upright in his chair. "Did Andre Parrish tell Karl Ramsay law enforcement were about to pick him up?"

Drummond nods. "Yes."

"Did you know that at the time?"

"No…"

"Did you intend to shoot the two occupants of the Toyota sedan that left out of Pike Street the morning of the attempted apprehension?"

"My client did not, and that's a leading question."

Whicher looks at the lawyer.

"He was acting in a fully lawful manner."

"You shot them," Whicher says. "Did Parrish put you up to it?"

Drummond speaks, his voice dry. "Look. He psyched me up..."

"In what way?" Ferguson says.

"He kept on... about not giving anybody a chance to do damage..."

Ferguson regards him. "He encouraged you—to shoot first?"

"Parrish was clearly influential," Sterling says, "in setting the tone on this."

Drummond swallows. "He just kept at it—the night before, and on the day..."

"Mister Drummond accepts no fault in the shooting." Sterling leans forward. "And furthermore, I repeat, it was a fully legal action."

Whicher holds up a hand.

"However," the lawyer continues, "I want to highlight that it was this incident—and its unfortunate consequences..."

Ferguson cuts in; "Two people getting killed?"

"Which led to Deputy Parrish exerting even greater influence over my client," Sterling says, "specifically in regard to..."

"The abduction of Gregory Joyner." Whicher looks at him.

"Exactly." Sterling sits back.

"I read your statement," the marshal says.

"Well, then you'll know our position..."

"I'm not investigating the shooting," Whicher says, "or your client, or any misconduct, criminal or otherwise. I'm here on behalf of the Marshals Service and the DA's office—in respect of the case against Karl Ramsay."

Ferguson looks at Billy Drummond. "Tell us what happened with Gregory Joyner?"

The young deputy stares up from the bed at the ceiling. "Parrish heard a kid had seen him. On Pike Street. He just flipped..."

"What happened?" Whicher says.

"I told him there was nothing I could do—they already put me on admin leave."

"He went looking for Gregory?" Ferguson says.

"Did he tell Ramsay?"

"Hell, yeah," Drummond says.

The marshal notes the detail. "What'd Ramsay say?"

Drummond closes his eyes, opens them. "He told Parrish to offer them money. A couple hundred. Just to leave, to get out, go someplace else..."

"Two hundred thousand?" Whicher says. "Did Parrish have that?"

"He could get it." The deputy looks at him. "But he couldn't find them anyplace. He told me he looked up where they were living—they weren't there..."

The marshal thinks of moving Annaliese and Gregory to the home of Grace Pires.

Drummond exhales, turns his head away. "He started spending all his time looking; staking out the house, whenever he was off duty..."

Whicher thinks of the state of Parrish; of the food and garbage amassed in his truck.

"Finally, they came back," Drummond says, "he followed them. Got the boy on his own. He took him."

"What for?"

"He said he wasn't going to hurt him..."

"The boy said he was held against his will," Whicher says, "at your address."

Fulton Sterling breaks in; "This was all under duress..."

Ferguson's voice is testy; "Let's just hear it."

Drummond blanches, shifts his weight on the bed. "It was extra leverage, Parrish said. To make them leave, make them go someplace else—far away. Scare the boy's mom. Give her the money, but make sure—make sure they were frightened, make sure they went away. I told him it would never work..."

Ferguson says, "Then why agree to help him?"

Drummond's eyes move onto hers. "He told me he'd pin both the shootings on me—make everybody think it'd been deliberate..."

"We have text messages," Sterling says, "phone calls which back this up."

Whicher writes a note on the pad. "What did Karl Ramsay know about it?"

The young man's face is hollow. "I don't know. He knew about the money."

"Was he involved in Gregory's kidnap?"

Drummond shakes his head. "I mean, Parrish told me Ramsay got arrested. He got picked up out on the rez. I don't think he told Andre to do it. But by this time Parrish was gone, man, he was losing it, I didn't know what he was going to do. But I wouldn't have let him hurt the kid..."

"My client was an unwilling participant in all of this," Sterling says, "acting under extreme duress, a victim in his own way."

Whicher levels his eyes on the lawyer. "You want to save that? For the judge?"

Drummond struggles to sit up from the bed, flops back down. "I never meant for any of this to happen."

The marshal only eyes him, says nothing.

Fulton Sterling speaks. "Other law force enforcement personnel have been implicated in taking bribes," Sterling says, "in being part of a network controlled by Andre Parrish. My client was just the most junior member, the most vulnerable here..."

Ferguson angles her head. "Maybe he should've just said 'no' to the money..."

Whicher sits back in his chair. "So, you don't know that Karl Ramsay had any part in Gregory Joyner's kidnap?"

Drummond's voice is small in his throat; "It was Parrish.

He just lost it… he knew he was going down, he wasn't thinking straight."

The marshal glances at the hazed sky out of the window. Catches Ferguson's eye. Addresses the lawyer. "Alright. I think that's all we need here."

———

The sun is low over the mountain country on the Mescalero Reservation, the late afternoon growing cold.

Whicher descends a forested ridge on a snow-covered road to a clearing among the pine and fir—sees Officer Roanhorse's Ram pickup—a farm truck parked alongside it.

Beyond the truck is a run-in shelter, sheet canvas stretched over rusting steel hoops.

He sees the stocky figure of Officer Kee inside it, Officer Roanhorse talking to two men. Recognizes Daniel Tessay, operator of the high-country ranch—and Nathan Henry, the hand, black hair loose to his shoulders.

The shelter is half-filled with bales of aging hay—several pulled out, dragged into the snow.

Whicher rolls to a stop in the Silverado, cuts the motor. Gets out as Officer Roanhorse steps toward him. "I got your message."

The men in the clearing regard him.

"Been out in court?" The BIA officer eyes the city suit beneath the wool coat.

"Interviews," the marshal says.

"With Ramsay?"

"Seeing him after this."

Roanhorse grunts. "Well, there's a bunch more black tar of his here."

The ranch operator takes a step forward.

Whicher takes in the battered-looking shelter.

"There was more of it out by Pajarita Canyon," Tessay says.

Stepping to Roanhorse's pickup, Whicher sees the wrapped packages in the bed. "Ramsay's cooperating? Fully? Giving up all this?"

The BIA officer nods.

Whicher steps through the snow to the shelter.

Officer Kee pulls a tarp cover back—exposing a heavy-duty plastic storage sack. Visible inside are individual packages, tightly wrapped. "You can tell him," Kee says, "and tell his friends—to dump their garbage elsewhere."

The ranch operator stares at the sack, at the wrapped bundles within it, resentment in his deep-set eyes. "Nobody comes out here…"

Nathan Henry speaks; "That hay is old, last year's."

"We hardly come here," Tessay says. "They must've sneaked around all over…"

"Some of the places he told us about, we couldn't find them," Roanhorse says. "Had to get Mister Tessay here to show us."

Tessay turns, regards the mountain and forest. "Leaving all this. It's like an insult to the land."

Officer Kee takes a shovel, starts to dig at the earth. "Some places it's buried, covered up."

"We've had to hunt," Roanhorse says. "Daniel took us out —to the canyon, a couple other places."

"You think you're getting it all?" Whicher says.

"If there's anymore, we don't know about it."

"Ask him again," Kee says, "if you're seeing him."

Tessay's voice is gruff in his throat. "Don't ask nice."

The marshal steps back to the Ram pickup, eyes the contents of the bed. Tallies it, silent.

Roanhorse walks over.

"Leastways," the marshal says, "nobody else should come trying to find it."

The BIA officer's face is hard. "If they come, we'll be waiting."

The marshal nods.

Roanhorse looks off along the snow-covered road. "Jena Velasquez is back."

"She came back?"

"Moved in with a girlfriend. On the rez."

The marshal thinks about it. Looks at Roanhorse.

The BIA officer's expression is uncertain.

"They nol prosed," Whicher says. "Declined to prosecute."

"You got her off?"

The marshal listens to the sound of Kee working the earth, digging in the floor of the shelter—the metal blade of the shovel singing against the frozen ground. "I just made a recommendation. Told her to give up what she knew. Prosecutor agreed to file a motion to discharge, the judge dismissed it."

"The girl got lucky."

Whicher regards the wrapped drugs in the pickup bed. "This all… it's not on her."

Roanhorse shoves his hands into his uniform jacket.

"This way, she gets another chance," the marshal says.

Roanhorse turns back for the shelter. "Sure hope she'll use it."

At the gas station in the Mescalero business district off the four-lane highway, Whicher tops off the tank in the Silverado—sun behind the ring of hills, twilight turning the sky from cobalt to a deepening blue.

A chill wind blows across the expanse of asphalt plaza fronting a post office, a diner, a tribal store.

Cars and trucks pass on the highway; headlamps lit, the sound of their motors a low moan reflected around the sides of the hills. He thinks of Ramsay—at the Otero County Detention facility. Scant thirty miles more to go.

The fuel nozzle in the truck clicks to a stop, the marshal pulls it from the filler neck, replaces it on the pump.

He fits the fuel cap, heads for the store.

Sees a woman in a camo pattern jacket, stepping out. Chewing on a hunk of fry bread, an open grocery bag in her hand.

She stops. Regards him.

Jena Velasquez's eyes come flat onto his.

He sees hostility in her face.

She shifts the grocery bag to her chest, swallows the food in her mouth.

"Ms Velasquez."

"What're you doing here?" She stares at him.

"Just passing through," he says, "on business."

The door to the store opens, a man in a sweat top and snapback exits.

The marshal steps aside to let him pass.

He waits for Velasquez to say something—or continue on her way.

She takes a pace into his eyeline. "What business?"

Whicher looks past her into the lit-up store. "Headed to Alamogordo."

She nods silently.

"There something on your mind?"

Tearing off another piece of fry bread, she chews. Stares at him. "What's going to happen with Charlene?"

The marshal glances at her. "Nobody's charging her on account of me."

"I heard they're sending her to prison."

"What I heard," Whicher says, "they were charging her with possession."

"The drugs in that house weren't hers—none of that belonged to her…"

"I know that."

Velasquez juts her chin, searches his face.

"Possession," Whicher says. "That's all they're going with. Not trafficking. That's not the same. She'll be alright, she'll get a year, eighteen months."

"How is that okay?" Velasquez sets her face to the cold wind blowing across the weathered plaza. Water wells in her eye. "How is that okay…"

The marshal watches headlamps moving on the highway in the gathering dusk. "Look, she's cooperating. I told her to get herself a deal. She gets a year, that's minimum. It was never going to be less…"

"What about Karl?" Velasquez says. "What happens to him?"

"Karl Ramsay will disappear."

"Oh? For him it's okay?"

Whicher shakes his head. Eyes the first of the evening stars. The vault of sky stretching vast above them. "He'll go into witness protection. For state's evidence to convict."

Velasaquez leans into the wall of the store building, pulls her jacket about her against the wind. "All he has to do is talk?"

"Has to give up everything," the marshal says. "Tells us everything he knows. Everybody gets cleaned out; everybody on the take in this…"

Jena Velasquez looks at him, eyes glassing with tears. "He goes free…"

"Not free."

"Sure, he does…"

"The life he had," Whicher says, "is over."

Velasquez pushes up off the wall. "Charlene goes to prison. For nothing. For being around him." She glares at the ground, something of the flame in her dying. Water streaming from her eye. "You know that's a crock…"

Turning her back, she walks out onto the deserted plaza.

The marshal breathes the night air, watches.

As she disappears, step by step into a measureless dark.

He nods a silent acknowledgement.

In the stark-lit corridor of the maximum-security wing in the county detention center, suspended observation cameras monitor every angle as Whicher follows a corrections officer to the secure entrance of an interview room.

The CO unlocks the door.

Whicher steps through.

Sees Karl Ramsay behind a thick glass insert in the dividing wall of the room.

The CO waits at the threshold. Indicates a metal panel with a single switch. "Buzz on that, you get done."

The marshal nods. Takes a seat in front of the window.

Ramsay's face is clean-shaven now, etched with stress, his head buzzed almost bald.

He sits hunched behind the glass, in a set of faded orange scrubs, wrists cuffed.

"Mister Ramsay."

The man behind the glass only looks at him.

"I'm here on behalf of USMS Texas, Western District."

"My lawyer told me I'm dealing with the DA's office in El Paso, now."

"Right."

"Then what're you doing here?"

"One of ours was shot, injured."

Ramsay says nothing.

"Marshals Service submits a report—to the DA." Whicher unfastens the wool overcoat. Takes the notepad and pen from the jacket of his suit.

Ramsay shifts side to side on his seat.

"I saw the BIA police today. They say you've given up the narcotics you had stored on the reservation."

The man nods.

"You tell Andre Parrish about it? That stash of black tar heroin?"

"He knew about it," Ramsay says.

"I saw some of it today. Did you tell him about that old sawmill?"

"Yeah."

The marshal thinks of Gregory up there.

"So?" Ramsay says. "Listen, I'll keep my end of the deal. So long as the prosecution keeps theirs. I'm giving them people hooked up with half the cartels on the border here." Ramsay's face is accusatory. "You told me I'd be in a WITSEC wing." He glares, pulls his cuffed wrists against the chain at his waist.

"You're secure."

"Not what I had in mind…"

The marshal ignores him. Opens up the notepad. "I need to know about the sequence of events, the first morning."

Ramsay makes a face. "Like what?"

"Andre Parrish told you we'd be coming. Parrish was seen on Pike Street…"

"By this witness, right. This kid who's now safe…"

"No thanks to you…"

"I had nothing to do with any of that…"

The marshal stops him with a look.

"What do you want from me?"

Whicher leans in closer. "Did Parrish know who gave you up to law enforcement?"

The man behind the thick glass screen only stares.

"Did he know who the informant was?"

Ramsay's face is slack, weighing his answer.

"You hold out on me," Whicher says, "I'll take it back to the prosecutor's office."

For a moment, Ramsay's eyes are calculating. He nods, slowly.

"Parrish knew?"

"He told me it was… that 'Mexican'."

The marshal doesn't react.

"Rios. Luis Rios. What difference does it make?"

"That's why you went after him?"

"He was gunning for me. He heard I was already on the run. He couldn't wait to stick the knife in."

"He went after the heroin you stashed away?" Whicher says. "Went after your weak links? Like Jena Velasquez?"

"That's the level he's at." An ugly look steals across his face as Ramsay stares from behind the secure screen.

"So, Parrish knew. And you knew." Whicher writes the detail onto the pad.

"You know something else?"

Whicher looks at him.

"Only two people knew I'd even be there that night."

"On Pike Street?" The marshal considers it.

"Antonio. And Salazar," Ramsay says.

The marshal sits back in his seat.

"It was Salazar set me up."

"How you figuring that?"

"Because the house was Antonio's."

Whicher turns the pen in his hand, pictures the address; Pittman's place.

"Think about it," Ramsay says. "It was full of ice. You think he would have sold me out to that Mexican son of a bitch? Triggered a bust? Have cops come in, tear up the place —with what was in there?"

The marshal draws a line on the pad at the end of his notes. Runs the pen back over it. Then over it again, the line thickening, darkening every time.

"After Parrish came around that night, I called him. Told him what I was going to do."

Whicher only eyes the line, silent.

"Three o'clock that morning," Ramsay says, "they were both asleep. Parrish told me you'd be coming at daybreak. I left the house. Told him I wouldn't mind if Salazar came to some serious harm…"

The marshal thinks of Drummond's account—of Parrish riling him, psyching him up.

"I called Salazar soon as it was light," Ramsay says. "Told him I had to go out. Told him to come meet me. Turns out they both came out," Ramsay says. "And you blew 'em both away. Too bad."

Whicher plays the sequence over in his mind—pictures Salazar, in the passenger seat of the Toyota, going for a gun. "Parrish knew who'd be in the car?"

From behind the screen he hears a barked laugh. "Hell, yeah."

The marshal leans his back into the chair. Sees his own reflection superimposed over Ramsay in the orange scrubs. Thinks of spiraling damage. Every compromised action, each corrupted step. A wrecking ball to anything in its orbit. Drug money like a poison. Creeping death.

"How long is this all going to take?"

"I'm about done," Whicher says.

"No, I mean this," Ramsay says, "this whole thing? The inquest, people's trials. My thing; everything."

"I'm about done."

"I mean all of it."

The marshal stares at the man for the longest time. "I don't know, Karl." He traces the line a final time, closes the notepad. "Is it ever going to be over?"

Snow hangs in the night air on the mountain, floating dreamlike in the hi-beams of the Silverado over the Osha Trail

Road.

In the rear-view mirror, the lights of the village of Cloudcroft are behind him. Ponderosa pine and Douglas fir and Gambel oak crowd the deserted road climbing into the woods.

In the blackness beyond the windshield, he pictures Andre Parrish.

The injuries to his body.

Torn open from the fall.

From his belly to his throat.

He thinks of Annaliese Joyner's words, hears them. Thinks of her on the timber deck at her house. Pacing. Fierce light in her eye. As if summoning some force. As if somehow, she'd known.

He sees Parrish, in his mind's eye, the way he was found.

I'll bring him into my world. Cut him open.

From out of the dark is the sign for the Joyner property.

He shifts his grip on the wheel, slows—takes the turn up the white-over drive.

―――

In the doorway of the A-frame house, she regards him.

Whicher waits in the wind in his suit and hat, the collar of his coat turned up.

From the house is warmth, light. The sense of sanctuary.

"Sorry to call late," the marshal says.

She steps back slowly from the door. Ushers him inside.

"I was passing. On my way home to Texas."

Gregory descends the wooden staircase.

"Thought to see if you were alright…"

The boy's eyes widen in his face. He stops on the stair.

"Evening." The marshal nods to him. "It's alright. Everything's okay."

Annaliese Joyner eyes her son. Turns to step through into the living area.

Whicher follows into the low-lit room—flames bright behind the glass in the wood stove. "I just came from the prison." The marshal takes off his hat. "The place they're holding the man I came here for."

Head canted, she folds her arms over her chest, stands silent by the stove.

Gregory enters the living room. Takes in the marshal, searches his face. He stands dead still, thoughts at work behind the quick eyes.

Whicher gives a muted smile. Lets the boy sense him; feel out the lack of alarm.

Unmoving, Gregory studies him. Then just as suddenly, turns to his mother. "How much stuff do I need to take?"

"Think about what you'll need," she says. "What you want to wear. Just find things, for a start…"

Gregory glances at Whicher. Expression shifting. Lifting. He brushes his shoulder length hair from his face.

Stepping from the room, he runs back up the staircase.

The marshal turns to Annaliese.

"We're leaving in the morning."

He looks at her.

"For California. To be with Gregory's father."

"You don't need to go."

She unfolds her arms. Draws a hand across her face. "He's pretty shaken up. About all of this."

Whicher holds her eye a moment. "The only person that might've wished your son harm is dead. I want you to know that."

She breaks off looking at him, stares into the light from the stove.

Whicher lets the Resistol hang between his thumb and finger.

Annaliese speaks her words to the flames. "Something like

this happens, you start to reconsider... a lot of things. His father wishes he would have been here—wishes he could've been around him—to protect him."

"So, you're going out there?"

"Maybe that's just how things ought to be."

The marshal surveys the room. The mismatch of furniture, the paintings, pieces of art. "There's good people here. This place. Here and on the reservation."

"I know that."

"Got to make a stand, someplace."

"Is that what you do?"

He doesn't reply.

"Place is one thing," she says. "People are who you stand with."

The marshal dips his head. Puts on his hat. "Well. My job here is finished."

She looks up from the fire.

He steps back, turns for the hallway, eyes the staircase, thinks of Gregory.

Annaliese follows him to the door.

She lifts the latch, opens up.

He steps out, turns back.

She stands in the frame. "Thank you," she says.

He lets his eyes meet hers again.

"For finding him."

The marshal doesn't speak.

"You think we'll be alright?" She gives a fleeting smile.

"I do. Yes, I do."

Annaliese eyes the snow swirling in the night air, puts a hand to the door. "You have people waiting for you? In Texas?"

He nods.

"Go home, then."

He takes the truck keys from his pocket.

She says, "That's where you'll stand."

Printed in Great Britain
by Amazon